What Happened to Evie Del Rio?

Sarah Watts

To Susie,

Enjoy the 80s nostalgia!

Sarah Watts

x

Cahill Davis Publishing

Cahill Davis Publishing Limited

ISBN 978-1-7398015-3-3 (eBook)

ISBN 978-1-7398015-2-6 (Paperback)

Cahill Davis Publishing Limited

www.cahilldavispublishing.co.uk

To my husband Jay, for always believing.

Chapter One

Cassie

June 2018

Do you know what it's like to find out your mum is the woman who inspired one of today's most iconic indie love songs? Bloody weird, that's what...

My mum's name is Genie McNamara. Nothing special really about that name, but she was formally known as Evie Del Rio and, as it turns out, she's the inspiration behind the song "Used to Be" by '90s indie band The Mountaineers. The song was written by their lead singer Ed "Nasher" Nash, who Mum dated when they were teenagers. Ed wrote "Used to Be" for her after they split but only recorded it in 1995 when it appeared on the band's debut album, *Past Times*. It's actually quite a good song—slightly cringy lyrics when you know they're about your mum though. This song has been played everywhere: on the radio, at weddings and more recently used as the theme tune for a TV drama series. That's how my brother Will and I found out about "Mum's Song", as we started calling it. Everyone kept using Shazam to find out who the song was by, and by the time the TV drama finished, "Used to Be" was one of the most downloaded songs of the year. Then, "Mum's Song" was featured on a documentary called *Musical Muses: The Girl in the Song.* That's really when our lives started to change.

Mum keeps being contacted about whether she really is the girl in the song. The press somehow found out that Mum's maiden name was Del Rio and have pursued her ever since. She changed her name to Genie just before she met Dad, as she said that she thought it sounded more grown-up than Evie. Our dad said he thought it was hilarious that Mum had been the inspiration for such an iconic song. Secretly, I think he was a bit hurt, because when I was looking through his record collection, I found a copy of The Mountaineers' debut album. I think Dad might have been a bit of a fanboy of the band.

It's really unsettling to suddenly have your family's private life thrust into the limelight. Will was quite impressed by it all at first, but since the publicity has increased and the boys at his school have kept teasing him about Mum's past, he's become very distant. I, on the other hand, can't believe that Mum never told us about the song. I mean, how cool must it be that someone was so completely in love with you that they wrote a song about you? It's like having your own "Wonderwall" moment. Although, after Noel Gallagher split up with Meg Matthews, he said the press had got it all wrong and she wasn't the inspiration behind the song after all. Ed, on the other hand, can't say enough about the song and his inspiration. He's made an awful lot of money out of it.

Loads of old photos of Mum have resurfaced, and it's funny to see what Mum looked like when she was around my age. Her hair was really blonde and spiky at the front,

and she always wore loads of black eyeliner and red lipstick. She looked more like she should have been in a band
than Ed did. They did look quite cool together. There's a
particular photo that has appeared in the press and on
social media numerous times, where Mum is sitting on
Ed's lap, clearly laughing at something he just said, with a
cigarette dangling from her thin, elegant fingers. He too is
holding a cigarette, gazing into her eyes while some band is
playing in the background. They are both clearly besotted
and obsessed with each other—completely oblivious to
everyone else.

Chapter Two

Genie

June 2018

I really can't believe my past has come back to haunt me. And to be made so public too. I have worked so hard to reinvent myself as a respectable wife and mother, and I really thought I'd finally achieved a life that my parents could be truly proud of. If only Ed hadn't released that song. I remember him telling me that all the songs he'd written about me would one day make him famous, and I suppose he was right. Although unfortunately they've also made me somewhat infamous, which is really not what I want. Everyone keeps looking at me in a different light now—my own family, the children's teachers, my hairdresser, the lovely beautician who did my manicures. Not to mention my cleaner, who very kindly sold a story on us about how my husband Gray and I have separate bedrooms. We don't, by the way, we have a spare bedroom that doubles as an office when Gray has to work late.

I've basically stopped going out. You see, Ed has really exaggerated and embellished our story, and although most of the stuff he said has an element of truth to it, I really don't want to be reminded of my past.

Poor Gray. My lovely big hunk of a husband who has made me respectable has a look of disappointment in his eyes whenever we're alone together. My darling daughter, Cassie, is absolutely fascinated and somewhat impressed by my past. Then there's my precious son, Will. He's crushed that his school friends think I'm some kind of former sex kitten, and that's putting it politely.

I thought my secrets would remain safe after all these years, but with Ed's resurgence of popularity, he's lit the touchpaper, sat back and watched it burn. Thankfully, his uncle Paul seems to have vanished off the face of the earth, so at least that's one less person to worry about selling his story to the press.

I honestly don't know how much more I can take of this. Gray says I should just embrace it, weather the storm or maybe give a reputable newspaper or magazine my side of the story. I know he's right but, at the moment, I don't even want to remember all of the truth so it's best to say nothing. Printed words can be changed and manipulated, taken out of context. I have been considering being interviewed by the makers of *The Girl in the Song*, as they were the ones who started this whole thing off, but I'm really not in the right headspace right now. I'm just trying to carry on as best I can.

The ironic thing is that Gray has a copy of that wretched album in his vinyl collection. I noticed it when we moved into our most recent house and I was helping him sort out his precious record collection. I should have said something to him then about knowing Ed, especially when he picked the album out to play that night. I made an excuse about needing to go down the road to pick up some extra milk so I didn't have to hear "my song". By the time I got back, he'd packed the album away and my secret was safe for a little while longer.

Ed is relentless in his pursuit of fame, and he's now got the recognition he's always craved. I don't suppose he even realises how much I've changed over the years—I have so much to lose. I'm not the same wild Evie he met all those years ago who didn't give a damn about the future. Evie just lived for the moment and to hell with the consequences. It's only since I met and married Gray and we had our children that I realised what real, true love is. What Ed and I had all those years ago was complete infatuation and pure lust.

Chapter Three

Will

June 2018

To find out your mum once dated a singer in a band and had a song written about her was quite a novelty at first, but now that Ed Nash keeps talking about his relationship with my mum when they were young, it's become a bit embarrassing. My mates Alex and Tommy think it's hilarious and keep taking the piss.

"What other rock stars has your mum shagged?" is the normal chant on the football field. I try not to take too much notice but it's hard not to take offence. Then they start on my sister, asking if she's a slag too. Last time someone asked me that, I punched him square on the nose and broke it in several places. He had to go straight to hospital. To be fair, he didn't grass on me. He said that my head had collided with his nose while playing football at lunch time. He's kept away from me since then.

So, now I have a bit of a reputation of being a hard nut. I don't mind. I'll take it. It's made me quite popular with the girls at school. A couple of them have told me they like the song and that my mum should be flattered. To be honest, I haven't talked to Mum about it much. Her and Dad are always talking in hushed tones whenever Cassie and I are within earshot. I think my dad is pissed off with this Ed bloke. My mum is just embarrassed. Sometimes, I catch her crying. She always pretends she's not.

Dad said we're all going to take a holiday once Cassie has finished her GCSEs, which is any day now, but I've asked if we can wait until the World Cup has finished, as England are doing quite well. Mum said it's because of the manager's lucky waistcoat. I think she's deluded. What does she know about football? Dad has said he's not waiting that long to go away.

Mum's had loads of her ex-school friends releasing old photos of her to the press. It really doesn't look like her, although sometimes the photos remind me a little bit of Cassie when she's got loads of makeup on. Our now ex-cleaner, who worked for us for years, sold a story on the state of Mum and Dad's marriage, and Mum cried for two days solid. Perhaps a holiday would be good for all of us. I finish school on the eleventh of July and the World Cup final is the fifteenth of July. I'm sure I can find somewhere to watch the final in Orlando. I'll mention it to Dad. It'll show him that I'm thinking about the family and not just about myself. Dad loves watching England play football, and sometimes he even manages to get us tickets for some of the England games through his mate Jonesy, who's also my godfather. It's brilliant because you get all the hospitality too and the food is amazing. I'm obsessed with football and my dad has that same obsession but with his precious record collection.

Chapter Four

Gray

June 2018

I absolutely adore Genie, and I have done since that day I set eyes on her in that quirky little bar in Brighton where she was working all those years ago. She is as beautiful now as she was back then, and I will do anything and everything in my power to keep her and our family together.

Ed Nash has got a fight on his hands if he thinks his love song is going to make her go back to him. It's a shame really, as I've always liked that song, but I've always thought that Ed "Nasher" Nash is a bit of a prat. Seems I was right all along. Always trust your gut. That's what my old dad used to say.

Genie has been so quiet since that song was re-released, and there has been quite a media storm surrounding it. It didn't take long for the press to find out exactly who "Evie" is, and Ed's been so enjoying being back in the limelight. His old band is now reforming and going on a reunion tour in the autumn. He's been on every daytime TV programme you can think of, and he really is the darling of the tabloids right now. Cassie brought home a magazine the other day with his face looking up smugly from the front cover. Even in my own home, I can't get away from that self-satisfied-looking bastard.

Genie has always been quite vague about her youth. She was apparently a bit of a rebel at school, always flaunting the rules, and she got expelled from her secondary school for smoking and bunking off. We've tried to keep that from the children for obvious reasons. I now wonder if Ed Nash was the cause of most of the trouble Genie found herself in all those years ago.

Now that Cassie's exams are coming to an end, I plan on taking the family to Florida. My old mate Hugh Jones—or Jonesy, as we all call him—has a secluded and very private villa that he's promised me we can stay in. I think we all need to get away from London for a while, let Genie rest and relax and then maybe we can work out our next move with the whole Ed/*The Girl in the Song* debacle. I still think she should give her side of the story to the makers of the original documentary, but Genie is quite reluctant to talk to anybody about that point in her life. I'll give her time. She'll open up soon enough. I just want my beautiful, witty and happy wife back again.

Chapter Five

Evie

December 1984

Mum and Dad are so mad at me. They've just been called in to see Sister Maria, my headmistress, yet again. She's a frigid old cow who just hates us girls because we're young and pretty and have the world at our feet, whereas she chose to be married to the church. She caught me and Ed, from St Augustine's School, snogging at the bus stop around the corner from our school, and although we managed to get away from her by jumping on the bus, I knew she had clocked me. Ed and I ran up the stairs to the upper deck and managed to get the back seat of the bus, where we had a bird's-eye view of Sister Maria shaking her fist as if she were possessed by the Devil, rather than being a devout sister of Christ. Ed didn't help things, as he flipped her the finger. I thought she was going to have a fit.

We got off the bus a couple of stops later, quite close to Ed's house. Amazingly, his mum and dad were out, so we had the whole place to ourselves. I love Ed's house—it's so cool and bohemian. Both his parents are artists, although his mum is also a teacher and his dad's a part-time singer in a band, so there's always something happening. Sometimes his dad has his mates round for a smoke and a jam. I like it when Ed joins in and his dad lets him play the guitar. He said he's gonna write a song for me one day so everyone knows just how much I mean to him, which is kinda cool.

As soon as we got in and Ed realised no one was around, he dragged me upstairs to his bedroom. He put one of his mixtapes into his stereo. With the melancholy and haunting sound of The Smiths singing "This Charming Man", he pushed me onto his bed, with his kisses becoming more and more forceful. He somehow expertly managed to unhook my bra. He discarded his clothes and the rest of mine. I tried to slow things down—we'd never gone this far before—but we just couldn't stop ourselves. Before I knew it, we'd done it. My first time. It really hurt but at the same time I liked it, and I was just glad it was out of the way. Afterwards, Ed made a joke that if he had his way, he'd be my last too. My only. He's just so passionate about me. I really do like him and I'm glad he was my first.

We lay there for what seemed an eternity and then Ed rolled a joint, took a big drag and passed it to me. I tried to copy what he'd just done but ended up coughing my guts up.

"You really do have to put in a bit more practice, you know?" Ed laughed as he sat up in bed and traced his finger around the contours of my face, finally resting on my lips. He kissed my mouth once again and smiled at me.

"I'd better get going. My mum will be looking out for me. She gets really annoyed when I'm late, and I've got a ton of homework to catch up on," I said, suddenly feeling rather self-conscious of my nakedness. I managed to locate my school shirt and skirt together with my bra, but to my horror I couldn't find my knickers.

"Looking for these, Miss Del Rio?" Ed teased as he held up my rather tatty, off-white school knickers.

"Give them back, Ed," I shouted.

"Make me," he replied, waving my knickers high above his head.

"I hate you, Ed Nash, I really do," I protested, trying my best to retrieve my underwear.

"Oh, I do love it when you get angry. I might have to keep these for my special collection, you know." He smirked.

"Ugh, that's gross. Give them here. I can't go home without them," I pleaded. He relented and allowed me to snatch them back. I managed to put them back on as discreetly as I possibly could.

"You off now?" Ed said, pulling me so close I could feel his heart beating next to mine.

"Yeah. I gotta go," I replied, trying half-heartedly to release myself from his tight embrace.

"One more kiss."

"Just one more," I agreed, knowing I had to get home quickly, my body betraying me by just wanting to stay here with Ed.

He grabbed me roughly, pushing me back down on the bed. We kissed again, him only releasing me when he heard a key in the door.

"Wait here," instructed Ed.

"Mum, Dad," he called out, stumbling into the hallway as he rushed to put his discarded clothes back on.

"Hi, Ed. It's Paul," a gruff, raspy voice replied. "Your dad said to use the spare key, as I need to lay low for a couple of nights."

Ed is always talking about Paul. He's Ed's uncle, his dad's half-brother. Apparently, he's really cool and doesn't treat Ed like a kid. He's nearer in age to Ed than he is to his own brother, as Ed's dad and Paul have different mums. Ed says that Paul is more like an older brother to him than an uncle.

"Alright, mate. Just coming down." Ed signalled for me to quietly follow him.

I grabbed my school bag and silently followed Ed downstairs. I managed to sneak out the front door as Ed kept Paul busy in the kitchen with small talk.

I have never run so fast in my life to get home. All that training I'd done for Borough Sports was clearly paying off. As I turned the corner, my bus had just arrived at the stop. I did a final sprint and managed to jump on just as the bus started to move. That time, I sat downstairs on one of the long seats near where the conductor normally stands and thought about the fact that I was no longer a virgin. *Just wait until I tell Ginny*, I thought. She'd be fuming, as she's always fancied Ed, but he decided that it was me he wanted.

Chapter Six

Ed

December 1984

My mates and I have always had great success with the girls from the local Catholic girls' school. There's this one blonde girl called Ginny with enormous tits. She's always coming on to me. She seems nice enough, but I only keep her sweet, as I really fancy her friend Evie. Evie's one of the girls that everyone wants to be their girlfriend. She also has blonde hair but hers looks really natural against Ginny's brassy peroxide blonde colour.

Evie is a classic beauty. The type of girl who looks good dressed in anything. As her and Ginny are always together, I've managed to get to know her quite well. There's a small group of boys from my school and some girls from hers who kind of hang out together in the local park, smoking and sometimes sharing a couple of cans of Fosters one of us has managed to nick from home.

Eventually, Evie and I started hanging back from the rest of the group. We meet from school. I wait with her at her bus stop, and we get off with each other. She doesn't seem to care who sees us. She's wild!

We never actually managed to have sex until the day her headmistress caught us snogging at the bus stop. We gave her the slip and then went back to my house. Thankfully, my parents were out, and to be honest we just couldn't stop ourselves. We probably would have done it again if my uncle Paul hadn't showed up at the house unannounced. I'm always fascinated by Paul, as he never seems to work but always has loads of cash. He often pushes a crumpled tenner into my hand with a wink so my mum and dad don't see. While I was chatting to Paul, Evie managed to slip away.

I can't wait to tell all my mates about what happened between me and Evie, and I'm sure she'll be telling Ginny. Evie wasn't my first. I've had sex before but not with anyone as beautiful and special as Evie. My first time was when I went on holiday with Paul to a caravan down in Hayling Island. He set me up with an older girl who worked behind the bar at the social club. She took the lead, as I didn't have a clue. Sharon. She was a bit on the chubby side, but she was kind and showed me exactly what to do.

Not long after Evie left, Paul asked if we have any beer. He's always asking about beer. Always drinking. Always smoking.

"Yeah, sure. Dad's got a load in the fridge. Just help yourself," I replied.

Paul grabbed a can of beer from the fridge and took a swig from it. It left a frothy foam moustache above his upper lip, which he wiped away effortlessly with the back of his hand. I made a note of how cool Paul looked just by opening his beer and decided I would try that one out on Evie the next time I saw her. He then sat down on our leather sofa and put his muddy old Dr. Martens on Mum's favourite cushion. She'd be fuming if she found out. She's not overly keen on Paul at the best of times, as she thinks he always gets Dad into trouble. She's probably right, but I think that every time Paul is here, there's kind of an air of excitement in the house—well, there is for me and Dad.

Paul and I spent the rest of the afternoon chatting, smoking and drinking our way through Dad's beers. It wasn't until I heard a key in the door that I realised how late it was. Unfortunately for us, it was Mum returning home from work.

"Paul, Ed, what on earth do you think you're doing? Ed, have you been smoking and drinking?" she shouted.

I went to stand up but, in my rather drunken and stoned state, I lost my balance and fell flat on the floor, which in turn made Paul collapse on top of me in a fit of laughter. My mum looked at us both in disgust, turned on her heel and stormed out of the house. We just lay there laughing uncontrollably.

"Fancy another beer, Ed?"

"Yeah, why not?" I readily agreed.

"How about another joint?"

"Sure."

"Tell you what, you get the beers and I'll teach you how to roll a joint properly. I think you could do with the practice," he slurred.

Chapter Seven

Cassie

July 2018

I've been enjoying some time off now that my GCSEs are finally over. It's so good to not have to look at another flash card or revision book for the rest of the summer. I won't throw them out though, just in case. Emma and Lucy from my maths class burned all their schoolbooks in Emma's back garden on the last day of their exams, but as they are straight-A students, they definitely won't need them next year. I'm not so sure, however. We've had such a disruptive time lately, what with all the publicity surrounding Mum and this Ed guy. The press interest has been quite distracting.

It's weird to think that Mum was going out with Ed when she was around my age. I don't even have a boyfriend. Most of the guys in my class are idiots, although Danny Bailey is quite easy on the eye. I'm hoping I might see him at the gym, as he's really into his fitness.

Dad wants us all to go away to Florida soon, but Will wants to be in London to watch the World Cup final with all his mates. I think a change of environment could do us good, especially Mum, who is really living on her nerves at the moment, wondering what new revelations Ed is going to expose about their teenage relationship. If you Google Mum's maiden name or do a search for *The Girl in the Song*, all manner of things pop up about Mum: drug taking, underage drinking, underage sex etc. You name it, Evie Del Rio seems to have done it.

Sometimes, I can't believe they're talking about my mum. She's so sensible and normal, but then I guess that could be why she's so strict with us—she doesn't want us to repeat the same mistakes she made. She said the reason she makes us revise and comes down hard on us when it comes to studying is because she flunked her exams and really regrets that part of her life.

Another reason I'm so pleased not to be at school anymore is all the bitchy gossip about Mum and Ed Nash. It's amazing how much people gossip.

Mum has virtually stopped going out. No gym visits, no manicures and definitely no lunches with the girls. Auntie Maura, who's one of Mum's closest friends, still comes over. She's a star. She always comes laden with home-cooked food for us all, and it seems to be the only way we can get Mum to eat. Dad has been trying really hard to coax Mum to eat a bit more but it's as if every single mouthful chokes her. She's got ridiculously thin. That documentary has turned our lives completely upside down.

I wish Mum would open up a bit to me. I've seen loads of old photos of Mum when she was going out with Ed which have surfaced in the press. She looked incredible with her bright blonde hair carefully coaxed into defiant spikes, heavy black eyeliner and mascara and the reddest ruby-coloured lips, normally with a cigarette between them. Will and I now know why she's so anti-smoking—because she used to smoke herself. The press always compares her looks to a young Debbie Harry. She's still a very attractive woman but so conservative now compared to her younger days.

Chapter Eight

Genie

July 2018

I'm sick to the back teeth of Ed Nash. I really do wish that he would crawl back under the rock from which he came. I know we have history together, but to be honest it's a history I would rather forget. I'm also getting quite anxious about what Ed's going to reveal next if the price is right from the press. I've got to tell Gray absolutely everything about my past, which is something that I really don't want to do. I don't think I can bear him finding out the real truth about me. It'll be just like being sixteen years old all over again, when my parents found out what I was really like.

Gray is trying his best, love him, and the children have coped in their own way, but I think I'm going to have to deal with the aftermath of my past myself. Grown-up Genie Mc-Namara is going to have to sort out Evie Del Rio's youthful mess once and for all. I still haven't quite worked out when or how I'm going to do it, but I want my nice, safe, ordinary life back. I'll start by calling Maura. She's such a breath of fresh air and always so positive too. I could have done with having Maura in my life sooner but she's with me now and she's always on my side. I think I'll tell her everything and see what she thinks I should do. I'm hopeful that she won't judge me too harshly.

I reach for my mobile and call Maura. Gray is going to be out tonight at some work thing and Cassie's staying at a friend's, so that just leaves Will here, who will be so engrossed in his Xbox he wouldn't even notice if the roof caved in. With a near empty house, I'll tell Maura to pack an overnight bag too, just in case.

Maura arrives in an Uber in typical "Maura style"—her unruly curly red hair is loosely tied up in a scrunchie. She flashes a big smile at her Uber driver as he dutifully carries her overnight bag all the way to our front door.

"Thanks a million, Ahmed. You're a real star."

"You are most welcome, Miss Maloney. Have a pleasant evening."

"I'm sure I will. Now, don't you work too hard, Ahmed. I'll see you again soon."

I open the front door before Maura has even pressed our Ring doorbell. Gray upped our security once the press got hold of our address, and it's good to be able to see who's at our front door. He also changed the locks on all our external doors and installed a new house alarm and another security camera in the back garden. It does make me feel a bit safer but I'm beginning to feel like I'm being held captive. I miss my old life.

"Thanks so much for coming over. I..." I start to say but my tears cut me off.

"You're fine, my love. You're fine. I've got you," says Maura, enveloping me into her enormous bosom. "Let's get ourselves inside and open one of Gray's expensive bottles of wine." She cajoles me with a conspiratorial wink.

Maura knows my house almost as well as she knows her own, and she soon has me sat on the sofa, a large glass of rosé in my hand. She sits beside me, takes a big sip from her glass and waits until I'm ready to talk.

Chapter Nine

Ed

July 2018

I can't believe my luck and change of fortune over the last year, and it's all thanks to that TV series using my song "Used to Be" and then the documentary *The Girl in the Song* featuring my song together with classics like "Layla" and "Wonderful Tonight" by Eric Clapton, written about Pattie Boyd. It certainly has stirred up quite a media storm, which I'm really benefitting from, but I've also started thinking back to those heady days when I was with Evie. It's such a shame we were forced apart, but I guess we were so young. I do sometimes wonder if we would have got married and had kids had we stayed together. Or perhaps our relationship would have just run its course.

At times, I feel a bit guilty that I've turned Evie's, or should I say Genie's, life upside down, but I'd really love to see her again. Just to see if the spark is still there. She still looks gorgeous but so conservative in terms of looks—her spiky blonde hair has been replaced with carefully high-lighted waves and her makeup has been toned down to a much more natural look. I still would though. Her old man might have something to say about it. Can't believe she got married. He seems a bit older, and he looks as if he's got a bob or two. He's got what I should have had: Evie and the two kids. One of each. Just what Evie and I used to talk about wanting all those years ago. That's my one regret. Not having any kids.

After pretty much coasting along in life—just like my uncle Paul, as Mum always used to say—I've suddenly got a purpose. The band have been offered a reunion tour, and the lads and I are well up for it. We're not young anymore, we're all nearly pushing fifty, but I'm convinced we've still got the stamina to go on tour. It's all going to be televised by the documentary makers of *The Girl in the Song*. Perhaps Evie might come along and listen to her song? Somehow, I don't think that's going to happen though. She doesn't want anything to do with me or the song. Her lack of comment to any of the articles that have been written about us, whether by me or by some of our old friends or my family, has been very consistent. She hasn't said a word.

I've been contacted by Ginny, who used to be really good friends with Evie way back. I feel a bit guilty about the way I used Ginny to get to Evie all those years ago, but she doesn't seem to hold a grudge. She's suggested meeting up privately, as she's just discovered some more old photos of us all from when Evie and I were together. She thinks the press will be really interested to see them, but she wants to run them by me first. I asked her to message me the photos privately, but she was very insistent in meeting up to show me the photos in person. And to be honest, I'm quite intrigued to see Ginny again and see how life has treated her, so we've been messaging each other on Instagram to arrange a meeting. She seems keen to meet me at my flat but I'm not so sure, so I may try and arrange to meet at hers or somewhere more neutral. The press are all over me currently and they are closely monitoring who goes in and out of my flat, so I need to think of a way for us to meet up discreetly. Quite a few of our old school friends have sold stories already with a few old photos, which is fine as far as I'm concerned. Why should I be the only one to make a few bob out of the current hysteria? But Ginny has hinted that the recent photos she's found could be interesting. I'll sleep on it.

I need a good night's sleep, as I'm being interviewed by a new morning TV magazine show called *Wake Up and Smell the Coffee*. I'm looking forward to showing them a bit of the Ed "Nasher" Nash charm. I'll give Ginny and her photos some more thought tomorrow.

Chapter Ten

Virginia

July 2018

I still miss Evie Del Rio's friendship, and I have done since the day she left. It was all because of me that Evie got to know Ed. I was the one who introduced her to him, as my cousin used to go to the same school as him. Ed used to chat to me at first but of course Evie just had to bat her baby blue eyes and he went running towards her. Saying that, it didn't last too long. Once her parents found out they were sleeping together, they split them up. Pulled her out of school right before her O levels too, which everyone found very odd. They moved house and cut all contact. I didn't even have a new landline number for her. We had no social media back then, so if you wanted to disappear into thin air, then you could do just that. It was as if she'd never even been there at all—well, except for in all my photos.

I moved on from Ed being with Evie and started dating Jamie, one of the other boys from St Augustine's. He was one of Ed's friends who wasn't in Ed's band and was a bit like me—kind of on the sidelines. We used to go to all their gigs. Jamie and I would stand right at the front, singing along word for word to all their songs. The hardcore fans like us sometimes were the only ones who turned up. The music was great though.

Ed was, and still is, a very charismatic rock frontman. The type most women want to be with, to be the one who tames him. Most guys just want to be him. Chiselled good looks, dark hair, the obligatory stubble and the most piercing blue eyes you have ever seen. It's just a shame Evie was the one he really wanted and not me. I wouldn't have just left him in the middle of the night. I would have fought tooth and nail to be with him.

Jamie and I stayed together after Evie left and all through that summer after our O levels. It was a great summer just hanging out, going to gigs, smoking and drinking in the local parks or at people's houses if their parents were at work. We split up when I started sixth form to do my A levels and he decided to work as a trainee mechanic at his dad's garage. By that time, Jamie and I really didn't have anything in common anymore apart from the sex. It was an amicable split, and since all the recent press about Evie and Ed, we've become friends on social media.

He's married now with kids and he took over his dad's garage, so he's done pretty well for himself. He even has a villa in Spain, and I'm pleased for him because he is one of the good guys. Obviously back then I didn't appreciate that. I've always gone for the bad boys. I suppose I've always been looking for my "Ed". I mean, I have two bad boy ex-husbands, but then I also have two beautiful daughters. Sasha and Shannon are the bright shining lights in my life, and I don't regret being with either of their dads for a single moment. They gave me the most precious gifts ever.

Shannon particularly is really enjoying reading all the press about *The Girl in the Song*. She thinks it's wild that her mum used to hang out with Ed and Evie. Just wait until they see my new photos. It will blow their minds.

I must remember to set my Sky+ for tomorrow's *Wake Up and Smell the Coffee*, as I know that Ed is going to be on it. I think it's all about The Mountaineers' big reunion tour, but I'm sure they'll manage to ask him some more probing questions about Evie being his muse. Perhaps soon it will be my turn on the sofa, getting all cosy with the presenters Rachel and Ethan if the press takes an interest in my old photos. Evie—or should I say Genie—should be so grateful that someone loved her enough to be inspired to write a love song all about her and their doomed relationship. I would be thrilled if Ed, or indeed anyone, had written a song about me.

Sometimes when I listen to the words of "Used to Be", I imagine that Ed wrote those words with me in mind. Perhaps if I play my cards right and Ed and I do meet up, he'll realise he chose the wrong blonde all those years ago. I know I'm no Evie Del Rio, but the new, improved Virginia Baker is looking so different to the Ginny Weathers that Ed used to know.

Chapter Eleven

Gray

July 2018

I've decided to give Genie some space by going to a work function alone. She's so anxious all the time, and every time I bring up the subject of her perhaps putting her side of the story to the press or to the documentary makers, she just clams up. One of our company's longest-serving salesmen is leaving and we want to give him a good send-off, so it's a great excuse for me to have some time out too.

I really want to take us all on holiday, but I can't get her to commit to a date, and then there's Will who is adamant that he wants to watch the rest of the World Cup in London. I'm going to just make an executive decision and book the tickets. Jonesy says his villa in Florida is free for most of July and August, so we can just escape and reassess exactly what to do as a family. It will be good for the kids to get away from London and all the press. I'll chat to the family tomorrow. Perhaps we'll get away as soon as the World Cup is over. Dear Will is so convinced that England are going to get to the final, but I've lived through enough years of disappointment since 1966, although I was far too young to appreciate that particular win.

I don't really like leaving Genie alone at the moment, but Will is there, and I know Maura will always come over if she's needed. She's a godsend that woman. They both worked in a small dive bar in the centre of Brighton when I met Genie all those years ago. It was where all the cool kids hung out, and I'm not including myself in that same breath.

I had gone to stay with Jonesy, who was studying art at Brighton Poly. I had my first job in advertising sales in London, so I used to work all week in Soho and then would go and see Jonesy and his mates in Brighton on Friday nights. We'd be partying all weekend and then I'd leave on the Sunday to get ready for work on Monday. It was like being a student but with money. I lived for my weekends.

Jonesy had told me about a great bar called The Hidden Snicket, named as such because to get there you had to cut through the narrowest of alleyways and it was fairly off the beaten track of all the normal traditional pubs and cheesy wine bars. It was on my first visit to The Hidden Snicket that I met both Genie and Maura. Genie was a breathtaking beauty with the bluest eyes I had ever seen, long blonde hair tied up and piled on top of her head with just a couple of strands of loose hair either side of her face. I purposely chose to be served by Genie, but it was so difficult to even get her to crack a smile back then. I persevered and, obviously, eventually it paid off. I still remember the first thing I ever said to her.

"Two Sapporos, please," I said, trying to appear sophis-ticated with my choice of Japanese beer. Not very inspired, I know. "And a drink for yourself."

"Thanks," she replied with only a hint of a smile. "I'll have mine later on if that's ok?"

"Of course. What time do you finish?"

She looked at me as if trying to work out whether I was just your normal lecherous Friday night punter or an ok kind of guy. "The bar closes at eleven, but I've got a break in five minutes. I might have a drink then."

"Fancy some company?" I boldly asked.

"If you like." She gestured with her head towards Jonesy. "You'd better give your friend his drink, otherwise he'll think you've ditched him."

I passed a Sapporo to Jonesy, who was mid-conversation with a couple of Italian girls. It was clear they didn't have a clue what he was saying with their basic knowledge of English and his lack of Italian, coupled with his strong Welsh accent.

"Cheers, Gray. This is Carla and Sofia. Did I get that right?" he asked the giggling girls.

"Si, si," they both replied.

"I'll leave you to it, Jonesy."

"Please yourself, mate," replied Jonesy as he returned his attention to his newfound friends.

I managed to get a seat at the bar, close to where Genie was, and I waited. After a while, she came around to the other side of the bar with what looked like half a lager. She lifted her glass towards me and took a sip of her lager.

"Thanks for that. I really needed it." She smiled.

"My pleasure. I wasn't sure if you were up for company. You must get blokes buying you drinks every night of the week."

"Sometimes. But tonight I was just thirsty," she joked.

"Oh, and I thought I was special," I replied, pretending to clutch at my wounded heart.

"Maybe you are, or maybe you're not."

"I'm Gray," I formally announced, holding out my hand to her. Taking my hand, she introduced herself.

"Genie."

"Nice to meet you, Genie."

"Good to meet you too, Gray, but I've got to get back behind that bar, as we're really short-staffed at the moment." And with that, Genie took another sip of her drink and returned to her side of the bar.

The rest of the evening went by in a blur. I chatted a bit to Jonesy and the Italian girls, who were so Jonesy's type, but my head had been completely turned by Genie. Last orders were called and Jonesy got another round in, served by Genie. I could see them chatting, which was always a worry because once Jonesy has a few drinks inside him, you never know what he's going to say. Thankfully, on this occasion, he had my back.

"Your barmaid wants to get you a drink after closing," he whispered in my ear as he handed me yet another beer and returned to his Italian girls.

"Really?"

"Really."

I chatted a bit more with Jonesy and the girls as I slowly finished my beer, aware that I might be waiting a while for Genie to finish up.

After what seemed an age, Genie and Maura had managed to shoo away the last of the Friday night stragglers, including Jonesy and his Italian girls, and it was now time for the staff and their chosen friends to enjoy a late-night drink.

"Another Sapporo?" Genie asked me.

"Yes please. That would be great."

Genie passed me a Sapporo, and this time her drink of choice was a vodka and tonic, her glass full to the brim with crushed ice. She shyly took my arm and ushered me to a couple of seats slightly tucked away from the main bar.

We started with some small talk, and I told her all about how I worked in Soho in the week but came down to visit Jonesy most weekends.

"I've seen your mate in here before. He's one of our regulars, but I've never seen him with the same girl twice. He seems like a bit of a player to me," Genie said as her brow furrowed. She clearly wasn't too impressed with Jonesy and his antics.

"He just hasn't met the right girl yet," I replied, taking another sip of my beer for Dutch courage, not wanting Genie to think that I was just like Jonesy.

"How about you? Have you got a nice girl waiting for you back in London?" she asked cheekily, fiddling with one of the alcohol-soaked beer mats.

"Me? No such luck. Just me and my black cat Woody."

"Woody? Cute name." I looked into her eyes, trying to detect if she was being sarcastic, but all I saw was sincerity and intrigue.

"I thought so. He was a stray," I continued. "Kept hanging around in my garden, so I started feeding him, and now we're inseparable."

"Who looks after Woody when you're in Brighton?"

"Oh, my neighbour Bessie pops in and feeds him. I think she loves him as much as I do." I laugh.

Genie paused and took a breath, all cheekiness dropping from her face. "And what's this Bessie like?"

"Uh, she's adorable. Not only does she look after Woody, she even leaves me a loaf of her delicious home-cooked bread whenever I've been away," I said with a big smile.

Genie swirled her drink around the glass, as if she'd suddenly gone off the idea of alcohol. "How come you two aren't dating? She sounds like perfect girlfriend material to me."

I almost spat out a mouthful of my rather overpriced beer. "Maybe because she's as old as my grandma."

"Oh," replied Genie, looking somewhat sheepish.

"Were you imagining some busty blonde with a penchant for baking?" I teased.

"Err, no. Well, possibly," she stammered as her face flushed cherry red with embarrassment. We both looked at each other and burst out laughing.

Chapter Twelve

Cassie

July 2018

I went to Saskia's party in Petersham last night with some of my school friends to celebrate the end of our GCSEs. I used to go to primary school with Saskia, but I'm convinced she only invited me to find out all the goss on my mum. I kind of overreacted by getting absolutely pissed out of my head, and Mel had to take me back to hers in an Uber, which apparently I was sick in and now her mum's account has been charged with a one hundred pound cleaning fee.

Trouble is, I can't remember anything about last night. Well, apart from a pile of sick-smelling clothes by the side of the bed at Mel's. Thankfully, her mum and dad were still out when we got home, but I've still got to give Mel's mum the money to cover the Uber cleaning fee. Mel's mum Cath is quite cool, so I don't think she'll tell my parents. She knows what we've all been going through as a family recently, so she won't want to add to our worries.

"Morning, sleepyhead. Or should I say pisshead?" Mel laughs, handing me a glass of water.

"Morning. Oh God. I completely embarrassed myself, didn't I?" I moan, retreating under the sheets again.

"Yes and no."

"What the hell does that mean?" I reply from beneath the sheets, feeling like death.

"Saskia was goading you all night about your mum and that Ed bloke. And, well, basically you just lost it, as anyone else would have. You told Saskia that she should look a bit closer to home before criticising the state of your parents' marriage."

"I did *what*?" I say, uncovering my head from the sheets. God, my head is pounding. What on earth did I drink last night? My mouth feels as dry as the Sahara Desert.

"Well, you told Saskia that her mum has been banging her tennis coach for months right under her dad's nose." Mel bit her bottom lip, waiting for my response.

"O-M-G, I said that?"

"Well, you were knocking back the prosecco and then Alfie was offering everyone Tequila shots and you did three in a row, as you were so wound up. I called an Uber soon afterwards, as I didn't want things to escalate. The Uber driver was actually quite nice and understanding considering you puked in his car. I bunged him an extra twenty pounds as well as the fee that will be added to my mum's account, as he was very concerned about you. He said he has a daughter the same age as us. I actually said you had food poisoning, but I'm sure he knew you were just pissed."

"God, the shame of it all," I mutter, wishing I could go back in time.

"You're fine. No one knows about you being sick. There's nothing to worry about," Mel reassures me.

"I so need a shower," I croak.

"Yes, you do. And you bloody well need to clean your teeth as well. Your breath honks." Mel laughs as she leaves the room.

"Thanks, Mel," I shout out after her. "I can always depend on you to tell me the truth," I say, climbing clumsily out of bed.

I make my way to Mel's ensuite and step into her shower. After a few minutes of just standing under the water, enjoying the soapy bubbles of Mel's rather expensive and delicious-smelling shower gel, the pounding in my head starts to subside.

I'm completely mortified that I got so drunk. I really don't want to be making a habit of losing control. If Mel hadn't been there for me, God knows what might have happened. I think all the pressure of my GCSEs and all the publicity involving Mum and Ed has got on top of me. Saskia just got the brunt of it. I do feel guilty about revealing the fact that her mum's been shagging her tennis coach. I know how much gossip about your family can hurt and how it feels when everyone is talking about you.

Once I step out of the shower and put on some clothes Mel has left out for me, she makes me some breakfast and then suggests that she should come back home with me just in case I bump into anyone from the party. I'm so lucky I've got Mel on my side. She reminds me a bit of Auntie Maura. Nothing is ever too much for her, and she always has my back.

Mel and I get the bus back to my house and let ourselves in. The alarm is on, so I know we're alone. Dad's definitely at work, Will's still at school for another week and I guess Mum's probably with Auntie Maura.

I get a couple of mugs from the kitchen cupboard and make us both a coffee. I put them on the kitchen table, one in front of Mel, and switch on the flatscreen TV. Ed Nash's charming smile fills the screen. Mel nearly spits out her freshly made coffee. I open my mouth to comment about how it won't be long until Mum is mentioned, but quickly close it again to listen as Ethan speaks.

"So, Ed, what's your current relationship with Evie Del Rio?"

My point is already proved.

"Well... I don't really have one at the moment."

"Too right you don't," I add, glaring at the screen.

"I mean, we've both moved on over the years, but who's to say that if we met up again one day the spark wouldn't still be there?" Ed shrugs but the shrug comes off as confident... almost cocky.

"Are you joking? My dad would swing for you if you ever came anywhere near my mum," I yell at the TV screen as Mel pulls me close with a reassuring squeeze.

"Calm down. He's just playing on the situation for his own benefits."

"Would you say Evie Del Rio was your first true love?" asks Rachel. *"I'm sure lots of our viewers would love to know."* She stares right into the camera and smiles, her teeth gleaming white, as if she's looking into the eyes of each viewer, giving them exactly what they want.

"Well, of course. When we were fifteen/sixteen, we were always together. Almost inseparable."

"Exactly. How many years ago was that?" Mel comments, shaking her head. "He's living in the past. It's pretty sad really."

"Oh, we all know what that young love feeling is like." Ethan laughs and sighs reflectively. "Why do you think 'Used to Be' has been such a popular song?"

"As you just touched on, I think it's because we all know what first love is like." Ed places his hand on his heart.

"Cringe." I roll my eyes.

"There's nothing more real than the first time you fall in love," Ed continues. "All your senses come alive, and you're counting the hours, the minutes, the seconds until you can see that special person again."

Mel pushes two fingers into her mouth, faking a gag. I snort.

"Oh, you are spot on with your analogy of first love. I think everyone can identify with that," Rachel says encouragingly. Ed flashes her one of his killer smiles.

"That Rachel bloody fancies him, doesn't she?" I say, turning towards Mel for her opinion.

"Yeah, she does. He's a bit young for her, isn't he? I don't think Ethan's too impressed by her flirting though."

"Do you remember your first love, Rachel?" Ethan teases to his partner on TV and in real life too, pretending to be outraged.

"Well, yes, I do actually," Rachel replies, blushing ever so slightly.

"Enough said about that until we get home," Ethan concludes, faking a grin. "So, Ed, if Evie Del Rio were to get in touch, you'd definitely be up for meeting up again?"

"Of course I would. It would be great to catch up after all these years, but I completely respect that she has a family now."

"Oh, so now he's trying to be Mr Nice Guy, is he?" I huff.

"She's got a rather gorgeous husband," adds Rachel somewhat provocatively.

"Err, yes. Yes, of course, she's married. I, er, am completely aware of that." He clears his throat and scratches the side of his head. "Myself and some of the gang from the old days are hoping to have some sort of reunion soon around the time The Mountaineers are starting their reunion tour, you know, catch up, find out what's been going on, so it would be great if Evie could join us."

"Oh, that sounds interesting. Any idea what date that might be?" gushes Rachel.

"I'm just in the process of sorting something out with an old friend."

"And does this old friend have a name?" Ethan coaxes him.

"I couldn't possibly say at the moment, but rest assured you'll be the first to know," Ed cleverly retorts.

"Well, that's something to look forward to. And the reunion tour starts in October?" asks Rachel, seeking clarification.

"Yeah, that's right. We're starting in Newcastle on the eighth."

"We'll make sure to put a link to all the tour dates on our website," adds Ethan.

"Perhaps you and Rachel would like to come along to one of our London dates?" suggests Ed.

"We might just do that. Thanks, Ed."

"Yeah, I don't think they'll be there for some reason," I observe.

"I don't think Ethan will want to watch Rachel drooling over Ed," Mel agrees.

"Unfortunately, that's all we have time for right now with Ed, as we've got to go to the news. Please do come back and see us again soon," says Rachel.

"Thank you," replies Ed, flashing a huge smile to the camera.

I grab the remote and switch off the TV, ridding myself of the offending grinning smile of Ed Nash.

"He loves himself, doesn't he?" I exclaim, rolling my eyes. I finish the rest of my coffee, looking straight at Mel to gauge her reaction.

"He really does. I can't seem to picture your mum and Ed together. He seems a bit of a bad boy, doesn't he? Your mum is so ladylike and your dad is just so lovely. I can't imagine either of them being with anyone else," says Mel reassuringly.

"I bet they'll be discussing all the latest gossip on *Loose Women* again about Ed and my mum. This'll set Mum back even further, I just know it will. Once Will has finished school, I think Dad wants to take us away to Florida to get away from all the fallout," I add, taking our empty coffee cups and putting them in the dishwasher.

"Sounds good to me. Do you think you'll come back for your GCSE results or get the school office to email them?" quizzes Mel, trying to steer the conversation away from Ed Nash.

"I haven't even thought that far yet. I don't think I've done too well, what with everything that's been going on. I'll try to discuss things with my parents if I can catch them both together. Honestly, they're like passing ships in the night," I confess, hunched forward, elbow on the counter, resting my chin on my palm.

"You might surprise yourself, you know. And there are alternatives to A levels, especially at college. My cousin did animation alongside art, so there's lots to choose from." Mel pauses, as if giving me time to weigh up options in my head. "You don't have to stay on at school for sixth form, you know. I know I'm not staying on."

"Oh, Mel, I'll work it out nearer the time. Right now, I just want to know my mum is ok. Hopefully, Auntie Maura will have taken her out somewhere where there are no TVs."

Chapter Thirteen

Evie

December 1984

I'm so glad it's the Christmas holidays. Ed and I are still going strong, spending every spare moment we have together. It's difficult though, as my parents and my school are really ramping up the amount of studying I have to do for my O levels, which I'm due to take next summer. Ed's parents are much more relaxed about his revision schedule, but as his mum is a teacher, Ed almost has a ready-made tutor on hand if he needs it. He's also one of those students who doesn't really have to try too much with their studies, unlike me. If I don't study, I won't pass.

My best friend Ginny is having an early birthday party. Her actual birthday is Boxing Day, but no one is really allowed out on that particular day what with family Christmas gatherings, so Ginny always celebrates on the twenty-second of December. She's hired out the local church hall and invited nearly all of the boys we know from St Augustine's. The plan is that Ed and Jamie are going to smuggle in a load of alcohol with Ed's uncle Paul's DJ kit, as he's going to DJ at Ginny's party. He's also promised that he'll supply us some weed for the after-party at Ed's house.

None of our parents have a clue about our plans and that's half the fun of it.

Ginny and I spent months planning what to wear and, in the end, we're both pretty pleased with our choices. We bought our outfits from Kensington Market over several happy Saturday afternoons, mooching around the different stalls, soaking up the atmosphere. Even the food smells are so exotic. We looked in awe at the eclectic bunch of stallholders—they seem so mature and sophisticated to a couple of young and impressionable girls from Barnes. I've got the shortest black dress you have ever seen, which has a scooped low-cut back, so I'm not going to wear a bra. I've teamed it with some cowboy boots and a black leather biker jacket. Ginny's got a Grecian-style red dress. Her boobs look even more enormous than usual, thrust forward in a gravity defying bra. Her peroxide hair is piled high on her head. She looks stunning. No one would guess that she's just a few days shy of her sixteenth birthday.

The plan for after the official party is that Ginny's told her parents she's staying with me and I've told my parents that I'm staying with her when in fact we're all staying at Ed's house. Ed's parents are away for the night, but Paul will be there. Paul's cool. He isn't like any of our parents. Paul is a rule breaker. He treats us all like we're his equals, not fifteen- and sixteen-year-olds trying too hard to grow up too soon.

The party's amazing. Paul's choice of music is incredible, so the dance floor is never empty as he plays our favourite songs from The Smiths to The Police, The Cure, Siouxsie and the Banshees to New Order. There's something for everyone. You can almost smell the testosterone in the air as the single boys vie for the prettiest of the single girls, plying them with cheap booze and pulling them closer as the music starts to slow down towards the end of the evening. God knows how Ginny's parents don't have a clue about what's going on but they've mainly stayed in the little kitchenette area, handing out cokes and lemonades, which little do they know are being mixed with varieties of Cinzano and Bacardi. The tension is mounting as Ed and his band, The Propellers, do their soundcheck and Paul helps them set up their kit. Ed's fairly drunk but he still knows how to work a crowd.

They're nearing the end of their set when Ed decides to say a few words to the audience. "Thanks to everyone for always supporting us and to the lovely birthday girl Ginny for allowing us to play at her sweet sixteen birthday party. I've just written a new song, and I'd like to dedicate it to my girlfriend, Evie," Ed slurs to the audience, swaying ever so slightly.

He throws me one of his special smiles, and everyone's eyes are suddenly upon me. The band starts up, and the beginning of the song is just a riot of loud drumming from Mark coupled with Jez's bass guitar repeating the same riff over and over again before Ed cuts in with the vocals, his voice slightly gruff and husky from an evening of smoking and drinking. The words are raw and personal, and Ed doesn't take his eyes off me once as he sings every word directly to me. It's as if no one else exists in this precise moment of time.

The song ends in the same way it started—with Mark's heavy drumming and Jez's repetitive riff as Ed's voice repeats the same chorus line of "Forever mine, forever mine" again and again until the music comes to an abrupt stop. The crowd claps and claps and cheers for the band, and Ginny and I just look at each other in complete awe.

"Oh my God, Evie. That song was absolutely beautiful. Have you heard it before?" asks Ginny, giving my hand a squeeze.

"No, never." I shake my head, still in complete shock, beaming. "Ed's always saying he writes songs about me, but I'd never heard any of them until just then. That really was quite something."

Ed saunters towards me, wraps his arms around my waist and kisses me so passionately he nearly knocks Ginny's mum over, complete with a sagging tray of soggy egg mayonnaise sandwiches. Once we come up for breath, Ginny's mum looks at us both, slightly wide-eyed.

"Sandwich anyone? There are loads left over," Ginny's mum asks, trying to regain composure after being taken aback by the kiss.

Ed flashes Ginny's mum one of his killer smiles, patting his taut stomach whilst muttering something about needing to keep his figure in check, politely declining the neglected egg sandwiches.

"Oh, Ed, you're such a lovely young man and a very good singer too. Although all that drumming and guitar noise has given me quite a headache," witters Ginny's mum.

Ed's uncle Paul manages to interject rather cleverly, saying that he'll lock up and that her and her husband are to get themselves home and rest up after all their hard work putting on such a good spread. He even says he'll make sure everyone takes a piece of Ginny's birthday cake home. They don't need to be asked twice. I've never seen Ginny's parents move quite so fast. On their way out the door, Ginny's mum asks me to thank my parents for having Ginny to stay over. I nod and smile politely, stifling a giggle.

Paul plays "Come on Eileen" for one of the closing songs and finishes with "New York, New York", which typically results in most of the crowd falling over as everyone links arms and kick their legs higher and higher as the song comes to an end. Thankfully, Ginny and I remain upright. It really has been one of the most brilliant parties I have ever been to. Ginny begged her parents to let her have one of her presents early. She'd been hankering after a Polaroid instant camera so she could take loads of photos at the party. Of course, her parents caved in and the latest must-have camera was in Ginny's possession just in time for the party. We had great fun taking photos of each other in various stages of undress while we got ready. The boys managed to get hold of the Polaroid for a while and took some photos of the band together with quite a few cleavage shots. We spend ages poring over the photos later that night back at Ed's.

Chapter Fourteen

Virginia

July 2018

I sneakily managed to watch Ed on *Wake Up and Smell the Coffee* at work. I made an excuse about checking out the TV in the conference room for an upcoming meeting. My boss, Mr Bruce, was fine with it. He is very easy-going and, as far as bosses go, is really nice to work for. All the other PAs say he's mesmerised by my boobs. Well, he isn't the first man. But I'm not complaining. I enjoy the attention and all the more now that I'm older. I'll take whatever attention I can get.

Ed looked incredible. His hair is a bit shorter now, but he still has that same twinkle in his eyes and that charming, killer smile. I think Rachel was very taken by him and Ethan went quite easy on him. He even mentioned me—ok, not by name but he did describe me as a "friend". Hopefully we can get together and get to know each other all over again. I can't wait to show him my other photos. My next plan is to get a definitive date to actually meet up with Ed. If I can't engineer a meeting at his flat, then maybe we can discreetly meet in a hotel. I still live fairly local to where we were all brought up, although I have now moved to Hampton Hill, having been outpriced by Barnes' ever-spiralling house prices. I've got a nice thirties house, which I managed to secure after my first divorce.

To be honest, Jon, my first husband, was only too happy to let me have the house. All he wanted to keep was his beloved motorbike so he could indulge his midlife crisis with his bimbo girlfriend Jacey and tour around Europe with them both. He never really contributed to the house anyway. I put down the deposit from the money (an early inheritance present) that my parents had given me, so Jon didn't really have a claim on the house. He occasionally used to send money to me for Sasha, but once I married my second husband, Callum, and had Shannon, Callum was happy in the beginning to provide for both of my daughters. Jon was a posh boy— privately educated, dark-haired with a passion for all things to do with motorbikes and heavy metal— whereas Callum was a bit of a chancer, blonde hair, muscles and tattoos, with the gift of the gab. He could charm the birds off the trees. And that was the problem. He was always having affairs, and his last affair resulted in another daughter. That was it for me. And just like how Jon had quite happily disappeared from our lives, so did Callum. Then, it was just me and my girls.

Don't get me wrong, I've had boyfriends since Jon and Callum, but nothing really serious. I work hard and I still play hard, but something has definitely been missing from my life. I miss having a best friend. I've never got over Evie just upping and leaving. No goodbye. No messages. No postcards. Just a big fat void in my life.

My then boyfriend Jamie helped a lot when Evie first left. We all tried to help Ed at the beginning, as he was as bereft as I was. It brought us closer together at first, and Ed and I even had a little fling behind Jamie's back, but both of us missed Evie so much and seeing each other just intensified our mutual loss.

Ed left soon after Evie did once he'd done his O levels. I heard that he went to live with his uncle Paul and formed a band, but when Paul got arrested for dealing and went to prison, Ed lost his way a bit. He drifted in and out of a series of dead-end jobs before forming The Mountaineers with the guys from his original band, The Propellers. Once they split up again, he fell off the radar for a while. And then, of course, Evie's song "Used to Be" was featured in *The Girl in The Song* documentary after that TV series, and I guess the rest is history!

The remainder of my working day went by fairly quickly, as Mr Bruce was out at meetings for most of the afternoon, so I was able to daydream and plan my next course of action in meeting up with Ed once again. I've sent him a DM on Instagram and now I'm waiting. I've kept it light, complimenting him on his TV appearance and casually suggesting setting a date to discuss my photos. I've even checked to see if he's read the message—he has.

Well, I'm not going to hang around forever for him to get in touch. I will have to take matters into my own hands. I've laid out all my old Polaroid photos in a circle, carefully putting them in date order as best as I can remember. We all looked so different then: so young, so carefree and so very happy.

I pick up the photo of me with half a face of makeup done, taken as myself and Evie were getting ready for my sixteenth birthday party. God, that party was a right laugh. I got great kudos for holding that party. I think that was probably the last time I saw Evie let her hair down and really enjoy herself. That girl really knew how to party back then.

Chapter Fifteen

Ed

December 1984

After we pack Uncle Paul's DJ equipment and our kit safely away, we all leave the church hall and go back to my house. My parents are away, thankfully. Dad would have been fine about Paul and everyone else staying over but anything whatsoever to do with Paul and my mum always disapproves. So, I've said that I'm staying at Jamie's, and she seems happy with that. She thinks Jamie's parents are very respectable, what with Mr O'Connor owning his own garage and Mrs O'Connor being a dentist. Mum and Dad are staying with Mum's sister in North London for a pre-Christmas party, so she's far too preoccupied to think too much about me.

We manage to store Uncle Paul's DJing equipment in his van together with our kit. There's a crook lock on the steering wheel, so everything is fairly safe overnight. The lads and I carry the rest of the booze back to mine, and we fill up every spare space in our fridge with the leftover drink from the party.

Ginny's gained a newfound confidence now that she's almost sixteen and is drinking, smoking and snorting whatever she can lay her hands on. Evie's the same. They crank up my parents' old stereo and put on one of Uncle Paul's mixtapes. They take to the makeshift dance floor in the living room, dancing and gyrating provocatively to Siouxsie and the Banshees' version of "Dear Prudence". Every single guy in the room is transfixed by the girls' antics, and it feels good as I smugly think that I'll be the one going to bed with Evie tonight. Jamie looks at Ginny with a wry grin, obviously harbouring similar feelings to me, about the reality of him finally spending the whole night with Ginny. We turn to each other, clink our drinks together and smile, as if to say that we really can't believe our luck.

The partying continues late into the night and then a few people start to head home. Soon enough, there's just the usual crowd left: me and Evie, Jamie and Ginny, Mark and Jez from the band and a few girls from Evie and Ginny's school who have kind of latched on. Uncle Paul's hooked up with one of the barmaids from the local pub, and she seems perfectly happy serving drinks to everyone despite having just finished her shift. It might have something to do with Paul providing her with enough speed to last most people a whole weekend. Every time Paul, or indeed anyone else, wants a drink, she's there, content with a little arse squeeze from Paul as a reward for all her sterling efforts.

By 3 a.m., both Evie and Ginny are starting to flag, so we decide it's time for bed. Jamie and I make several attempts to get both girls upstairs but a combination of partaking in too many drugs and drinking to excess makes the easiest of tasks seem near impossible. Jamie gives up, and Ginny and Jamie end up crashing on the sofa. I eventually pick Evie up and carry her up the remaining stairs to my bedroom. I lay her down gently on my bed and take off her cowboy boots. Even though we've been sleeping together for some time, I don't think it's right to undress her while she's out cold. I strip off to my boxer shorts and join Evie in bed.

It takes me some time to drop off, as I'm completely wired. I can still hear Paul and his barmaid friend talking downstairs and the distant sound of Paul's mixtape as I eventually drift off to sleep.

It seems like I've only just dropped off when I feel Evie's arms around me. She's now completely naked and tugging at my boxer shorts. I turn towards her, and we start to kiss with more and more urgency as she climbs on top of me. I don't know if it's the drugs, the booze, timing or maybe just the perfect mix of all three but tonight with Evie has to rate among one of the most incredible nights of my life sex-wise. Tonight, we don't have the constraints of school, homework or anyone busting in on us, so I guess we just really take our time, experimenting and exploring each other's body. Evie gives me one more kiss and rolls off, exhausted. I sit up in bed to roll a joint as Evie settles back to sleep.

"I love you, Evie Del Rio," I whisper, not realising she's listening.

"I know you do. Me too," Evie sleepily replies.

I abandon my joint and lie back next to Evie, watching the rise and fall of her chest as she drifts back off to sleep.

Chapter Sixteen

Genie

July 2018

I'm so glad Maura came over to rescue me last night. I really needed her company and her practical advice. I can't believe I almost told her my biggest secret from before I met her. She knows I messed up my exams and had to leave home, but that's about all she knows. She's been a part of my life since we met in Brighton all those years ago and, luckily for me, she employed me first as a cleaner and then in the evenings I would help to collect all the empty glasses in the pub that she was managing. She let me serve behind the bar once I turned eighteen.

I really am almost ready to share my secret with both Gray and Maura, but as Will was home last night, I really didn't want him to overhear our conversation and find things out before Gray.

Today is the first day I've felt relatively normal since *The Girl in the Song* came out. Maura insisted on treating me to lunch, so we're now at a little pub that Maura knows. We've hardly bumped into anyone, let alone anyone we might know. This beautifully kept secret of a pub overlooks the River Thames.

"God, we lived on this sort of food back in the Brighton days," Maura comments, as if reading my mind, helping herself to a huge dollop of mayonnaise for the chips we're sharing. Maura followed me to London not long after I moved from Brighton, a larger client base for her venture of advising failing pubs. We always joke that she's like the non-sweary version of Gordon Ramsay.

"Unfortunately, nowadays, my metabolism isn't quite the same," I snort, taking a bite of my cheese and ham toastie.

"Come off it, Genie. There's not a pick on you currently. You can afford to indulge yourself once in a while. I don't want you fading away on us."

Maura has only ever known me as Genie. When I moved to Brighton at seventeen, I changed my name from Evie to Genie. I wanted to reinvent myself and distance myself from all things "Evie". Although I had actually been christened Genevieve, I felt it never really suited me.

As I struggle to finish my food, I catch a middle-aged woman with sleek black, bobbed hair a couple of tables away giving me a second look. "It is you, isn't it?" she calls out to me.

"Sorry, I think you must be mistaken," I falter, a trickle of cold sweat running down my back. The woman gets up from her table and approaches ours, still convinced.

"You're Will's mum, aren't you? I'm Marcus' mum. They were at primary school in Richmond together. We moved to Dubai about ten years ago. I'm just back visiting my parents. God, those two were as thick as thieves back then," she says with a warm smile, as if remembering all the scrapes the boys used to get into.

"Yes, yes, of course," I reply, my tense shoulders relaxing a little as my brain tries to place her from all those years ago.

"Oh, well, I'll let you enjoy your lunch in peace, but please do take my card. Marcus will be thrilled to hear that I bumped into you. He always talks so fondly about your Will," she says, standing up to hand me her card, which she removes from her beautiful Mulberry wallet. "You look great, by the way," she adds, gently touching my arm.

I glance down at her glossy embossed gold and white card and take note of her name. Sandra Mariner, MD, Goldcrest Holdings. It does vaguely ring a bell.

"Thank you, Sandra. You too. Say hi to Marcus."

"Do you have a card?" she asks, lingering near the table.

"No, not on me. I'll text you," I hastily reply, not wanting to divulge any further personal information. If the last few months have taught me anything, it's to trust no one. Apart from my nearest and dearest.

Lunch out ends with a glass of champagne each, at Maura's insistence, to toast the fact she managed to actually get me out of the house. It's a monumental achievement for me, and I almost feel normal again. Maura settles the bill, once again at her insistence, and before long, we've ordered an Uber and are making our way back to South West London. Thankfully, it's Ahmed, Maura's usual Uber driver, and after initial pleasantries, he leaves us to our conversation while he concentrates on the road.

"Thanks for today, Maura. It's been great. Just what I needed. I loved that pub. How come I've never heard of it?" I ask. I slouch in my seat, next to Maura in the back, relaxed for the first time in ages. It's probably that glass of champagne that's taken the edge off.

"The whole reason I love going there is because it feels like my own little peaceful haven. You only get to know about it if someone introduces you to it. It's almost like a private members' club," Maura discloses, face animated with personality and excitement.

"Well, someone must have introduced Sandra Mariner to it." I glimpse out the window, my mind stuck on her, not taking in any of the scenery. "I do vaguely remember her and her son Marcus from Will's primary school days."

"Do you think you'll contact her?" asks Maura.

"I don't know. It might be nice to chat to someone who hasn't heard all about my scandalous past," I muse.

"Well, just be careful. Admittedly, she's been away from the UK for ten years, but she may well have read all about you and Ed online or indeed watched the documentary. Plus, her family are still here. They'd know."

"Don't worry, she's not going to become my new best friend," I say, giggling.

Maura's face remains expressionless despite the teasing. "You know how I worry, Genie."

"Yes, I know. You've always had my back," I reassure her.

We get back to Richmond quickly and both climb out of the Uber.

"I won't stay long, Genie, as I've got to get back to the cats. I just need to grab my bag and then I'll be off," Maura says, following me to the house.

I put the key in the door and, not hearing the usual beeps of the alarm, I realise it's off and that someone is home.

"Cassie, are you home?" I call out. At least, I've deduced it's her, as Will still has about a week or so of school left before the summer break and it's far too early for Gray to be home. "Auntie Maura is just picking up her bag and then she's off. Can you come down and say hello?"

Maura places her hand gently on my arm. "Don't bother her, Genie. I'll knock on her door when I get my bag." She smiles and starts up the stairs.

I busy myself in the kitchen unloading the dishwasher, buoyed up by having spent such a nice afternoon with Maura. I even find myself humming along to the radio.

Chapter Seventeen

Ed

July 2018

I have to say that I think my appearance on *Wake Up and Smell the Coffee* with Rachel and Ethan went rather well. I managed to flirt a little with Rachel, but not so much as to upset Ethan, and I plugged the band's reunion tour. I hope I seemed considerate in regard to Evie's feelings, but our teenage relationship, although brief, still seems to make headlines and I'm going to milk it for as long as I can.

Loose Women was doing a feature about first love off the back of my appearance on *Wake Up and Smell the Coffee*. There was quite a discussion about whether or not you really ever forget your first love. Do any of your future relationships ever match up to the thrill of that first love?

I make myself a coffee and take a seat on my balcony, taking advantage of another beautiful sunny day, and begin to scroll through my social media feeds. Ginny's privately messaged me on Instagram again, congratulating me on my appearance. She's keen to catch up and probing for me to give a definitive date to do so. Ginny was always a nice enough girl, but not a patch on Evie. I have a vague recollection of us having a bit of a thing way back, not long after Evie left. I just remember it not feeling right at the time. It was too soon after Evie. I left the area where we all used to live not long after. I send her back a quick message confirming that I can meet her at her house one evening this week. It will be more discreet this way, and I also don't really want her to know exactly where I live just now.

I have a quick scroll through social media while I sip my coffee. The general consensus was positive after my TV appearance, which I'm really happy with. Mission accomplished.

I look out over the balcony and admire the pleasing view of the carefully manicured gardens below. I could never have afforded to live somewhere like this if Used to Be hadn't been picked up for the theme song to that TV show. And if *The Girl in the Song* hadn't picked it up afterwards. Life's good again right now.

I glance at my DMs again to see if Ginny has replied yet. Nothing. It would be interesting to catch up after all these years. I've lost touch with most of the old gang except for my fellow band members. When we were growing up, it wasn't as easy as it is nowadays to keep in touch. If you moved without a forwarding address or a new telephone number, then you could more or less disappear. Which is exactly what happened with Evie and then again with me.

After Evie left, I just wanted to get away, to try and reinvent myself and not be reminded of her every single day. I spent a whole month after she went just answering questions as to her whereabouts. No one around me understood what it felt like to be sixteen and for your girlfriend to just up sticks and leave without saying a word. It destroyed my self-confidence. When Uncle Paul offered me a way out, I took it. My mother was heartbroken when I left with him. My father, however, would have loved to have had the guts to come with us, but he knew it would break my mother's heart to lose both her only son and her husband. They're still together to this day. My relationship with them is somewhat strained, but we've been in touch since *The Girl in the Song* media storm. My mother will never forgive Paul for taking me away, but at the time it seemed like my only choice: to get away and start over.

Paul, unfortunately, has been in and out of prison over the years. Not surprisingly mainly for dealing, some shoplifting and for being drunk and disorderly, as he's always getting into fights when he's drunk. I keep in touch, bung him a bit of money every now and again because I owe him for being there when I needed him. I also like to keep him away from the press. I don't need some journalist probing Paul about my past. Paul was the one who first introduced me and all my friends to drugs. I was quite a mess by the time Paul went to prison. I couldn't hold down a job, as I was either pissed or high, normally both. I couldn't hold down a relationship, and I was always getting asked to leave bands that I'd joined. They used to love me at first, but once I'd made that first good impression and they got to know the real me, they would let me go. I just couldn't sustain being sober long enough to do the one thing that I was actually good at: being the frontman in a rock band. Thankfully, I've got my second chance now with being in a successful band.

It's strange to think that all my misfortune started with Evie leaving me and yet somehow my resurgence today is all to do with the song that I wrote for her all those years ago. I just wish I could talk to her to find out what happened. To get closure. Maybe then I could finally move on. I'm almost fifty, and I've never been married or had a family. I feel like I've missed out. Don't get me wrong, I'm so grateful for a second shot at getting my music heard but my personal life's a mess.

My phone beeps with a DM from Ginny inviting me over to her house in Hampton Hill tonight, with the promise of a home-cooked meal. It does sound rather inviting. I message her back, agreeing to meet. I'm not meeting her until 8 p.m., so I have the rest of the day to myself. I decide to hit the gym, do some weights, go for a run and relax in the spa in readiness for my dinner date.

Chapter Eighteen

Virginia

July 2018

Oh my God, I let out such a shriek when Ed finally replied that I got some very strange looks in the office. Thankfully, my boss had called me earlier to say he wouldn't be returning to the office, as his last meeting had been cancelled, and he was now nearer to his home than he was to the office. He also very kindly said that if everything was up to date, I could leave early. I didn't need to be told twice. I had my bag packed and was out of there before anyone else realised. I'm grateful for the extra time, as Ed is due over at 8 p.m. and, in my wisdom, I offered to cook dinner for him.

Now, my girls will tell you I'm not the world's best cook but I do cook a great roast, and I'm guessing that Ed, being a single man, probably hasn't had a good home-cooked roast or indeed any other sort of home-cooked meal for some time. A slightly odd choice, I know, for the middle of summer, but it will have to do. I also picked up some fresh strawberries for dessert and some wine and beer before driving home at such a pace to try and miss the school traffic.

Both the girls are out at work and college, so I have time to tidy the house, take a shower and start to prep the meal. Once everything is sorted food-wise, I will style my hair. My hair colour has changed over the years. I was a brassy peroxide blonde the last time Ed and I saw each other. Nowadays, courtesy of my very expensive hairdresser Mario, I'm a kind of sun-kissed honey blonde. Thankfully, Mario worked his magic on my roots just last week.

Clothes-wise, I'm going to be casual: tight cropped capri pants and a silk vest, with natural, light makeup. If the weather holds up, perhaps we can have a drink in the garden.

I finish the final touches to the house and have a final check on my precious Polaroids. I actually unearthed a bunch more over at my parents' house. Ed's obviously intrigued enough to take time out of his busy schedule to come and see them for himself, and I hope secretly that he's just a little bit curious to see me after all these years. I've called the girls to ask them to make themselves scarce tonight, and they happily agreed. Sasha and Shannon know the importance of this dinner.

I glance at the time: 7:45 p.m. Just fifteen minutes to go. I pour myself a small glass of chilled prosecco and take it out in the garden, enjoying the last bit of evening sun. The garden is one of the reasons I bought this house. It's big enough for entertaining, always sunny—it's south-west facing—and despite being just off Hampton Hill High Street, it's fairly private and secluded, as over the years, the various climbers I lovingly planted have taken root and offered some much-needed shade and privacy.

I'm at my happiest just pottering about in my garden, pulling up any rogue weeds that dare to try and take up residence. I really want to do some repairs on my summerhouse and maybe even get a hot tub. Perhaps my old photos might help towards that financially in some way? I'll see what Ed thinks of them.

My thoughts are interrupted by the faint sound of the doorbell. 8:01 p.m. He's almost on time. I put down my glass of prosecco and walk to the door, opening it. My whole body turns weak. I thought with the years that have passed, maybe my attraction and pull to him would have at least become manageable. It doesn't help that he looks better in person. As good, just aged, as when I used to know him.

"Hi, Ed. Great to see you. Please do come in. Welcome to my humble abode."

"Hello, Ginny. You look great," says Ed, leaning over to kiss me on both cheeks. My heart is beating so loudly, I'm convinced he can hear it. I feel like I'm sixteen years old all over again. I've dreamed of being this close to Ed Nash for a lifetime and here he is on my doorstep!

"Actually, I've reverted back to Virginia again. It seems more grown-up than Ginny," I explain, flushing slightly at his compliment.

"Sorry, Gin… I mean, Virginia. Yes, you're right. Virginia really suits you. Oh, and these are for you, Virginia," Ed says, handing me a beautiful bunch of gerberas together with a chilled bottle of champagne as he steps inside.

"Thank you so much. The gerberas are just beautiful. Come through to the kitchen while I put these in water, and

I'll fix you a drink. Dinner will be ready in about half an hour," I say.

Ed follows me through to the kitchen.

"What would you like to drink? I've got beer, prosecco and now, thanks to you, champagne."

"Oh, I'll grab a beer to start off with, please. We can maybe have a glass of bubbly later," he replies.

"Sure." I take a beer from the fridge, open it and hand it to him before getting a vase out from the cupboard under the sink. "Let me just put the gerberas in a vase and then we can go through to the garden. It's still lovely and warm out there."

"How come you know what flowers they are? I didn't; I just thought they looked nice." Ed laughs as he watches me carefully arrange my flowers in a vase.

"I'm no expert but I really do love gardening. It's my guilty pleasure. I could spend hours in my garden, and in all weathers too, just nurturing the plants." I step outside and lead Ed over to some chairs in the garden.

"Do you know it's been over thirty years since we last saw each other? I never expected after all this time to be sitting in Ginny Weather's garden discussing horticulture," he teases as he leans back and looks at the sky, bathing in the last of today's sun.

"Yeah, I guess we've all changed a bit over the years. Although, look at you, you're still getting your music heard. And then you've got the tour to look forward to, haven't you?" I say encouragingly.

"I guess so, but to be honest, if it weren't for that documentary, I'd probably still be struggling." He sighs.

I smile weakly. "No point dwelling on that. You're here now. I'm just going to check on dinner. I'll be back in a couple of minutes."

"Sure. It's rather relaxing sitting in your garden. Do you need any help?" Ed asks somewhat reluctantly.

"No, I've got it covered. I'll call you when it's ready."

Chapter Nineteen

Ed

July 2018

I reached Virginia's house just after 8 p.m. and discovered her to be a very pleasant surprise. Obviously, it's the first time we've seen each other in over thirty years but we've picked up quite effortlessly, and I'm really enjoying the evening. She cooked an amazing roast beef dinner with all the trimmings. I haven't eaten such a delicious home-cooked meal in years. Virginia's two ex-husbands must have been fools to let her go. She's filled me in on her daughters, who she's more or less brought up single-handedly. You can easily tell how proud she is of them. They sound like a nice, tight family unit. The more I hear about her family, the more I regret the choices I made over the years and the fact I'm fundamentally alone.

"I'll just go upstairs and get the photos," says Virginia, leaving the kitchen.

"Sure thing. Shall I open the champagne?" I boldly suggest with the support of a fair bit of alcohol.

"Yes, why not. Although, it is a school night. Some of us have to adhere to office hours, you know," she says with a playfully raised eyebrow and a smirk as she turns back to look at me.

"What time do you have to be in work tomorrow?"

"About nine-thirty. It's not too bad. And my boss is very flexible. I think he's just grateful that he has someone to look after him. His previous PA was a bit of a tyrant." She continues down the hallway. "What are your plans for tomorrow? Do you have an early start?" Virginia asks, waiting for a response with her foot on the bottom step, ready to climb the stairs.

"We start our rehearsals for the upcoming tour and we've got a meeting with our manager, so it will be busy but hopefully nice and productive."

I fetch the champagne and manage to locate a couple of champagne glasses. Just as I'm pouring the second glass, Virginia returns from upstairs with a bunch of Polaroids on a tray. Within seconds, she's carefully arranged all the Polaroids in a row across the tray.

"I've tried to put them in date order as best I can. You might be able to shed some light on some of the ones that I can't remember the dates of," says Virginia.

We spend around twenty minutes laughing and joking about the state of our haircuts and clothing choices from the '80s until Virginia focuses our attention on a couple of the later photos of me and Evie. I remember the day quite vividly, as it was an unusually warm day in early April. A big crowd of us had gone to hang out in Mark's garden. His parents had installed their own swimming pool in their garden, inspired by them having a pool with their Spanish villa. It was a great novelty back then, and Mark's parents were more than happy to have us all over to share in the fun of having an outdoor swimming pool.

"Look at Evie in this photo," says Virginia, pointing a carefully manicured nail at Evie, who was sitting on the side of the pool, dangling her legs in the water, watching and laughing as the rest of us splashed around in the pool. "Don't you think it's odd that Evie is the only one of us not in swimwear?"

I shake my head. "Not really. I think she forgot her swimsuit that day, if I remember. She'd had another argument with her mum about going out when she was grounded, and she stormed out of the house without it."

"Well, the Evie I used to know would have just jumped in the pool in her underwear, but she seemed very hesitant on that day to undress and get in the water. Don't you think that's odd?"

"Err no, not really. Maybe she was on her period? I dunno. Evie was a girl with her own rules," I say, feeling slightly uncomfortable as to where this conversation could be heading.

Virginia continues to scrutinise Evie in the photo. "Don't you think she looks like she's got a bit of a tummy on her?"

I stare harder at the photo. "Umm, I didn't really notice, to be fair. Maybe a bit. As I said, she might have had her period and been a bit bloated?" I reply. I had forgotten that once "Ginny" has a bee in her bonnet, she won't let it go.

Virginia leans back, taking her eyes from the photo to me. "Well, Ed, I have a theory. Top up my glass, and I'll explain."

Virginia doesn't waste any time once I've topped up her glass. She takes a big sip, wrinkling her nose from the champagne bubbles. "I think Evie was pregnant, Ed. That's why she left. I guess her parents found out. Did you have any idea?"

Virginia's comments are like a sucker punch. A family is all I've ever wanted. Surely that can't be the reason Evie left?

"I don't think she was. I think I would have known," I reply somewhat defensively, not really knowing quite what to say to Virginia but trying to shut down this awkward topic of conversation.

"No disrespect, Ed, but you were never and probably will never be an expert on pregnancy," says Virginia, completely dismissing my view. "I've had two babies. I know what it's like to be pregnant, the changes that your body goes through. You can see how her waist has slightly thickened here." She points to it in the photo. "She definitely looks bigger than she normally did. Her boobs look bigger too. I'm surprised you didn't notice them. I can't believe we didn't notice all those years ago, but I guess we were young," she concludes, staring at me, waiting for me to respond.

"Well, I'm not so sure. I'd like to think I would have noticed if Evie was pregnant, but I suppose it does explain a lot. I guess I'll never know. I can't exactly ask her, can I?" I eventually say, completely dumbfounded by Virginia's suggestion that Evie might have been pregnant. This is definitely not what I expected from tonight's meet up. I just feel emotionless, my brain struggling to process, still wanting to deny the whole thing because... the idea of nearly having everything I've ever wanted and losing it is harder than thinking I was never even close.

"No, but I could. I could try and reach out over Instagram like I did with you," suggests Virginia, her eyes shining brightly with anticipation.

Chapter Twenty

Genie

July 2018

I feel so much better after my lunch out with Maura. That woman is a tonic. She should be used by the NHS to alleviate depression and anxiety. I know she's certainly saved my mental health on many an occasion over the years. She's the sister I never had.

I walk through to the sitting room and settle in my favourite chair overlooking the garden, which is looking rather resplendent with the vibrant, bright colours of summer. I have so much to be thankful for: a loving and loyal husband, two great kids and my health.

My silent thoughts are interrupted by Cassie, who's come downstairs. She enters the room rather reluctantly and bites her bottom lip. I wonder why she's looking so sheepish.

"Hi, Cassie. How was last night?" I ask, trying to figure out if something happened last night to make her seem so not herself.

"Yeah, ok," Cassie mutters.

"Just ok? Did you have a few too many proseccos?"

"Yeah. About that…"

I smile, thankful to have reached the cause of her sheepishness. "Don't worry, darling. It happens to the best of us. It's all a learning curve, but, bizarrely, it never puts you off, as you'll find out for yourself," I say, laughing.

Cassie still won't look me in the eye, and I'm beginning to realise it has nothing to do with her hangover. My laugher drops off.

"What's happened? Is everything ok with Will and your dad?"

"Yes. Fine. Absolutely fine," replies Cassie. "But I do have something to run by you."

Brilliant. Even in my head, it comes off sarcastic. "Ok. Shoot. I'm all ears."

Cassie takes a deep breath before explaining that she saw Ed on *Wake Up and Smell the Coffee* to mainly promote his forthcoming tour.

"You ended up coming up, as you always seem to do. I mean, compared to some of the stuff that's been in the press, what he said about you was quite tame. But I really think you should sit down and watch it on catch up," she suggests.

I nod slowly. "Perhaps when your dad gets back. Thanks for looking out for me. Now, please don't be so nervous in the future about approaching me. I get it. It's not nice, but nothing for you to get so hesitant about," I say, getting up to wrap Cassie in my arms.

"I'm sorry, Mum," she whispers, hugging me back.

"It's fine, darling. We know Ed isn't going to go away, and with his increasing fame and popularity, my name will always be linked to his." I let go of Cassie and step back, my eyes dropping to the floor. "I'm probably going to have to give my own version of events one day soon, but I don't think I'm quite strong enough yet."

"It might be a good idea, Mum. Until you comment back, everyone will take all the comments about you as truth. And for what it's worth, I think you're strong enough."

"I know. I'll discuss things with your dad when he gets back tonight. He's been suggesting that I get in touch with the makers of the documentary, so I might consider that going forward." I lick my lips and fake a smile. "In the meantime, what do you think everyone would like for dinner tonight? It's been ages since I cooked a proper family meal."

"Homemade lasagne," shouts Cassie without any hesitation.

"Lasagne it is, then. With a nice crisp salad and some very garlicky bread."

"Do you need any help, Mum?" Cassie asks, her hand on the doorframe, not sure whether to make her way to the kitchen or go back to her bedroom.

"No, I'm fine. You go upstairs and have a rest; nurse that hangover of yours," I tease. "I'll bring you up a cuppa."

"Will do. Thanks, Mum." She goes to walk upstairs, pauses and turns back to face me. "How do you know I'm hungover?"

I snort. "It's in your eyes, darling. Don't forget, I do remember what it's like being sixteen, you know," I reply with a wink.

I internally giggle as I watch Cassie clumsily climb the stairs back to her room. She really is a fantastic daughter.

Not perfect in some people's eyes, but she's my version of perfect, along with my beloved Will. I would do absolutely anything to protect my children from the outside world. I've always vowed to be a loving and caring parent to my children. I've never wanted Cassie or Will to feel like disappointments to me or not good enough. I spent a lifetime trying to make up for my youthful misdemeanours to my parents. They were just beginning to be proud of the life I've made for myself when Ed stormed back in and smashed my newfound life and respect to smithereens.

I've made a decision. I'm finally ready to put my side of the story out there. But I will have to talk to Gray first. I'd hoped to run through things with Maura first to gauge her reaction but that didn't really pan out last night, as Will was there. For the first time in ages, I feel quite positive and strong. I can handle anything with the support of Gray and the children. I will sit down with Gray after dinner and finally tell him everything. He is a good husband and father and the backbone of this family. I thank my lucky stars every day for bringing him into my life.

Chapter Twenty-one

Gray

July 2018

We've given Peter a great send-off and are all certainly feeling the aftereffects of the previous boozy night this morning. In fact, it's only after consuming a cheeseburger meal with a coke from Maccy D's at lunchtime that I began to feel more on an even keel.

I feel bad that I ended up staying out last night at the company flat, as I've had a couple of texts from Cassie saying that Ed was on TV this morning. Cassie managed to break the news gently to Genie. Amazingly, she took the news quite calmly, and Cassie said that she's even cooking a family meal for us all tonight. Late last night, she sent me a text wishing me a great evening and that she understood why I needed to stay out. She also sent me another text this morning saying we need a family meeting. I'm not convinced that tonight is the right night to have a family meeting, as it's the eleventh, which means it's the World Cup semi-final between England and Croatia. If I'm honest, I don't think Will will be in the mood for a family conflab. Perhaps Genie and I can have a bit of a chat first before we involve the kids. I've been waiting for Genie to open up and talk about this *Girl in the Song* business for so long. I might give Maura a call to see if she has been given the heads-up on any revelations.

I push shut my office door and dial Maura's number. She answers within two rings.

"Gray, how are you? Have you recovered from all your partying last night?" Maura asks, amusement in her voice.

"Hi, Maura. Well, let's say once I consumed some of the finest fast-food cuisine, I was as right as rain," I joke, hastily pushing the empty fast-food cardboard cartons deeper into my office bin.

"Genie will be horrified to think you've been frequenting McDonald's again, you naughty boy." Maura laughs.

"Well, she doesn't really have to be privy to that information right now, but seriously, I just wanted to talk to you about Genie's current state of mind after Ed's recent TV appearance. I'm assuming you've heard?"

"I have. She messaged me to let me know and said Cassie told her. She's actually doing ok. She seems calmer and more like her old self. She took it all quite well. He seems to have run out of salacious things to say about her, I guess. The old git might be mellowing."

A chesty "ha" escapes my throat. "I doubt that, Maura. *The Girl in the Song* has been such a lifeline to Ed, and I'm not naïve enough to think he's run out of steam quite yet. But I did want to ask you something. Genie has called a family meeting tonight, and I wondered if she's given you any clue as to where her head's at right now?" If my phone was corded, I would be nervously wrapping the cords around my fingers right now.

"To be honest, I think she wanted to tell me something yesterday, but as Will was at home, she seemed hesitant to really talk. A family meeting is good progress, isn't it?" Maura's voice rose in pitch with her question. "She did seem much more like her usual self at lunch earlier. She bumped into someone she knew from Will's primary school days and handled herself really well, not like the jumpy Genie of late."

My eyebrows raise. "That's good to hear. Maybe she's coming around to my way of thinking and is now willing to put her side of things to the press."

"Well, if that's what she wants to do, good on her. She's been suffering in silence for too long, and neither of us really know what she went through before she arrived in Brighton."

"Very true," I agree. "Thanks again, Maura."

"Cheerio, Gray," she says just before I hang up.

Chapter Twenty-two

Genie

July 2018

I can't wait to see Gray. I just want him to hold me and never let me go. I feel now is the time for the whole truth to be told and I'm going to tell Gray first. He deserves to finally know. It looks like I couldn't have chosen a worse day to call a family meeting, as Will hasn't been able to stop talking about a certain World Cup semi-final. I guess my revelation will have to wait until the match is over. In the meantime, I'm going to busy myself with organising a family meal. I really used to enjoy cooking from scratch, and I know that the children certainly appreciate my efforts when I do cook. I think Gray will be secretly pleased too, as I've neglected all things domestic since *The Girl in the Song* aired, and I've noticed that Gray has lost quite a bit of weight recently. If it weren't for Maura, I think we would all have faded away.

I need to go to the supermarket to pick up the food and some wine for tonight, so I decide to see if Cassie will come with me. It'll be good to have a bit of time with my girl. She's been managing so well with everything. She's had her GCSEs to contend with, she's been worried about me and she's experienced the dark side of fame, courtesy of my youthful misdemeanours.

I call upstairs to Cassie, and thankfully she's awake. Soon enough, she joins me downstairs, nursing a coffee. She jumps at the chance of coming shopping with me. I drive into the main part of Richmond and park up.

"Fancy a cuppa and a nice bit of cake before we start shopping?" I ask Cassie as we climb out of the car.

"Yeah, go on. Where do you want to go?"

"How about that little café on the hill?" I tilt my head in the direction of it. "You can work up a bit of an appetite on the walk and I can work lunch with Maura off."

Cassie laughs. "I definitely don't need to work up an appetite but sure, Mum, there is fine."

We leave the car park arm in arm, mother and daughter walking in the hot July sunshine as if we don't have a care in the world. Even before I left, my mother would never show me any affection, let alone walk out in public with me arm in arm. Thankfully, affection has always come easily to me concerning my children. God, just thinking about my mother brings me out in a cold sweat, which seems at odds with the heat of yet another sunny day.

After I met and married Gray all those years ago and I was first pregnant with Cassie, Gray helped me reach out to my parents, and up until recently we had a fairly cordial relationship. They seemed to be far better grandparents than they ever were parents, Mother in particular. But as soon as Ed surfaced, our relationship has once again become strained. My mother can barely tolerate being in the same room as me. I suppose I only have myself to blame, but I still maintain that I would never continue to punish Cassie or Will for mistakes they made when they were young years down the line.

Cassie and I reach the café, both out of breath from the uphill walk, and are lucky enough to find a nice table in the shade. We quickly order, and before long Cassie's tucking into a slice of delicious homemade carrot cake, washed down by a nice pot of tea we're sharing.

"You do realise we could have easily just sat in the garden with a cuppa, you know," I remind Cassie with a wry grin. "We probably should have picked something fancier that we don't have at home."

"I know, Mum, but we haven't got any carrot cake at home, so surely my cake order makes up for that," Cassie responds, greedily shovelling the rest of the cake into her mouth, hardly able to close it.

I focus on my cup, my mind starting to flip through serious thoughts, and wipe a stray drip of tea from the side of it. "I'm so sorry I've put you through so much, Cassie, especially during your GCSE year."

"It's not your fault your first boyfriend happened to write a song about you. I mean, it's flattering and everything but it's not really something that you want to be reminded of over thirty years later, when you're not even with that person anymore." Cassie dabs at her mouth with her napkin before pushing her plate to the side and crossing her arms on the table. "If someone wrote a song about me right now, I'd be thrilled if it were successful, but years later it would be a big no-no. The girl you were then is so not the woman you are now."

"How did your dad and I manage to raise such a wonderfully wise and beautiful daughter?" I proudly say, holding back the tears. It's almost as if Cassie understands exactly why I'm so nervous about Ed being in my life again, which, of course, is ridiculous. No one knows the real reason why his reappearance disturbs me so much. I open my mouth and quickly close it again before the secret slips from my lips.

"I learnt from the best," Cassie says, beaming.

I call over the waiter and pay the bill, then we start to walk back down the hill to the supermarket to stock up for tonight. Cassie and I spend ages choosing ingredients for the next couple of meals, as well as getting what I need for lasagne. I leave Cassie with all the bags of shopping while I bring the car round. As the traffic is light, we're back home within ten minutes.

Shopping successfully put away, Cassie and I grab a couple of iced waters from the fridge and sit outside on the patio, enjoying the afternoon sun. I've tied my hair back and put sunglasses on. I bought a newspaper with my shopping earlier—something I rarely do after all the recent tabloid gossip about my youth—and I happily thumb through the pages all insisting that "Football is coming home!"

"It's that big football match tonight that Will's been banging on about for ages, isn't it?"

"Yes, it's a biggy, Mum. Even I know that it's no mean feat that England have got through to the semi-finals of the World Cup," Cassie says, laughing.

"Sorry, darling. Despite having a football-mad son, I seem to have no interest in the game whatsoever. It's something that seems to have passed me by. Well, apart from that manager's gorgeous waistcoats." I tilt my sunglasses down and wink.

Cassie shakes her head, chuckling. "Would you and Dad mind if I watch the match over at Mel's after dinner? Her parents said she could have a few friends over. They're having a bit of a party to celebrate the football."

I try to make sure what I'm feeling internally doesn't reflect on my face as disappointment inwardly takes over. "Umm. I guess so. Do you know if Will has any plans? I really wanted to have a bit of a family meeting tonight."

Cassie shrugs. "I think he mentioned something about watching it at Tommy's."

"Well, I'll still cook early and then you two can go your respective ways. Unless I postpone the meal and you eat at Mel's and Tommy's? We can all catch up tomorrow. I'm sure your dad's keen to watch the game himself." My big secret has waited this long to be told, so I don't think a few more hours will really make that much difference, and Gray, although not the biggest football fan in the world, always loves watching England play.

"Would you mind, Mum? Mel's parents are doing a barbecue, and I think Tommy's parents are too."

"It's fine. Why didn't we think of having a barbecue tonight and having a few friends over?" I say, kicking myself that I've been so distracted recently. "I know I've been all over the place, but I promise you that things are really going to change from now on. I'm feeling stronger every day, and you have all helped me with that. And your auntie Maura, of course."

"It's fine, Mum. It's what families do, isn't it?" says Cassie, kissing my cheek, just like she used to when she was small.

"Thank you. I appreciate everything you all do for me," I reply, wiping my happy tears away.

"Oh, you're not going all soppy on me, are you, Mum?" jokes Cassie, playfully pushing my shoulder. "No need to cry, happy tears or not. You are spoiling your makeup, and you know whenever you cry, the tip of your nose goes red," she reminds me.

"OK. Point taken. No more tears."

"Can I call Mel to let her know that I can come over later for the barbecue?" Cassie places her hands palm to palm, in the pleading position, and pushes out her bottom lip.

"Of course. I'd better text Will to let him know that he's got a pass for Tommy's tonight."

I pick up my phone to message Will, Cassie moving to one of the sun loungers, already on the phone to Mel, giggling away.

Watching her chat to Mel reminds me of my relationship with my friend Ginny from school. Gosh, I wonder what happened to her? We were as thick as thieves back then. She was my first best friend. I've always felt like I let all my friends down just leaving like I did, but my parents made a knee-jerk decision at that particular time in my life and chose to send me away once they found out what sort of daughter I really was. My life from then on wasn't my own.

I thought I'd shelved all those negative thoughts and feelings of being scared and vulnerable, but what with the reappearance of Ed, I feel just like I'm sixteen years old all over again. It will be a risk to finally tell Gray absolutely everything, but we've been together since I was eighteen, he's the father of my children, we love each other and there shouldn't be any secrets between us. I need to tell him everything, and tonight, after the football and with the children both out, is surely the perfect time.

Chapter Twenty-three

Ed

July 2018

My meet up with Virginia was very enlightening, and I take my hat off to her. She's made a good life for herself and her daughters despite having had a couple of deadbeat husbands. I also think, a bit like me, she has been badly hurt by her supposed best friend just disappearing from her life, and that void has never been filled for either of us. I lost my first love, and she lost her best friend.

It's the World Cup semi-final tonight, and the whole of the country is buzzing. Virginia is quite a revelation, as she absolutely loves football—something I wasn't aware of all those years ago. Her daughters' boyfriends are both avid footie fans, and Virginia, who is still always up for a party, offered to host a garden party at hers if the boys managed to reach the semi-final. She said she was unsure whether to invite me, but I'm so glad she did, as I felt so at home and at ease in her company when we had dinner. And to be honest, I really want an excuse to see her again.

We haven't quite decided what to do about the newly discovered photos, as I'm not convinced that Evie was pregnant when she left. I feel that, as we were so close, I surely would have known she was pregnant. Why wouldn't she have confided in me? It's a bit of a mindfuck, to be honest, so I think an evening of beer and football is just what I need. Virginia has promised not to do anything about the photos until I've had a bit more time to process all the facts. I'm not even sure what I can do to find out if Evie was pregnant all those years ago, as she clearly doesn't have a grown-up son or daughter. I've seen photos in the tabloids of her children, and they're both teenagers. Unless her parents made her have a termination?

Anyway, for the first time in ages, I'm going to try to have an Evie Del Rio night off. Tonight's all about the football and enjoying some time with an old friend and her family. Virginia said she can't wait for me to meet her daughters, and I am actually really looking forward to meeting them too. The idea of being part of a family, even just for an evening, sounds good. Sometimes I look back with such affection about my childhood before Evie left. Mum and Dad used to host such great parties: the music and drinks would be flowing, and everyone seemed so at ease and comfortable just hanging out at ours. Why did things change? I guess my mother would blame it all on Paul's bad influence. I know Dad is proud of me, as he's set up a very active Facebook fan page for me and the group. He's always posting and contributing to the page. Mum thankfully doesn't do social media, so she doesn't get involved, which is just as well, as I think she would be a bit shocked at some of the discussions and comments that appear from time to time.

I promised Virginia that I'd pick her up some bottles of her favourite prosecco along with some beers for the lads, and I've decided to throw in a few bottles of bubbly just in case we have cause to celebrate getting into the World Cup final. Well, a man's got to have hope, hasn't he?

I pop into my local off-license, order the drinks and give them Virginia's address for delivery. She told me she's taking a half-day off from work, so I've arranged delivery after 3 p.m. I fortunately have a day off from rehearsals, so I'm thinking of surprising Virginia by getting there a bit early. Perhaps she could do with some help moving furniture or something? Who am I kidding? I know I'm making excuses to see her again, and this time it really doesn't have anything to do with Evie. Virginia seems so sorted, so happy in her own skin and so content. All I know right now is that I want to spend more time with a woman that I barely gave a second glance to all those years ago. Perhaps I chose the wrong girl?

Evie and I had something special all those years ago but we were just kids. We didn't know about real life back then. Everything was about the next big thrill—where the next drink, smoke or shag was coming from. It was all-consuming, but it felt so real at the time. At least we didn't have social media when we were growing up. It's bad enough looking at some of the Polaroids Virginia has of us all, complete with dodgy haircuts. Just imagine if our every move had been Instagrammed like it is for today's generation.

With England reaching the semi-finals of the World Cup, football mania has certainly arrived in the UK. The streets and cars are decorated in red and white, and there's an air of optimism throughout the land. Us Brits are used to being disappointed in the world of international football, but this current young team has given us hope again.

Armed with some of those gerberas Virginia liked so much the last time we met, I'm in an Uber, on my way to her house, as I'm not sure what time things are going to finish up, and I also fancy a few drinks tonight. I can't go too mad, as we have rehearsals tomorrow for the tour, but I thankfully now know my drinking limits—something that eluded me in the past.

My drug use has lessened too after seeing the state of my uncle Paul. All those years ago, he seemed so cool, so anti-establishment, but now he just looks like an old bloke who's really neglected himself. You can smell the alcohol on him, as it just oozes from his pores. I'm not going to end up like him, which has always been my mother's worry and, in hindsight, completely justified. I just didn't see it back then.

I thank the Uber driver as I arrive at Virginia's and walk slowly to her doorstep. I ring the doorbell and take deep breaths as I wait for an answer, shocked at how nervous I am.

The door opens, revealing a young woman. "Hello, Ed." No need to ask for sure if that's who I am, clearly having seen my face plastered everywhere of recent.

"Err, hello. You must be Shannon, or is it Sasha?" I ask, desperately trying to remember Virginia's daughters' ages to work out which daughter this one is.

"Right the first time. I'm Shannon, the younger one," she says with a glint in her eye.

"Great to meet you, Shannon. Your mum has told me so much about you," I stammer, suddenly tongue-tied, looking at a mirror image of Ginny at a similar age. I'm taken aback by her confidence. If I remember rightly, she's only about eighteen.

"Come on in. Mum's just in the kitchen making up some more Pimm's."

I follow Shannon through to the kitchen, where Virginia is expertly chopping a selection of fruit for the Pimm's. I lean in to greet her with a double kiss, and we awkwardly clash noses.

"Good to see you again," I say with a big smile.

"You too. And thanks so much for the drink delivery. My neighbour already tuts when I put out my recycling. God knows what she'll say after tonight." Virginia giggles.

"These are for you as well," I say, handing her the handtied gerberas.

"They're absolutely beautiful. Thank you, Ed. I just need to find a vase for them," she replies, placing the flowers gently to one side.

"Can I help with anything?" I ask, feeling slightly redundant.

"You could fix us both a drink while I get the Pimm's sorted," Virginia answers as she continues cutting up the fruit.

"Sure, what do you fancy?"

"A glass of prosecco, please. There are buckets of iced beer in the garden if you want one of those."

"Actually, I'll join you in a glass of prosecco," I reply, for some reason not wanting to leave Virginia's side.

"The glasses are in the cabinet behind you." Virginia points towards a well-stocked glass cabinet attached to the wall as she lovingly arranges the gerberas.

I fix us our drinks, and Virginia gets Sasha's boyfriend, Josh, to take the Pimm's into the garden, which has been transformed into a sea of red and white—from tablecloths to napkins, flags and balloons—it's a patriotic paradise.

One of Shannon's friends has lent Virginia a projector with a screen, which is set up on the patio, shaded by an awning. The build-up to the semi-final has started, and the BBC are doing a sterling job interviewing the crowds on the streets, asking them where they're going to be watching the match. On the way over to Virginia's, I noticed people smiling and talking to each other. The atmosphere is electric, the anticipation that we're possibly just about to witness something incredible almost palpable.

The booze is flowing, and Virginia's garden is starting to fill up as more and more people squeeze themselves in. I've now met both Shannon and Sasha and their boyfriends, Micky and Josh, who both seem like nice guys. The girls teased me a bit about exactly how many years I've known their mother. They clearly think both me and Virginia are positively ancient.

Finally, the match starts. Within five minutes, we've scored from a free kick, and I'm convinced we're off to the final. We get some really good chances but our luck seems to have run out. Unfortunately for England, Croatia's sixty-eighth minute equaliser in the second half sends the match into extra time.

Shannon and Sasha do their dutiful hostess bit just before the extra time starts, making sure everyone has full glasses and plenty to eat. Virginia has done herself proud, the table almost groaning under the amount of food on offer. From salads to hotdogs, burgers and chicken, every taste has been catered for. Virginia has such a great family and set of friends, and it's really nice to feel so welcomed by a bunch of people, most of whom I've just met. Apart from the guys in the band, I really don't have a group of friends.

The extra time starts, and Virginia edges herself closer to the screen. I usher her gently in front of me so she can see properly, drinking in the minty smell of her hair, which she has loosely tied back. The evening feels almost perfect but for the football. We have a few chances, but it doesn't seem to be our night, and you can see the game slipping away from England as they start to lose momentum, whilst Croatia's confidence seems to grow. With just eleven minutes to go, their striker gets the better of us, and our goalie can do nothing to save the goal. And with that goal, the dreams of a nation are crushed, but on the upside, our young team has given us an unforgettable summer of wonderful footballing memories.

I'm gutted with the result, but I guess not too surprised, having got used to the disappointment over the years.

"What a shame," Virginia whispers softly, still looking at the screen, as if she can somehow rewind the match and change the result.

"I know. Gutting. Fancy a glass of champagne to commiserate?"

"Thank you for those extra bottles. Sir, you are really spoiling me," jokes Virginia, fluttering her eyelashes, the disappointment from the match already drifting away.

"You are very welcome. Sorry I forgot the Ferrero Rochers though." I laugh.

"Yeah, sorry, that was a really bad impression..." Virginia says. "I haven't seen the advert since the '90s."

Virginia takes my hand and leads me inside to the kitchen. "I put the champagne in my secret wine fridge," she admits.

"So you did. Clever. You get the glasses, and I'll pour."

We take the champers into the sitting room at the front of the house. It's good to get away from the main body of the party and spend some time with Virginia alone. I sit on the seat of the sofa nearest to the table and pour out a couple of glasses of champagne. We clink glasses and sit back on the sofa, listening to the distant hum of voices and music from the garden. I can feel the warmth of her skin when our arms almost touch as we recline on the sofa.

"You certainly know how to throw a party, don't you?"

"I've moved on since my sixteenth birthday, haven't I?" Virginia replies with a giggle, placing her hand on my knee.

"If I remember rightly, your sixteenth was pretty legendary." I put my arm around her shoulders, breathing in her perfume, the smell of which is starting to become familiar.

"I guess so. Well, apart from the soggy egg sandwiches." She laughs, throwing her head back.

"Oh God, your poor mum couldn't give those bloody egg sandwiches away for love nor money," I say with a smile.

"That party was one of the last times Evie really seemed herself, don't you think?"

My body clenches. "I thought we weren't going to talk about Evie tonight."

"We're not. It was just an observation. That's all. Sorry if I touched a nerve," Virginia snaps, sitting bolt upright, as if the proximity of our bodies was close to burning her skin. "We actually said we wouldn't do anything about the remaining Polaroids quite yet, but I didn't realise the subject of Evie Del Rio in general was a no-go area."

I can't decide whether I feel guilty, embarrassed or both. "Oh, it's not really, but I've had such a great evening with you and didn't want to spoil what I thought was a couple of old friends having a rather enjoyable evening together." I sigh, putting my champagne glass back on the table.

"So, I've gone and spoilt things, have I?" I'm sure I see her discreetly trying to wipe a solitary tear away from her eye, as if the sudden anger is seeping out as quickly as it appeared, replaced by hurt.

"No, no. Don't be silly. I just didn't expect us to get on as well as I think we are. Unless I've completely misread the situation?" I nervously try to read her face.

"Yeah, we do get on," she admits. "And you know I've always kind of liked you, but I guess the timing's never really been right."

"Our timing has never been great. Until now." I lean forwards and glance at her lips. She doesn't pull away. I slowly move closer until our lips are touching. My hand moves to the back of her neck as I firmly kiss her.

A sudden noise interrupts us. Virginia snaps her head away and turns to the door, greeted by one of Micky's mates, dressed head to toe in red and white, including deely boppers perched somewhat precariously on top of his head.

"Uh, I was just wondering where the bathroom is? It's ok. I'll find it." Our interloper awkwardly leaves the room.

We look at each other and burst out laughing.

"What were we saying about timing?" Virginia says, rolling her eyes towards the heavens. This time, all I see are tears of laughter.

Chapter Twenty-four

Cassie

July 2018

I had a really great afternoon with Mum. We went food shopping, and Mum, bless her, has even let me and Will hang out with our friends, despite wanting a family meeting. I'm so excited that Danny's here. Mel already said he'd be coming, as her dad works with his. I still couldn't believe it until now though.

Mel and I bought a couple of England T-shirts, which we've customised by cutting away the sleeves to make them sexier and then knotting them at the side, teamed with denim shorts. One thing I'm determined to do is monitor my drinking tonight, as I really don't want a repeat of Saskia's party.

I don't really know too much about the rules of football but the atmosphere was electric when the match was playing, and even I got carried away jumping up and down when England scored so early on. Once the second half started, England lost their way and Croatia scored, which meant they had to go to extra time. Everyone still believed England could finish the job, but not long before the end of the extra time, Croatia scored again. It was as if time stood still while we all secretly prayed England would score again and at least then we would go to penalties. It wasn't to be, but Mel and I enjoyed persuading Danny and his friend George that we're die-hard footie fans.

Mel's brother cranks up the music, and Mel and I dance as provocatively as we can. We both have our sights set on two certain boys tonight. I can feel Danny's eyes on me, so I know I'm close to achieving. It doesn't take long for Danny to saunter over and take me by the hand. He ushers me to the drinks table and pours me another glass of prosecco while Mel and George dance.

Danny sits on one of the beanbags that's been laid out at the back of the garden and pulls me onto his lap.

"Mind my drink," I protest as half of it spills down my shorts. I gasp as the cold liquid soaks through to my legs.

"I can always get you another one, you know. Don't stress. I just wanted to get to know you a bit better away from everyone," says Danny, slurring slightly.

"Well, here I am," I say, blinking somewhat erratically as I try to keep in control after having at least three glasses of prosecco and not much food despite Mel's parents having catered for the masses. My head is spinning the same way it did at Saskia's party before I reached the point of memory loss.

Danny's hot, beery breath is on my neck, and although I've dreamed about getting up close and personal with him for ages, something just doesn't seem right.

"I'd like to go and find Mel, please, Danny," I demand with as much authority as I can muster, sobering slightly.

"Ok. No worries. Keep your hair on," he jokes before adding something else which I don't quite hear properly.

"What did you just say?" I question bluntly.

"I said, you don't take after your mother, do you?" he repeats with a smirk.

"What on earth do you mean by that?" I reply tersely, removing myself from his grasp. Danny clearly isn't the nice guy I thought he was.

"I thought you'd be a bit friendlier, that's all," he says quickly, trying to backtrack, holding his hands up.

"If your idea of being friendly is sticking your tongue down my throat, then you've got the wrong girl," I say through clenched teeth.

"Clearly." Danny stands up and walks away, leaving me sitting on the beanbag all alone. I tip the rest of my drink onto the grass and take deep breaths, composing myself. I leave my glass on the ground and storm into the house.

Unfortunately for me, Mel is engaged in a full-on snogging session with George. Danny, though, thankfully is now nowhere to be seen. I approach the food table and help myself to a few bits and pieces to try and soak up the prosecco and also to lick my wounds. Danny might be sporty and good-looking but he's still a dickhead. I won't be bothering to pursue him anymore after his snide, underhand comment about my mum's past. He obviously had "like mother, like daughter" in his head. I won't confide in Mum about this experience—she'd be mortified. I can handle myself. I don't want my first time to be with some guy who thinks I'm fair game and doesn't really want to get to know the real me.

I can't face eating any more food, so I decide to go back to where the main throng of the party is. Danny has now turned his attention to a girl with long peroxide blonde hair, wearing even shorter denim shorts than me or Mel dared to. She's welcome to him.

Mel worriedly rushes over to see me, having successfully managed to extract herself from George's lips. "Has something happened?"

"Danny's a prize prat. Not worth talking about," I reply, glaring in his direction.

"Ok." She nods, her face relaxing. "You can tell me in your own time. I really like George. He's asked me out over the weekend. I'm so excited," she gushes.

"Good for you," I say somewhat begrudgingly.

"I'm sorry things didn't work out between you and Danny, but I thought you'd at least be pleased for me." Mel frowns, clearly hurt.

"Of course I'm pleased for you, but don't expect any double dates," I say with a smile, trying to lighten the mood and make amends for my earlier grumpy response. Mel smiles, going back to her usual self. My eyes flit back to Danny. George is now with him, talking to him. I can't help but wonder what they're talking about.

Chapter Twenty-five

Evie

December 1984

How the Christmas holidays have dragged without seeing Ed or Ginny. My parents have kept me under lock and key ever since Ginny's party. We had a deal: if I was allowed to go to the party, then I had to do loads of revision for my mock O levels over the holidays once we returned from Auntie Maureen's house on the twenty-seventh. Ginny's party was amazing. I can't believe we all got away with staying at Ed's house. His uncle Paul is a right laugh, and he certainly knows how to throw a party. And because he's older, parents seem to trust him. Well, apart from Ed's mum, who thinks he's an idiot. She'd go mad if she knew we all stayed at their house overnight.

Ginny took loads of photos with her new Polaroid camera at her party. Because of my enforced incarceration, we still haven't managed to catch up and go through them. I remember taking one of Ginny where she was just going to blow out the candles on her cake. She looked amazing.

I haven't even been able to use the phone to call Ginny. To be fair, our calls do go on a bit. We normally chat about what we've just been up to despite having just seen each other earlier that day. But I've formulated a plan to try and meet up with everyone.

Mum's in the kitchen, fastidiously ironing bedsheets, so I take out the remaining bottle of milk from the fridge and purposely knock it all over the kitchen table. She's outraged by my clumsiness, and as I half-heartedly clear up the mess, I suggest popping to the corner shop to buy some more. Incredibly, Mum falls for it, mainly because she's addicted to coffee. I'm out that door before she has the chance to change her mind.

I run to the corner shop and straight past it, hoping the fact I'm running has given me extra time away from the house. I'll call in the corner shop on the way back. I leg it over to Ginny's, as she lives the closest, and ring the bell impatiently.

A very sleepy-looking Ginny answers the door. "Hello, stranger." It's only 9:30 a.m., but clearly Ginny doesn't have to get up at the crack of dawn like my mum makes me, as she's still dressed in her nightclothes.

"Can I come in? I haven't got long," I say breathlessly.

"Sure. Come in. Mum's gone to visit Gran, so she'll be ages." Ginny yawns and steps aside for me to enter.

We go through to the kitchen, and Ginny pours us both an orange juice.

"I've been wondering what's happened to you," says Ginny, handing me a glass.

"Well, you know there were conditions for me to go to your party, don't you?"

Ginny nods.

"They've kept me indoors since we got back from my aunt's house so I can revise. I'm going mad. They won't even let me use the phone. Can you believe that? Mum's put a lock on it. I mean, I know I agreed to restrictions but... this is not what I thought at all."

"Bloody hell, that's a bit extreme, isn't it? Oh, you poor thing," says Ginny, giving me a hug. The hug lingers more than it usually would, probably because of how sleepy she is. It seems as if I've pulled her away from her bed and she's still seeking comfort.

"So, what have I missed?" I say, eager to catch up on all the latest gossip, knowing I don't have much time.

"Not a lot, to be honest. Everyone's been forced to see family over the Christmas break, although there's talk about a party on New Year's Eve."

"No, I can't believe it. Whose party?" I ask impatiently.

"Mark's. The band are going to play a few numbers."

"Oh, bloody hell. It's so not fair that I'm locked in the house all over the holidays." I pound my fist on Ginny's kitchen table with pure frustration.

"I know. They are really being overstrict, aren't they?" agrees Ginny. "Do you want my mum to have a word with your mum to see if you can stay here for the night?" she adds, desperately trying to find a solution to my latest set of rules.

"I don't think it will make any difference, to be honest. They have basically banned me from going out anywhere so I can study. I only managed to get out the house just now because I purposely spilt the remaining pint of milk and offered to buy a new one. Which reminds me. I'd better get to the shops, otherwise she'll be sending out a bloody search party," I say, eyes on Ginny's kitchen clock.

"Why don't you take a pint from our fridge? We've got loads. Mum won't miss it."

"Thanks, Ginny. You're a star."

"No probs," she says, opening the fridge. "Listen, why don't we send letters to each other as a way of contacting each other whilst you're grounded. Once I've found out a bit more about the New Year's Eve party, I will leave a note in some clingfilm under that big flowerpot where you keep your spare key outside your porch. If you want to contact me, you do the same. I'll pop along to check for messages when your mum's car isn't on the drive."

"Sounds like a plan," I agree. I go to cross my fingers that no one will forget their key and have to look for the spare before remembering that I'm completely caged there and they'll only have to knock. "I'd better run. Love you, Ginny."

"Right back atcha," she replies, thrusting the pint of milk into my hand.

I run as fast as I can to get back home, stopping at the end of my street to catch my breath. Once I reach the house, I spot the curtain twitching. Mum is obviously looking out for me.

"You took your time, Evie," she scolds as she opens the front door.

"I bumped into Ginny at the shop."

"Well, get inside and make me a coffee. I trust you remembered the milk?"

"Of course," I say, holding the pint of milk aloft as I step past her, into the house.

I make Mum a coffee and a cup of tea for myself and spend the remainder of the day pretending to revise whilst listening to a compilation tape that Ed made me. One side has all our current favourites on it like The Smiths, Depeche Mode, Aztec Camera and New Order. On the B-side, he's recorded some of his own music with The Propellers, including the song he played at Ginny's party. Listening to that tape keeps me sane whilst my parents still insist on keeping me at home.

It's not so bad when Dad's at home. He can always be persuaded to see both sides of an argument or discussion. But that can also be a problem. It depends on who's the most persuasive. Me or Mum? I'll try and get Dad on my side once I know a bit more about the New Year's Eve party. I think Ginny's secret letter idea is genius, but I'm really worried we'll get rumbled by my mum. She seems to have a sixth sense whenever I'm planning anything.

I've been incarcerated in my bedroom for what seems like an eternity, although it's only 12:30p.m., so I decide to venture downstairs for some lunch. Mum's busy meticulously ironing Dad's work shirts in the kitchen, almost trance-like. I can't work out my mum. She's a pillar of the community: she helps at church every Sunday, she always bakes for the Holy Communion breakfasts and she regularly does charity box collections for our local children's charity door to door. I used to help her when I was younger, carefully peeling off the smiley stickers to give to the people who kindly donated, but she's a cold fish towards her own family. I can't remember the last time she held me close or kissed me when I was upset. I often wonder why Dad's stayed with her all these years, as she's as cold to him as she is to me. It's only Phillip, my older brother, who has long since flown the nest, that makes Mum happy and can make her smile.

That's why I like staying at other people's houses, as it's nice to see how other families live. Ginny's parents, although a bit fuddy-duddy, always hold hands whenever they go out, and you can see how Ginny's completely adored by them. A kind of brightness shines out from their eyes. Even Ed's parents are very tactile.

"Don't make a mess in the kitchen. I've only just finished cleaning it after you spilt the milk earlier," snaps Mum, momentarily looking up from her beloved ironing.

"I won't." I snap back, reaching up for the Breville toastie maker in one of the high cupboards.

"I asked you not to make a mess, Evie. Don't use the Breville, dear. It takes ages to clean, and I don't suppose you'll be the one cleaning it, will you?" she says with a snarl.

I grit my teeth against what feels like the start of an argument. "I will clean it out, Mum. I really fancy a toastie."

"No, it's not happening today. Use the normal toaster."

"What is the point in having a Breville if we can't use it?" I shout, slamming the door of the cupboard with as much force as I can manage. The door bounces off its usual closed resting place and settles slightly ajar.

"Don't use that tone with me, young lady. I have given you an option. If you don't like it, you can do without and go to your room." Mum crosses her arms and moves to stand right in front of me.

"Stick your Breville, Mum, I'm going out." I push past her, flouncing out of the kitchen.

"You are not allowed out. We agreed. You have to..."

I don't stay long enough to hear the rest of what she has to say, but I've heard it all before, and I'm not willing to hear anything more of what that damn woman has to say. Grabbing my jacket, I slam the door, making sure the whole house vibrates. Fuelled by pure rage, I run all the way to Ginny's, cursing my mother, knowing full well that Ginny's mum would let her use the bloody Breville. Despite ringing on Ginny's doorbell numerous times, there's no reply. I sit on her doorstep in the hope she'll reappear, but after about ten minutes, I give up and walk over to Ed's house.

It's been ages since we've seen each other, and I'm really missing him. It takes me a good twenty minutes to walk to Ed's house from Ginny's. I ring the bell and wait. I'm just about to leave when I hear someone walking towards the front door. The door opens. It's Paul.

"Who do we have here, then?" he says with a wry grin. "Well, if it isn't Ed's favourite girl Evie. Come in. Come in. Ed's not in right now, but please come in and wait."

"Umm, don't worry, I'll come back later." I smile awkwardly and start to turn away.

"He won't be long. He called earlier and said he'll be home soon. We're going to have a bit of a jam when he gets back. He's been working on some new material. He'd be cross if I didn't insist that you stay." Paul opens the door wider, the wry grin still on his face.

I bite my bottom lip, trying to decide what to do. I don't currently have anywhere else to go, and it's not like I don't know Paul. It couldn't do any harm to just wait for ten minutes or so.

"Thanks, Paul. I'll come in and wait if it's no bother," I relent.

"No bother at all," he says, ushering me through to the sitting room.

"Fancy a drink?"

"No, I'm fine," I reply as I sit.

"You don't mind if I carry on, do you?" asks Paul, pointing at the guitar propped up in the corner of the room.

"No, go for it."

Paul starts to play his guitar as I stare out the window, wondering how much longer Ed will be. It seems odd being in the same house as Paul without Ed or the usual hangers-on. Plus being sober. I don't think I've ever seen Paul without a drink in his hand or a spliff between his lips. Normally, he seems quite cool. Today, in the harsh daylight, he just looks old. I watch as Paul's yellow nicotine-stained fingers whizz all over his guitar. I can definitely see where Ed gets his musical talent from.

I glance at the time: nearly 2 p.m. I haven't had any lunch yet, and I'm starving. Ed surely won't be much longer?

"Do you play, Evie?" enquires Paul.

"No. I just like music in general. I wish I had a musical talent like you and Ed."

"I'm sure you've got some other special talents." Paul licks his top lip, showing his yellowing teeth. I immediately pretend not to notice or indeed hear what he just said. "Well, I could always teach you the basics of playing the guitar if you ever wanted to learn, you know," he adds.

"Oh, I'm fine, thanks. How much longer do you think Ed will be?" I ask, swiftly changing the subject.

"He said he wasn't going to be long when I last spoke to him."

"How long ago was that?"

"Maybe an hour. Stop stressing. Here, have a beer. It will chill you out," says Paul forcibly, opening a couple of cans of Foster's.

"It's a bit early for me, and I haven't had any lunch yet."

"Well, just sip it. It'll pass the time until Ed gets here."

"Umm, ok. Thanks," I say, reluctantly taking the can.

Paul takes a big swig of his beer, leaving a residue of beer froth on his top lip, which he licks off with the tip of his tongue, looking straight at me as he does it. I take a little sip from my can, feeling the bitterness of the beer burning the back of my throat as I swallow it. This whole situation doesn't feel right. Even being back at home being shouted at by Mum seems preferable to this. I can't put my finger on it but for the first time ever Paul unsettles me.

I don't know if it's telepathy or just good timing but within a minute or so, I hear a key in the door, and in comes Ed. I'm so pleased to see him that I nearly knock him off his feet as I rush towards the door to greet him.

"Woah, that's a great welcome," says Ed, giving me a big kiss. "How did you escape your mum?"

"We had a row, and I walked out," I explain.

"I see good old Uncle Paul has been looking after you," Ed remarks, noticing my beer.

"I always treat the ladies well. You know that, Eddy boy. Do you fancy joining us for a beer?" he says.

"I might later, but right now I'm bloody starving. Have you eaten, Evie?"

I shake my head. "Not yet. That was what the row was about. Mum wouldn't let me use the Breville."

Ed frowns. "What's up with that woman? I think we've still got one in the back of the cupboard. Let me have a look."

It doesn't take long for Ed to locate the sandwich maker, and we're soon happily eating delicious ham and cheese toasties together at the table in the living room. I'm relieved to be away from Paul. I purposely left my beer behind too. Although I enjoy a drink with my friends, drinking in the middle of the day with a grown man doesn't seem right.

Ed and I finish off the toasties and then Ed makes us both a steaming hot chocolate, which we take upstairs, leaving Paul with just his beer and guitar for company. We lie back on Ed's bed and just enjoy being together once again. I close my eyes and snuggle up to Ed, feeling relaxed for the first time in a long time.

"Evie, your mum called to see if you're here."

I jolt awake at the sound of Paul's voice. I can't believe I fell asleep. How long was I out for?

"Did you tell her I'm here?" I anxiously shout back, mouth dry, wishing I'd actually drunk my hot chocolate as I look at it cold on the bedside table.

"No, of course not. Said I haven't seen you in ages."

"Ok, thanks for that."

"She sounded properly pissed off though," he adds, his voice getting quieter as he wanders away from the bottom of the stairs.

Ed yawns and stretches next to me. "I suppose you'd better get going. Where are you going to say you've been?" he enquires.

I sigh. "I'll say I went window shopping. I can't say I was at Ginny's. My mum may well have phoned there as well, although she was out earlier when I called round."

"I do hope I wasn't the second choice to hang out with today," Ed says playfully, running his hand through his tousled hair.

I roll my eyes. "You know Ginny's house is closer than yours, you dingbat. That's why I tried her house first."

"I'm only sorry I wasn't here earlier. I can think of loads of things we could have got up to this afternoon." Ed pins me on his bed with a forceful and passionate kiss.

"Don't," I try to object, unlocking my lips from his. "I really want to stay here with you. But this really isn't helping..."

Ed slips his hand under my top and begins kissing me with more and more urgency. Needless to say, I don't leave Ed's house for at least another forty-five minutes. Searching his bedroom for my clothes is no mean feat. I eventually locate my underwear tangled up in his sheets.

Ed and I slip downstairs, greeted by the sounds of Paul playing guitar and singing the same lines over and over.

"Uncle Paul, Evie's leav—"

"Oh, don't disturb him on my account," I say, trying to sound as though I'm being polite, when in reality I just don't want to have to see Paul again.

"He'll be annoyed if I don't let him know you're leaving; you know how much he likes having you around." Ed grabs my hand to lead me to Paul, leaving me no chance to protest.

We walk through to the back room. I wave and mouth "goodbye" to Paul, who has now stopped singing and is busily rolling another joint.

"See ya, Evie. Don't worry, your secret is safe with me." He grins, and I fake a grin back.

"Cheers, Paul." I make a swift exit towards the front door. I give Ed one last kiss and leave.

Mum will still be fuming from earlier and the fact I stormed off and spent the whole afternoon out. It's also looking extremely unlikely that I'll be able to make it to Mark's New Year's Eve party, as Mum will definitely punish me for today. I'll have to try to make amends and get Dad onside. I can usually talk my dear old dad round, as I've always been the apple of his eye. My mum and I, however, have never been close. It's as if she resents my youth. When she met Dad, she was a natural blonde with aquamarine eyes and an hourglass figure. Dad always says he had to fight off many an admirer to finally get Mum to himself. She's still an attractive woman but family life seems to have sucked her dry. She never lets herself have any fun.

They met at the local dance when they were both seventeen, and since that day, they've never been apart. I don't think Mum has ever been a girl's girl. She has two much older brothers and then there's her older sister Maureen, who's a bit of a religious nut. Mum adores my older brother Phillip—he's the brainy one, a straight-A student who is already at university in Liverpool—but she always bemoans that it was me who ruined her figure. "Sorry, I didn't ask to be born," is my staple reply, much to her irritation.

A mere twenty minutes and I'm home again. An all-time record. It's amazing what an afternoon with Ed can do for a girl's energy levels. I push the garden gate open and walk up the path. I reach for our spare key, which is always kept under the flowerpot outside our porch, but it seems to have mysteriously disappeared. I ring the bell and wait for Mum to let me in, but she doesn't come to the door. I sigh and seat myself on the doorstep. There's no point ringing the bell again—Mum's definitely inside, definitely knows I'm here and is definitely ignoring me. I bring my knees to my chest and wrap my arms around my legs, trying to protect myself from the cold December evening. Thankfully, Dad returns a little bit earlier than normal from work, although my whole body is practically numb at this point.

"Evie, what on earth are you doing outside in the cold?" Dad frowns, taking his coat off and gently draping it around my shoulders.

"I had an argument with Mum, and she's locked me out." I wipe my runny nose with the back of my hand as Dad's coat envelops me like a warm hug.

"I'm sure your mum wouldn't have locked you out on purpose. There must be a logical explanation why she hasn't answered," says Dad, who never thinks the worst of his wife. He opens the door, ushering me into the warmth. "Put the kettle on and make some tea to get yourself warmed up."

I dawdle to the kitchen. The kettle's still warm, so Mum can't be too far away. I busy myself in the kitchen whilst

Dad calls out for her. With no sign of her downstairs, Dad sprints up the stairs. I listen to his footsteps and can tell by the different creaks that he's gone straight to their bedroom. I can hear my mum's raised voice being softened by my dad's hushed tones. I make myself and Dad a cuppa, remembering to add two sugars into Dad's favourite mug, which I bought for him a few years ago for Father's Day, emblazoned with "World's Greatest Dad".

I sit at the table, drinking my tea, enjoying the feeling returning to my fingers and toes. Ten minutes later, Dad comes back downstairs. He sits opposite me and takes a big swig of his tea.

"Thanks for this. You even remembered the extra sugar," he says gratefully. "Don't let your mum know; I'm supposed to be on a diet." He winks.

"Your secret's safe with me," I say with a furtive smile, happy that he wants me onside. "Where's Mum?" I ask. I don't want Dad to think I was listening in in any way, even though I couldn't hear what was being said.

"She's got one of her migraines, you know, the ones that keep her practically bedridden. That's why she didn't answer the door when you rang the bell," Dad explains, and I think he genuinely believes his words. I don't. "We'll talk later about what happened earlier because right now I want to change out of my suit and have some dinner. I'm starving. I don't think Mum had time to sort out any dinner, but we could pop down to Wimpy if you fancy?"

"I'd love that. We haven't done that for ages." I stand and put my empty mug in the sink. "I'll just change into some warmer clothes." Somehow, my clothes feel as if they've gripped the freezing air from outside and are keeping it hostage against my skin despite my warming cup of tea.

I pop upstairs to grab my new black and red stripy mohair jumper, glancing briefly through the crack in my parents' bedroom door. Mum's propped up in bed, reading the latest Jackie Collins paperback. She clearly doesn't have a migraine, as I suspected, she's just sulking after today. Just an excuse not to have to spend time with me and Dad. Well, sod her. Dad and I will have a nice meal out without her. I will definitely broach the subject of Mark's party. I'm sure I'll be able to talk Dad round without Mum being there.

Chapter Twenty-six

Genie

July 2018

Well, tonight is the night I will finally tell Gray the whole truth. He deserves to know absolutely everything, and I think I'm just about ready to confess. I am so grateful to Gray for rescuing me all those years ago. In fact, moving to Brighton was the catalyst in changing my life for the better, because not only did I meet my future husband, I also met my best friend, Maura. I never believed in fate until I moved to Brighton and met them both. They were clearly sent to save me.

I've got in a selection of his favourite beers and a couple of bottles of his current favourite rosé. By the time Gray arrives home, I'm already halfway through my first glass of rosé. Dutch courage, I suppose.

"Hi, gorgeous," Gray says, planting a kiss on the top of my head. "How are you doing?"

"I'm ok. Let me get you a drink. What's your poison?" I say, getting off the sofa.

"I'll join you in a glass of rosé, although I must confess, I did have a couple of beers at work with the lads. You sounded quite serious earlier about calling a family meeting." He pauses, as if listening for movement upstairs. "But the kids aren't here."

"Well, I didn't want to spoil their football fun with a family meeting. I've waited so long to tell you all everything, so one more day isn't going to make much of a difference."

"Well, why don't we have something to eat and see how you feel? Maybe talk just me and you."

"Sure," I agree, knowing my secret's still all mine for now. To be honest, I'd probably rather talk to Gray alone first anyway.

I fetch some food I cooked earlier from the kitchen and bring it to the conservatory, placing it on the table I already set up there. I put the radio on low, hoping "Used to Be" doesn't make a musical appearance tonight.

"Do you want to chat now or after we've eaten?" enquires Gray.

"No, we'll talk after. We have the whole evening to talk," I reply, taking a seat opposite him. I know I'm holding the inevitable off. Maybe a glass or two of rosé will lighten him up in preparation for the news. I mean, he seems to be in a good mood anyway but just to be sure.

Gray gets stuck into the assortment of salad, cold meats, homemade pasta and my infamous potato salad. I've shelved the idea of lasagne until the children are back. That man can eat for England. I pick at a bit of salad, pushing the same couple of leaves around my plate, my throat dry and prickly with apprehension. I take another sip of rosé, enjoying the slight burn of the alcohol as it slips down my throat.

We mostly eat in silence. Luckily, silences between us have never felt awkward. I don't think Gray has time to talk between the amount he's shovelling in per mouthful and the quickness at which he's eating. His second plate of food is nearly empty and he's part way through a second bottle of rosé. Our talk is looking less and less likely to happen.

"Come on, Genie. What's the great revelation, then?" Gray slurs, trying to pour me another glass of rosé. I put my hand over my glass to show I don't want any more, but Gray doesn't notice and manages to pour the wine all over my hand and partly over the table. I go to the kitchen to get a cloth to clear up the mess.

When I return, Gray isn't there. I watch him through the glass, pacing at the bottom of the garden. I walk down to join him, wrapping my arms around his waist. He envelops me in one of his special bear hugs.

"Sorry, Genie, the drinking's got to my head, and I just needed some air. I'm feeling a bit better now." His words are coming out less slurred. "Now, what did you want to tell me? I guess it's important, and as per usual it's probably got something to do with that bloody Ed Nash." He huffs, letting go of me.

Gray's handsome face looks flushed from all the rosé, and I'm really not sure I should reveal all while he's drunk. "I-I-I don't know that now is the right time after all, Gray. You've had quite a lot to drink and—"

"Oh, for God's sake, Genie, I'm sick to the back teeth of pussyfooting around you. Spit it out, woman. Perhaps you should have another glass of wine to loosen you up a bit. I want to help you and look after you. That's all I've ever wanted to do. But time and time again, you close down, and I feel as though you've never fully given yourself to me." Gray leans back against the fence and looks up, clearly agitated. "I've always been honest with you, but you have always held something back. I'm giving you that opportunity here and now. Yes, maybe I've had a little too much to drink tonight but I'm here and I'm ready to listen to whatever you need to tell me."

I've never seen him so riled up, so passionate and so bloody honest. I love that man with every bone of my body, and here I am ready to break his heart. But he needs to know the truth. I owe it to him.

I take a deep breath. "It all started when I was fifteen..."

Chapter Twenty-seven

Evie

April 1985

"What are you looking for in such a hurry?"

I jump and turn to look at Mum, who's standing in my bedroom doorway, arms folded. Mum should be out. She's meant to be out. She's meant to be doing charity work. What is she doing here? I search my brain for a story. One she'll hopefully agree to. Not that I think she'll agree to anything—I'm supposed to be grounded. Again.

"Ummm... my swimming costume. I'm going swimming with Ginny." It's not a complete lie. I am looking for my swimming costume, and I am going swimming with Ginny, I just leave out the fact it's at Mark's house in his newly built swimming pool.

"Have you forgotten you're grounded?" she snarls.

I'm glad I'm back facing away from her, searching through my drawers again. If she'd seen the eyeroll, I would have been in deeper trouble than I'm already in. "I just want a bit of fun, that's all. Everyone else's parents let them have a life, you know. It's just a trip to the swimming baths," I spit back at her.

I've gotten incredibly used to lying. Unfortunately, Mum's got incredibly used to my lies. She doesn't know what's truth or lie anymore when it comes to me, so she just deems everything a lie. Even when I'm telling the truth, I can't win. Not that this is one of those times.

"You're *not* going." She says it slowly, accentuating the "not".

"Oh, but I am going. You just try and stop me," I growl, finally locating my old swimsuit. I defiantly stuff it in my bag.

"Put that back," she shouts.

I've had enough, and with no detection of a motherly bond from my mum, I can't help but feel nothing but hate and an unwillingness to do anything she tells me. "No. Why should I? You can't keep me locked up like a prisoner forever, you know?" I reply, my cheeks flushed with rage.

I barge my way out of my room as my mother screams obscenities at me. I run down the stairs as quickly as I can—not that I think she'll chase me, and even if she does, I know she won't be able to keep up—slamming the door behind me. I'm literally shaking as I sprint all the way to Mark's house, knowing that this time my mother really will make my life a misery once I finally return home. Not that I'll notice; every day with her already feels like a misery.

Ginny's already there parading in her new lime green bikini, which accentuates her fabulous figure. None of the boys can take their eyes off her. She looks amazing.

"Evie, you made it!" Ginny grins and ushers me over to the side of the pool. "Did you manage to get your swim-suit?"

"No," I lie, thinking about my faded dowdy pale blue swimsuit that I just risked everything for, stuffed at the bottom of my school bag. It's no match against Ginny's beautiful new bikini. "Can you believe my mum was at home? She caught me red-handed looking for my swimsuit and kindly reminded me that I'm grounded. We rowed, as per usual, and I stormed out. At least I'm here though. I'll just roll up my skirt and shirt sleeves and dangle my legs in the pool. It'll be fine."

"You know, Evie, you look great in whatever you wear anyway," she says graciously, immediately making me feel guilty for coveting her beautiful bikini.

Ed soon joins us, grabbing me by the waist and kissing me.

"Come on, you two lovebirds, let's get in the pool," shouts Mark.

Ed and I reluctantly part locked lips, and I go off to find Ginny. Ed, who's already wearing his swimming trunks, spectacularly divebombs into the pool with Mark, soaking all the girls, all of whom are sitting at the side of the pool. They all frown and grumble, their carefully styled hair ruined by the chlorinated water. Ginny was clever enough to sit on one of the sun loungers slightly away from the pool, so her makeup and hair have remained beautifully intact. And thanks to her, my makeup and hair remain intact too.

"Budge up, Ginny," I say, perching on the end of the lounger.

"Did you see the boys' divebombs?" She laughs. "The look on Meredith Jenkins' face when her hair and makeup got ruined was priceless. She's had her eye on Mark for ages, you know. She doesn't stand a chance though. He only ever goes for dark-haired girls."

"Yeah, I know what you mean," I say, momentarily feeling a little sorry for poor mousey-haired Meredith.

Ginny and I move to the side of the pool, dangling our toes in the water. Ed and Mark soon join us at the side of the pool, Ed squeezing himself between me and Ginny whilst Mark starts chatting up the very dark-haired Veronique, who's just moved in next door after relocating from France. Her grasp of English is almost as limited as Mark's grasp of French, but within moments they're kissing quite passionately by the side of the pool whilst a heartbroken Meredith looks on despondently.

"You girls getting into the water?" Ed asks as he slips back into the inviting pool.

"I haven't got my swimsuit with me. I forgot it this morning and then when I went back after school, Mum was there, so I just stormed out," I explain to Ed.

"Another row? I thought she was supposed to be doing her charity work this afternoon?"

"She was. It must have been cancelled. I'm quite happy just dangling my feet in the water, to be honest," I bluff as Ed stands between my legs as they dangle in the water and leans in for a kiss, neither of us caring that my school clothes are now completely soaked. We eventually pull apart as Ed swims off to the other side of the pool.

"How about you, Ginny? Fancy a dip?" he calls out.

"I'll be in in a minute. I just want to get some photos taken first. I'll ask Meredith to take some."

Ginny sashays over to where Meredith and her friends are sitting. "Meredith?"

"Y-yes," Meredith stammers, completely intimidated by the beautiful Ginny.

"Any chance you could take a few photos of us all? Would you mind?" Ginny asks in her most persuasive voice.

"Sure. Just show me what to do. I've never used a Polaroid before," she replies nervously.

"It's really simple. You just look through here, point the camera and click. Then the photo pops out here," Ginny explains patiently, pointing to where the photo comes out.

Ed, Jamie, Ginny and I sit together at the side of the pool, Mark and Veronique kneeling just behind us. Meredith takes the first picture. As we wait for it to develop, Ginny encourages her to take another one. Poor Meredith now seems to have the job of "official photographer". By the end of the afternoon, Meredith has accumulated quite a collection of Polaroids for Ginny.

"Thanks, Meredith. These are awesome. Tell you what, as a thanks, I'll take one of you and your friends," says Ginny, not taking no for an answer.

Meredith and her friends Dionne and Charmaine all sit together on the sun loungers. Ginny takes a quick photo of the girls as they squint against the April sunshine. The photo develops, and Ginny hands it over to Meredith and her friends, who study it religiously, anxiously looking at themselves in all their Polaroid glory.

Ed spends the rest of the afternoon alternating between sitting by the side of the pool with me and showing off his admirable diving skills whilst messing about with Jez, Mark and Jamie in the water. Ginny and I spend most of the afternoon people-watching. Ginny and Jamie still seem to be getting on famously. He's really into her in a big way and hangs off her every word.

I glance at my watch and realise I'll have to make a move, as Dad will be back from work soon. I want to get to him before Mother does.

"Ed, I've got to get back and face the music," I shout over to him.

"Give us a sec, and I'll walk you back." Ed starts swimming in my direction.

"It's fine. Stay here and enjoy yourself. I don't want my bloody mother shouting at you as well. She's going to be fuming as it is," I reply.

"As long as you're sure?" Ed jumps out of the pool and half-heartedly dries himself off with a towel. He takes my hand and leads me through the house to the front door.

"Are you sure you can't stay?" he asks, grabbing hold of me, leaving another damp patch on my school shirt.

"You know I'd love to, but I've got to get back around the time Dad gets home. I have to at least try and get him onside." I give Ed a quick kiss on the lips, keen to get going.

"Evie Del Rio, that was a rubbish kiss. I want a proper one," he demands, grabbing me for a far more passionate kiss.

I arrive back from Mark's house before Dad gets back from work, and I manage to get upstairs to the bathroom without my mother catching sight of me. She's having a lie down in her bedroom, probably suffering from another one of her imaginary "migraines".

Locking the door behind me, I run a bath, liberally pouring some of Mother's expensive bath oil into it that Dad bought her at Christmas. She's still not used it. The bath somehow feels nicer having used the forbidden bath oil, the temperature perfect, the feel of the water a pleasant change. As I immerse my whole head into the water, I wish I could wash away all my problems. I spend ages in the bath shaving and then wash my hair using the special French highlighting shampoo and conditioner set Ginny bought me for Christmas.

My skin is soon in danger of resembling a wrinkled old prune, so I get out of the bath, grabbing some fresh fluffy towels from the airing cupboard, and wrap a towel around my body and then towel-dry my hair before combing it through. Letting the water drain away, I wash the bath out, erasing any evidence that I've used Mother's bath oil. With Dad not home and Mother in bed with a "migraine", I chance leaving my body towel on the side of the bath to dry.

I've just opened the bathroom door and I'm furtively walking across the landing when Mother comes out of her bedroom. It's been years since she last saw me in any state of undress, let alone starkers. Mum's eyes pop, and I try to protect my modesty as best I can by covering myself with my arms.

"You've put an awful lot of weight on, Evie," she states, taking a long look at me.

"Ummm, thanks," I say, sprinting to my room. "Apparently, I boredom eat when I'm grounded. Which happens an *awful* lot." I open my bedroom door.

"Stop," she shouts. "Let me look at you properly."

I pause in the doorway to my bedroom and turn around, moving my hands away. "Here. Is this what you want to see? What's your problem? Now, if you don't mind."

Within moments, she's hurling abuse at me. For a woman who spends so much time in church, her language is becoming increasingly aggressive, littered with the most unchristian words I have ever heard come out of her mouth.

"Change into your nightclothes and then get back here. Your dad will be home soon," Mother orders.

"But—"

"Just do it," she screams at the top of her voice.

Already in enough trouble as it is, I do as I'm told and nervously join her back on the landing. She makes me lift up my top, revealing my clearly expanding waistline. She shakes her head and laughs. But it's far from happy laughter.

"Are you pregnant?" She raises her eyebrow and stares at me expectantly for an answer. I focus on my breathing and don't respond. "I said, *are you pregnant*?" Her spit hits my cheek as she screams in my face.

"No." I mean, I'm not, am I? I can't be. I'm way too young.

"We all know you've been spending time with that Ed boy. Clearly, you've been doing more than spending time with him, haven't you?" She puts her hand on her forehead, as if feeling lightheaded. "I can't believe it. My daughter is a sl—"

"Felicity, you stop right there before you say something you'll regret," Dad's voice booms from the downstairs hallway. Caught up in our own world, neither of us heard him come in. The stairs sound louder than usual as he makes his way up them. "What's going on?"

"Thank God you're home, Dad," I say, relieved. I try to pull my top back down, but Mum grabs hold of it and keeps it lifted.

"Look at her stomach. She's pregnant," Mum shrieks.

"I'm not," I yell.

"Calm down, Felicity. Shouting at Evie isn't going to get us anywhere." He kneels in front of me, trying to remain expressionless at the sight of my stomach, and asks calmly, "Evie, sweetie, are you sure you're not pregnant?"

"I..." I stop. There's no point lying anymore. To myself or anyone else. "I'm so sorry, Dad, but I'm not sure," I reply quietly. I feel like I want to cry but Mum has this aura about her that makes me hold in my vulnerabilities. I don't want her to see I'm shocked. I don't want her to see I'm so worried about Dad seeing me in a different way. I don't want her to see I'm petrified.

"I'll book you an appointment with a private local doctor tomorrow. Go and rest now, Evie, dry your hair, and I'll fix us all some dinner," Dad calmly says, taking control of the situation. "Felicity, let's have a bit of a chat downstairs."

Amazingly, Mother obediently follows Dad downstairs after her foul-mouthed tirade as I retreat to the sanctuary of my bedroom.

Chapter Twenty-eight

Ed

May 1985

I'm really missing Evie. The last time any of us saw her was at Mark's pool party. She had, of course, had another row with her mum and wasn't able to get her swimming stuff. Once she'd arrived at the pool, she just dangled her feet in the water, with her school skirt and shirt rolled up. The weather was brilliant, and us lads had a right laugh divebombing into the pool, literally soaking anyone nearby. Evie stayed fairly close to Ginny, just enjoying watching everyone having a laugh. Towards the end of the afternoon, Evie had to leave. We kissed briefly and then she was gone.

According to Ginny, she never showed at school the next day. About a week later, the teacher told her that Evie and her family had relocated due to her dad's job, but Ginny swore blind she was seeing Mr Del Rio at their house still. Whenever Ginny or I ring their bell, there's never an answer.

I still see Ginny from time to time, including tonight at our gig at the local youth club, because she's now officially going steady with Jamie. I pour all my emptiness and sadness into my music. I decided to rewrite "Used to Be", as it's always the song that everyone shouts out for at our gigs.

It's been a couple of hours since the gig finished. Ginny had to wait for me and the rest of the band to finish packing away our stuff and then talk to a few one-night-only fans, as she needed some help with a certain boyfriend who hit his drinking limit and then some. I had to leave my equipment at the venue. I'll pick it up tomorrow. It's been a long walk, which should have been a short walk, to Jamie's home to offload him to his parents, and now we're stood on his doorstep awkwardly, alone together for the first time since Evie left.

"Well, that was eventful," I say, chuckling.

"Yup. At least his parents were cool about it, as per usual." Ginny puts her hand on one side of her waist and leans to the side, as if she has a stitch. "I wish my parents would put my drunkenness down to silly, youthful misde-meanours."

"And they thanked us for getting him home safely, which is always appreciated," I add. "Not like I make a career out of pretty much carrying people home." I blow out an unsteady breath, my heart rate still trying to settle back to its usual rhythm.

Ginny nods and smiles meekly.

"Fancy coming back to mine for a drink and a smoke?" My parents are out and I'm not quite ready for the night to end. Since Evie's left, I've not really liked being alone with my thoughts.

"Sure."

We walk back to mine, and I fix us a couple of beers and roll a joint, which we take with us to the back garden to share. We sit next to each other on the grass, me with my legs straight out in front of me, Ginny cross-legged. Although it's been a stifling hot and sunny day, now, sitting in the garden, the temperature has definitely dropped. Ginny's breaths are apparent in the air as she shivers, only a thin denim jacket to protect her from the plummeting temperature.

My empathy and loyalty to Evie fight against each other, somehow feeling as if giving my jacket to Ginny is a betrayal to Evie. In the movies and books, it's always the partner giving his missus his jacket, like a sign of romance. I decide that Evie wouldn't want her best friend to freeze and let my empathy win. I take off my leather jacket and wrap it round Ginny's shoulders.

"Thanks, Ed. It's bloody freezing. God, isn't it strange without Evie being here?" Ginny says, and I decide then that giving her my jacket was the right thing to do. Far from a gesture of romance, her mind is still where mine is. "It just doesn't seem right without her. I miss her so much, but it must be so hard for you as well. I mean, you probably spent just as much time with her as I did."

"You're right. It's so weird that she just left without telling either one of us. Something awful must have happened for her to leave so suddenly," I agree. My mind has gone to a million different places, a million different scenarios, and I'm still no closer to working out what happened.

"I miss her every single day. Life's just not the same without her," Ginny mutters, a tear rolling down her cheek.

"I understand, Ginny, I really do. Come here. Please don't get upset." I put my arm around her shoulders and pull her against me. She stays there, her head against my chest as I rub her back, trying to comfort her.

Ginny pulls away and looks at me, fresh tears in her eyes. I stare back, both silent. We both lean forward slowly at the same time, until our lips meet for an innocent, comforting kiss. My arms wrap around Ginny and one of her hands reaches round to the back of my head, pulling me closer as the kiss gets deeper, and we revel in the comfort.

"Oh my God. I don't quite know how that happened," Ginny whispers. She moves my arm from around her and pulls the quilt tighter, making sure everything is covered.

"I'm sorry. I don't know what came over me." I look away from Ginny's sad eyes.

"It wasn't just you, Ed. It was me as well." I wonder if she blames herself more than me, just as I blame myself more than her.

"Listen." I hold her cheek, making her look at me, then quickly pull my hand away, the innocent move not feeling quite so innocent in this moment. "I won't say anything to anyone. You have my word. Now, let's get dressed and then I'll walk you home."

I pick my clothes up off the floor and get changed quickly.

"I'm going to lock up and then I'll get you back home, ok?" I say, trying to take control of the situation and get us out of it as quick as possible.

"Thanks, Ed. It'll be our secret; I won't breathe a word." Ginny squeezes my hand, as if to seal the deal. I go downstairs to give her some privacy, shutting the bedroom door behind me.

It's not long before Ginny comes downstairs, her smudged red lipstick freshly applied and her tousled hair in place once again.

It's about a twenty-minute walk to get back to Ginny's house. We walk together through the streets of South West London, and to anyone who sees us, we look just like any other teenage couple returning from a night out rather than two friends who have just betrayed the most important person in both of their lives.

We reach Ginny's house, and I go to give her a hug goodbye and wonder if that's too much after what just happened, so we both just stand there awkwardly, a decent amount of space between us.

"Well, goodnight." I wave uneasily, not knowing what else I can do. Ginny nods, opens the front door of her house and goes inside.

I jog all the way home, keen to get back before Mum and Dad. I tidy away the evidence of our smoke and our beers and lie in my bed, where my sheets now smell of Ginny's musky, heady perfume. I can't even remember what Evie's perfume smells like. She's been gone for exactly four weeks and two days and it's not getting any easier to deal with. What sort of person am I that I've already slept with her best friend and betrayed one of my best friends in the process? No wonder she left. Evie deserves so much more.

Chapter Twenty-nine

Evie

June 1985

The day after the visit with the private doctor, where they confirmed my pregnancy, Dad took the day off work and drove me and Mum to Auntie Maureen's house in Bournemouth. I was told I was to stay there for the remainder of the pregnancy.

Auntie Maureen's house is on one of the soulless, new housing estates about a twenty-minute walk from the seafront. There's a tiny paved garden where she has a selection of uninspired planted containers and a plastic green patio set with an umbrella, where I'm allowed to sit as long as I don't talk to any of the neighbours. I often sit outside if the weather's warm enough and try to revise or read one of Auntie Maureen's Mills & Boon books where some handsome, hunky doctor always comes and rescues a damsel in distress. I know no one's coming to rescue me.

I often wonder what Ed, Ginny and the rest of the gang thought when they realised I was gone. I guess they would have been upset at first, but at least they all have each other, whereas I'm stuck in an unfamiliar area with a couple of middle-aged mean-spirited sisters.

Auntie Maureen and Mother make me go to church every Sunday. We always sit in the front row, as if being so close to the altar and the priest will help wash away my sins. I can almost feel the hostile parishioners' eyes burning into my swollen belly every time we go, which is further accentuated by the flowing gingham smocks Auntie Maureen has been obsessively sewing for me ever since she heard about my pregnancy. As the weeks progressed, I began to recognise particular parishioners. There's one family with two daughters—one's my age and she has a younger sister who's about eleven. They always smile at me when they think their parents aren't looking.

The months in Bournemouth have bizarrely flown by so far despite my enforced incarceration. My mother accompanies me to any hospital appointments I have, and Dad comes and visits us every other weekend for dinner and a quick walk along the seafront. I live for his visits, as he's the only person in the family who treats me with any compassion. I secretly cry when he returns to London on Sunday evenings.

Sometimes, I dream Ed's with me, supporting me all the way with my pregnancy. Other times, I become resentful that he's just carrying on with his life as if nothing's changed. I long for my freedom. If giving away my baby gives me freedom, then surely it's the right thing to do? Auntie Maureen has put us in contact with a Catholic adoption service that apparently has loads of worthy parents longing for a child. I don't really have any choice in the matter and just silently agree to anything Auntie Maureen and Mother suggest about the fate of my unborn child.

My mother arranged for me to take my O levels at the local comprehensive school, so every day I have an exam, Auntie Maureen drives me to the school in her beloved pale blue Ford Fiesta. During schooltime, the other pupils just stare at my ever-expanding belly and whisper disapprovingly in the corridors when it's time for break or lunch. After each exam, Auntie Maureen returns to collect me. Today is the last of those days. Today is a bittersweet day for me. While I'm glad to get away from pretty much all the other students, there is one who I'm really going to miss: Emma. Emma, who just so happens to be one of the sisters in the church.

I've spent these last couple of months looking forward to seeing Emma at breaktimes and again at lunch, as she makes me feel like I'm a normal sixteen-year-old again. It's good to talk to someone my own age. We swap music suggestions, and she made me a mixtape of all her current favourite songs, which I listen to secretly on my Walkman. The words of "When Love Breaks Down" by Prefab Sprout take on a new meaning as Ed clouds my thoughts by day and keeps me from sleeping at night. Well, that and a baby who enjoys wriggling and moving inside me constantly. And just when I get into a comfortable position, especially at night, the baby gives me a hearty big kick, as if to remind me they're very much still there.

Emma never judges me, and she's never once asked who the baby's dad is either. She just gives me her friendship and buys me endless supplies of sweets to satisfy the sweet tooth I've developed throughout my pregnancy. We've spent many a breaktime stuffing ourselves silly with flying saucers, Fruit Salads and if I was really lucky, she'd produce a Curly Wurly, which we would happily share. Mother allowed me to join in with the revision sessions at school between exams, so it gave me and Emma a bit more time together to hang out. I even have Emma's phone number. She knows I'm unable to use the telephone at Auntie Maureen's but she said it's useful to have at least one person's telephone number when you move to a new area. I've stored the little piece of paper that Emma has neatly written out her telephone number on in my jewellery box, having folded it several times so that it will fit, hoping and praying Mother won't find it.

My last O level was history, and now it's finished, Emma and I are enjoying our final lunchtime together before it's time to say goodbye, as the dreaded Auntie Maureen will be waiting to drive me back to her house. We've managed to find an empty classroom, out of earshot of the other pupils. We've both just stuffed down half a ham sandwich each, Emma chucking the foil covering towards the bin, spectacularly missing. Neither of us bother to pick it up and actually put it in the bin. I'm not sure I could actually even bend down that far to do it.

"I can't believe we won't be able to hang out anymore now school is over," Emma says, pulling me close.

"I know, but Mother doesn't want me forming any ties down here. God knows what plans she's got for me once I've had the baby," I reply, enjoying the physical contact of Emma's much-needed hug. It's been months since anyone other than Dad has showed me any affection.

"We can still see each other at church though, can't we?" says Emma, linking one of her arms through mine.

I nod. "We can, although we won't be able to talk. We'd probably get excommunicated," I joke. Well, I'm sure it's a joke in Emma's case, but maybe not in mine.

"Just imagine that. No more boring Sundays at church." Emma laughs.

"Once I've had this baby, I'm never going to set foot in a church again," I vow.

"I know what you mean. They always go on about forgiveness, but your mother just seems to enjoy punishing you." She pauses, as if she's wondering if she overstepped the mark. I'm just glad someone else sees things the same way as me. "I've never asked you, and I hope you don't mind, but if you could, would you want to keep your baby?"

I look down at my pregnant tummy and stroke it, sighing. "Yes, but I realise I have nothing to offer them. The baby's dad doesn't even know he has a child. They made me leave London before I was able to tell him. I've been told my baby will be going to a good Catholic household through the church, so they will be loved and looked after. Who am I to prevent my child having that sort of life?"

"You're so brave, Evie." Emma stares at me with adoration. I'm not sure whether she means I'm so brave giving up my baby or I'm so brave coping with a pregnancy without the dad around.

"I'm not brave; I'm just a silly girl who got caught out. My boyfriend and I took a few too many risks, and this is the result." I point at my swollen stomach.

"Well, I think you're brave, and you've got my number if you feel you ever need it," Emma says loyally.

"Thanks, Emma. I really have appreciated your friendship over the last month."

Emma unlinks our arms and reaches inside her school bag for something. "I've uh... I've actually got something for you," she says, handing me a small money bag.

"What's this?"

"There's about ten pounds all in all. There's a five pound note, and the rest is in coins. Think of it as your emergency fund in case you need to call me if you ever manage to sneak off," Emma says, her cheeks blushing.

"I can't take this, Emma," I protest.

"You must. Half of it is from my piggy bank, but the coins are from the missionary box that we were given at church months ago. I've been taking a few coins from it for weeks. I was going to save up for some new records, but I think your need is greater than mine. Doesn't the church say that charity begins at home?"

My hands shake as I slip the small money bag into my pocket, holding back tears. "I hope that I can repay you one day. I can't tell you how much I've appreciated your friendship since I've been in Bournemouth. You've given me hope, Emma, and I will be forever grateful for your kindness."

Emma smiles and nods, clutching my shaking hand.

"Look, I've got to go, as Auntie Maureen will be waiting. I'll see you on Sunday. Thanks again," I say, hugging my new friend as if my life depends on it.

We walk together... well, Emma walks, I kind of waddle, as the baby seems to have had a growth spurt recently and I'm finding it hard to walk properly. We go through the corridor towards the double doors at the front of the school. We briefly hug again, only pulling apart when we spot one of the teachers tutting in our direction.

I walk out of the school for the final time and spot Auntie Maureen's car almost immediately. I open the passenger door and climb in.

"Well, that's it now. You can concentrate on delivering a nice healthy baby for that lovely Catholic family who are going to raise your poor illegitimate child," Auntie Maureen says spitefully.

"Thanks for that, Auntie Maureen. And how was your day?" I reply sarcastically as I buckle my seatbelt.

"Goodness knows how Felicity managed to raise such a rude, arrogant daughter. I blame your father's side of the family completely," she hisses, driving out of the school at a respectable twenty miles per hour.

Chapter Thirty

Genie

July 2018

I take a breath and look at Gray, who has tears in his eyes. I can tell he's heartbroken now he knows the truth. But I can't work out if he's heartbroken at what I went through or the fact I kept it from him. Maybe he thinks I don't trust him, which is really not the case at all. I had to put my secret baby behind me and move on for my own sanity.

"Did you have the baby?" Gray asks, barely a whisper as he struggles to get the words out.

"I had complications at just over eight months, and I lost a lot of blood as I gave birth. I had a blood transfusion. We were both very weak and poorly," I reply. "But yes, I had a little girl. Because I was so out of it, I didn't get to see her properly. Milly. At least, that's what I would have called her if I'd been able to keep her."

"Oh, Genie. I'm so sorry," he says as he pulls me in close. I breathe him in, tears coming to my own eyes.

"It was all my fault she was so small," I murmur. "I had smoked, I had carried on drinking and taking drugs, as I had no idea I was pregnant. She never stood a chance. And now Ed is back, I'm frightened that he'll find out I was pregnant. I feel bad that he never knew he was a dad, but I thought he'd never get the opportunity. At the time, I wished he knew, but now..." I bite my bottom lip. "So much time has passed. I'm so sorry I never told you about Milly," I say, arms wrapped around Gray, desperately hoping he won't judge me too harshly. Although, no one can judge me as hard as I've judged myself.

"I can't believe you went through all of that and you never told me," Gray says.

I immediately feel my body clench at the words

"You've carried all that guilt for years, but it does make sense why you have such a fractured relationship with your parents," he continues, shaking his head in disbelief. "What happened to Milly?"

"The original plan went ahead: she was adopted by a lovely Catholic family. Or, at least, that's what I was told. Apparently, they could give her all she'd ever need. Everything I couldn't provide," I reply sadly.

"Kids need love. You could have provided that."

I look up at Gray, love in my teary eyes. Part of me, a big part of me, wishes I'd told him years ago. He would have understood my erratic behaviour, fought with me through this mess and helped me emotionally in every way I needed, rather than in every way he could try. All this fear I've built up over the years is now crumbling before me. Fear that didn't even need to be there in the first place.

"And you've not had any further contact since then?" asks Gray.

"No." I lean my forehead against his chest, shame running through me. "I've always thought about her, but I try to remember that I gave her a good life by letting someone

GENIE 145

else bring her up. I had literally just turned sixteen when she was born, and I had absolutely nothing to offer her." I look up at him, trying to read his face. "I'm sorry, Gray, that I wasn't honest with you when we first met. And the longer I left it, the harder it seemed to actually tell you the truth."

"It's a lot to take in, Genie. You have another daughter. The kids have a grown-up half-sister. I can't quite get my head around it all." His arms loosen around me as the information sinks in. "You've been so brave telling me about Milly. Thank you for being so honest. It explains so much..." says Gray, deep in thought, a single tear rolling down his cheek. A single tear for the stepdaughter he never had, or a single tear for my dishonesty?

The secret I've been harbouring for over thirty years is finally out, but this is just the beginning. I have to tell the kids, and Gray could still decide this is all too much and he can't be with me anymore. I just feel so emotionally drained.

"I'm so tired, Gray. I need to go to bed."

"You go on up. I'll tidy up," Gray replies, kissing my cheek gently.

Chapter Thirty-one

Gray

July 2018

Genie has always intrigued me, kept me interested and made me laugh since the day we met, but nothing could have prepared me for what she said today. It explains the broken girl I met all those years ago in that Brighton bar. She's always said Maura and I saved her from the brink of despair, but I don't think either of us knew how important those chance meetings were for her.

I'm so surprised that Genie hasn't tried to look for her firstborn. Genie had just turned sixteen when she had Milly, and I met her when she'd just turned eighteen. We married within two years, but we struggled to conceive when the time came. I had always wanted a family, but I wanted Genie more, and if that meant a life with it just being us, I would have been just as happy. Would I still have been happy in a childless marriage with Genie now, knowing she had a child before me?

I can remember the complete joy when Genie's period was late. Now I'm wondering if part of that happiness from Genie's behalf was realisation that she had a second chance at motherhood. Nine months later, we were blessed with Cassie. Cassie was such a contented baby.

Genie blossomed as a new mother; nothing was too much for her. Being a mother seemed to come naturally to her. Just over a year later, we became that perfect family of four with the arrival of Will. I had been more than happy with just one child, but Genie had seemed hellbent on having a sibling for Cassie.

The fact Genie had a baby all those years ago with Ed would be dynamite if the press ever found out. We need to have an honest conversation as to what our next move is.

My head is scrambled, so I find the physical act of tidying away the dinner plates a welcome relief to the turmoil in my mind. I'm not ready for sleep quite yet. After meticulously washing and putting away our wine glasses, I walk out into the garden and sit down on the decking, light a cigarette and sip a whiskey, wondering just how our lives are going to change. I gave up smoking years ago, but with this whole situation, the stress and not knowing how to deal with Genie, I've been having the odd one here and there. The bad habit has been taking over recently and I've been keeping a pack of them in my pocket, not that Genie's noticed yet. She'd be fuming. I guess when you slip up in childhood and do a lot of things you know you shouldn't, it can turn you the other way as an adult. I will keep this a secret for now. Maybe for always, if I manage to give it back up. I guess we all have our secrets. Just some aren't as big as others.

The thought of Cassie in a similar position as Genie found herself all those years ago breaks my heart. I hope I'd deal with that predicament in a more reasonable way than Genie's parents. It explains her difficult and almost toxic relationship with her mother. Her father is far more reasonable. Genie often talks about him with great affection. To be fair to them both, they have been exemplary grandparents. Cassie and Will have wanted for nothing.

I neck the rest of my whiskey and stub out my cigarette, then go inside to lock up. As I approach our bedroom, I can hear Genie's usual light snore. I slip into the ensuite to clean my teeth and splash my face with cold water before I undress and go back into the bedroom. I slip in beside Genie, our bodies so perfectly in tune with each other, my legs fitting into the bend of her legs as they do every night. I kiss the back of her head and try to sleep but find that every time I close my eyes, I see Cassie and Will as small children being chased by Milly, shrieking with delight as she swoops in to try and catch them.

Chapter Thirty-two

Virginia

July 2018

My garden party for the football was a great success. Ed was the perfect guest: attentive, generous, outgoing and actually quite humble, which was quite a surprise.

We also had a bit of a moment, which I almost bloody ruined by mentioning Evie. I've always had a soft spot for Ed but seeing him again as an adult has really intensified my feelings for him. It doesn't feel like an unrequited school-girl crush anymore either. It's funny how things turn out.

After our kiss was interrupted and the moment passed, I had the task of clearing up as the guests started to leave. To be fair to Ed, he stayed and helped, together with Sasha and Shannon and Josh and Micky, who all thought Ed was "pretty cool for an old dude". For goodness sake, neither of us have even celebrated our fiftieth birthdays yet. But I suppose when you're under twenty, anybody over twenty-five seems positively ancient.

Ed left not long afterwards, as he had quite early rehearsals for the tour in the morning and I had work anyway. We arranged to meet again, probably at the weekend. He said he'll contact me about timings, as he wasn't sure what time off he was going to get over the weekend. It really depends on how their rehearsals go. It's mad to think that Ed, Mark and Jez are still playing together in the band. Ed has certainly been through a fair few bands, but it's good to see their friendship has endured the years.

We haven't talked since about the new photos I unearthed at my parents' house and my theory about Evie possibly being pregnant. I'm probably wrong anyway. Perhaps I was clutching at straws just to see Ed again. I'll leave things be for now and wait to see if Ed mentions anything. I just can't wait to see him again and maybe see both Mark and Jez after all these years. They were such a good bunch of mates to have back then, and I'm looking forward to some serious reminiscing.

After the excitement of the football last night, being at work is dragging. I think the whole country has a hangover after the disappointment of the football. No one's returning calls and even my boss has kept himself to himself, so I'm alone with my daydreams. I'm keeping myself busy by reorganising the filing system to distract myself from daydreaming too much about Ed. He wasn't particularly interested in me when I was in my prime, so why would things change now that I'm almost fifty? Although people can and do change. And we've all certainly had a lifetime of changes.

The reorganisation of the filing system doesn't keep me occupied for too long, and to pass the time, I idly scroll through Instagram. Evie, or should I say Genie McNamara, has an Instagram account but she hasn't posted any photos for some time, which seems to tie in with the resurgence of the re-release of "Used to Be" and *The Girl in the*

Song documentary. There are photos of her children and her husband. They're certainly a very photogenic family: all blonde-haired and blue-eyed. Her husband is a tall and very distinguished-looking man, with piercing blue eyes and slightly greying, dark blonde hair. She has two children, one of each, who both look the perfect combination of her and her husband. It's a shame really that we weren't able to stay in touch. Would it hurt to send Evie a quick DM? I know I said to Ed that I wouldn't do anything about the photos but surely it wouldn't hurt to just send Evie a quick message?

Hi Evie/Genie,

It's Ginny, although I am now known as Virginia! Just wanted to reach out and say hello. It's such a shame that we lost touch. It would be great to maybe catch up sometime.

Cheers, Virginia.

Oh well, there goes nothing. Unless she replies, I needn't tell Ed I've been in touch. By the look of her Instagram account, she never uses it anyway.

The rest of the afternoon drags even slower than the morning, but Mr Bruce lets me leave early, as he has to leave the office himself due to an event at his daughter's school.

It doesn't take me too long to drive home, and I decide that rather than doing some gardening—like I normally do when I have some spare time—I'll read the latest book I've downloaded on my Kindle. I make myself a cup of tea and take it with me to sit under the shade of the umbrella of my patio set.

I'm absolutely exhausted after last night; all the organisation for the party, the tidying and then an early start this morning for work has taken its toll. After only reading one chapter, my heavy eyes get the better of me and I finally give in to my tiredness. I close my eyes. Just as I'm about to drift off to sleep, I hear a banging on my front door and a continual ring of my doorbell. Surely it's not one of the girls? I hurry back inside and open the front door to be greeted by a courier delivering a parcel.

"Miss Virginia Weathers?" the courier enquires with a big smile.

"Yes, that's me. Thank you," I reply whilst signing the courier's digital notepad.

Once inside, I hurriedly tear open the parcel. It's obviously from Ed, as there's only one person who still knows me by my maiden name. There's a beautiful box inside with some homemade, delicious-looking Belgian chocolates and a single bottle of champagne. I rip open the gift card, which is attached to the box.

Virginia,

Thank you for another great evening. Shame about the footie result! Talk soon.

Ed x

There's a permanent smile on my face, knowing he's thinking of me as I am him. I put the chocolates and the champagne in the fridge, chucking the wrapping in the bin. The card goes into my purse, away from prying eyes. I return to the garden, unable to read, my thoughts consumed with Ed. I open Instagram to thank him, deciding to keep my message light and chatty.

Thanks so much for the chocolates and champagne, Ed. Hope rehearsals are faring better than the football did. Catch up soon. Virginia x

I go back to reading, able to concentrate again now I've reached out to Ed.

"Mum? You out here?" Sasha calls out through the open back door. I didn't even hear her come home. Oh well, I managed a sentence. I'll have to count that as bookish progress.

"Hi, yes, I'm here," I say, discarding my Kindle on the grass underneath my chair.

"You're home early. Is everything ok?" Sasha comes outside to sit beside me.

"Yes, fine thanks, love. Mr Bruce has a do at his daughter's school, so he let me leave early, as there was nothing much happening at work today. Too many hangovers after last night, I expect."

"That Ed bloke is nice, isn't he?" says Sasha as more of a statement than a question.

"Yes, he is. He's very nice," I agree with a smile. And there Ed is again in my head.

"Do you fancy him, Mum?"

"Do I what?" I snort. "Sasha, you can't ask me that," I exclaim, pretending to be outraged.

"I've never seen you so happy as last night. You couldn't stop smiling when Ed was here. He's quite good-looking for an old bloke, you know. You could do worse, Mum." She grins, laying her head on my shoulder.

"Well, I can't say I disagree that he's 'quite good-looking for an old bloke', and yes, I do like him," I reply, a warm flush rising from my chest to my neck.

"Did someone receive a parcel today?" Sasha probes. She's obviously clocked the gifts in the fridge.

"Yes, a thank you for a nice evening."

Sasha pauses, clearly wondering if she should ask what's on her mind. "What happened to Evie? Do you know?" She looks at the ground, presumably hoping not to upset me by bringing up the past.

"Well, as far as I can tell, she's married with two kids and lives in Richmond. I don't know much more, to be honest, as she's never commented publicly about her relationship with Ed or anything else, for that matter." I'm kind of glad the sun is facing me and giving me a reason to slightly squint, otherwise Sasha would see the sadness in my eyes. I spent years with Evie pushed to the back of my head, but now the media is so focused on her and I'm back in contact with Ed, I think about her all the time and can't help but feel a deep devastation that our friendship went from everything to nothing, Evie now a stranger.

"Do you think Ed still holds a torch for her, Mum?" Sasha says, bringing me back to the present. "I don't want you to get hurt again. My dad and Shannon's dad were pretty useless husbands, and you deserve to be treated like a queen."

I can't deny that the thought hasn't crossed my mind. In reality, they were together for such a short time, but with how much he's focused on her musically and spoken about her, it's not something I have a definitive answer to. "I don't know, love, to be honest. The only thing I know right now is that Ed and I get on. It's easy, I suppose, because we've got a shared history. I like the man he is today much more than the boy that I used to know, if that makes sense?"

"I understand, Mum. Ed seems like a great guy, but I just want to look out for you, that's all. Shannon seems so impressed that you used to hang out with someone who is kind of famous, and I wonder if that stops her seeing any further." She gets up from her seat before continuing. "I'm gasping for a cuppa. The salon's been full on today. Fancy joining me?" she says, walking towards the kitchen.

"Yes, please," I call after her. "And thanks, Sasha. I know I can always depend on you to have my back, but I'm old enough to make my own mistakes," I say, closing down this particular topic of conversation for now.

I haven't done too badly with either of my daughters really, considering both their dads thought with their cocks rather than their brains throughout both marriages. And up until now, I've been happy enough with single life, but with my fiftieth birthday approaching at an extremely rapid pace, I'm ready to possibly allow a new man into my life. Perhaps that's Ed? Then again, maybe it isn't. Time will tell.

Chapter Thirty-three

Ed

July 2018

The rehearsals for the forthcoming tour have gone pretty well on the whole today. Mark's drumming is perfection as per usual, Jez's bass playing is as slick as ever and my vocals haven't been too shabby considering all the shouting I was doing last night at the football, but I'm not overly happy with the backing singers, Cindy and Chyna, who've just joined us. They've apparently done loads of session work but I'm just not gelling with them musically. Cindy is the better singer; she can really belt out a tune. She's all big hair and has a very impressive cleavage to match, the daughter of a Jamaican reggae star, whereas Chyna, who is originally from the Philippines, is apparently just there to look sexy, as she seems to spend most of her time pouting into her microphone, and I can hardly hear her vocals at all. They are really lovely people, I just don't think they're a good fit with the band, but I fear we are stuck with them, as our manager, Toby Tucker, won't have a bad word said about them. There's a rumour that he's shagging one of them, or maybe even both of them, and that's fine if everyone's happy with that situation, but they're simply not fitting into the sound of The Mountaineers. The session musicians Toby has hired for the tour, however, are cracking, and they fit right in.

Today has flown by, and I feel bad that, apart from sending Virginia some chocolates and some champagne as a thank you for last night, I haven't managed to speak to her. I'm quite pleasantly surprised that since we've met up again, we've got on so well. Virginia is a breath of fresh air compared to most of the women I've met over the years. There have been young ones, older ones, married ones and groupies but no one has ever matched up to Evie until now, and to think she was there all along.

Toby walks back into the rehearsal room, clutching the smallest takeaway coffee cup I've ever seen, bought from one of those new hipster coffee shops that seem to have cropped up around the city. He sits down and turns to the backing singers.

"So, Cindy, your voice needs to blend with Ed's. Remember, it's not a competition to see who can sing the loudest. I want you two to work together. When you get it right, your voice can really complement Ed's. And, Chyna, I want you to bring all your sassiness to your performance. Don't forget to join in with your tambourine and keep your backing vocals light. Let's take it from the top," says Toby. Maybe that's why I can hardly hear Chyna—I was right, she's purely here for sexiness and most likely can't hold a tune.

I'll certainly give it to the girls because after Toby's instructions, their voices start to sound as if they've always been on the more recent tracks. By the time we come to sing "Used to Be", Toby instructs the girls to hang back and just dance. "Used to Be" is always our last song, and I still get a buzz when the audience sings my words right back to me.

"With your blonde hair and ruby red lips, you were every schoolboy's dream, looking like a movie star staring out from a magazine.

Oh, my head's in a state, why, oh, why did you make me wait?

Let's be together forever, just you and me, no one else matters.

They say we're too young to know (too young to know), but this boy's dream eventually came true because it was always you and only you.

The plan was to be together, forever, forever.

My love for you will never fade, our love was tailor-made.

Let's get back to how we used to be (how we used to be, used to be).

Let's be together forever, just you and me.

No one else matters.

They say we're too young to know (too young to know).

Our love was tailor-made, why, oh, why did you have to leave?

We shoulda proved them wrong—it coulda just been you and me.

Please come back to me, let's get back to how we used to be... how we used to be... used to be."

I wrote this song years ago, when Evie and I were together, but when she left, I revised the words slightly. Nothing like a broken heart to get the creative juices flowing.

"Loved it, guys. Girls, that was exactly what I wanted from you. Just brilliant," Toby enthuses.

"It all seems to be pulling together," I agree.

"I think that's enough for today. Get yourselves out of here," Toby instructs.

"Anyone fancy a drink? My treat as a thank you for everyone working so hard today," I enquire.

Toby makes his excuses, as does Cindy, but Chyna says she's up for a drink, as do Andy and Simon. Mark and Jez are always up for a drink. There's a pub just around the corner from the rehearsal room. I get the drinks in, and we're lucky enough to find some seats at the back of the pub. Andy and Simon chatting to Chyna whilst I fill Mark and Jez in on my recent meetings with Virginia.

"I remember Ginny. She was a right laugh. Wasn't she going out with Jamie back in the day?" says Jez, leaning back in his chair.

"Yes, that's right," I reply, taking a sip from my pint, remembering how Virginia and I betrayed both Jamie and Evie one fateful night. I've tried to cast that particular night out of my mind, as neither Jamie nor Evie deserved that.

"Her and Evie were as thick as thieves. Are they still in touch?" asks Mark, interrupting my thoughts.

I shake my head. "Virginia never heard from Evie again. Same as me."

"Ooh, that's a strange one. I thought you two were going to last the distance. It was odd the way she just kind of disappeared," Mark continues.

"Yep. One day she was there, the next day she was gone. No note. Just lots of unanswered questions." I scratch out small splinters of wood from under the table with my thumbnail, trying to keep myself in the present, afraid to face the reality of the only woman I've ever loved walking out of my life all over again. "The only reason people have started talking about her again is because of "Used to Be". I know we've capitalised on the meaning of the song and she has, somewhat unjustly, gained a notorious reputation from all of that, but people keep asking about our relationship, and quite frankly, I'm grateful, as it's kept us in the public eye."

"Yeah, you're right. If it weren't for the song, we'd still be playing small pubs and clubs," Mark agrees.

"Anyway, enough about Evie." I pat Mark on the back. "I'd like you all to meet Ginny again. I mean, Virginia. I think I might message her to see if she can join us, if you're happy to stay for a few more drinks?"

"Yeah, that would be great," says Mark as Jez nods.

"I'll get another round in," Jez offers, getting up from his seat and making his way to the crowded bar.

Chapter Thirty-four

Virginia

July 2018

Sasha and I both enjoy the last few rays of sun in the garden before it disappears behind our neighbour's trees, giving our garden some much-needed shade.

"I'm going to meet Josh at the gym later, and I think we're going to eat something healthy in the café afterwards. We've both decided we need to work off some of the excesses from last night," says Sasha, letting out a big yawn.

"Sounds like a good idea to me." I move my sunglasses to the table between us, the sun now unable to blind me.

"You could always use one of my guest passes to go and relax in the spa, then join us for dinner?" Sasha kindly suggests.

"Don't be daft. You don't want me cramping your style," I say, trying to put her off as politely as I can.

"Honestly, I mean it, Mum."

Sasha's just about to almost frogmarch me to the gym when an Instagram message flashes up on my mobile. It's from Ed.

Rehearsal finished. Just in the pub with Jez and Mark. Fancy joining us? They'd love to see you again. Will send an Uber. Just let me know x

"Well?" enquires Sasha, raising one of her perfectly arched eyebrows.

"It's from Ed. He wants me to join him and the guys from the band for some drinks."

"What are you waiting for?" she says, smiling. Sasha has always encouraged me to get back out there in the dating game since Callum left.

"He said he'd send an Uber," I add.

"Say yes," says Sasha encouragingly.

"Do you think I should go?" I ask as I start to panic slightly about seeing Ed again, not wanting to look weird by sniffing myself but unable to not worry that I smell of sweat from when I had the sun beaming down on me.

"Err, yes, of course," Sasha says, as if saying no is completely out of the question.

"Oh God, what will I wear?"'

"Just reply and then I'll help you get ready. I'll do your makeup for you," says Sasha, taking control of the situation.

I speedily reply to Ed's message: *Sounds great. What time and where?* x

Ed responds swiftly: *Uber coming in twenty. Pub is The Dog and Duck in Bateman Street. See you soon* x

Sasha and I sprint upstairs, and within quarter of an hour, she's helped transform me. She's given me smokey eyes and used a bronzer so I look like I've just returned from two weeks in the sun. I put on cropped jeans and a Bardot top, with white Converse pumps. With just a couple of minutes to spare, Sasha curls my hair.

"You look stunning, Mum."

"Thanks, Sasha. I couldn't have done it without you." I stare at myself in the mirror, hardly able to believe how much she's transformed me in such a short amount of time. "Make sure you lock up when you go to the gym. I'm not sure what time I'll be back."

"Well, just text me if you're going to be late or if you decide not to come home."

"Cheeky cow, of course I'll make it home," I exclaim, slightly embarrassed that my eldest daughter thinks there's a chance I could be a dirty stop-out tonight.

Sasha peers through the shutters in my bedroom, keeping an eye out for the Uber. "No sign yet. Late as always. Let's go down and wait. Do you fancy a quick drink for some Dutch courage?"

"No, darling. I don't want to turn up half-cut, as I haven't eaten anything since lunchtime."

The Uber finally arrives, and I kiss Sasha goodbye. My driver isn't at all chatty, so I just sit back in my seat, watching the world go by. I love summer evenings in London when the weather's this good. We get through the traffic with little effort from Hampton Hill, but by the time we reach Hammersmith Bridge, the traffic has started to back up. Thankfully, as we approach the West End, the traffic starts to clear. My driver huffs as he tries to turn left but finds the main road closed, so he turns off down a smaller road. He certainly knows his way around the backstreets of Soho, and I arrive at the pub in next to no time.

I walk into the pub and do a quick scan around the bar to see if I can locate Ed. I look all along the long bar to try and spot a familiar face in the sea of strangers, only to be greeted by a smiling Ed.

"Ahh, you made it," Ed says, swooping in with a kiss on my cheek. "We've got a big table at the back of the pub. Jez and Mark can't wait to see you. I'll get you a drink first. What do you fancy? Prosecco?"

"Yes, please," I reply, taking in my surroundings.

Ed orders our drinks, grabs them off the bar and ushers me to the back of the pub.

"Everyone, this is Virginia," Ed announces.

I recognise Mark and Jez straight away. They're older, but apart from that, they're just the same as the six-teen-year-old boys I used to hang out with.

"Wow, Virginia, you look great," says Mark.

"Thank you. You guys look pretty good yourselves," I reply.

"And this is Andy and Simon, who have joined us for the tour, along with Chyna."

"Hi, everyone," I say in what I hope comes across as a friendly and approachable manner as Ed makes room for me next to Mark.

Ed hands me a glass of prosecco, which thankfully calms the butterflies in my stomach.

"It's amazing to think you guys have remained friends all these years," I comment to Mark and Jez.

"We still haven't been able to shake Ed off, however hard we try. Every time he joins a new band, he somehow manages to piss them off and then he comes running back to us originals," jokes Jez, sticking his tongue out at Ed in jest. They're still like a bunch of kids.

"Oi, you. It's only because no one else ever matches up to you guys, you know that," Ed responds, giving Jez a jovial pat on the back.

"So, guys, you've only got a few months before the big tour," I say, wanting them to know that I'm up to date on what's happening with the band, that I actually take interest and actually care. "How are the rehearsals going?"

"Yeah, that's right. Things are going really well, and these guys have settled in nicely," says Mark, looking over at Andy, Simon and Chyna.

"You all make it easy for us. We do feel very much part of the band," Andy says as Simon and Chyna nod in agreement.

I warm to Andy straight away. He says he's a Londoner, if you count Staines as being in London. He isn't particularly tall and has a very similar personality to my ex-husband Callum with the complete gift of the gab. He's skinny, has receding strawberry blonde hair and wears John-Lennon-style glasses, which always seem to be perched right on the end of his nose. He's quite the ladies' man. And Chyna, along with many other women in the pub, can't take her eyes off him.

Chyna is a petite Asian goddess with a figure to die for and doesn't look much older than Sasha, but she has nothing much to say for herself, I find.

Although quieter than Andy, Simon has a maturity that belies his years. He can only be about thirty. He's a big presence with long, dark, curly hair. His voice is booming when he can actually get a word in edgeways against Andy's constant chatter.

The conversation turns to Jamie, as both Mark and Jez lost touch with him over the years. I fill them in as much as I can about taking over his dad's garage and his villa in Spain, and as the only social media he's on is Facebook, they each decide to send him a friend request, both of them needing some Dutch courage from yet another round of drinks.

All the talk about social media reminds me that I sent Evie a message earlier. She hasn't touched her social media accounts in months but my message is out there now somewhere. I'm a bit concerned that I haven't told Ed what I've done, but seeing that she hasn't even read my message, I cast any worrying thoughts or repercussions aside.

Ed finally sits down with me after being so busy making sure everyone in the group is ok and have what they need. "You and the boys seem to have picked up nicely from where you left off," he remarks.

"Yes, it's as if the last thirty years never happened," I say, laughing. I'm really enjoying myself tonight, hanging out with old friends. It's easy. It's comfortable.

"Has it really been that long?" asks Ed, shaking his head in disbelief.

"You do the math, Ed. It's weird but they still seem the same. Obviously, a bit older and wiser, I guess, but I'd be able to recognise them both anywhere."

"I'm not so sure about them being any wiser." He chuckles. "You do know that Mark is on his third wife, don't you?"

"Watch your mouth, Ed Nash, you seem to have forgotten that if I ever get married again, I'll be on my third husband," I retaliate with a smile.

"Oh God, Virginia, I didn't think. Anyway, your situation is totally different to Mark's," says Ed, desperately trying to backtrack.

"Don't worry, I was only teasing." I playfully dig my elbow into his ribs to show him that all is forgiven and no offence was taken. I know by the look on Ed's face that he's truly sorry for what he said. "Everything in life is a learning curve, and if I hadn't met my two husbands, then I wouldn't have Sasha and Shannon, would I? And I can't imagine my life without them."

"They're a real credit to you, Virginia."

"Thanks, Ed. They're great girls. I'm very lucky." I always like to think I've brought the girls up well but to hear that someone else thinks so too feels good.

The evening continues with much merriment and banter, just like the old days, as the four of us almost revert back to being sixteen again with stories from way back when. Nothing is said about Evie though. It's as if she never existed, which, to be honest, is exactly how we all felt when she upped and left all those years ago.

Ed gets a final round in, but I decline, as I'm feeling slightly woozy from too much prosecco and no food, so I opt for a glass of water.

"Do you fancy dinner out somewhere, just the two of us?" whispers Ed.

"I really could do with something to eat to soak up the prosecco you've been plying me with all evening." I wink cheekily.

"Sorry, I should have ordered you something." He looks at the empty packets of crisps in front of Simon and Andy and then his eyes drop away guiltily.

"It's fine. We can grab a bite to eat now," I reassure him. "It's not like I'm not old enough to buy my own packets of crisps anyway. It's not on you."

Everyone says their goodbyes, and we all promise to meet up again soon. Ed and I walk side by side to the end of Bateman Street, trying to decide what food to eat. Ed suggests going back to his and ordering some food in. I'm secretly delighted to finally be invited to Ed's inner sanctum.

Chapter Thirty-five

Genie

July 2018

I wake up early, greeted by another beautifully sunny day. Gray's still fast asleep, so I tiptoe around him, not wanting to wake him, as I know that once he's awake, today will be a day of deep discussions, and we still have to tell the children about the existence of their big sister Milly.

I go downstairs, and I'm pleasantly surprised to find that Gray's tidied up everything from the previous night, even remembering to put out the recycling. He really did stay up to tidy, it hadn't just been an excuse to avoid me. All I needed last night was to just go to bed and sleep. I was so exhausted from everything.

I make us both a cup of tea, take Gray's upstairs and leave it on his bedside table. He sleepily acknowledges it and closes his eyes once again. I decide to have my tea in the garden to enjoy the early morning solitude before everyone gets going with the day. The sunrays are just beginning to hit the patio, and I contentedly watch the birds greedily feeding from the bird table. It's a good half an hour before Gray joins me, his hair sticking up all over the place, wearing his old trackie bottoms and an ancient Metallica T-shirt.

"Good morning, Mrs McNamara. How are you on this fine and beautiful morning?"

"Not too bad. I slept remarkably well. How about you?" I reply as Gray sits beside me at the garden table.

"I'm good. I'm going to book the flights to Florida today now that both kids have finished school. Think we could all do with a break. Jonesy said his villa is free any time over the next few months," Gray continues.

I nod, knowing I need to push myself by getting away from here, hoping it will help clear my mind. "When shall we tell the children?" I ask tentatively. I mean about my secret, not the holiday, my mind still focused on last night.

"How about when the kids get back? Or shall we wait until we get to Florida?" Gray picks at a thread from his tatty trackie bottoms.

"I favour today, although there will be an awful lot of questions to answer," I say, wanting my secret to finally be out there, not wanting to hold on and dwell on the what ifs any longer.

"Today it is, then. I'm not going into the office today. I've decided to take a day's leave to spend with my beautiful wife," says Gray with a big, reassuring smile.

"I'm ok, Gray. I don't need babysitting, you know."

"I know you don't, but I would like to take you out to brunch before the kids get back with all their questions." Gray sighs. "To be honest, I've got some questions too."

"I don't really know what else I can tell you," I say somewhat defensively, looking away from him.

"Well, I just can't believe you haven't tried to find Milly for one," Gray says. "There are loads of different websites where you input all your information together with any known information about your child, and they do the rest. There have been loads of successful reunions."

"I know, Gray. But I wouldn't have even known where to start looking for Milly." I screw my face up, wondering why he's bringing up about the websites. Has he been doing his own research? I'll drop it for now, just in case I'm wrong. I've already kept a massive secret from him, I don't need to now come across accusatory. "Before I met you, I knew what I did was best for Milly at that time. My parents told me that she went to a lovely family who couldn't have children. And then once Cassie came along, I didn't want to burst our little family bubble. I thought you might leave me for not being totally honest with you all these years. I mean, you might still leave me now you know the truth, but it's a risk I had to take. I couldn't let you find out any other way."

Gray shakes his head vigorously. "I could never leave you, Genie. I love you too much for that. We have Cassie and Will together. We're a family who needs to stick together. I'm only sorry that you felt you couldn't confide in me sooner, but I do understand, Genie, I really do." He reaches over the table to hold my hand.

It feels good to have Gray by my side. I always feel safe with him. Telling him was a risk, but so far it seems to have paid off. But I feel guilty, so guilty about all the lies, all the half-truths I've told throughout our marriage, but dear Gray still just wants to help me, to try to fix me and put me back together again. I wonder if I would have been as strong if things were the other way around.

"Both children messaged while you were still asleep. Neither will be home before lunch. Let me freshen up and then you can tell me where you're taking me for brunch. I don't mind where, just make it somewhere quiet. I'll try to answer everything you want to know," I say reluctantly.

"Leave it with me. The Bingham is nice and discreet. I could request outside seating," Gray suggests.

"I'd better wear something decent if we're going to The Bingham."

"You'll look gorgeous whatever you wear."

I pop upstairs and pull out a couple of possible dresses from my wardrobe before changing my mind and settling on some pale blue linen trousers and a crisp white shirt. I loosely tie back my hair and apply some more lipstick and some bronzer to perk up my pale skin. I grab my bag and make my way into the garden.

Gray gasps. "Wow, you look amazing," he says, overexaggerating as usual.

"Thank you." I roll my eyes but can't help but smile. "You, however, look like you've just got out of bed," I say, looking at the state of him.

"Good point," Gray agrees. "The table's all booked."

"That's great. Now, go and shower. I'll lock up," I instruct, shooing him upstairs.

I secure the patio doors and sit in the coolness of the sitting room, idly flicking through yesterday's paper while I wait for Gray. Within ten minutes, I hear him coming down the stairs.

"That was quick," I say, closing the paper and putting it on the coffee table.

"I didn't want to leave my beautiful wife waiting too long, did I?"

"I guess not. Shall I go and find her?" I smirk.

"Oh, you'll do," says Gray, laughing.

We lock the front door behind us and make our way to The Bingham for our brunch date. The sun is blazing hot as we start our walk to get there, and after just a few minutes, I long to be in the shade. Once we do reach The Bingham, thankfully, we're ushered to a nice shady table on the outside terrace, overlooking the River Thames.

We order a couple of salads with some bread and a couple of glasses of rosé.

"This is lovely. I should really take more time off work on days like this," says Gray, looking out over the terrace at the perfect view of the river.

"It would be great to have you around more often but I know how much the company means to you."

"Well, for starters, I'm definitely booking those flights to Florida later for as soon as possible. I've put it off enough, but I'm owed some time off and I think you need me more right now. My brain has been in overdrive after last night, and I think we should delay telling the children about Milly until we are away. If we tell them everything tonight, they're going to have so many questions to ask, and I don't fancy that on a nine-hour flight."

"I agree." I'm just relieved that Gray has stopped cross-examining me about Milly for now. I'm exhausted by talking, and I know that there will be so many more questions to answer once the children know, most likely going over the exact same ones Gray has and is bound to ask. I think he senses my reluctance, because I can see in his eyes that he has so much to ask and yet none of what he wants to say is coming out of his mouth. I know the point of going out was to talk but I'm not going to make that move. Our brunch is a welcome distraction from everything that's going on for me.

Once we've finished eating and paid the bill, Gray and I decide to go for a walk along the riverside. We walk hand in hand, just enjoying being together.

"We certainly don't need to go abroad for hot weather, do we?" I observe, trying to steer the subject away from Milly before she's even mentioned.

"We don't, but I think two weeks away from everything will recharge everyone's batteries and give us some space to think. The kids are knackered, as am I, and you could definitely do with a break. You could invite Maura out for the second week if she's free. I know how much you ladies enjoy the shopping outlets in Florida."

"You wouldn't mind?" I ask, turning towards his kind, handsome face to kiss him.

"Maura is family as far as I'm concerned. The children adore her, and she'd be doing me a favour. You know how much I hate clothes shopping," he says, kissing me back.

Chapter Thirty-six

Cassie

July 2018

After the disappointment of last night, and I'm not talking about the football, I keep going through things in my mind about what a prick Danny's turned out to be. I shouldn't really let him bother me but the whole situation has made me feel very exposed and vulnerable. I can't imagine ever having a serious boyfriend at my age like Mum did.

Mel was so caught up with her forthcoming date with George that she wasn't really there for me last night, but she didn't know the whole story, so I can't really blame her. I've since filled her in on Danny's behaviour, and she was horrified and now feels somewhat guilty. But I'm fine. It's made me realise that I can't really trust any guys, and at sixteen, I'm more than happy to be on my own.

Mel's mum's cooked us a full English breakfast, which we're greedily wolfing down with a never-ending supply of tea. Their house was in a right state after all the partying, but Mel's mum seems to have everything under control, and with the help of one of her friends, they've managed to get everything back to normal.

Mel has been religiously checking Snapchat, as there's talk of a load of our ex-classmates all meeting up on Richmond Green around lunchtime. Mel has managed to hide a few bottles of beers from last night to take with us, so we're all set.

"I'll just message my mum to let her know what I'm up to, as I know she'll be keen to catch up," I say, quickly sending Mum a message on WhatsApp.

"Sure. God, our parents just don't have the stamina anymore for a late night and a few drinks, do they?" Mel laughs. "Did you see the state of my dad last night, slurring his words? And Mum's friends from work were so drunk." She leans closer, eyes wide. "Anna Murphy's mum had to be carried home by her boyfriend. Oh, the shame..." she bitches.

"I don't think Anna's mum had anything to eat, you know. That's always the problem. I mean, look what happened to me at Saskia's party. I skipped dinner. But you'd think by their age, they would have worked that out," I say, still completely puzzled by our parents' generation.

Mel's dressed to impress on the off-chance George might show up, whereas I'm hoping and praying Danny won't be there after last night. I decide to cast him from my mind and focus on the fact I'll be catching up with some old friends for a few drinks in the sunshine. He's not going to ruin my day.

Mel and I leave her house, hop on a bus and make our way to the green. A big crowd of girls and boys from various secondary schools in the area are gathered on the green already. We join some of our ex-classmates and excitedly catch up on everyone's news. Most of us have plans to meet up at Reading Festival at the end of August.

As Mel and I sit with Emily and Katie from our former tutor group, I catch sight of George and Danny arriving. Danny's hand in hand with the girl in the shorts from the party. She's welcome to him; I had a lucky escape there. I notice that George is looking for Mel, so I nudge her and nod towards where the boys are.

"Will you be ok if I go and speak to George?" Mel whispers.

"Yes. Go on. It's not his fault his mate's a dickhead," I say, laughing.

"As long as you're sure?"

"I'll be fine," I reassure her.

Mel goes over to where George is, and he greets her with a big hug. Danny and his companion nod a brief hello to Mel just before she manages to get George on his own. I really hope she isn't telling him about what happened last night.

I chat with a few other friends for a bit longer while I finish my beer. Mel's still happily hanging off George's every word, and who can blame her really? George is a great guy, good-looking, funny and is clearly besotted by her. I'm genuinely pleased for her, but I just want to get home now and see Mum. I quickly send a message to Mel on Snap, say my goodbyes to the rest of the girls and start the walk home.

Chapter Thirty-seven

Genie

July 2018

We take a leisurely stroll back home and then I sit back out in the garden with a sobering cup of tea as Gray checks on some work stuff and calls his work's travel agents to finalise the flights to Florida. Ever the shrewd businessman, Gray is holding out for the best deal on our flights.

As I drink my tea, I idly scroll through my phone. I've rarely checked my social media since *The Girl in the Song* furore, and I'm quite shocked to see the amount of unread notifications. I notice that I have several direct messages, along with a couple of direct message requests. Most are random spammers but one in particular catches my eye. Well, the name in brackets does. Could it really be Ginny after all these years? I accept the message request.

Hi, Evie/Genie, It's Ginny, although I am now known as Virginia! Just wanted to reach out and say hello. It's such a shame that we lost touch. It would be great to maybe catch up some time. Cheers, Virginia.

It really is my Ginny from all those years ago. I quickly look at her profile and find a very attractive woman. Gone is the peroxide blonde hair and heavy makeup, replaced by honey-coloured blonde hair with gentle curls and sun-kissed skin. It seems she has reverted to her original name, wanting to reinvent herself from Ginny to the more grown-up and sophisticated Virginia, just like I tried to shed the skin of Evie Del Rio and replace her with the very respectable Mrs Genie McNamara. I really can't believe we haven't tried to find each other sooner. We were such good friends back then and I've always felt guilty about just leaving, not that I had a choice. There's a definite element of guilt on my side for leaving both Ginny and Ed. It must have been quite hurtful to never hear from me again. In the first few weeks when my mother moved me to Bournemouth, I cried every day for the friends and the life I'd left behind.

I compose a quick reply.

Hi, Virginia. So lovely to hear from you after all these years! I've always been so sorry that we lost touch. I agree it would be great to catch up one day. Take care. All the best. Genie xx

I send it before even thinking it through properly. It's such a nice surprise to hear from Ginny that I don't consider any repercussions. I quickly put my phone away in my bag, as I can hear Gray coming into the garden.

"Are the kids home yet?" asks Gray, looking rather pleased with himself.

"Not yet, but Cassie's just texted to say she'll be home in half an hour and Will is just about to leave Tommy's."

"I've managed to get us flights for tomorrow lunchtime from Heathrow," Gray announces.

"Wow, that soon? I haven't even phoned Maura yet." I push myself up from my seat, my excitement contained by my overruling thoughts of all the things that I needed to do by tomorrow.

"Well, call her now. I really hope the kids will be pleased. I'll have to work a bit late tonight to finish things off, but Gerry will pick up any slack for me if need be while I'm away." The fact he has to work late tonight already shows me that I'll probably have to pack for the both of us.

"Right, well, I'd best call Maura and start packing. Jonesy's villa has a washing machine, doesn't it? We might have to take suitcases of dirty clothes, as I haven't done any washing recently," I confess.

"Jonesy's villa has all the mod cons, but we can buy new in Florida if we need to. Just pack the basics."

"You know that's easier said than done," I grumble. I know I should sound more grateful but I could've done with a few more days to get organised. I've let so much washing and so many chores slip, so caught up in shying away from this whole *The Girl in the Song* attention. Usually, I'm prepared for anything. And I should have known to be prepared for this, Gray forever impulsive.

I grab my phone and send Maura a text about her joining us the second week. She's probably at work and won't be able to answer her phone.

I go upstairs and start looking through my wardrobe to see what I can pack. I sort out a few sundresses, some shorts, vest tops, a couple of swimsuits, underwear and sandals and then do the same with Gray's clothes. I will leave the children's until later once they know we're going away. Will has grown so much over the last few months and I don't have a clue as to what clothes still fit and Cassie changes her mind so often as to what she likes wearing that it would be a thankless task.

Just as I'm racking my brain as to whether the suitcases are in the loft or in the spare room, I hear the doorbell go.

"Can you get that?" shouts Gray. "I'm on the phone to work."

"Will do," I shout back.

Typically, it's Cassie, who always finds it impossible to take her keys with her whenever she goes out.

"Hi, Mum. Sorry, I left my keys at home. Again." Cassie says, walking inside and starting to climb upstairs. I shut the door behind her.

"I've noticed. Good night?" I ask.

"Yeah, it was ok, I suppose. Shame about the football. Everything ok here?"

"Yes, fine, darling. Your dad and I want to talk to you and Will once he gets back," I shout out as she disappears from view into the upstairs hallway.

Right on cue, Will arrives back too, using his keys to open the door.

"Hi, Will. Great timing. Once your dad has finished on the phone, we need to have a bit of a chat. We've got some news."

"Oh ok, sure. When's dinner? I'm starving," says Will, ruled by his stomach as always. I roll my eyes.

Will goes upstairs to his room, and within minutes, I can hear his booming voice talking to his friends on the Xbox. Children today seem obsessed with technology, whereas in my day our obsession was music. How times change.

Gray finally emerges from his office with a big grin on his face.

"You look very pleased with yourself," I say.

"I am. Gerry is all up to speed, the flights are booked, I've got all the codes for Jonesy's villa and I've organised car hire," Gray replies.

"We'd better tell the kids, then, as they'll need to pack. I'll call them down," I say.

Finally, after neither child responding to me calling their names, I resort to an announcement via their Alexas. That does the trick.

Both children come downstairs, phones in hand, and we all sit around the kitchen table.

"I've booked tickets for Florida. We go tomorrow afternoon," Gray announces.

"Yes," says Will, punching the air. "Excellent. I can't wait to tell Tommy. We'll be there for the World Cup final, won't we? Jonesy's got an outdoor TV, hasn't he? Imagine watching the final in the pool or the spa in the sunshine."

"Cassie? What do you think?" I ask, noting her silence.

"Sure. It will be great," she replies flatly.

"You could sound a bit more excited, Cassie. It's just what we need as a family," scolds Gray.

"Sorry, Dad. Think I'm just a bit tired after last night. I'll go and start packing," she replies with a forced smile.

"Sure, darling. Off you go. Just let me know if you need any help," I add, concerned that Cassie doesn't seem her normal self. I'm kind of hoping she'll accept my open invitation to help her pack at some point so I can speak to her about what's going on inside that mind of hers.

Cassie and Will disappear upstairs to supposedly start packing, whilst Gray complains about the amount of clothes that I've packed.

"Surely no one needs that many shoes. Or indeed that much underwear," he says, looking in disbelief at my attempt of packing, even though I've pretty much packed bare minimum. "I've already told you there's a washing machine," he adds.

"Well, you might be able to survive on a small amount of pants, but I, however, like to have some sort of choice with my underwear selection," I reply as Gray grabs hold of me and pulls me close.

"You know I'm only teasing you, Genie. You take whatever you like, darling. But don't forget that you and Maura will get to do some fairly serious shopping once we're there."

I nod, purposely adding a couple more sets of underwear. Tomorrow can't come soon enough, but once we're away, I'll have to reveal my true self to my children. I only hope they'll understand.

Chapter Thirty-eight

Ed

July 2018

Our taxi makes good progress through the streets of Soho, and we eventually find ourselves outside my new rented flat in Teddington. I can tell Virginia's impressed by the location, as she hasn't stopped talking about how lovely Teddington is since I told her where I live, just as I was to the estate agent those six months ago when they first showed me around. I'm fortunate to be on the top floor, which gives me stunning panoramic views over the River Thames, with two balconies to choose from, one which leads off from the sitting room and the other from my bedroom.

"Oh my God, Ed, what a stunning flat," says Virginia when we walk through the door. "The views of the river are just incredible." She peers through the glass, like a child at Christmas, taking it all in.

"Let me open the patio doors, and I'll sort out a take-away. Do you fancy a drink?" I ask.

She turns back to face me. "Ummm, maybe a glass of water, but I am starving. What shall we order?"

"Do you like Thai food?"

"I love it. But nothing too hot. I'm a bit of a wuss when it comes to spicy food."

I pull up the menu for the local Thai takeaway on my phone and we pore over it, choosing enough spicy and non-spicy dishes to suit us both. I also order a couple of Singha beers. Then, I lead Virginia to the balcony, where we sit, breathing in the night air and enjoying the continuing evening heat.

"How long have you lived here?" Virginia asks.

"About six months. As soon as I saw it, I just knew I had to live here. I love the views. Everyone keeps themselves to themselves, although they are neighbourly enough to take in a package for me if I'm not around. The shared gardens are a bonus if I need to get outside, but it was the balconies that sold it to me."

"It's stunning. There's so much space too." Her brow creases. "I have to ask, whatever happened to your uncle Paul? Where does he live now?" The question comes out of nowhere, and the mention of Paul unnerves me, but I find myself answering anyway.

"I think he's renting a caravan on Hayling Island. He always loved it there, and we used to holiday a lot there when I was younger. He was inside for a while for drug dealing, which probably doesn't surprise you. I bung him a few quid every so often into his bank account to tide him over. Now that I'm in the public eye, I'm trying to distance myself from him, to be honest," I say, voice lowered, hoping beyond hope that she keeps that information to herself.

"Ahh ok. I remember Paul and his love of all things narcotic. I can't believe how we used to dabble back then. I'd be mortified if my girls did drugs," Virginia confesses, her face flushing, potentially embarrassed about her past.

"I've tried to keep that side of my past from the girls. Thankfully, they're both into their fitness, so they seem to be quite clean-living. Well, apart from the alcohol. You have to have some vices," she adds.

"Oh God, can you believe the amount of drink and drugs we used to do?" I run a hand through my hair, thinking back. "I can't believe we got away with it. How come our parents didn't notice? Paul has a lot to answer for. I had a really bad substance problem a few years ago, but thankfully that's all behind me now," I confide.

"I'm sorry to hear that. I read that Paul has been in prison, but I didn't know things had got so bad for you. Did you go to rehab at all?" Virginia asks gently, placing a comforting hand on my arm.

"No, I didn't. I think I was too scared that they'd make me give up alcohol as well. Once Paul was inside, it made it easier not to use, although my drinking did become a bit excessive, but I've managed to cut back quite a bit. Gone are the days when I used to blackout, thankfully. I find it makes me more creative when I'm song writing though."

"Maybe limit your drinking to just weekends and special occasions?" Virginia suggests.

"Fancy joining me?" I challenge.

Virginia shrugs slightly and tilts her head. "Sure. Why not? We're not getting any younger, are we? As you know, I do love my prosecco, but I'm always looking for ways to improve my health and fitness. So, after tonight, we'll just drink at weekends."

"And don't forget the special occasions," I add quickly.

The takeaway arrives, and we set it out on the table on the balcony. I hesitate before offering one of the Singha beers to Virginia.

"Our restricted drinking starts on Monday," exclaims Virginia.

"Thank God you said that. You must have read my mind," I reply, popping the caps on the beers and handing one to Virginia.

After we finish every single morsel of food, we both sit back, slowly nursing our beers and our full stomachs, just taking in the beautiful, still and starry night.

"Ed, I've had such a great evening," Virginia begins with a smile, "but I should really think about getting back home. The girls will be waiting up for me."

"It's Saturday tomorrow. Are you sure you can't stay?" I blurt out, not ready for the night to end quite yet.

"No, Ed. I can't. Let's just take things slowly," Virginia says firmly. I can sense her reluctance to leave despite her words.

"Ok, let me at least get you an Uber."

I check my Uber account for any nearby drivers to pick Virginia up. I can't help but feel delighted when I find there to be no one currently available in the area.

"No luck. Let's have another drink while we wait for one to become available."

"Are you sure it's not just a ruse to make me stay the night, Ed?" Virginia winks.

"As if I'd do something as underhand as that," I reply, taking my chance to kiss her at last. I think the kiss takes her by surprise at first, as she pulls away and gasps. I go in for another one, and this time she kisses me back, and it takes my breath away. I don't remember a kiss ever making me feel this good. Not even with Evie. Until now, nothing has ever measured up to Evie. What's going on with me?

Virginia eventually pulls away and leans back in her chair, laughing, breaking the sexual tension in the air. "God, what are we like? Snogging like a couple of teenagers on your balcony. I'm sure there's some sort of risk assessment we should be adhering to."

"I think we've both got better with age, don't you think?" I reply.

"Possibly," says Virginia with a wry smile.

"Any chance I can persuade you to stay?" I persist, pulling her close again for another kiss. The giggle and the way she kisses me back is all the answer I need.

Chapter Thirty-nine

Virginia

July 2018

Despite all my good intentions, I didn't make it back home last night. My night with Ed was everything I had hoped for—so much better than our post-Evie fling when we were sixteen. Ed was definitely right when he said we've improved with age. Rather than being completely infatuated by him, I'm beginning to get to know the real Ed. He's a different man to the selfish boy I knew all those years ago.

He even woke me up with tea in bed and fresh towels so I could take a shower, plus the promise of breakfast on the balcony to take full advantage of another beautiful summer's day. After a luxurious shower—so much better than mine—I join Ed on the balcony.

"Breakfast is served, madam," Ed says with an exaggerated bow.

I'm greeted with a warm buttered croissant and an assortment of jam and marmalade, together with a large cup of steaming coffee.

"Well, I wasn't expecting this," I say, sitting myself down at the small table.

"You're lucky I've actually done some shopping. It's very rare that I get the chance. I should really sign up for a delivery service, but I'm so often not here it never seems worth it," Ed says, taking a seat opposite me. He drains the rest of his coffee, having already started his before I made it to breakfast.

"Well, it's really appreciated after all the alcohol we consumed yesterday. I really mean what I said last night about us both trying to cut back on our alcohol consumption," I say, spreading a liberal amount of strawberry jam on my croissant.

"Don't worry, I'm still up for it. I really need to get fit for the upcoming tour anyway. Toby, our manager, will start putting us through our paces fairly soon. There's talk about me getting a personal trainer to help me shape up," Ed replies.

"As I said, I'm up for just having a drink at the weekend. If we do it together, it will help us keep on track. I want to be fit and healthy for my fiftieth," I say encouragingly.

"Oh God, don't mention the dreaded five-oh." Ed winces, as if in pain, then laughs. "Mine is in January. God knows what I'll do for it, although at least we'll have just finished the tour by then."

"Finding myself single at almost fifty, I'm planning on going to New York for my fiftieth with the girls. New York around Christmas looks magical." I feel my eyes light up with all the hopes and plans I have for the holiday. "The girls are really looking forward to the shopping."

"You consider yourself single, do you, Virginia?" Ed enquires with a smile.

"Yes. I don't have a husband or boyfriend right now," I say in a matter-of-fact way, wiping the corners of my mouth for stray strawberry jam.

"What about last night?" Ed asks, avoiding eye contact, fiddling nervously with the spoon on the side of his saucer.

"What do you mean?"

"Well, I thought after last night we might kind of be seeing each other?" he mutters awkwardly.

"Oh, I see," I say, almost choking on that last mouthful of croissant. I really didn't see this coming. I mean, I was hoping last night did mean something, but I've always found Ed hard to second guess.

"I've been really enjoying getting to know you again recently, and I just kind of presumed... thought you felt the same..." he says tentatively.

"I do really like you, Ed, but I'm so scared you'll hurt me again, just like when we had our fling back when Evie had just left," I confess.

"I know I was a right shit back then, but I was so messed up when Evie just upped and disappeared and I felt guilty for shagging one of my best mates' girlfriends. It was the wrong thing to do back then, but now that we're older, this seems right." He takes my hand and gives it a big squeeze.

There are butterflies in my stomach for the very first time in years. I put my arms around his neck and kiss him gently on the lips before our kisses merge into one. I feel like I'm sixteen again, but this time Ed isn't thinking about someone else.

"I guess that kiss means that perhaps you're not currently single?" Ed says with a wink.

"I'll get back to you on that one."

We spend the rest of the day back in bed, just enjoying being with each other, stopping only when the hunger pangs get too much and then Ed decides that he'll treat me to a late lunch. We get dressed again and leave the apartment, making our way to The Anglers—a nearby pretty pub overlooking the river. We grab a table in the shade and order burgers and chips. I will be the size of a house what with croissants for breakfast and burgers for lunch. As it's still the weekend, we order a glass of prosecco for me and a beer for Ed and then we just enjoy being together, watching stressed families trying to get their little ones to eat their overpriced kiddie meals.

"Gosh. Kids look like hard work to me. Goodness knows how you managed on your own with your two," Ed says, shaking his head as he sees yet another child having a tantrum as the mother pleads with him to be quiet and just eat his chips.

"To be honest, it wasn't that bad. Callum—Shannon's dad—treated Sasha like his own because Jon was off having his midlife crisis on his motorbike around Europe. Neither of them wanted for anything until he fathered another daughter and then that was the end for me. He still sent money for both of them until the mother of his youngest daughter demanded more money and then he didn't have enough for both of my girls as well," I say, pausing only to take a sip of my prosecco. "Callum is a bit like Andy, your session musician, he can sweet talk anyone," I continue. "Unfortunately for me, Callum just couldn't keep it in his pants. Fidelity is everything to me. I've never forgiven myself for cheating on Jamie with you all those years ago, so I decided to make sure I never cheated again and that if I found out anyone had cheated on me, like both Jon and Callum did, then that was the end." I wonder if I've said too much, but if things are to progress with Ed, then he needs to understand that I won't be messed about.

"Wow," he says, finally managing to get a word in. "That told me, didn't it? Just to let you know, there is no one else in my life right now. I'm enjoying getting to know you all over again."

"Well, I hope you mean that. Time will tell. Now, where's that burger?" I laugh, trying to soften the serious edge to the conversation.

Our food eventually arrives, and we make quick work of our burgers. I insist on settling the bill, as Ed was so generous yesterday. It's only when I leave to go to the ladies that I notice Ed is getting a lot of attention. Of course people would recognise him, I don't know how I managed to not see it. It also explains the extra-special attention we received when our server brought out our food. He doesn't seem to really notice the furtive looks and nudges people are giving each other but he does keep his mirrored Ray-Bans on.

Once I make my way back to him, we decide to take a walk along the river by crossing the pretty little iron bridge over to the other side of the river and walk hand in hand to Kingston. The towpath is full of people: families walking and cycling, joggers and people like us walking and just enjoying the sunshine. We reach Kingston Bridge and walk along the riverside before cutting through Bushy Park and eventually making it back to Ed's flat.

"I'd forgotten how lovely it is around here. Since I moved into the flat, I haven't really explored the area properly. It's not much fun on your own," says Ed.

"You chose well here, Ed. It's idyllic."

We spend the rest of the afternoon sitting on the balcony, chatting, drinking tea and generally finding out all about our lost years. Ed kind of already knew all my life stories, as I'd been quite candid with him when we first reconnected. Piece by piece, I'm learning more about Ed from the man himself, away from the headlines. I'm surprised he's never, in his almost fifty years, shared a home with a woman. He's either lived with Paul or with Jez or Mark and then more recently with friends of friends before being able to afford the rent on his current apartment after his recent popularity resurgence.

I was in touch with the girls earlier via our family WhatsApp group, with lots of winking faces from both of them due to my non-appearance last night. I'm desperate to get back home to change into some fresh clothes and to see the girls, but I'm equally more than happy to be in this current perfect bubble that I've found myself in with Ed. At the back of my mind, however, are my Polaroids and the fact I only yesterday messaged Evie. I promised Ed that I wouldn't do anything with the photos, and I haven't. But I never promised that I wouldn't contact Evie. She probably won't reply anyway, but it won't harm to just check to see if she has responded. I have one new unread DM on my Instagram account just begging to be opened and read.

"I'm just going to check in with the girls," I lie.

"Sure. Go through to the bedroom for some quiet if you like," Ed says, gently touching the small of my back as I leave the balcony. As things seem to be going so well with Ed, I could surely be excused for my slight duplicity. I close the bedroom door and check my unread message. I'm so surprised to see a reply from Evie.

I will leave it for now and perhaps reply to her in a couple of days. Ed doesn't need to know everything...

Chapter Forty

Will

July 2018

I was dreading getting back from Tommy's yesterday, as I thought Mum would still be upset and Dad would be trying to cover up for her like he always does. Adults think we don't get things, but truth be known, we do. I know there's more to this Ed bloke than Mum is letting on. I hate seeing her upset, as I'm not very good at dealing with other people's feelings. I want to help but I just don't have the words. I'd rather be kicking a football or playing Xbox, so when Dad said we're going to Florida, I couldn't pack fast enough.

Dad surprised us with an airport lounge when we got to the airport. I could see the relief on Mum's face to be away from the crowds. Mum still gets recognised a bit, and if we are with her, we get people taking sneaky photographs of us all. I do love airports though. There's always something going on, and when we were younger, we used to play a game with Mum where we looked at people and tried to decide where they were going. I tried to get Cassie to play the game, but she just wasn't interested. She's been a right moody cow since she got back from Mel's.

We got seated in the airport lounge at a table close to the window, where we could watch the planes come and go. I was starving, so I ordered a full English and a cappuccino. I'd stayed up really late playing *Fortnite* with Tommy, so I needed a caffeine fix. Mum doesn't like me drinking coffee, as she says I'm too young, so she always makes me a decaf. Thankfully, she was in the loo when I ordered.

Dad ordered himself and Mum a glass of champagne to toast the holiday. I could tell Mum didn't really want any, but she took little sips as she picked at her breakfast. Cassie had a full English and a green tea, which looked like pond water. She thinks it will help her lose weight. I mean, she's not even overweight but one of her friends said that if you drink green tea after eating lots of food, it somehow helps you. I just don't get how girls' minds work. Dad says he's still trying to work them out too.

After we finished our food, Dad was busily reading the financial pages of the newspaper that he'd picked up on the way into the lounge, while Mum flicked through a glossy women's magazine and Cassie was pretending to read *Grazia*. I'd had enough of reading from school, so I took a few photos of myself in the lounge to put on my Insta story. In just a couple of minutes, about eighty people had already viewed my story. Tommy called me, and I left the table to speak to him.

The time went quite fast when I realised that the lounge had an Xbox, and in the end, Dad had to almost drag me away from it, as we were being called for our flight. Dad had another surprise for us, as he had bought us upper-class seats. I couldn't believe our luck. We were one of the first people to board the plane, and it was great to be able to read through the inflight magazine and find out what films and TV programmes were being shown onboard. And then there was food and drink being dished out at every opportunity. It was my idea of Heaven.

Once we had been in the air for some time and had eaten lunch, the flight attendant asked us if we wanted to have our seats turned into beds. I didn't need to be asked twice and took a load more photos for Instagram. Mum had her seat turned into a bed and actually went to sleep, whereas Dad and Cassie were happy as they were. I can highly recommend flying upper class, as before I knew it, the captain said once we'd had our afternoon tea, we should get prepared for landing. Mum had slept most of the way. I think she'd taken some sleeping tablets, as I saw Dad give her a big nudge to wake up just after the captain had made his announcement. Cassie hadn't said a word to me the entire flight, as she had her headphones on, just watching films and listening to music. That suited me. I had eaten so much food and watched about three movies, and I'd even managed a little nap when my seat had been converted into a bed.

We cleared customs quite quickly, and Dad ordered a super-sized taxi to take us to Jonesy's villa, as he'd enjoyed a few drinks on the flight. He planned to pick up his hire car the next day. We'd stayed in Jonesy's villa when I was about ten, so I could remember it a bit. It's only about twenty minutes from all the parks, so a great location, but it's on one of those posh communities where they have their own security guards at the gate before you get into the estate. It has eight bedrooms, so Cassie and I had the pick of the rooms. There's a huge master suite downstairs with an amazing jacuzzi bath, but Dad said he'd prefer us all to sleep upstairs for security reasons. I chose a bedroom overlooking the pool area, which has a king-size bed for me to sprawl out on, and Mum and Dad chose the main master bedroom upstairs, which has an en suite bathroom. Cassie chose a room as far away from me as possible, overlooking the front of the house.

The particular sweet spot was seeing that Jonesy had updated the games room, complete with an Xbox with more games than I have at home. There's a basketball hoop, a snooker table and a foosball table. There's plenty to keep me occupied. The outside pool area is the perfect setup too with an outdoor screen. There's a jacuzzi big enough to hold a party of six. Dad really has come up trumps with this particular holiday.

It's good having Jonesy as my godfather, as he's well minted and is always really generous with his close friends, like Dad. Dad and Jonesy used to be at school together and have always kept in touch. My dad has done well with his advertising business, but Jonesy's life is out of this world. It's something to do with hospitality—that's all I know. But what I do know is that Jonesy doesn't have a regular girlfriend and doesn't have any kids. I think Cassie is a bit pissed off that Jonesy isn't her godfather. Her godfather is Uncle Phillip, Mum's older brother, who lives in Hong Kong, or maybe he's in Thailand now. I can't remember. He rarely keeps in touch.

Granny adores Uncle Phillip and can't stop talking about him, which I think pisses Mum off. He's not married yet and he doesn't have any kids either, but he does have a really hot girlfriend, who is probably only about thirty. I think she's in PR or something, but we've never met her. Mum and Granny are always really snappy with each other whenever they meet. Mum says it's because Uncle Phillip has always been Granny's favourite. She's said it on numerous occasions. Mum didn't do very well in her exams at school, whereas Uncle Phillip is a bit of a brainbox and even has a degree. Everyone's different, I suppose. I'm good at maths and sport, whereas Cassie's got a great singing voice and likes drama. I couldn't sing myself out of trouble.

Grandad's cool, although he gets bossed around by Granny all the time. He always takes Mum's side if they argue though. I bet he gets it in the neck from Granny when they get home. Granny and Grandad have always been great grandparents, and when we were really young, they would often babysit.

Luckily for us, Jonesy arranged a brilliant welcome pack, so we have plenty of food for our first night. While Cassie and I check out the pool, Mum's busying herself unpacking and has started to prepare omelettes for everyone. Dad has already familiarised himself with the villa's alarm system, set the aircon, located the safe and, most importantly, made sure all our phones, iPads and laptops are connected to the Wi-Fi.

The pool is warm, as it has had the whole day to heat up in the scorching Floridian sun. The forecast for the next few days is similarly hot, which suits me. I got Cassie, somewhat begrudgingly, to video me doing backflips into the pool, with a couple of slo-mo to put on my Instagram story. Now she's done filming me, Cassie is sitting on the side of the pool, dangling her feet in.

"Are you coming in?" I shout, jumping off the side of the pool, covering Cassie in water.

"Will, you prat. My hair's soaked now," she screams.

"Oh, come on, Cassie. Loosen up. We're on holiday." I go underwater once again, resurfacing right beside her.

Cassie huffs and storms off into the villa.

Mum calls me inside for my omelette, so I reluctantly grab a towel and follow Mum inside. We all sit at the kitchen table and tuck into delicious ham and cheese omelettes.

"God knows how any of us can still be hungry after all the food we consumed on the flight. I guess I just felt guilty only making Will one, as he's always hungry." Mum laughs, picking at her omelette. She offers the rest to me, which I gladly accept. I mean, she's not wrong.

"So, one major rule for you two. No fighting. Now, this holiday is just what this family needs, and I want everyone to get on. Agreed?" says Dad.

"Agreed," Cassie and I both reply, Cassie running her fingers through her damp hair. She has a face like a slapped arse, so I know she doesn't mean it. Game on.

Chapter Forty-one

Genie

July 2018

It's such a relief to get away from London. I keep going over and over how I'll break the news to the children that somewhere out there they have an older sister. I just can't tell how they're going to react. Cassie seems so withdrawn since she got back from Mel's but, wrapped up in my own drama, I've neglected to really talk to her about what's wrong. Cassie and Will have already had a bust-up over Will splashing Cassie with water from the pool. Hopefully, they'll settle down. Everyone's probably tired and jet-lagged, so things will seem better in the morning, after we've all had a good night's sleep.

It's 10:30 p.m. The children have retreated to their rooms, so Gray and I are enjoying a glass of wine outside, under the lanai, looking out over the glistening pool, listening to the comforting sound of the mini waterfall flowing from the jacuzzi, into the pool.

"Fancy a dip?" Gray asks suggestively, moving his chair closer to mine.

"Are you sure that's all you're after?" I reply with a tired smile.

"Well, at my age, I'll take anything I'm offered." Gray winks.

"Gray! Don't forget the kids are here, you know."

"Come on, Genie. We're on holiday..." Gray says, kissing my neck gently but passionately.

"I'm not sure where my swimsuit is," I protest weakly. I know I'm making excuses but all I want to do is have some glasses of wine and then go to bed.

"Who needs a swimsuit?" Gray pulls back slightly and shrugs, starting to read my mood.

"I do. I'm not going skinny dipping, Gray, so you can get that idea out of your head." I mean for it to sound like a gentle rejection but it comes out harsh.

"Spoilsport. Don't worry, we've got two weeks," Gray says, finally giving up on the idea of skinny dipping but only for tonight.

Gray pours us another couple glasses of wine as we sit, enjoying the water on our tired feet. When the wine's all finished, we stay outside, taking advantage of the warm night air and then dry our feet on a couple of towels and make our way inside.

Gray checks the locks, sets the house alarm and looks in on the kids—an old habit that seems hard to break—before he gets ready for bed in our ensuite bathroom. We each have our own vanity basin, so I have plenty of room for all my pots and potions. Within a couple of minutes, Gray has undressed and brushed his teeth. By the time I've taken off my makeup and cleaned my teeth, Gray's already fast asleep, letting out a very light but equally annoying snore.

I climb into bed beside him, switch off the bedside light and fail miserably trying to find the curve of his legs, Gray usually finding the curve of mine. I toss and turn for what seems hours, but when I check the time, I've only been in bed for about half an hour. Thankfully, Gray's in such a deep sleep and I'm physically so far away from him that my constant tossing and turning doesn't seem to trouble him. I try to switch my brain off and think of anything but the upcoming conversation with the kids, eventually falling into a restless sleep filled with flashback dreams from my teenage years and visions of my children telling me they hate me and that I'm a horrible mother.

Chapter Forty-two

Ed

July 2018

Things between Virginia and I seem to be moving along so quickly that I think we've both been taken by surprise. I conveniently forgot how I'd used her to get to know Evie all those years ago. But that was then.

I'm now beginning to wonder why I didn't realise how amazing Virginia is before. I mean, she was very much part of the gang back then but it had always been Evie for me. I suppose when you're fifteen or sixteen, being in a band holds some sort of fascination. Mark and Jez seemed to swap girlfriends every few weeks and there was never any shortage of willing volunteers. Jez eventually settled down with Poppy, a girl he had known since primary school. But the one real constant was Evie and me. We were the power couple of our group. Girls would always try and chat me up, but I only ever had eyes for Evie.

The last time I saw Evie was early April. We had a great day hanging out at Mark's house, me jumping in and out of the pool. I remember the day quite well, as Evie had rowed with her Mum yet again and had just run out of the house to come and join us. If only I'd known at the time that that was to be my last day with Evie. I would have paid her more attention. Unfortunately, us lads were more concerned with showing off to each other by divebombing into the pool. I remember kissing her goodbye and offering to walk her home, which she refused, as she was anxious to get back.

The photos Virginia showed me are the last ones of us all together. I'm still not sold on Virginia's hunch that Evie was pregnant when she left. I really want to take another look at them but I don't really want to spoil things with Virginia by bringing the subject of Evie up again.

Virginia's popped home to check on the girls. The plan is for her to get some fresh clothes and then come back to mine and stay the night, then we're going to have a barbecue at her house for the World Cup final on Sunday. It's good to have plans for a change rather than just going with the flow like I always do. I'm going to have a session at the gym whilst I wait for Virginia. I need to keep my fitness up for the forthcoming tour.

I've decided I'm going to drive to the gym, as the car needs a run. I've been so busy recently that I haven't done much driving, and my leased Mercedes has been gathering dust in the communal garage. I'm lucky that we have tight security here. Sid, our security guard, is a right character: an ex-policeman who can sniff out a wrong-un a mile off. He always has time for a chat and is constantly ready to dish out some advice, whether you ask for it or not. He has his finger on the pulse, and if he likes you, you're sorted. He got rid of a lot of tabloid photographers who were hassling me when the press found out where I live.

"Good afternoon, Mr Nash," Sid calls out from the other side of the garage, where he's using his litter picker to rid the garage of any bits of rubbish that have dared to take up residence.

"Hi, Sid. Please call me Ed. Mr Nash is reserved for my dad," I joke. He often calls me Mr Nash despite my persistence to get him to only use my first name. It's like he needs fresh permission every so often to use my first name.

"Of course, Ed. How's life treating you? You're not having any trouble with the press at the moment, are you?" he enquires.

"It seems to have quietened down. I think people have been so wrapped up in the World Cup that I'm old news," I reply. "I've been so busy recently that I've been neglecting my car, so I thought I'd give it a run. I'll catch you later, Sid," I say, climbing into my car. I drive up the ramp from the car park, giving him a wave as I leave. I know that if I don't leave now, Sid, who likes a chat, would have me there for at least another fifteen minutes.

It's good to be behind the wheel once again, and as the weather's still really warm, I decide to have a slow drive through Richmond Park. What's the point of having a convertible if you don't have the roof down now and again? I love Richmond Park. There's a sense of freedom when you're there, whether you are jogging, walking, cycling or driving. I must remember to bring Virginia here one day. And there she is again. She's always on my mind lately. I must be going soft in my old age, but I've never felt like this before. Well, not in my adult life.

Women have tended to come and go in my life. No one has ever put up with me for more than a couple of months. It's always the drinking, the drug taking and the inability to keep it in my pants, so who can blame them really?

Virginia is so different to how I remember her. She's so grounded and sorted, and she makes me feel good about myself again. She's lived a proper life. She's been married, she's a mother of two great girls and she's got a proper job and a great home that she's worked hard to get. What have I achieved really? Not a lot. I've written a bunch of songs that have only become popular because of a TV show, drank too much, taken far too many drugs and let people down along the way. Not much of a catch really. But Virginia seems to enjoy spending time with me, so I suppose I should just enjoy spending time with her.

The drive around the park has definitely given me some headspace, although I sometimes think far too deeply about everything. Maybe that's what helps me write my lyrics. I find it easier to say what I feel through my music.

I arrive at the gym and park up. I keep my sunglasses on as I walk through reception, as all the receptionists know who I am and I'm beginning to think one of them leaked my home address to the press. I mean, I can't prove it; it's just a hunch.

I really bust it out in the gym. I hit the cardio machines, do some weights and also spend time in the outdoor jacuzzi and sauna after. Once I'm done working out and relaxing, I go to the changing rooms, where I get showered and then get dressed.

With no word from Virginia yet, I grab a coffee from the café and sit outside. I scroll through my social media accounts. There's a link to a story on one of the tabloid sites that catches my eye: "Evie Del Rio, the inspiration behind the hit song "Used to Be" by The Mountaineers, jets off for fun in the sun with her family."

I press on the link and find a slightly blurred photo of Evie, her husband and her two kids arriving at Heathrow Airport. I don't have time to read the article, as my screen lights up with Virginia's name. I touch the "answer" button.

"Hi there, you ok?" I say in a hushed tone, conscious about who might be listening in.

"Hi, Ed. I'm back home now," says Virginia in her now familiar husky voice.

"Sure thing. I'll be there in five."

"Great. See you then."

I end the call, grab my gym bag and my unfinished coffee, and walk towards the car.

Not a minute late, I arrive outside Virginia's five minutes later. I park over her driveway and ring the doorbell. As she opens the door, I'm almost taken aback by just how gorgeous she looks. Her hair is loose and wavy and she's wearing a sundress. I don't think I've seen her wearing a dress since her sixteenth birthday party.

"Hi. You look amazing, Virginia," I say, drinking in everything about her, greeting her with a quick kiss before being ushered inside.

"Thanks. You don't look so bad yourself. Shall we stay here or go straight back to yours?" she asks.

"You look so gorgeous that I just want to take you out and show you off to everyone, but the other half of me wants to take you upstairs," I admit.

"Well, I'm easy either way." She throws back her head, laughing. "Oh my God, I can't believe I just said that."

"Seriously though, would you like to go out?" I ask.

"I'm a bit like you. I'd love to go out but I want to keep you all to myself," she confesses.

"What about another takeaway? We could sit in your garden until the sun goes down and then I'll drive us back to mine. Or we could just stay here? Especially as we're going to watch the football here tomorrow. But equally, I don't want to make you feel uncomfortable if the girls are here."

"They're both staying at their boyfriends' tonight, so if you want to partake in a little sleepover, that would be great," Virginia says with a smile.

"I guess that's our decision made. Now, come here so I can say hello properly. I've missed you," I say, kissing her again. Once we surface from the kiss, Virginia's beautifully styled hair is looking a little worse for wear.

"What are we like?" She giggles. "Let's sit in the garden. Do you fancy a drink? We're allowed; it's the weekend."

"The abstinence doesn't start until Monday anyway, so who am I to say no?" I wink.

"Grab a bottle of prosecco from the wine fridge, or there's beer if you fancy in the main fridge, and head out to the garden whilst I sort out my hair and reapply my lipstick. Maybe you should take a look at the state of your face in the hallway mirror while you're at it." Virginia does a cute little snort.

I turn to look and hold back a gasp. I genuinely look like a clown. "I thought the colour would suit me, but I have to admit it looks better on you." I grab her for another kiss, keen for this moment not to end quite just yet.

I manage to remove the lipstick from my face and busy myself in Virginia's kitchen, sorting out the drinks. I even know where she keeps her wine glasses now. Her house is beginning to feel as familiar as my own flat. The garden is so peaceful despite the proximity of other houses due to the abundance of plants and flowers that shield it with privacy. With the continuing hot weather, if you were to close your eyes, you would think you were in some tropical paradise rather than being in a suburban garden just off Hampton Hill High Street.

Virginia soon joins me, looking refreshed and, dare I say it, even more gorgeous than before. I simply can't get enough of her. Things have really moved forward at an increasing speed but I'm enjoying this perfect little bubble we've created for ourselves. I'm equally concerned about keeping our relationship private though. It's my own fault the tabloids have taken such an active interest in my personal life. I've always courted the press, using them to my advantage when *The Girl in the Song* was broadcast. I'm thankful for everything it's given me but my blossoming relationship with Virginia is private and I want to keep it that way for as long as possible.

"Shall I just fix us something to eat? Unless you want to go out?" Virginia asks.

"I want to spoil you. You always seem to be cooking and looking after everyone else, so I'm going to take you out for dinner and then I'm going to very selfishly keep you all to myself until the girls get back tomorrow," I announce in an almost growl-like voice, biting my lip.

"Oh, I do like it when you go all masterful on me. There's a great Italian restaurant around the corner. I'll call them now and make a reservation," says Virginia, grabbing her mobile.

"Sounds good. I'll just put the rest of the wine in the fridge for later."

She wasn't joking when she said the Italian is round the corner. Within five minutes, we've locked up, walked there and been seated. We're sitting opposite each other at a private little table towards the back of the restaurant. We place our orders, the restaurant quick to serve our food, the wait time less than quarter of an hour: garlic bread to share and a couple of freshly baked sourdough pizzas. I hold back on the chilies, remembering that Virginia isn't keen on spicy food. We're equally quick at eating, us both more ravenous than we realised.

The restaurant is fairly busy, but people seem to be keeping themselves to themselves. It's only when I settle the bill that I notice a couple of girls glancing over at our table and then whispering amongst themselves. I thank the waitress and usher Virginia quickly out of the restaurant. As I turn around, I catch one of the girls taking a photo of us on her phone. I'm fuming but desperately trying not to react. Virginia obviously realises something's wrong, as I practically frogmarch her back to her house.

"What on earth was all that about, Ed? I've never been so embarrassed in my life. You more or less dragged me out of that restaurant," Virginia shouts, her cheeks flushing.

"I'm sorry. I just want to protect you, that's all," I stammer, unused to someone questioning my behaviour.

"What do you mean?" Her eyes are wide, her arms flailing. I hold her hands in mine to stop her arms moving and try to explain.

"There were a couple of girls that clocked me when I paid the bill. And then when we left the restaurant, they took a photo of us leaving."

"Are you ashamed of being seen with me?" Virginia asks with tears in her eyes. Her hands slip from mine.

I stare into her eyes and frown, unable to comprehend how she could think that. "Of course not. Far from it. I just don't want your life turned upside down just because we're dating."

"Look, I'm a big girl, and I've looked after myself and the girls over the years. And although I'm flattered that you want to look out for me, I can deal with it. Do you know how much gossip there has been about me having two husbands who have both left me for someone else?" she says, her vivid, bright blue eyes almost burning into me.

"I know you can handle yourself, Virginia, but this isn't just local gossip; this is the tabloids. They have the ability to ruin people's lives."

"I know they do. And you, Ed, have to take some responsibility for how you have disrupted Evie's life since that documentary came out. All that you have now is because you traded in on the notoriety of your short-lived teenage romance. *You*"—she jabs me in the chest with one finger, her long fingernail most definitely leaving a dent in the skin under my top—"were lucky that you just happened to write some bloody good songs about it. You can't have it all your own way." Every word that comes out of her mouth is the absolute truth, but I'm too much of a selfish prick to just admit she's right.

"Wow, that's told me," I reply heatedly. "I didn't know that's how you really feel. I think it's best that I leave now, don't you?" I shout as I turn my back on Virginia and storm off towards the front door.

"The choice is yours, Ed," she challenges. "I've really enjoyed spending time with you recently but, seriously, you do need to grow up now. It's not all about you."

Chapter Forty-three

Virginia

July 2018

Evie has been on my mind since she messaged me back. I remember the laughs we had, with and without the boys, the sleepovers and the shopping trips. And now I feel guilty for having put the idea that Evie could have been pregnant when she left into Ed's thoughts. I mean, it would explain an awful lot, but I can't publish those photos or release them to the press. I gather up all my old photos and lock them away in the little book safe on my bookshelf. Only Ed knows about these latest photos, although the girls saw them briefly when Mum found them in her attic, as they were staying over. I think I've always missed having Evie as my best friend. If we'd remained friends, who knows, we would probably have been godmothers to each other's children.

I spend the rest of the evening just sorting things out, as I haven't been around much over the last couple of days. The house is eerily quiet with the girls away but, being so used to my own company over the years, it's also quite therapeutic. I do some washing, unstack the dishwasher—the girls still seem incapable of doing that particular task—and make myself a cup of tea, which I enjoy in the cool of my garden, lit up by an assortment of pretty, twinkling solar lights.

I glance at my watch, surprised to see that it's after 10 p.m. I decide it's time to lock up for the night. I left my phone on charge while I was in the garden. Before I unplug it, I notice there are a few missed calls from Ed. He'll have to do better than that. I switch my phone off. The girls can phone me on the home phone if they need me.

I kick off my sandals and settle down to finally start watching *Stranger Things* on Netflix. The girls have been nagging me for ages to watch it. I soon get caught up in a world of a terrifying Demogorgon and extremely familiar dodgy '80s outfits, where no one has ever heard of Ed Nash. I'm just about to start the second episode when my doorbell rings and then the letterbox rattles.

I jump at the noise, jarring against the quiet of the house, the darkness seemingly making it louder. I peer around the room, the knowledge of someone outside leaving me with that feeling of being watched, knowing I'm not alone. The girls have keys, so it can't be them. It's way after 11 p.m., so I'd hope Ed would have the decency to call first if he were ready to make an apology rather than make the situation worse by scaring me senseless. I now wish he was still here though and that we hadn't argued. I'd at least feel protected.

I peer cautiously through the crack in the living room door. From here, I have a partial view of the front door. I can see a blurry figure through the frosted glass. The doorbell goes again and then the letterbox opens, a very familiar, desperate voice entering through it.

"Virginia, babe, let me in. I've been locked out."

I blow out a long breath, walk into the hallway and open the door to be greeted by my ex-husband Callum. Even in his drunken state, his cocky swagger remains. My fear soon turns to anger. Before I can speak, he's already opening his mouth again.

"Thanks, doll. You're a lifesaver." He grins before brushing past me and marching clumsily towards the sitting room. It's almost as if he still thinks he lives here.

"Bloody hell, Callum, I really don't need you here right now," I shout, closing the front door, following him into the sitting room.

"She's only gone and kicked me out, 'asn't she? Silly cow thought I'd been chatting up the new barmaid at the pub. She bloody changed the locks an' all," Callum explains, plonking himself down on my sofa, making himself extremely comfortable. He's fairly drunk, which is nothing new, the smell of the alcohol oozing from his pores, and I know from past experience that I don't have a chance of moving him when he's like this.

"That's all well and good, Callum, but you can't keep turning up here every time Amy chucks you out. Surely, you must have some mates that you can call on?" I say sternly, hands on hips, trying to convey some sort of authority.

He waves my comment away with a flick of his wrist. "Are my lovely girls 'ere?"

"No, they're both staying over at their boyfriends' houses."

"Oh, shame. It would have been great to catch up. I miss those girls," he says with a mournful edge. I know he's only thinking about them because he can't exactly not when he's in their house.

"You should have thought about that before you started putting it about," I snap.

"Oh, come off it, Virginia. We were never really compatible. I was always your bit of rough after that posh prat Jon did a runner on you, wasn't I?" Callum slurs.

"Thanks for that, Callum. I think it's probably time you left, don't you?" I say, standing as upright and as tall as I can without my heels on.

"Ahh, you don't mean that, do you, darlin'? I know you've missed me," Callum mumbles, the numerous pints he obviously consumed earlier making him sound slightly incoherent. I didn't realise quite how drunk he really is.

"Can I stay the night, Virginia? I'll kip on the sofa. You won't even know I'm 'ere."

"It's not a good time, Callum," I mutter.

"What do you mean? The girls will be upset if they find out you kicked me out in me hour of need," he says, trying to convince me by using my two weaknesses.

"I'm just not in the mood for you and your domestics." I enunciate the words, hoping Callum will understand and get the hint.

"I've got nowhere else to go, Virginia. I'll talk Amy round eventually, and I'll be gone in the morning. I'm seeing Jimmy tomorrow, and he's only round the corner from 'ere. I'd stay with Jimmy if he weren't on the night shift. It will be the last time I ask you for a favour, I promise. Do it for the girls, please?"

"Ok, on one condition: you are gone before the girls get back. I don't want them seeing you in this state," I say as I finally give in to Callum, against my better judgment.

"Alright, babe. Understood," Callum readily agrees, not really having any other suitable options available to him.

"I'll get you a blanket and a pillow. But I don't want any funny business, ok? Amy deserves better. Hell, I deserve better," I warn him.

"Thanks, babe. I knew I could rely on you. You're a star. Don't worry, I'll be gone in the morning. You won't even know I was 'ere."

I sort out his bedding and leave him a bottle of water for the morning. I had many years of dealing with Callum and his excessive drinking. Within minutes, he's snoring away without a care in the world. Callum isn't really my problem anymore but the girls would never forgive me if I turned him away. Unfortunately, he also knows this.

I switch off the lights and head to bed. This is not the end to my Saturday night that I pictured just hours earlier. I briefly think about Ed and wonder how he's feeling before sleep finally comes to me.

Chapter Forty-four

Genie

July 2018

"Good morning." I open my eyes to a very cheery and very awake Gray, cup of tea in hand.

"Good morning," I say groggily, sitting up in bed, propped up by several plump pillows. I try to wake myself up, feeling like I've not slept at all. Taking the tea from him, I glance at the time. My eyes widen, and if I'd taken a sip of tea, I probably would have spat it out. "Gray, it's only 6 a.m. What on earth are you doing up?" I pause. "What on earth are you doing waking me up?"

"Well, I'm obviously still working on London time. Sorry, I just thought I'd treat you to a cup of tea. I never normally have the chance to treat you, so I thought why not now?" Gray genuinely looks like a wounded puppy.

"Gray, it took me ages to get to sleep. I had to listen to you bloody snoring for ages," I grumpily reply.

"Ok. Point taken. I'll take myself back downstairs and let you sleep," he says, kissing me gently on the top of my head.

I drink my tea and then snuggle back under the covers. I manage about another hour of sleep and then decide to join Gray downstairs. I'm still tired but I'm certainly not going to get any more sleep this morning, what with Gray crashing and moving about downstairs. Our bedroom is directly above the kitchen, which is just where he happens to be. Incredibly, the kids are still managing to sleep through all the noise.

I slip on my kimono-style dressing gown over my nightdress, complete with a pair of flipflops, and walk downstairs. Gray, bless him, is trying to cook poached eggs and bacon. I've not seen such a mess in a kitchen before though. Well, not since he last "cooked" a breakfast, which was for my last birthday. I'm dreading the washing-up and cleaning.

"I thought I would cook you some breakfast," he says, looking at me with a big smile. He adds, somewhat sheepishly, "Sorry. As per usual, I've made a bit of a mess."

How could I be cross with him? He's always trying so hard to do nice things for me. Although, to be honest, looking at the mess, I would have been grateful for just another cup of tea. I could have cooked and cleaned and it would have probably taken me less time than this will take to clean.

"It looks wonderful. Thank you. Is it warm enough to eat outside, do you think?"

"You go and check, let me know, and I'll bring you your breakfast in a minute."

I slide open the patio doors. It's warm enough to sit outside, although the sun hasn't quite come over the pool yet. The villa overlooks a tranquil lake where, if you're lucky enough, you can see different species of birds swooping down to try and find fish. I call out to Gray to bring the breakfast outside. He's managed to find a tray and is carefully trying to balance poached eggs on toast with a couple of glasses of orange juice. I close the door behind Gray, and we tuck into our breakfast.

"Sorry, the eggs aren't really up to your usual standards, Genie, but I am trying," Gray says.

My heart aches with love that after what he's recently found out about me, he somehow feels he's the one who needs to make an effort. How did I get so lucky? "They taste all the nicer because you cooked them, Gray." And they really do. The love put into this breakfast really changes the whole appeal.

"Really? You're not just saying that to not hurt my feelings?"

"Really. It's all just perfect. Thank you." I lean over to plant a kiss on his cheek, but he turns his head, so gets a gentle peck on the lips instead.

"Gray!" I begin as he artfully kisses me again just as Cassie comes outside to join us.

"O-M-G, you two, get a room," she shouts, shielding her eyes, pretending to be embarrassed.

"You should be happy that your parents still fancy each other," says Gray.

"Ok, Dad, just stop. I really don't want to hear any more."

As if on a Cassie rescue attempt, Will joins us, rubbing his eyes whilst looking at our empty plates. "Have you had breakfast already without me?" he says indignantly.

I nod. "Your dad treated me."

"Nice. Is there any more, Dad?" Will looks at Gray expectantly.

"Sit yourself down, Son, and I'll cook you the same. How about you, Cassie?"

"Don't bother. I'll help myself to some yoghurt. I want to look good in my bikini," Cassie replies curtly.

"You're on holiday, for God's sake, Cassie. Have some-thing a bit more substantial," Gray says encouragingly. "Plus, who you trying to impress? Me? Your mum? Will? Because I don't see anyone else here."

"Oh, go on, then," she relents. Finally, there's a smile from her.

Gray causes yet more havoc in the kitchen as he cooks for the children whilst I discreetly try to tidy up after him. We then all sit outside under the lanai, happily watching as the sun finally comes over the pool. It's not long before Will is splashing around in the pool again. Cassie sits on a sun lounger, shades on, busily messaging Mel whilst Gray and I sunbathe. I sent Maura a message last night just so she knows we've arrived safely. She messaged to confirm she's able to join us and just needs to sort out a cattery and flights. I also left a voicemail for my parents to let them know we decided to go away. It was more for my dad's benefit, as I know he'll now pop over to water the garden and take in the post. Mother probably won't approve of us going away at such short notice, but she no longer controls my life.

It must be about 10:30 a.m. when Will suddenly gets out of the pool, excitedly shouting that with the time dif-ference, the World Cup final will be starting shortly. Gray jumps up with almost as much vigour as Will. After five minutes of trying to work out how to use the outside screen, we have success and rather special first-class seats for the football. Neither me nor Cassie are particularly bothered about who will win, but both Gray and Will are completely gripped by the on-screen action.

I half-heartedly pick up a novel that I've been "reading" for months but failing to make any headway with. No fault of the book itself, I've just been too on edge since Ed and his music re-entered my life and turned it upside down. I don't blame him for exploiting our teenage relationship to further his music career. By the sound of things, he's drifted for pretty much most of his life up until recently, and he probably just needs the money. When I had to give Milly away, I shelved any feelings I had for Ed, as it was just easier that way.

As I was quite weak after having Milly, my mother used that as an excuse to keep me at home. I wasn't allowed anywhere by myself. To be honest, it was worse than when she didn't allow me out after Ginny's party. At least then I could see my friends at school. Stuck in Bournemouth, I was like a prisoner, as I didn't know anyone there but for my mother and my auntie Maureen. Dad was still working in London, and as they'd sold the family home in Barnes, he was renting a bedsit close to where he worked, coming down to see us in Bournemouth every other weekend. I would have loved to have spent more time with Emma, but friendships weren't allowed.

Nothing I ever did was good enough for Mother. I'd flunked my O levels after all the upheaval, but I amazingly managed to just pass both my English exams. So, there

I was, sixteen, penniless, alone and locked up with two malicious middle-aged women.

"Mum, France won," Will shouts, interrupting my teenage memories.

I nod and smile, deep down not the least bit interested. Will jumps into the pool once again whilst Cassie continues to sunbathe.

Gray grabs a beer from the fridge and goes to the spa. I follow and join him, undoing my sarong.

"This is just what we needed, isn't it?" says Gray, moving closer to me in the water.

"Yes, it's perfect. Thank you. Although I think Cassie is very quiet, don't you?" I ask, wanting reassurance that Gray too has realised things with Cassie aren't quite right.

"Oh, she's probably just a bit jetlagged. You know it takes a while to acclimatize and what with the time difference and the fact she probably didn't get much sleep at Mel's the other night. She must be just feeling a bit off."

"Yeah, maybe. But call it Mother's intuition—I don't think she's her normal self. And we're just about to drop a bombshell on them," I continue, refusing to be placated by Gray.

"Is tonight the night?" Gray whispers.

I nod. "I'm so scared about what they're going to say though."

"It'll be ok. They're good kids. I'm sure they'll understand," Gray says, always the optimist.

"I really hope so."

"We've brought them up well. I'm sure there'll be a lot of questions but we'll get through it."

"You think?" I say, desperately wanting to believe him.

"Positive," he replies, leaning over to kiss me. "You taste of sun cream." He laughs.

"And you taste of beer." I laugh back at him.

"What do you expect? I'm on my holidays."

When Gray's away from the stresses of work, he's just like a big kid. I can see so much of Gray in Will. They're both so refreshingly uncomplicated and full of fun, whereas I fear that Cassie has inherited all my worries and anxieties. Time will tell how they will both cope with my latest bombshell.

Chapter Forty-five

Ed

July 2018

I awake with a start, momentarily reaching out to find Virginia. But of course, she's not here. She's cross with me for bundling her out of the restaurant somewhat unceremoniously when those girls took a sneaky photo of us together. I probably overreacted—I normally do. Virginia pulled me up on the fact I've played the press to my advantage with my recent success. Everything she said to me was spot on. And she's right again that I haven't given a thought to Evie and her family, of how all the unwanted publicity has been affecting them. It's all a complete nightmare, but the one thing I do know is that I miss Virginia and I need to put things right. I've wasted years just drifting, never committing to any one person or place.

I shower, make myself some coffee and have some cereal on my balcony, just watching the world go by. One of the Australian girls I often say hello to in the lobby area is busy doing some exercises in the communal garden. She's my usual type: young, pretty, athletic and blonde. Normally, I would have chatted her up by now and managed to get her into bed, but I'm just not interested. What on earth would I have in common with someone her age? Perhaps I'm finally growing up. Laughable, considering I'm almost fifty.

I finish my breakfast, lock up and take the lift down to the garage, bumping into Sid, who's carefully checking for anything untoward.

"Morning, Ed."

"Morning, Sid. Everything ok with you today?"

"Not too bad, thanks. I still can't believe how some people live, leaving their litter in the car park like this," he says, shaking his head whilst picking up several abandoned crisp packets with his litter grabber.

"You'd think if you could afford to live somewhere like this, you would know how to behave," I agree.

"It's beggars' belief, it really is, but enough of my woes. How are things with you?" Sid asks.

"Not too bad, Sid, but I've got some making up to do with my girlfriend," I confide.

Sid stops litter picking and uses his litter picker in the same way people who talk with their hands do as he starts turning the conversation to a fuller one. "Got to treat your woman like a queen. It's worked for me, as me and my Janice have been together for nearly forty years. I'm going to take her on a cruise to celebrate. She's always fancied going on one."

Time for me to leave before I'm here all day. "Thanks for the tip, Sid. This one's a keeper," I say with a smile, getting into my car.

I have to park at the top of Virginia's road, as everywhere else is busy. I walk towards Virginia's house as a man walks down Virginia's path, whistling away to himself.

He's blonde, well-built, with a selection of tattoos on his muscly arms. I crouch on the pavement, pretending to do up my shoelaces as he walks past me. His phone rings and he answers it, talking quite animatedly. I only catch a few words. But they are enough to stop me in my tracks.

"Yeah, mate. I crashed at Virginia's cos Amy kicked me out. Yeah, Virginia's alright. She'll always give me a bed for the night, if you know what I mean... and have I got some gossip for you," says the man, with a dirty laugh.

I stand and watch the man walk to the top of the road with a swagger. Clearly, she didn't waste much time, as he obviously stayed the night.

I walk back to my car and sit in it for a while. Am I making a mistake with Virginia? I thought she was so genuine, but I really don't like the look of that bloke. I sigh. I came here to see Virginia and apologise for being a dickhead, and that's exactly what I'm going to do. Irrelevant of what she did or didn't do last night, I still made her feel like crap yesterday. I lock the car again and walk back to Virginia's house. I'll see if she mentions her mystery man. That's if she'll even talk to me. I walk up the path and ring the doorbell.

I think I can just about see Virginia walking up the hallway as I peer through the frosted glass in the door. In my head, I've got so much that I want to say to her, but my mouth has gone dry. I just want to apologise, to put things right.

She opens the door with a look of surprise on her face. I'm obviously the last person she expected to see this morning. "Oh, hi, Ed. I didn't expect to see you again," she says flatly.

"Hi. I just wanted to see you and to apologise," I start.

"Do you want to come in?" I'm not sure if she really wants me to come in or if she's concerned about the neighbours seeing us talking.

"If that's ok?" I question. She nods and leads me down the hallway, into the kitchen. "Fancy a coffee?"

"Yeah, go on. Thanks," I say, thinking how awkward this all now seems. It doesn't often happen but I literally don't know what to say.

"So, the whole reason you're here, the apology..." She rests her elbow on the table, chin in palm, and waits.

"I'm sorry, I really am. I don't even know why I stormed off last night. I should never have left you like that." I touch her hand. I want her to believe that I really am sorry. I want her to give me another chance. And I'm just really hoping she didn't sleep with that guy.

Virginia walks away from the table and over to the kettle, seemingly satisfied. "I really wish you didn't leave last night. I could have done with you being here."

"Really? Why's that?" I probe, cocking my head. Is she going to admit to that bloke being here last night?

"Well, after you left, I had an unexpected visitor. Callum—Shannon's dad." Far from how he made out the night went, she seems more irritated than happy. Definitely doesn't look like someone who just had a night to remember in any good way.

"What did he want?" I ask, getting closer to what I want to know.

"A bed for the night. He had a row with his girlfriend and she locked him out. He used to do this all the time. I only let him in because I knew the girls would be cross if I turned him away." Kettle boiled, she pours the hot water into both mugs and stirs.

"Where did he stay?" I try to ask it casually but it unfortunately sounds more like an accusation. I've only just apologised and have a feeling I'll be doing so again if I keep questioning.

"Really, Ed? Where do you think he stayed?" She raises one eyebrow sternly as she places my coffee in front of me.

I shrug. Hopefully not where Callum was suggesting to his "mate".

"He stayed on the bloody sofa. I'm not in the habit of sleeping around and definitely not with Callum," she shouts. She takes a deep breath to calm herself. "We were over long ago but, as I told you, he was always good at supporting both the girls before he had another daughter with Amy. Lauren. She's only five."

And now I feel utterly terrible and guilty all over again. "I'm sorry, Virginia. I keep putting my foot in it. I'm just not very good at this relationship stuff," I say sheepishly.

"Are we in a relationship, Ed? I thought we were just kind of casually seeing each other," Virginia says with just a hint of a smirk.

"I'd like to think we could be. Can we start again?" I wince, as if waiting for rejection.

"I'd like to be, but I won't be controlled by anyone, and you've got to face up to the consequences of your actions. Perhaps you should try to reach out to Evie, either privately or publicly, to apologise for all the hurt you've caused her." Her words are stern and sharp. Maybe this is why I've fallen for her. Years of bad influences around me, selfishness and easy women. And now I have this woman in front of me. A moralistic, fiery woman. A good person to put me on the right path.

"I know I've fucked up, and I'm sorry. At least let me show you I'm sorry properly?" I pout dramatically.

"Don't think you can get round me that easily, Ed." Virginia laughs, kissing me passionately.

"Can I presume that the World Cup final barbecue is back on?" I ask cheekily.

"How could I say no to you? Sasha and Shannon will be back soon with Josh and Micky, and I've bought loads of food. You can help me set up as your punishment for being such a drama queen."

"Your wish is my command, mistress," I joke, bowing to Virginia.

We spend the next hour or so prepping the food for the barbecue. Virginia shows me how to marinade the chicken, and we chop a selection of vegetables for the kebabs.

"Shall I go to the offie and get some more beers in, or have you got enough?" I ask.

"Actually, we could do with some more prosecco, if you don't mind?" she says with a grin.

"I'm beginning to think this house runs on prosecco," I banter.

I give Virginia a kiss goodbye and walk to my car, whistling all the way, thrilled to be given another chance. I'm not going to blow it this time.

I drive to my usual offie and buy twelve bottles of prosecco, thinking that at least Virginia will have some spare bottles for a future occasion this way. I'll be back here tomorrow otherwise with how much that household blimmin' drinks it.

By the time I get back, both Sasha and Shannon have returned home with Josh and Micky in tow. The lads set up the bar in the shady part of the garden whilst I help Virginia with the barbecue.

"We should have invited Mark and Jez over. I would have loved to have seen them both again," Virginia says as she searches in her garden shed for some extra coals for the barbeque.

"I think they're both going to the pub to watch the match. Mark uses the football as his escape from the new baby," I say. "An excuse for some 'him' time."

"Wow. I didn't realise he had another child. What did they have?" She bends down, moving items out of the way, finding a bag of coal right at the back of the shed.

"Another girl. He was desperate for a boy but is now on girl number four." I take the bag of coal from her and carry it over to the barbecue, Virginia remaining at my side.

"Good luck to him for the early teenage years is all I can say." Virginia laughs like only a mother of girls who has come out the other side can.

"I think he's already finding that quite a challenge, as his twin girls Tia and Teagan from his first marriage are now sixteen, his third daughter Marnie from his second marriage is eleven, and coupled with new baby Luna, it surely all has to be a logistical nightmare." Thinking of Mark and his tribe of kids is the only thing that ever makes me feel better that I never got the opportunity to be a parent. I'd take no kids over what he has to go through.

"Thankfully, both his ex-wives and his current one get on famously. I don't know how he manages it all," I muse.

"Mark's such a great guy though. He's just so chilled—although I can't imagine living with someone like that would be easy," she admits. "He's lucky they all get on. My two exes can't stand each other. Callum despises Jon for abandoning me and Sasha but then he went and abandoned all three of us when Lauren was born."

"I can only assume both your ex-husbands need their heads examined, leaving someone as amazing as you," I say to Virginia, pulling her close.

"I'm not that easy to live with, you know. I'm a right cow until I've had at least two coffees in the morning. Just ask the girls." She snorts.

"You're just too nice. You never say anything bitchy about anyone, do you?" I kiss the top of her head as she leans into my chest.

"Oh, I have my moments. I tore you off a strip yesterday, didn't I?" she reminds me.

"Yes, well, the less said about that, the better. I deserved it. It's just that I've been really enjoying spending time with you recently."

"Me too, but right now, you can get the television on and sort out the drinks whilst I start cooking," she says, moving away from me to take control of all the preparations for the barbeque.

I busy myself with my assigned jobs and fix drinks for everyone whilst Sasha and Shannon help their mum make the salad and butter the rolls for the burgers and sausages. I'll have to be careful not to overindulge on the food and drink, as Toby wants us to be fit and healthy for the tour. I've cut out the drugs already and stopped smoking about six months ago. I just need to restrict my drinking to the weekends and special occasions, like I've agreed with Virginia. How hard could it be?

We spend a great afternoon laughing, eating, drinking and watching France and VAR shatter Croatia's dreams of winning the World Cup. Shannon, Sasha, Josh and Micky are great company, and my plan to not overindulge hopelessly crashes. By the end of the afternoon, we are all quite drunk.

"So, Ed, how come that song you wrote ages ago about that Evie has made you so rich and successful?" Shannon asks, feeling somewhat bold by consuming far too much prosecco.

"Shannon, that's enough," Virginia warns.

"I'm just asking the question everyone wants to know the answer to," she slurs.

"It's fine, Virginia." I put my hand on her knee to show her I'm ok. "I was in a band when I was younger than you and was going out with Evie, who incidentally was your mum's best friend at the time." I squeeze her knee gently, hoping to reassure her, wondering if her mind has jumped to that time we betrayed Evie, just as mine has. "Evie inspired quite a few songs back then. I re-recorded 'Used to Be' about two years ago when my old band reformed as The Mountaineers. It ended up being used for the theme tune on that drama series about that cult and then people started downloading it," I explain.

"Yes, but how did it get featured on *The Girl in the Song*?" Shannon leans closer, probing further.

"I did an interview about the story behind the song a while back, and the maker of the documentary thought it would be an interesting addition to the documentary."

"Everything leads back to Evie. Was it all so you could get back with her?" Shannon continues. Despite the fact she's being direct and really digging, for some reason, I find it quite refreshing.

"Yes, maybe at the beginning," I admit, internally wincing. It's definitely not the sort of revelation I wanted in front of Virginia but I also don't want to lie. "But things have changed recently, what with reconnecting with your mum—"

"Ok, ok, but how come you're now seeing Mum?" Shannon asks. "Sounds to me like she was your second—"

"That really is enough, Shannon." Virginia's glare alone would have stopped anyone's words from continuing.

"Sorry, Mum, just looking out for you." Shannon leans back in her chair and puffs her cheeks as she lets out a 'that told me' breath.

"I know, but it's really not the time to be interrogating Ed. Now, go and see if the boys want any more food. There's loads left," Virginia says, putting an end to Shannon's incessant questions.

"No offence meant, Ed. You're alright for an old rocker," Shannon says with a grin before jogging off to find Micky.

"Sorry, Ed. She's had far too much to drink and has no filter, just like her dad." Despite the apology, she's looking anywhere but at me. I can't blame her. It's not exactly what someone building a relationship with someone else wants to hear. And it's definitely not her who should be apologising.

"It's fine, honestly. It's refreshing for someone to be so transparent, and she's only looking out for you," I try to reassure her. "And for the record, just in case you are in any doubt, I want you to know that you're the one I want to spend time with, Virginia," I say, pushing a stray strand of hair behind her ear. "And I'm really sorry about what I said. It's true, Evie was my original goal, but me and my wants then are so different to now. I was living in a fantasy land. You've brought me back to reality and showed me what it actually is I need." I kiss her gently on the lips.

"Thanks, Ed. I really needed to hear that," she replies, reciprocating my kiss. "I'm not silly, I know you've held some sort of torch for her, and obviously you've shown that the torch has near enough flickered out, but it's not nice to think about."

We sit on the wicker sofa at the back of the garden, breathing in the heady aroma of the assorted herbs growing in varying-sized pots. I place my hand on her leg with what I hope she knows is a reassuring touch rather than a drunken randy grope. She doesn't seem to mind and leans her head on my shoulder. We sit there in blissful silence, just enjoying the peace and quiet. The silence doesn't last long, as Shannon comes rushing towards us, shouting words so fast that they come out as complete gibberish.

"Woah, woah. Slow down," Virginia says to Shannon.

"Quick, Mum. It's Dad. There's been a fight outside the pub. He's been beaten up," Shannon shrieks, arms flailing.

"What do you mean?" Virginia asks, mouth agape, sobering up immediately.

"Amy's brothers' mates have beaten him up for supposedly chatting up some barmaid," she wails.

"Where is he?" Virginia shouts, standing up, trying to calm Shannon down.

"Outside the pub. Can he come over?" Shannon asks, allowing her mum to grip her arms to hold her steady. "Jimmy called and said Dad's in a bad way."

"Ok. Get Jimmy to bring him over, and we'll have to patch him up."

Virginia turns to me as Shannon runs into the house. "I'm sorry, Ed. I haven't had any trouble from Callum for ages and then twice in one weekend."

"It's ok. He's Shannon's dad and she's worried about him. I understand. Do you want me to stay?" I ask, putting a protective arm around Virginia.

"Yes, if you don't mind. If you're here, I might be able to get rid of him easier. I've had years of clearing up Callum's messes on my own," she says, looking exhausted by everything.

Within minutes, Callum is being helped up the garden path by his mate Jimmy, his face bruised and bloodied.

Chapter Forty-six

Gray

July 2018

I call a taxi, taking Will with me to pick up a hire car. Will is keen for me to hire a Mustang. To be honest, the thought quite appeals to me, but it wouldn't really work now that both kids are adult-sized in height. I can just imagine the complaints from both Cassie and Genie about their hair if I had the roof down. So, that's a definite no.

We pick a hire car from one of the nearby hotels that has a car hire place attached. We're pleasantly surprised by the choice of cars available. After steering Will away from the Mustangs, we finally settle on a black Chevrolet Impala, which has plenty of room for everyone and for our suitcases on our return to the airport in a couple of weeks.

Will and I drive up and down the 192 so I can get used to the car, and I'm fairly easily persuaded to do a pitstop at Dunkin' Donuts for some cold drinks, coffee and doughnuts. We arrive back home to find the girls have hardly moved, lying side by side, sunbathing.

"We're back. And we've got doughnuts," Will shouts.

That's enough to get Cassie moving, and she happily helps herself to her favourite jam-filled doughnut, washed down by a raspberry smoothie. Genie and I gratefully drink our first proper American coffee of the holiday and share a glazed doughnut whilst Will proceeds to eat three in a row. I don't know where that boy puts his food because he's as slim as a rake. For the remainder of the afternoon, we all just laze in and around the pool, enjoying relaxing and generally doing nothing. Genie's reading, Cassie's completely engrossed in her phone and Will bounces from pool to spa before eating yet another doughnut.

"What does everyone fancy for dinner tonight?" I ask.

"Can we go to that new steakhouse near the big Walmart that Uncle Jonesy recommended? It sounds amazing," Will replies.

"Yeah, I don't see why not. I'll call ahead and book a table."

Genie and Cassie go off to get ready for dinner, and after Will and I have a last swim, I make the call to the restaurant before we both hit the showers.

As I come out of the shower and wrap my towel around my waist, Genie's putting the final touches to her makeup at the dressing table.

"You look amazing," I say, kissing the back of her neck. "Are you starting to relax?"

"A little, I guess, but I don't want to wait too much longer to speak to the children. Perhaps after dinner when we get back to the villa?" There's a slight shake to Genie's hand as she tries to apply her mascara.

"It sounds as good a time as any," I say, giving her free hand a squeeze.

It doesn't take me or Will long to get ready, although we still have to wait for Cassie to dry her hair.

"Come on, Cassie. I'm starving. No one's going to be looking at you anyway," Will says, deliberately antagonising his older sister, his shoes already on to leave.

A screech of annoyance sounds from Cassie's room. "Shut up, Will. No one's going to be looking at you, you mean. I bet you haven't even done your hair."

"I just rely on my naturally good looks..."

"Enough, you two," I interject before the pair launch into a full-on argument. "Let's get in the car before we lose our table at the restaurant."

The car's great, with plenty of room for all of us, and the children even manage to be civil to each other on the short ride to the restaurant. We announce ourselves to the cheery girl on the front desk, who gives us a buzzer. We go outside to join the rest of the fellow would-be diners. Within five minutes, our buzzer is vibrating. Less than a minute after that, we're sitting in a comfy airconditioned booth, perusing a menu of incredible steaks and burgers.

Will goes for a T-bone steak and chips, I have a New York strip and Genie and Cassie both go for fillet. All the steaks come with salad and either a baked potato or chips. By the end of the meal, we can hardly move, except for Will, who's already eyeing up the dessert menu. Will orders some traditional Key lime pie, but Genie and I just have a coffee. We're going to need our wits about us later. I settle the cheque—as the Americans like to call it—and we make our way back to the villa, stopping briefly at the pharmacy to stock up on some additional sunscreen and a few other bits and pieces that we need. The plan is to go to the big supermarket over the next few days.

Once back at the villa, we all rush to get changed and just let our food go down, except for Will, who's in the games room, shooting some basketball hoops. That boy has such an appetite, but I guess he does burn it off, as he can never stand still. As Genie and I get changed, we discreetly discuss how to broach the subject of Milly. Genie looks almost pale, even with her sun-kissed skin.

"I don't think I can do it," she croaks. "I feel sick."

"You'll be ok. I promise."

She leans forward and grips the dressing table, looking at me through the mirror. "You'll back me up, won't you?"

"I've always had your back, and I always will, whatever happens," I say, planting a kiss on the top of her head, desperately trying to reassure her that everything will be ok, hoping for this to be true.

Chapter Forty-seven

Genie

July 2018

I take my time by changing into a pair of joggers and a T-shirt, hanging up my dress, brushing my hair again and checking my makeup, doing absolutely everything I can to keep my secret from the children for that little bit longer. Even though I feel like a trembling wreck inside, at least I look ok outwardly.

Gray calls the children through to the living room area, telling them we need to talk to them about something really important. My stomach is in knots, my delicious steak meal threatening to come right back up again. This is really it.

I join Gray in the sitting area, walking in a much more confident manner than I really feel. I take a seat next to Gray, taking hold of his hand for absolute reassurance that we are in this together.

Gray calls the children again, and Cassie eventually emerges from her bedroom, Will finally walking away from the basketball hoops to plonk himself next to his sister.

"You both look like someone's died," Will observes.

"Oh my God. Did something happen to Granny or Grandad?" asks Cassie, her face full of concern.

Gray shakes his head. "They are absolutely fine, but we do have something very important to tell you."

"You're not getting a divorce, are you?" shrieks Cassie.

"No, of course not. Your mum and I are just fine."

"You're very quiet, Mum. What's up?" Will asks, much calmer than his sister. They both look at me expectantly. "Is it to do with that Ed bloke?"

"Mhmm," I manage, a solitary tear rolling down my cheek. I don't trust myself to speak properly right now without breaking down. My throat has closed up, and although I know the words are there, I physically cannot speak.

"I'd like him to do one, you know?" Will grabs his seat, knuckles turning white as he clutches the fabric. "All the hassle he's caused you."

I reach over to squeeze his hand, making him loosen his grip. I take a big breath. "The thing is..." I start before trailing off. I stop, noticing Cassie's body language. Her body is stiff, her arms folded across her chest, her face devoid of emotion. Gray gives me a reassuring nudge, as if to encourage me to continue.

"I know I've been so distracted since that documentary aired, and I'm sorry that I haven't been there for you both, but I've been struggling with things that happened to me when I was about Cassie's age. But before I fully explain everything, I want you to know that I absolutely adore and love both of you so, so much and would do anything for you. I only wish my parents had given me the same consideration."

Cassie's body language softens. She moves to sit next to me and strokes my hand softly, willing me on to continue.

"I was only fifteen when I first started going out with Ed. At first, everything was great. It was new and exciting. Stupidly, we both, and all our friends, started regularly drinking, and I'm ashamed to admit that we were dabbling in drugs too," I confess.

Both Will and Cassie's faces are in total shock. You really don't want to hear about your mother's youthful misdemeanours at their ages, but they need to hear the truth from me rather than some sleazy tabloid or magazine.

"I know this is hard for you to hear, but I want to be totally honest with you both, and I want to be the one who tells you the whole truth."

Both silently nod.

"Ed and I started sleeping together not long after we got together, and it's not something that I'm proud of. I now know with the benefit of hindsight that we were far too young. My parents tried to split us up, and they grounded me several times, but I still managed to meet up with Ed and my friends when Mother was doing her voluntary work and when Dad was at work.

"It wasn't until early April that my mother realised things weren't quite right with me. She caught sight of me coming out of the bathroom one evening and noticed that I'd put quite a bit of weight on. She got a bee in her bonnet that I was pregnant, asking me time and time again if I was. I didn't have a clue if I was or not, but the more she shouted at me, the more things suddenly started making sense. Dad arranged for me to have an appointment with a local doctor." I pause and swallow. "They confirmed that I was almost three months pregnant."

They still both look stunned, neither in any rush to respond, but I need to continue and explain everything.

"It's hard for me to find the right words to explain everything. My mother, as you know, is very religious, and she was absolutely horrified that I was pregnant, so she took me to stay with her sister, my auntie Maureen, in Bournemouth to continue the pregnancy in private. Dad stayed in London because of work. He also had to organise the sale of our house, as my parents didn't want anyone to find out about my pregnancy. He would come and visit us every other weekend, and those were the times that I lived for. I wasn't allowed to contact Ed or any of my friends. We basically just upped and left, never to be heard of again."

"What happened to the baby, Mum?" asks Cassie, her voice almost a whisper.

"My mother's plan was for me to do my O levels, have the baby and then have it adopted. I had no choice in the matter. Mother didn't want any shame brought upon the family. I took my O levels at the local comprehensive and tried to forget about my old life in London. I started to bleed at thirty-seven weeks, so they rushed me to hospital, where they realised the baby had decided to come early. She was born safely, although a little small. Milly, or at least that's what I would have called her. Mother and Auntie Maureen had been in touch with a local Catholic adoption agency who had lots of lovely childless couples only too willing to adopt a new baby. To be honest, I was so out of it I hardly even remember seeing her properly. And then she was gone."

"We've got a sister and you never even told us?" says Cassie, removing her hand from mine, rage starting to overtake her. I nod, concerned by her reaction.

"I'm sorry. I really am, Cassie. I don't know what else I can say. There are no words that can change this situation or make things any better."

"Where is she now?" Will asks gently.

I shrug sadly. "I don't know. Hopefully, she's had a good life with her adoptive family."

"How long have you known, Dad?" Cassie hisses at Gray. I've never seen her this angry, or hostile, ever..

"A couple of days," Gray replies calmly, understanding of her reaction, ignoring the way in which she's talking to him. "It's taken Mum a long time to come to terms with everything that happened to her."

"Didn't you ever try to find each other like they do on the telly?" Will asks thoughtfully. I feel relieved that at least one of my children is showing understanding and accep-tance. I don't know if I could handle double the negativity.

"I couldn't do that without telling your dad first. And... the longer time went on, the more I panicked that he'd leave if he found out."

"I completely support your Mum, and this doesn't change how I feel about her. I'm only sorry that she didn't feel she could tell me earlier so that we might have perhaps been able to track down Milly," says Gray loyally, once again showing me that I was wrong to hold secrets from him. Every time he shows he's here, I feel so lucky to have him. And then I have to swallow down a lump of guilt.

"I still can't believe you kept Milly a secret for all those years. How could you keep lying to us all for so long? It's like we don't even know you anymore. How can we ever believe a single word that comes out of your mouth?" Cassie shouts, pointing accusingly at me.

I feel physically sick. I want to make things right but whatever I say to Cassie now is just not good enough. The damage has been done. "I'm sorry," I whisper. I just want to hold Cassie, with all her hurt, and tell her everything will be ok, but she's looking at me like I'm a stranger. "I just shelved the idea that I'd even had a baby, but there was always a void in my life until you came along, Cassie," I continue, hoping she can see how much she means to me, that she *can* still trust me and the last thing I ever wanted to do was hurt her. "I couldn't get pregnant for years and then you came along, and we were so happy, and everything was just perfect and not long after we had Will. I've been so fearful since Ed has reappeared that he would find out somehow. I just want to forget that part of my life and concentrate on my family."

"But Milly is part of your family... of our family. What sort of mother doesn't want to find her firstborn child? All along, I've felt sorry for you that Ed Nash has destroyed your life when in fact it's the other way round." Cassie's spittle lands on my cheek. I'm silent. My heart literally aches for the pain that I've caused my family.

"Cassie, how dare you speak to your mum like that. Apologise immediately," Gray shouts as he stands in front of me, as if I'm some vulnerable object he needs to protect. But I don't need protecting. Cassie does. This is all my own fault. How can I be angry at her words when I caused this mess? What right do I have to fight against her or stand up for myself?

"No. She acts all high and mighty, when the truth is, she did all the things she's always told us not to do. She's a hypocrite," she screams, pointing at me. "And to think I had your side from the beginning, Mum. How silly do I look now?"

"Cassie..." Gray begins.

"It's fine, Gray. I know I'm a hypocrite." I put my hands on his arms, gently moving him to the side. "I wanted you two to learn from my mistakes," I say, eyes darting between Cassie and Will. "I've always tried to protect you both and shield you from making wrong decisions. You both know that I have a very odd relationship with Grandma, and I have always tried to not be like her. I'd like to feel you could both come to me for help, whatever the situation. I'm sorry I've disappointed you, Cassie, but all I know is that I love you both so much, and whatever you think of me, that will never change."

"You seriously think you're any better than Grandma after lying to your children and your husband for years?" Cassie marches off to her room, slamming the door. My insides tighten. She might as well have slammed my heart in the door as she left. Cassie's known for her emotions. That's what makes her so empathetic and caring. That's what also makes her hurt harder though. I could have handled an "I hate you" because she would never have meant it. Once Cassie calms down, she always ends up swept up in guilt. I've often held her like a little child in my arms after an emotional outburst. But being compared to *her*—my mum—with the image of her I've had my whole life... that somehow hurts more.

"I'm sorry, Mum, about everything that has happened to you. I'm trying to understand everything, I really am, but wow, that's amazing to think we've got an older sister. Don't worry about Cassie. She'll come around eventually. She's been such a moody cow since we left London," says Will, giving me a hug. I wasn't the only one who noticed her mood change, then.

"Thanks, Will. And if there's anything you want to ask me about what I've told you, I'll try and be as honest and open as I can. I love you," I say, giving my six-foot son a big hug back as he lays his chin on the top of my head.

"I love you too, Mum. I'll try to talk to Cassie," he says, leaving the room.

"Genie, I'm so sorry Cassie spoke to you like that. It was unforgivable what she said to you, but goodness, how amazing is Will? So accepting and so mature. I was sure it was going to be the other way round." Gray places an ever-protective arm around me.

"It's fine. I think Cassie is struggling in general, and this revelation is not what she expected. She was such a support when all the press attention started happening. I think she's in shock. Also, to find out you have a grown-up sister is quite a lot to digest."

"You're too understanding. She should never have spoken to you like that. I'll be having words with her later," Gray says, shaking his head in disbelief.

"Please, Gray, leave her. I think she'll talk to me in her own time, perhaps one-on-one?" I bite my bottom lip, dread entering my mind. "My only fear is that she talks to my mother."

"You don't think she would, do you?" Gray replies, his brow furrowed by the harsh reality of the potential consequences of my revelation. Neither of us thought much further ahead than just telling the children.

"Well, she's always been the apple of my mother's eye. A legitimate granddaughter she can be proud of, whose parents are actually married," I mutter.

"Let's hope Felicity doesn't get involved. But if she does, hopefully, Tony can smooth things over," Gray adds.

"Dear old Dad. He's had a lifetime of smoothing things over between us," I say wearily.

The children spend most of the rest of the evening in their respective rooms whilst Gray and I share a bottle of wine under the lanai, enjoying the peace and stillness of another hot and humid night. We've just finished our first glass when Will comes out to see us.

"How's Cassie?" I immediately ask.

"Sulking. She can't even speak to Mel because of the time difference," he says with a smug smile. I've been so wrapped up in Cassie not telling Mum that Mel didn't even enter my head.

"Neither of you must speak to anyone outside of the family about what Mum has told you," Gray warns, speaking quickly and sternly. "We are trying to decide together what the next steps are."

"Don't worry about me, but you'd better speak to Cassie, as she's bound to tell Mel. They tell each other absolutely everything."

Gray sighs. "He's right, Genie. I'll go and have a chat with her. You stay here, relax and have another glass of wine." Gray holds Will's arm gently as he passes and says softly, "You'll keep Mum company, won't you, Will?"

"Yeah, sure. Can I have a beer, Dad?" Will asks, taking advantage of the understanding child versus the angry child situation.

"Go on, then. But just the one, and don't think you're going to have one every night."

Gray leaves to talk to Cassie whilst Will goes off to get his beer. I'm left alone with my thoughts, wondering if things with Cassie will ever be the same.

Chapter Forty-eight

Virginia

July 2018

"Alright, babe? I bet you didn't expect to see me again quite so soon, did ya?" Callum says with a wince, his mouth all cut and bloodied.

"Come on, Callum. Let's get you sorted," I bristle.

"Aren't you going to introduce me to your friend, Ginny?" Callum deliberately doesn't use my full name, knowing how much it irritates me.

"This is Ed. And, Ed, this is Callum, Shannon's dad."

"Alright, Ed? I would shake yer 'and but, as you can see, I've had a bit of trouble today," Callum says, showing Ed his bloodied and blistered hands.

"Hi, Callum. You look like you've taken quite a battering there," Ed says in a friendly, blokey way. I wonder if the friendliness is fake.

"Yeah, I did. But you should see the other fellas." Callum laughs, blood trailing down his chin. I'm just glad we're outside, so the blood drips onto the grass instead of any of my carpets.

"I'll get my first aid kit, but I think you probably should get yourself to hospital, Callum," I suggest, not wanting

Callum to get too settled and knowing there's only so much I can do to fix this mess.

"'Ere, Shannon. Fetch us a beer, darlin'. There's a good girl." Callum settles himself into one of my wicker chairs.

By the time I've got the first aid kit, Callum has a beer in his hand and is entertaining everyone. I use the most astringent antiseptic wipes I could find, delighted every time Callum winces. I apply arnica to his bruised cheeks and fists.

"I've patched you up as best I can, but I really do think that you should get checked out at the hospital and then you should try to make things up with Amy, don't you?" I instruct Callum.

"I'm not going anywhere near that cow," he snorts. "She won't let me in anyway, and I don't want to frighten the little one," Callum replies swiftly.

"You'll have to go to Jimmy's, then," I say firmly. "Where is he anyway?"

"He's having a chat with Micky over there," Callum replies, pointing with a potentially broken finger.

"Well, you need to call Amy and apologise, then you and Jimmy can do one and go back to his. I really shouldn't be having to deal with this, Callum. You made your choice years ago, and I've moved on."

"Alright, Ginny. Keep your hair on. I'll have words with Jimmy, and we'll be out of 'ere. Let you and your new fancy fella get back to whatever you were doing," Callum says with a leer.

"We were enjoying a quiet afternoon after the football. Not that it's any of your business," I reply as haughtily as I can, just to wind him up.

"Let me just say goodbye to my girls and I'll be out of 'ere."

Callum calls the girls over and insists on having his photo taken with them both, despite the state of him. Shannon is cross with me for kicking her dad out, but my daughters have to understand that I can't keep rescuing him.

"Anyway, it was nice to meet you, Ed," Callum says, lingering in the garden. "You've got one of them familiar faces, you 'ave. How do I know you?" he asks, knowing damn well who Ed is.

"I'm a singer in a band," Ed replies flatly, also clocking the fact Callum is playing with him.

"What one's that, then?" Callum continues.

"The Mountaineers."

"Nice one, Ed. Thanks again, Ginny, for patching me up. I'll sweet-talk Amy, don't worry," Callum says with a smirk.

"That's ok, but don't make a habit of it. We're divorced, remember?" I remind him sternly, willing him and Jimmy to hurry up and leave.

"That we are. Most stupid thing I ever did letting her go," Callum mutters to no one in particular but loud enough for everyone to hear.

Finally, Callum and Jimmy leave, most likely to get themselves into more trouble.

"Well, that was an eventful evening, wasn't it?" I say, letting out a sigh as I close the door behind them.

"You could say that," Ed agrees.

"Now you know why I divorced Callum." I grimace. "He's a complete car crash. I really do feel for Amy. Callum can't help being Callum, and it's probably all true about him chatting up the new barmaid. He just can't help himself." I lean against the wall and shake my head. "He was never cut out to be a family man, but both my girls love him and tend to forgive him no matter what he does." I need Ed to understand the complexities of my blended family.

"I can see he can be very persuasive—a charming bad boy—but he was obviously a good dad to both Shannon and Sasha when you were married," Ed says, clearly starting to understand exactly what Callum is like but still trying to show his positives.

"You've got it in one." It's so frustrating thinking back to how amazing he was to my girls when we were married. I wish he could still be that same person now. Of course I see aspects of that same guy but he's clearly one of those men who has more time for his kids when he's actually with their mum. "I can't criticise him in front of Shannon. Sasha, being a bit older, is a bit more discerning, but she appreciates how he stepped up as a dad after her dad left." Ed nods.

"Does Sasha ever see her dad? Jon, isn't it?" Ed asks, turning the conversation away from Callum.

"Very rarely. Jon and his girlfriend travel a lot with their bikes. Sasha sees Callum as more of a dad to her than Jon is," I reply before asking, "do you fancy a sobering cup of coffee back in the garden?" I'm done talking about my ex-husbands.

"Sure, why not?" Ed replies as we walk together towards the kitchen. I use my posh coffee machine and reach for my proper coffee cups that are in the glass cabinet, rinsing them underneath the cold tap before adding the coffee and some milk. I hand one to Ed, and we walk back into the garden, sitting down on the wicker sofa where we were before Callum arrived.

"You've got a couple of great girls. They're a credit to you," Ed says, moving one of his earlier beer bottles aside to place his coffee cup there. "That's my one regret: that I never had any children. The more time I spend with you and the girls, the more I realise just how important family is, however it presents itself. My family, I guess, is the band. Mark and Jez are like the brothers I never had."

"Thanks, Ed. I worry that Shannon is a bit headstrong like her dad, but hey, you can't change genetics. You're lucky that you're still so close to Mark and Jez. How are your parents doing?" I ask.

"They're still together. Amazingly. Dad and I are close. He runs a Facebook account for the band. Mum is ok but as ever disapproves of anything to do with the music industry. She blames both Paul and Dad for getting me involved. But if music is in your blood, you've just got to go with it. I don't know anything else," Ed confesses.

"As you've just witnessed, my family is completely disjointed and not very successfully blended." I laugh. "But it's my family, and I have to live with the decisions that I've made. Once you have a child with someone, it binds you together, whether you like it or not," I say, maybe trying to justify why Callum is still in my life, however annoying he might be.

"I guess you're right. I'm grateful for the lads. I've lost track of how many of Mark's kids I'm supposed to be god-father to. It makes up for me not having any children of my own, I suppose. How are your parents? Are they doing ok?" Ed asks, seemingly deciding his coffee should be cool enough to finally drink now. He only takes a small sip, checking it isn't too hot.

"They're fine, bless them. As much in love now as they ever were. That's what I was looking for with both my mar-riages, I suppose. I just want what my parents have: un-conditional love. Can you believe that even now they hold hands when they go out?" I say proudly, already halfway through my own coffee.

"That's good to hear." He smiles sadly, and I wonder if he's comparing them to his own parents. I feel slightly guilty for bigging up how in love they still are now, when Ed's parents seem to be barely hanging on to their feelings. "I guess we're lucky to have our parents around, let alone that they're still married."

"Yes, we are." Although I never doubted it with my par-ents. It's always been obvious to me how made for each other they are. "My parents adore the girls but despise both my exes for leaving me as a single mum. It's not what you expect from a 'Barnes' girl, is it, being a single mum at almost fifty?" I laugh half-heartedly.

"Well, I still think both your exes need their heads exam-ined for leaving you. Callum more so after what happened to him today," he says with a grin, somewhat amused by his own joke.

"Maybe the fight's knocked some sense into him, but somehow, I doubt it." Callum has a knack for finding himself in some sort of trouble, wherever he goes.

Chapter Forty-nine

Cassie

July 2018

I wake up early. It's a mixture of jetlag and coming to terms with the bombshell Mum dropped. No wonder she's been super crazy since the press found out who she is. How could Mum and Dad have been married for so long without her ever saying, "Oh, by the way, when I was sixteen, I had a baby daughter, but I had to give her away"? I can't believe he's been so calm and accepting about it all, but Mum has always been Dad's Achilles' heel. She's always been able to talk him round whenever Will and I have misbehaved or broke anything, but this revelation is massive. Will and I have an older sister. I mean, Milly—or whatever she's called—is old enough to be our mum.

I was thinking all night since I stormed off about what our sister might look like. I look so much like Mum, especially when she was my age. Will looks more like Dad but he has the same eyes as Mum. They're almost turquoise in colour, whereas mine are like Dad's: a kind of pale blue. Ed also has blue eyes, if I remember rightly, and dark hair. I wonder if Milly looks like either of us, or maybe she looks more like Ed and his side of the family, whoever they are. I now feel guilty for taking Mum's side all the time. Surely, Ed has the right to know he has a daughter? Poor bloke. I don't think he ever got over Mum leaving him. God knows what he'll make of this if he ever finds out.

Once out of bed, I put on my new silver bikini, which fits my curves perfectly, bought on my last shopping trip with Mel. I decide to put on my matching silver cover-up over the top, as there's no one to impress here in the villa. With my hair tied back, I'm ready for another day of sunbathing. What I said to Mum is unforgiveable, but she's always telling us both to be honest, not to smoke, keep drinking to a minimum and tries to guide us from being tempted by having sex too soon or dabbling in drugs. It's like her mantra, and now we know why. How could she be so hypocritical when she herself has done all those things? And to top it off, she had a baby and gave her away.

I open my bedroom door to see if anyone else is up, and I'm pleased that, amazingly, it's just me. Will can sleep through anything... well, until his hunger overtakes him. I put on a pot of coffee for Dad and wait for the stovetop kettle to boil to make myself a cup of green tea. I scroll through my phone, reading the news headlines from back home. I'm greeted with a blurry photo of us all when we first arrived at Heathrow Airport. There's another headline that catches my eye: "Mystery blonde photographed with Ed "Nasher" Nash in West London Italian restaurant."

I click on the article just as the kettle starts to whistle. I nearly burn my hand in my hurry to remove it from the stove. Why can't Americans just have normal electric kettles for God's sake? I pour myself a cup of green tea and take it outside to the table under the lanai, remembering to disable the alarm. As I wait for my tea to cool, I watch the sunrise and read the latest about Ed and his new conquest.

There isn't any information about the woman in question. She's about Mum's age and has honey blonde hair. Ed looks his normal casual self, complete with obligatory rockstar sunglasses. At least he's dating someone nearer to his age. I've always been so critical about Ed Nash because of his revelations about Mum, but now I find myself really feeling sorry for him to have fathered a child and to have no clue. According to his Wiki page, he doesn't have any children. It's all a bloody mess. Things will never be the same now that we know we have a half-sister out there somewhere. I still can't believe Dad and Will have accepted everything so easily.

Dad is next to get up, and he joins me under the lanai, with a cup of freshly brewed coffee.

"Thanks for putting the coffee on. You know your old dad too well. I need at least two coffees to get the old brain cells going, even on holiday," says Dad, laughing, desperately trying to break the ice.

"You're welcome," I reply stiffly.

"How are you feeling after last night?" Dad enquires, reaching out to try and hold my hand, which I snatch away. Part of me feels bad, as I know Dad isn't in the wrong at all, but I just feel all flighty and like I don't want to be touched.

"Disappointed," I say, using the same expression Mum and Dad use when either Will or I fuck up. I look over at Dad to see his reaction, but his face is impassive. He's still protecting Mum despite everything.

"I know it's a lot to take in—it was for me too—but it does explain why your mum has been so stressed. We're a family, and we need to stick together and support each other," Dad attempts to explain, scratching at the stubble beginning to come through on his chin after a few days of not shaving. He looks exhausted.

"But part of our family is missing, and Ed has been denied ever knowing his only child."

"Since when have you been team Ed?" Dad asks, a sarcastic note in his voice.

"Well, I think Mum has gone about the situation all wrong. Surely, he has the right to know he has a daughter? He hasn't got any other kids. And Milly has the right to know who her real parents are." I'm beginning to regret making Dad a pot of coffee, getting increasingly irritated by his lack of understanding.

"Milly probably had a great life, with loving parents. She might even have some siblings too," Dad says, trying as always to justify mum's actions.

"Probably isn't good enough. What if she's had an awful life? She might even have some children of her own, Oh my God, I could be an auntie," I say, dramatically flicking my hair back.

"Ok, ok, Cassie. Let's not get too carried away. It's up to Mum as to what she wants to do, and I want you to apologise for the way you spoke to her last night," Dad says sternly, taking a big sip of his coffee.

"I don't see why I should have to apologise to her. She should be the one apologising to us for lying for years. Don't you think your marriage has been one complete lie?"

I ask, entering dangerous territory. If there's one thing I know about Dad, he has Mum's back irrelevant of whether he believes she's right or wrong deep down.

"Your mum had her reasons for not telling us the truth," Dad says calmer than I anticipated. "I think she's been in denial since she had to give her baby away. I couldn't have asked for a better wife or mother for you two. Show your mum some respect and some compassion, please, Cassie. I'm actually quite taken aback by your reaction, to be honest." I immediately feel just a little bit guilty about the way I spoke to Mum, not that I'll admit it.

"It's just a lot to take in, Dad. Our lives have been so disrupted since that bloody song was released. I think I've messed up my exams as well," I blurt out.

"It's ok. We know it's been tricky with all the press attention, and I'm sorry you've been so stressed about your exams, but it's not the end of the world if you haven't got the grades you hoped for. You can always do some retakes in November or the following year." His words feel gentle and rehearsed, as if he already knew all this. "Don't get stressed until you know what you're dealing with."

"I just don't want to disappoint you both, as I know you've spent a lot of money on my education, but I've just felt so distracted with everything that's been going on. Will and I have had to listen to people at school saying some awful things about Mum." I look at the beautiful view over the lake to avoid eye contact with Dad.

"I'm sorry, I didn't realise," Dad says, shaking his head. "But please don't worry about the money we've spent. My parents left me their house, which, although it wasn't a huge house, when I sold it, I decided to put the money into an account that was just for your education. I wanted you two to have the opportunities I didn't."

"You've done alright for yourself, Dad. You're a partner in your advertising firm."

"I've done ok, but I might have done better if I hadn't gone to the local comp. It was pretty rough at my school. If you were remotely academic, you got picked on, so I played it down," Dad explained. "How about I cook us all some breakfast? Or do you fancy going out for breakfast?"

"Let's have breakfast here, and maybe we could go out for some lunch?" I suggest, happy that dad and I are almost back to normal.

"Sounds like a plan," Dad agrees.

Dad whistles away as he prepares breakfast. I can always depend on Dad to calm me down when I really need it. I've felt like Mum's parent recently, always protecting her from what Ed or the press are saying, so much so that both Mum and I have forgotten that I also need to be protected and nurtured.

Dad soon joins me again outside with two perfectly cooked breakfasts. It's incredible how we can even be thinking about food after all we ate yesterday at the steak restaurant. I always want to eat when I'm stressed.

"How about a milky coffee just the way you like it? Give that awful green tea a miss," says Dad, trying to win me round.

"Fine. You're a bad influence, Dad." I laugh.

Dad eventually emerges with two steaming cups of coffee, longer than I know it would have taken to make them.

"I just checked in on your mum," Dad confesses.

"Ok," I reply curtly, my mood immediately dropping.

"She's still quite upset about yesterday, as you can imagine." Dad pauses, seemingly searching my face for a reaction to her upset. I keep my face blank. "She's been dreading telling you all about what happened to her, but she understands that it will take time for you to accept what she told you," he continues. "She'd like to come and join us. Do you think you'd be ok with that?"

"Sure," I say flatly.

"Thanks, Cassie," he says with a smile.

Mum comes outside with Dad, looking uncomfortable, as she tightly grips Dad's hand for support.

"Hi, darling. I hope you slept ok. I'm so sorry about everything. I really am." She looks at me intently as she sits opposite me, the table between us.

"I'm just getting my head round everything, Mum. It's all been quite hard to take in," I say, wanting her to understand that I'm not coping with everything... that I need my mum.

"I know. I know. The only reason I'm hard on you two is because I messed up my life at your age, and I just want you both to achieve as much as I know you are capable of. But above all, I want you to be happy," Mum tries to explain, running a hand through her messy hair. She looks as though she's been tossing and turning all night.

"I'm just upset that you didn't tell us sooner about Milly, and I don't like the fact you haven't tried to trace her."

Mum leans forward and sighs. "I think about her every day. Mother said she was better off without me, so that's what I started to believe. The longer I didn't say anything, the harder it became to say anything at all. Even Auntie Maura has no idea. She's due to come out to see us next week, so I'm going to tell her then," she says, her eyes clouding over as she struggles hard not to cry. Part of me wants to reach for her hand and tell her I forgive her, but I'm not sure I'm ready quite yet. That doesn't mean seeing my mum this upset doesn't squeeze at my heart.

"Cassie, do you want to see if Will is ever going to join us?" Dad asks, breaking the tension in the air.

"Sure," I agree, only too happy to get away from any more awkward discussions as I run upstairs.

Will's still asleep when I enter his room.

"Wakey, wakey," I shout.

"Oh, shut up," he grunts, putting his head under one of the numerous pillows on his bed.

"Everyone's outside having a chat about last night. Come and join us."

"Has anyone cooked yet?" Will asks.

I roll my eyes. Of course he's already thinking about food. "Dad and I have had a cooked breakfast. I'm sure he'll cook for you as well, as Mum hasn't eaten yet either. Not that she'll eat much. She hardly ever does. Oh, and Auntie Maura's coming out next week for the big reveal mark two."

"That'll be a right laugh with Auntie Maura here, and I'm sure she'll take the news ok. Go easy on Mum, yeah? It must have been hard for her. It's like you getting pregnant now and Mum and Dad making you give the baby away. But you'd obviously have to find a boyfriend first," he adds with a grin.

"Shut up, Will. You never take anything seriously," I snap, crossing my arms.

"I do. You've got to learn how to chill out a bit, Cassie."

I wait for Will outside his room, who manages to get ready in thirty seconds flat, as he just pulls on last night's shorts and T-shirt. We go downstairs and join Mum and Dad outside, who stop their private conversation as soon as we appear.

"Morning, Will," Dad says.

"Morning. Any chance of one of your fry ups? Cassie told me all about you cooking one for her," Will says cheekily.

"I guess I have to play fair. How about you, Genie?"

"Maybe a poached egg?" Mum replies.

Dad obediently goes inside to start the next breakfast shift, leaving me and Will with Mum. I can immediately tell that Mum's nervous and hesitant by the fact she's biting her nails. Will's obviously going for the "Best Son in the World" award, as he manages to chat away to Mum quite effortlessly.

"You alright?" he asks, giving her a reassuring hug.

"I'm getting there," Mum replies, smiling weakly. "If there's anything either of you want to ask me, then please do."

I have a thousand questions to ask Mum, but I just can't even begin to sort through the muddle in my mind right now.

"I just wanted to thank you for telling us about Milly. It can't have been easy for you, Mum, but it does explain why you've been so upset," Will says.

"Thanks, love. I really appreciate that."

We spend the next ten minutes trying to make small talk, fake marvelling about the birds swooping for fish in the lake behind the pool. Thankfully, Dad saves the day by coming out with Will's fry up and Mum's poached egg, so I don't feel obliged to say something positive. Will literally demolishes his in about five minutes, complete with a huge glass of orange juice.

"What does everyone fancy doing today?" asks Dad.

"I'd like to go kayaking. It doesn't have to be today though. There was a big feature about some lake close to here on one of those travel programmes recently where you can go jet skiing and kayaking. It looks awesome," Will says enthusiastically.

"Sounds like a definite plan for another day. We could look them up online and book something for later in the week," Dad agrees.

"Brilliant."

God, he's getting on my wick being so bloody nice and reasonable about everything. It makes me look like a complete bitch. "I guess it's another pool day. I'm good with that."

"That's fine," Dad says. "Although I do need to pop to the supermarket to pick up some extra food. I don't mind going on my own."

"I'll help," I swiftly offer, not wanting to be left alone with Mum. I can see right through Dad's plan of the three of us playing happy families.

"Oh ok, Cassie. That would be great. Genie, can you put a list together of what we actually need? You know I'll only bring back bacon, eggs, beer and wine otherwise," Dad says, laughing, the tension still feeling like it's out full force.

"Sure. Give me a few minutes." Mum goes inside to make a list, leaving the three of us outside.

"I thought you might have liked to spend some time with your mum," Dad says, frowning.

"Oh, I just fancied getting out of the villa, that's all," I lie. "Will went with you to choose the car, so I just thought it was my turn to have a trip out. It'll be quicker if I come with you. You take ages shopping, as you always get side-tracked by the wine aisle." Before Dad can say anything more, to maybe try and sway me to stay here instead, I add, "I'm just going to put something more suitable on for shopping." I run to my room.

To be honest, I would much rather be lazing by the pool right now in my new silver bikini but the thought of having to make polite conversation with Mum makes food shopping the lesser of two evils. I haven't even bothered to tell her that Ed has been spotted with yet another mystery blonde. I'm sure Auntie Maura will probably update her, as neither Mum nor Dad read the tabloids anymore for fear of reading yet another scandalous story about the life and times of Evie Del Rio.

I remove my silver cover-up, grab a pair of khaki shorts and team them with a white vest top, slipping them over my bikini. My flipflops and sunglasses complete my shopping outfit.

Dad is waiting for me, complete with Mum's lengthy shopping list.

"Bye, you two. Have fun," says Dad, waving.

"Mum's going to film me doing backflips into the pool for my Instagram story," Will replies like an overexcited puppy. Rather her than me.

We drive to Publix, which is the closest supermarket to the villa. It's going to take us ages to do the shopping, as the store is so big, which is typical with everything in the States. Bigger and better than back at home. There's a huge section at the start of the store with an array of inflatables. I persuade Dad to buy a couple of inflatable chairs, complete with cup holders. Jonesy's villa is well-equipped with a variety of inflatables, but he doesn't have any chairs, and Dad is only too happy to placate me.

We manage to pick up everything on Mum's list except for a particular facial sunscreen that she likes, but we can easily pop to one of the pharmacies that litter Highway 192 to get that later. A nice elderly shop assistant insists on packing all our shopping for us and then pushing our trolley to our car. I can't imagine them doing that for us back home.

We drive back along the 192, stopping for the now obligatory Dunkin' Donuts coffee and smoothies from the drive-through. As we're waiting for our order to come out, I can't hold back what's on my mind any longer.

"Dad, umm, someone took a photo of us at Heathrow. I found it online. It is blurred though, so…"

"Of course they did…" He sighs. "I'll take a look later."

"And apparently Ed's got a new mystery girlfriend. She looks a similar age to Mum," I blurt out quickly in case I change my mind.

Loaded down with a dozen doughnuts and our drinks, Dad drives us home. We unpack the shopping and join Mum and Will in the pool area, where Mum's belly laughing at Will's efforts of backflipping into the pool while she tries to film it. I don't think I've heard Mum laugh like that in ages. She's absolutely soaked through but, clearly, she doesn't seem to mind.

"You two look like you've been having too much fun without us," Dad jokes.

"We've got doughnuts and drinks," I add, sitting down at the table, helping myself to yet another sugary doughnut, washed down with an iced smoothie.

"Pass us one, Cass," says Will, pointing at the doughnuts.

"No eating in the pool, Will. You know the rules. Come out if you want to eat," says Mum.

Drinks and doughnuts finished, we all chill around the pool while Dad does a bit of research about kayaking. I put my AirPods in my ears, pretending to listen to music so I don't have to join in the forced and jolly "happy families" chat. We are far from that. I hear Dad mention the recent press to Mum, and I watch them searching online for the articles.

"I wonder who Ed's latest conquest is?" says Dad, peering at his iPad.

"Let me look, Gray. You know you can't read anything without your glasses on," Mum snaps. She's always nagging him to wear them, but she can't seem to push through his reluctance. She looks at the screen, frowns, then looks closer. "That looks a bit like my old friend Ginny. It can't be though. Surely?" She shrugs and leans back in her chair. "I forgot to tell you but Ginny reached out to me recently on Instagram. She said she's sorry we lost touch. I replied that maybe we should meet up," Mum confesses.

Dad shot her a quizzical look. "Why did you say you'd meet up with her? You've been so guarded about seeing people outside of the family since the documentary."

"I've always missed having Ginny in my life. We were practically sisters. Leaving Ed was bad enough all those years ago but leaving Ginny almost destroyed me."

Mum takes another look at the photo and is like a woman possessed as she carefully studies Ed and the maybe Ginny woman, opens Instagram on her phone and then cross-references it with photos from Ginny's Instagram account. I'm also intrigued as to why Mum's former best friend and ex-boyfriend are hanging out. It's weird. It's like me suddenly hooking up with George years later. Who does that?

I can't wait to talk to Mel about Mum's bombshell, but Dad has sworn me and Will to total secrecy. I guess I'll have to wait a while longer.

Chapter Fifty

Ed

July 2018

It's strange waking up in Virginia's bed, although she's already up, humming away to herself in her ensuite. She emerges with her freshly washed hair drying in a towel, wearing a multicoloured bathrobe.

"Morning, sleepyhead. You even slept through my alarm." She throws her head back, doing her now familiar throaty giggle.

"I must have been out for the count."

"Well, we did have a rather odd day. I still can't believe Callum just turned up like that." Virginia shakes her head as she wraps her bathrobe tighter around her.

"Don't worry. He's not your responsibility, but he is and will always be Shannon's dad, so I guess he's always going to be around," I say as much to myself as her. I've never really stuck around with anyone long enough to have to deal with dads, so this is all new to me. "But hopefully not as an unwanted guest every time he gets grief from Amy."

"Yeah, I guess you're right, and the girls should always try to maintain a relationship with their dads, even if I think they're a couple of idiots. I'm going to grab some coffee and breakfast, as I've got to get to work. Do you want anything?" Virginia asks, unwrapping her hair from the towel and combing it through.

"A coffee would be great. I'll grab a shower at home. Do you want me to drop you at work?"

"No, that's fine. I normally drive. I'll make us a coffee and then finish getting ready."

Virginia goes downstairs to make some coffee whilst I locate last night's discarded clothes and get dressed. I join Virginia downstairs and sit at her breakfast bar as she fixes herself some breakfast.

"Do you fancy something to eat?" she asks as she pours some milk over her cereal.

I shake my head. "The coffee is just fine, thanks. I'll grab something at rehearsals later."

"You've got a late start, haven't you?" Virginia asks.

"Yeah. Well remembered," I reply, impressed. It's nice to have a woman in my life who actually listens and cares. My mother always looks down on me and most women pretend to care, mind only on the fact they're about to bed a rockstar. But I guess that's my fault with my self-induced reputation. "We're not due in until eleven-thirty. Toby knows what we're all like in the mornings. Plus, Mark drops the kids at school every day. I don't know how he keeps up with them all."

"He's a good egg, Mark, isn't he? He's always liked keeping everyone happy. I'd say he is the one person out of us all that hasn't really changed," Virginia says thoughtfully, taking her first mouthful of cereal. I notice that her corn-flakes are practically swimming in milk and wonder if she's going to drink from her bowl once she's done. I wouldn't be surprised. She comes off all ladylike and then screams at the footie.

"Yeah. He's a good un, old Marky boy," I agree. "And clearly a great ex-husband."

"Wish the same could be said about my exes," says Virginia with a smile. She leans in for a kiss and then quickly pulls away. "Sorry, coffee breath." She laughs.

"I don't mind if you don't..." I grab her for one more kiss.

Virginia pulls away and puts her hand over my mouth, giggling. "Right. No more kisses for you, Mr Nash. I really need to get ready." She grabs her bowl and tips the rest of the milk down the side of the washing bowl before putting it on the side. I guess that answers my question. "As much as I would love to stay here with you, in my bed, I need to get to work."

"Spoilsport." I smirk.

Virginia just about manages to extricate herself from me and runs upstairs to get dressed. I finish my coffee and eat an apple from the fruit bowl, beginning to regret my "no thanks" answer to the offer of breakfast. Virginia reappears quarter of an hour later in a pale pink linen trouser suit, looking ready for business.

"Very impressive," I say, attempting a rather feeble wolf whistle.

"Why thank you. I do try. Hope your rehearsal goes well today," she says, gently touching her freshly glossed lips on mine. She clearly hasn't got time this morning to risk them smudging and having to reapply.

"Thanks. I'll try to call you later. Maybe I could take you for dinner tonight, depending on what time we finish?" I suggest.

"Can we take a rain check on that? Monday night is always our family catch-up night."

"Sure, no problem, but I would like to take you out for dinner one night this week if you're free," I say, feeling slightly deflated, not used to being told no.

"That would be good. Text me later and we'll sort out one night this week, but right now I need to kick you out and get moving, otherwise the traffic will be all backed up with the school run." Virginia opens the front door and beckons me out, as if I'm one of those children on the school run, needing prompting to leave the house for a day of boring lessons.

I slide my shoes on and follow her out. She locks up and gets into her car whilst I wave her off before driving back home.

True to form, Sid is tidying up the front of the flats, picking up a bit of litter that has dared to find itself in our communal flowerbeds. I put my window down.

"Morning, Ed. Another hot day ahead," he calls out to me as I approach the ramp to the underground car park.

I decide to go up the communal stairs rather than take the lift. I bump into one of the Australian girls getting ready for another epic exercise session. We nod at each other as I run past, up all ten flights of stairs without stopping. I feel physically sick by the time I get inside the flat. I bet that Australian girl wouldn't have been out of breath but, hey, that's the difference between being in your twenties and being almost fifty.

I shower and get ready, then grab another coffee and make myself some porridge to give me energy for the forthcoming day. I call Mark to see if he wants a lift to the rehearsal room, which he gratefully accepts, as he's worn out from doing the school run. The twins kept him waiting, which in turn made Marnie late for school. Both of his ex-wives are fuming that the girls were late for school. On top of that, the baby didn't sleep at all during the night, so Mark's looking forward to a nap in my car.

Mark lives in Richmond, so it doesn't take too long to get to him. I've never seen a man so grateful for the offer of a lift.

"Alright, mate?" I ask as he climbs into my car.

"Yeah, just knackered from last night. I'll get my head down for forty winks and then I'll be as right as rain."

Mark nods off with ease, and I concentrate on navigating my way to the studio, listening to the radio, which seems to be really championing our latest single "No More Tears" even though the majority of their listeners are definitely not in our age demographic. I still get such a buzz whenever our music is played on the radio. The journey to the West End is fairly uneventful, and I manage to do it within forty-five minutes. I park in the studio car park and give Mark a nudge. We make our way to the rehearsal room. Cindy and Chyna are already here, but Andy and Simon are still to make an appearance, as is Jez. He only lives just off Chiswick High Road, so I don't think he will be too long. Amazingly, Toby isn't here yet. I'm convinced he's shacked up with Cindy, but she's denying all knowledge of why he isn't here. Jez is the next one to arrive.

Toby's assistant Fifi comes through from her temporary office, informing us that Toby will be delayed by about half an hour due to having to go to an emergency dental appointment, and we are to set up and start practicing. We're already in the rehearsal room setting up when Andy and Simon arrive.

"You're lucky Toby's had to go to an emergency dental appointment. He doesn't tolerate people being late," Cindy warns them.

"Since when are you the boss?" Andy asks under his breath.

"Sorry, did you say something, Andy?" Cindy fakes a toothy grin, knowing damn well what he just said.

"I said, let's get started. Show Toby what we can do," he lies.

Everyone's in position, and we start off with some of the newer material. Cindy and Chyna's backing vocals work well on most of the numbers. Despite Mark's lack of sleep and his busy morning, he's on fire behind the drums. Simon's guitar playing complements Jez's now legendary bass playing, and by adding in Andy's keyboards on certain numbers, we are sounding very together. My voice seems to be holding up as I scream out some of the more shouty, rocky vocals and then I manage to reign it in on some of the slower, gentler songs.

"I'd like to practice 'Used to Be' once more, please," I announce. "Girls, you hang back on the backing vocals, but if you can do that dance routine you did last time, that would be great."

Everyone gets into place and does their thing. It's all sounding really slick and polished. Toby returns just as Mark's drumming signals the end of the song. Toby lets out a loud whistle and gives us a round of applause.

"I can hardly speak because of the injection they've just given me at the dentist but that was spot on. Just brilliant," he slurs.

It was definitely the right move to just have the one set of vocals on "Used to Be". Although Toby's really happy with our progress, he's a hard task master and has us go over some of the songs repeatedly. By mid-afternoon, we've all had enough, so we take a break, and Toby gets Fifi to order in some food for us. I keep it healthy—just a salad and bit of sushi—as I know Toby will be watching my calorie intake until the tour.

After our break, we don't finish rehearsals until nearly ten-thirty. We're all getting ready to go when Toby pulls me aside.

"I see from the press that you're seeing someone new, if the tabloids are anything to go by," Toby says with a big grin on his face, rubbing his chin and his ridiculous excuse for a beard.

"What do you mean?" I say, shrugging, car keys in my hand.

"There's photos online of you with some blonde coming out of some restaurant in West London. Haven't you seen it?" Toby asks incredulously, almost rubbing his hands together with the glee over the prospect of some more free publicity for the tour.

"Err, no. I've been a bit busy." Obviously, those girls from the restaurant must have sold their photos of us. I'm fuming but I don't want to show it. I wanted to keep my relationship with Virginia private. Things with her are different.

"So I see. It's all great press for the tour though. Who is your mystery lady?" Toby says with a slightly lecherous smile.

"Well, if you'd come out for drinks with us recently, you would have met her. She's an old friend."

"Anything I need to know about?" Toby asks, eager for any free publicity.

"No, not really. I'm trying to keep her out of the spotlight, as it's early days."

"Let's hope it doesn't dull the press interest in *The Girl in the Song*. Your youthful exploits with Evie Del Rio have really helped with selling this tour, you know. I don't want you spoiling your rock god status by settling down quite yet, especially with someone who isn't Evie," he says, his attempt at some sort of joke that's not really a joke.

"We're keeping things low-key, don't worry. Nothing's going to get in the way of the reunion tour," I assure him. In the back of my mind, I keep going over what if Virginia was right all along and Evie simply left because she really was pregnant. Every time Evie is mentioned, the thought resurfaces. I really need to see those Polaroids again. I need to know one way or another.

"Good stuff, Ed. I'll see you in a couple of days, but do keep your fitness regime up. I'll get the personal trainer sorted for you next month so you're in top shape for the tour. Now, get yourself out of here," Toby instructs as he clocks Cindy waiting for him. They are definitely shagging. She's so his type.

I walk out to the reception area, where Mark and Jez are both waiting for me.

"Any chance you could drop me off on your way home?" Jez asks.

"Sure, mate. Come on, you two. Let's get you home. Poor old Mark's got the bloody school run again in the morning, so he could do with getting his head down."

Mark opts for going in the back of my car so he can try to sleep, as he's worried Luna's going to be up all night again and he promised Rosita he was going to do most of the night feeds to give her a break. He's asleep and snoring by the time we exit the car park.

It's good to catch up with Jez. The chat is easy, as we've known each other since our school days. We chat about our respective health kicks in readiness for the upcoming tour.

"No nice new woman to tell me about?" I probe. It's about time Jez had a new girlfriend. He's such a decent bloke, and I know he could show someone the world.

"Nah, I'm giving them a miss. I haven't got the energy for it all. I quite like the look of Cindy, but I think she's shagging Toby, so I'm certainly not going anywhere he's been." He laughs. We're making good progress through the traffic despite the initial bottle neck around the streets of Soho.

"Yeah, I picked up on that too. Has Chyna said anything about it?"

"Chyna doesn't even give me the time of day. I think she's got her eye on Andy. I don't know what she sees in him," he ponders, shaking his head.

"He's just one of those guys with the gift of the gab, isn't he?"

"Yeah, I guess so. How are things going with you and the lovely Virginia?" asks Jez, swiftly moving the conversation away from himself.

"She's great," I say, and I find myself smiling like I always do at the thought of or any mention of Virginia. "We've had a few bumps in the road but I think we're back on track. She's incredible, although I'm worried for her about all the press attention. We got papped coming out of her local restaurant."

"Wow, has Virginia finally tamed the untameable Ed "Nasher" Nash after all these years?" Jez says, chuckling.

"I'm not sure about that. Did I really need taming?" I ask, not really knowing the answer myself.

"Probably not. You're not the guy the press always go on about. If they knew you, like me and Mark know you, they'd realise you're one of the good guys," says Jez, who, despite looking like a Hells Angel, is one of the most sensitive people I know. He married very young to his first proper girlfriend Poppy, a real hippy chick with the palest skin you had ever seen, bright green eyes and red hair. They first met at primary school, but she tragically drowned after a midnight swim on their honeymoon in Thailand.

They'd enjoyed the most blissful couple of weeks just being together—swimming, snorkelling, sampling exquisite Thai cuisine, rock climbing and hiking—but on the very last night, they went to a Full Moon Party and shared a Magic Mushroom shake. They apparently both felt very chilled at first, but as Jez was so out of it, he lay in the sand whilst Poppy danced her way to where the waves gently lapped the shoreline, paddling in the sea just up to her ankles. She called out to Jez to come and join her, as she wanted him to experience the beauty of the moon's reflection on the water.

By the time Jez managed to join Poppy, the water was almost up to her shoulders. Jez just couldn't seem to keep up with her, and the more he tried to, the more she seemed to be just that little bit out of reach. The last sighting Jez had of Poppy was her mouthing "I love you" as the waves finally took her.

They never recovered her body, and rumours of their extreme drug abuse and sex-fuelled orgies plagued Jez for years. There were even rumours that Jez had persuaded Poppy to take her own life so he could cash in on her life insurance. None of it's true, of course, but it made Jez a changed man. For a while, he joined a Buddhist retreat, where he tried to learn how to deal with his grief. Two years after Poppy died, he finally returned to London after travelling throughout Southeast Asia, which had always been his and Poppy's plan. He was older, wiser, didn't do drugs anymore and was ready to make music again, much to mine and Mark's delight.

We reach Chiswick High Road, and Mark wakes up just as Jez reaches his front door after leaving the car.

"Do you want to join me in the front, Mark?"

"Yeah, I need to wake up a bit, as I'll be looking after Luna when I get in. Rosita is exhausted." Mark decides to clamber into the front between the two front seats, over the handbrake. He collapses into the passenger seat and runs his hand through his hair. I wonder if he thought that would be the easier option due to his tiredness. I wonder if he still thinks that now.

"You look pretty done in yourself. Have you thought about getting someone in to help you with Luna?"

"I would pay for a night nurse just like that"—he snaps his fingers—"I tell you, but because it's Rosita's first baby, she wants us to do it all ourselves. There's no one giving out prizes for driving yourself into the ground," he mutters. He looks out the window and turns silent, seemingly to focus on staying awake for the rest of the car journey.

We reach Mark's, and he waves to me as he walks up the path. I drive home tired but still on a high from rehearsals. They went much better than I thought, and with a few tweaks, the British public are going to be in for a treat come October time. I quickly message Virginia to say goodnight and wonder if she's seen the photo of us in the press. I feel guilty that her life is about to change.

Chapter Fifty-one

Virginia

July 2018

As soon as I get to the office, I feel my colleagues' eyes burning into me as I fix myself and Mr Bruce a coffee. I knock on Mr Bruce's door, and he ushers me in, pointing to a bunch of papers that need attention. I return to my desk and sip my coffee as I systematically sort the papers into three piles. Caroline, one of the other PAs, pulls her chair up to my desk.

"You ok this morning, darling?" Caroline asks, with a big grin on her face. I feel like somehow I'm the only one in the office who seems to have missed out on an in joke or something.

"Yeah, I'm good, is there a reason I wouldn't be?"

It's clear from her tone there's a reason she's asking, and I have no idea what that reason is until she produces her mobile and shows me a couple of photos from an online gossip site. I reach for my reading glasses to take a better look. It's a series of photos of me and Ed coming out of my local restaurant. I feel exposed, vulnerable, my palms starting to sweat. Ed was right to be alarmed the other night.

"Have you seen these yet? You're a dark horse, aren't you, Virginia? I didn't even know you know Ed Nash. He's bloody gorgeous," says Caroline with a wink. Caroline is the real linchpin of the office. She never forgets anyone's birthday and is always the one who arranges the collections to buy the cards and gifts. She also loves a good gossip.

"No, I haven't. Ed is an old schoolfriend. We met up for dinner and someone papped us," I say almost robotically, tones hidden from my voice, as if it's the most normal thing in the world to be seen out with a well-known rock star.

"Oh, I wish I had an old schoolfriend like him. You're not going out with him, then?" Caroline asks with a giggle.

"As I said, he's an old schoolfriend. I'd best get on, Caroline. I've got loads to do today," I say, trying to close the conversation down. I'm definitely not going to give anyone anything to gossip about.

"Right you are, Virginia. Who'd have believed it—our Virginia knows Ed Nash," she continues as she makes her way back to her desk.

This is what Ed was afraid of: people seeing our photo in the press and putting two and two together. I understand now. I hope the rehearsals are going well for the band and the photos aren't going to cause us too much trouble. I keep myself busy with Mr Bruce's paperwork and type up a few letters for him, impatient to leave. Thankfully, Mr Bruce lets me go early again. I drive straight home.

As it's only 4 p.m. the girls are still at work and college, so I'm able to relax by doing some gardening. After all my hard work, I reward myself about an hour later with a cup of tea and sit under the umbrella, scrolling through some of my social media feeds. There are numerous links to the photos of me and Ed. Thankfully, no one seems to have named me yet, but I'm sure it won't be too long. I check our family WhatsApp to see that both Sasha and Shannon have sent me a link to the photos. There's nothing I can do about it, so I go back to enjoying the peaceful sanctuary of my garden.

Shannon's the first of the girls to get back home after a busy day at college. "Hi, Mum," she calls out. She joins me under the umbrella, kicking off her shoes. "You read the WhatsApp messages, then?"

I nod.

"Are you worried about them?" Shannon asks, moving her chair a little closer to mine.

"Not really, but I think this is what Ed was worried about: the press intrusion." Of course I'm worried, my stomach's been in knots since Caroline first showed me the photos, but I need to remain strong in front of Shannon.

"It won't be long before you're identified, you know."

"I know. I'll just have to deal with it. Caroline, at work, couldn't wait to show me the photos. I just said that Ed and I are old schoolfriends. She was rather impressed through." I shrug.

"A couple of my friends recognised you too," Shannon adds.

"Well, hopefully it will blow over. It's no one's business but ours," I say more for Shannon's benefit than my own, knowing damn well things will never be the same.

"You say that, but because Ed is in the public eye and up until now has courted press attention, I think you're going to have a hard time keeping it all quiet." Shannon runs her hands through her long hair.

"Well, it's out there now. We'll just have to cope with it somehow. What's new with you? Things ok with you and Micky?" I ask, steering the conversation away from my own love life.

"Yeah, all good. We're thinking about booking a holiday together. Only a week though. I don't know if I can put up with him twenty-four seven for any longer." She laughs loudly, rolling her eyes to the heavens.

"Any idea where you might go?" I enquire, thinking about how my baby is all grown up now, planning her first holiday with her boyfriend.

"Just somewhere hot with a beach. Oh, and a few bars, of course." She grins.

"Sounds like the perfect holiday when you're only eighteen." I say, feeling quite envious of the simplicity of life when you're young.

By the time Sasha arrives home, the sun has set and I'm busy in the kitchen dishing up noodles for us all. It's good and much needed for the three of us to sit down together.

"Thanks for sending me the link about the photos of me and Ed," I say to Sasha. "I told Shannon earlier that Caroline at work showed them to me. She's well impressed that I know Ed. She's quite the fan," I say, trying to add some humour to the situation.

"A couple of girls at my salon recognised you, Mum. I don't think it will be too long before you're named," Sasha warns. She's a beautician, and the girls there always have their fingers on the pulse of any tabloid gossip.

"We'll just play it down. Ed will probably just say we're old friends. I'm sure it will be fine. I think you're worrying too much," I say, trying to brush things off in front of my girls but secretly wondering what Ed will be thinking. I know he's been in rehearsals all day, so I'm not sure if he's seen the photos. He probably has. Surely, he has people that look out for any press attention?

"Sounds like you've got it covered, but I think we all need to be aware of not discussing Ed in front of anyone outside of the family. I'll have a word with Josh to keep his trap shut and, Shannon, you should do the same with Micky. He's got a mouth like the Mersey Tunnel when he's had one too many." As humorous as her words sound, there's a very serious edge to them.

"Point taken," Shannon agrees.

"Anyone fancy a cheeky glass of prosecco?" I say once we've all finished dinner. "Ed and I have decided that we are going to try to only drink at the weekends and on special occasions, but in my book, a Monday night dinner with my two gorgeous daughters is definitely considered a special occasion."

"Yeah, go on. One glass won't hurt anyone." Sasha's already eyeing up where she knows the glasses are.

"When have I ever turned down a glass of prosecco?" Shannon laughs. "I'll get the drink. Is it warm enough to sit outside, do you think, Mum?"

"I'll put the patio heater on," I reply.

"I'll clear the table and join you once I'm done." Sasha's already up, stacking our dirty plates.

I grab my shawl from the understairs cupboard and wrap it around my shoulders. Summer evenings in London are never as warm as you'd hope. I get the patio heater going and sit on my rattan sofa, waiting for the girls to join me. Shannon comes out first, juggling a bottle of prosecco and three glasses. Sasha steps outside a few minutes later.

"I love nights like this, just me and my girls," I exclaim, raising my glass.

"There's something quite liberating about living in an all-female household. Sometimes I forget what it's like to have a dad or stepdad in the house," Sasha muses.

"I'm sorry that both your dads ended up leaving, but always remember that they both left me, they didn't leave you. And, Sasha, you are very lucky that Callum, despite all his faults, still considers you as his daughter." I always find it so weird speaking about the complexities of my strange, little blended family.

"God, listen to you both. You've gone all soppy on me and you've only had a couple of sips of prosecco," says Shannon, breaking up the seriousness of the conversation. "We all know that Dad can be a bit of a dick sometimes, but at the end of the day, I know he loves and cares for both me and Sasha. I'm only sorry he wasn't a better husband to you, Mum. You deserve the best, you really do. And I really hope that things work out with you and Ed. If that's what you want."

"Thanks, Shannon. That means a lot to me that you approve of Ed. He's a great guy. He's not perfect, but neither am I. I enjoy spending time with him, so let's just see how things go."

I take one of each of their hands in mine, and smile to myself under the starry sky, knowing that irrelevant of what happens with Ed, I'll always have my girls.

Chapter Fifty-two

Genie

July 2018

We all had another fairly chilled day at the villa after my bombshell. I'm disappointed about how Cassie reacted, but I suppose it must be difficult for her finding out that I'm a complete fraud. She's always had my back since all the press attention, but to experience her being so hostile towards me is heartbreaking to deal with. Will, bless him, is a dream.

The oddest thing was seeing Ginny and Ed online photographed together coming out of an Italian restaurant in West London. Because, yes, the more I looked at the photo, the more apparent it was that it's definitely Ginny. In the photo, they both look amazing; life has been kind to them. Ginny is beautiful, her figure still slim and her much-envied chest seems more in proportion on a grown woman. Ed seems much more casual than in any of the previous photos I've seen or in his appearances on TV. His hair is now shorter. His vivid and mesmerizing blue eyes that I remember so well, covered up by the obligatory rockstar sunglasses. My stomach does a flip. I always thought that any feelings I ever had for Ed disappeared once he started trading on my name and our doomed teenage love affair but seeing him in those photos, which were obviously taken when he was off guard, has brought all those teenage feelings back. I quickly shut my iPad cover to put some distance between me and Ed, and I reach for my latest book.

"Genie, are you ok there? You look really flushed," Gray asks with such concern that I immediately feel guilty.

"I'm ok thanks. I think I just need some water. We all underestimate how strong the Floridian sun can be," I say, making an excuse to go inside.

Once inside the villa, the aircon feels incredible, and I take an iced water from the fridge, then go upstairs to lie down in our bedroom. The cold water helps but my face remains flushed. It isn't just the sun that's made it red, but my deepest, darkest thoughts of Ed suddenly resurfacing after a lifetime of denial. I've never even looked at another man in that way since being with Gray. He's my soulmate, my rock, my Mr Dependable who rescued me all those years ago. He deserves so much more. Of course, Ed will always hold a special place in my heart—he was my first boyfriend, my first love—but it wasn't real. Even if I hadn't got pregnant and been made to leave London, we probably wouldn't have lasted. First love rarely lasts. Meeting Gray turned my life around, and I will be eternally grateful for that. What I need to find out is what Ginny and Ed are doing meeting up. Perhaps I'll message Ginny again.

I nearly jump as Gray pops his head around the door to check up on me. "You ok, Genie?"

"Yes, I just needed to get out of the sun, that's all." I smile up at him as he walks over.

"Maybe a lie down will do you good, then. I'm probably going to book for us all to go kayaking tomorrow." Gray kisses me gently on my cheek and closes our bedroom door behind him, leaving me alone with my thoughts. Kayaking is probably just what we need. It will be good to do something as a family.

I put Ed and Ginny to the back of my mind and let myself drift off to sleep.

I wake to the sounds of Cassie and Will playfighting. I get up and go downstairs to the open-plan living room, checking the clock as I wander past it. I can't believe I slept until 8 p.m. Clearly, I must have needed sleep.

"Hey, Mum, you ok?" says Will, releasing Cassie from his vice-like grip.

"Oh, he's so annoying, Mum," Cassie complains, trying to brush her hair through with her fingers. At least she's talking to me.

"Will, try not to be so rough with your sister. I could help you sort your hair, Cassie, if you'd like?" I ask, trying to take advantage of the fact Will has completely ruined it.

"Yes, please," she says, much to my complete amazement. I was genuinely expecting her to either completely ignore me or outright reject me. I try to hide the shock on my face, my eyes only slightly widening.

She follows me upstairs, and she makes herself comfy in front of my dressing table whilst I heat the curling brush up. I brush and curl her hair, taking my time, making sure it looks perfect so she can't find another reason to have an issue with me. I work on her hair in silence, but even though we're both being quiet, the fact we're still spending time together feels like massive progress. I finish her hair off with a good dose of hairspray.

I turn the curling brush off as Cassie admires her newly styled hair in the large mirror in our bedroom. "Thanks, Mum. It looks great." She turns to me, scrunching her face up. "It's probably too late to go out for dinner now, isn't it?"

"How about a late-night trip to the outlet mall? We could have some Chinese food in the food court?" I suggest, desperate to please my daughter. I don't want the progress of us repairing our relationship to come undone. Plus, I can't deny I'm hungry and desperate for a shopping trip.

"I'll ask Dad." Cassie excitedly jogs off. If she were younger, she probably would have skipped.

Gray's outside, asleep on one of the sun loungers.

"Dad, can we go to the outlet place? Mum and I want to go shopping," Cassie asks loudly, making sure her voice wakes him up.

Gray darts up on the sun lounger, panting from sudden heart palpitations. "What's up? Where's the fire?" he stutters.

"Mum and I really want to go shopping. Can we go, Dad?"

He lies back down and frowns. "Right now?"

"Mhmm."

"Yeah, sure, I guess." He swings his legs over the side of the sun lounger and looks at Cassie. "I guess everything is ok between you both, then?" Right now, I'm sure Gray would agree to do anything involving us all spending time together. A sleepy trip for the sake of repairing a relationship is more than worth it. He's always been a peacemaker.

Cassie glances at me and lowers her voice, as if she doesn't want me to hear, even though she knows I can, or doesn't quite want to admit that she's starting the process of forgiving me. "I'm still cross with Mum for lying to us, but she's still my mum. We'll need to talk it all out at some stage, but that's after a bit of retail therapy."

Gray stands determinedly, even more convinced by the shopping idea now. "Give me five minutes and we'll get going. You'll only have a couple of hours though," he says before wandering inside to find his car keys, wallet and shoes.

I quickly change into one of my sundresses and just about manage to tear Will away from the games room, where he's shooting some basketball hoops. He's more than happy to join us if the end result is food.

Thankfully, the traffic isn't too bad, and we reach the outlets fairly quickly. Gray and Will go straight to the food court whilst Cassie and I hit the shops. We manage to pack quite a lot of shopping into just a couple of hours, spending out on makeup and some brand-new outfits.

"We'd best go and find the boys and grab something to eat," I suggest once we hit the last shop.

"Sure, Mum. Thanks for treating me," Cassie replies, linking her arm through mine. I'm hoping this means that I'm forgiven.

We finally make our way to the food court, through a maze of walkways between the various designer outlets, managing to dodge the numerous suitcases on wheels that many shoppers seem to have with them. We eventually find Gray and Will, where Will's finishing off his second hotdog.

"Hi, guys. Hope we weren't too long?" I say.

"Looking at all those bags, I would say that was a fairly successful couple of hours shopping," Gray observes with a smile. "We actually did a bit of shopping ourselves, as we knew you'd be ages. Just some sports gear and trainers," he confesses, pointing at several bags underneath the table.

"The real shopping will start next week when Maura joins us." I laugh, enjoying the company of my amazing family. I need to forget all about Ed and concentrate on the here and now.

Cassie and I share a box of Chinese food, with Will finishing off our leftovers, and we finally leave the outlets just as they're closing. Once we arrive home, the children go straight to bed whilst Gray suggests we have a cheeky glass of wine outside in the spa.

We quickly change, and I manage to find a couple of plastic wine glasses for our wine. By the time I join Gray, the spa's bubbling away. We sit back and let the bubbles work their magic.

"I keep thinking it would be good to have a spa in the garden, you know. How great would it be to relax in your very own jacuzzi at the end of a hard day?" Gray ponders.

"Do you think we'd ever use it?" I say, trying, as always, to be the practical one.

"Once it's there, we'd definitely use it."

"Ok, but you'll be responsible for all the upkeep and cleaning." He's always getting notions about buying extra bits and pieces for the garden. We already have a neglected office pod, which he was going to work from on the days he works from home (never happened); an indoor gym in the garage (never used); along with Gray's racing bike, which he was going to ride into work each day (now residing in the never used gym).

"Come closer, Mrs McNamara," Gray orders.

"Any closer, I'll be sitting on your lap."

"Maybe that's exactly what I want." He pulls me to him and kisses me gently on the lips. It's nice to spend time together and be able to relax, away from the stresses and strains of the past few months. We spend some time talking and reconnecting before sharing a more passionate kiss that gets our hearts racing.

Gray pulls his lips away from mine. "Much as I'd like to spend all night with you here in the spa, I fear my manhood will have shrunk away to nothing."

I tut playfully. "And that would never do."

"I'll grab the wine glasses, you go ahead and make yourself even more gorgeous for me. I'll join you once I've locked up." He climbs out first and hands me a towel. I wrap it around myself and head indoors.

I take a very quick shower to get rid of the chlorine and then climb into bed. Lying there, I think back on the day's events. Things ended pretty successfully after such a shaky start, but there's still a long way to go.

Gray seems to be taking ages, and as much as I want to stay awake for him and see where the night could lead, my eyelids feel so, so heavy...

Chapter Fifty-three

Gray

July 2018

Despite another late night, I'm awake early again. I let Genie sleep and make myself a coffee. I sit outside to watch the sunrise and catch up on some email and telephone calls. My mind has been in turmoil ever since Genie told me about her teenage pregnancy. I'm heartbroken for Genie that she was forced to give her baby away all those years ago. Despite my reservations about Ed Nash, he has a right to know he fathered a daughter. I'd want to know. I can't imagine being childless.

I've decided to at least try to find the Catholic adoption service Genie's mother used for Milly, but without actually talking to her, it's going to be difficult. I also don't want to upset Genie, especially as she's so fragile at the moment. I'm starting my search in Bournemouth, as that's where Milly was born. Genie's always been a bit vague as to how she ended up in Brighton, but I do remember that she mentioned that a girl from her auntie Maureen's church helped her get away from Bournemouth.

The sunrise is beautiful and well worth getting up early for. I finish off my coffee and then dangle my feet in the cool water of the pool, enjoying the silence whilst my family sleeps. But I don't have alone time for long, as Cassie's soon awake, and she comes and joins me outside.

"Morning, Dad, you're up early. Are you still suffering from jetlag?" She stands in the doorway and unties the hair tie from her hair, letting her hair flow, a kink in it where the hair tie was.

"Perhaps, but I just really think I'm learning to enjoy the silence that comes with early mornings," I say, still staring at the beautiful sky.

"How about I make you some breakfast for a change?" Cassie suggests, joining me on the side of the pool. She's got a genuine smile on her face, and she seems calm.

"That would be amazing. Maybe a poached egg with some smashed avocado? Oh, and another coffee, please," I reply, holding up my cup.

"I think I can just about manage that." Cassie laughs, taking the cup from my hand.

As Cassie leaves to fix breakfast, I return to my iPad and google *Catholic adoption services in Bournemouth*. The search returns quite a few more results than I expected, and I don't really have the time to go through them all right now, what with Cassie coming back imminently. I will have to level with Genie eventually. I close my iPad and wait for my breakfast to arrive, thinking about the day ahead. I've booked us all in for kayaking at the nearby lake for 11:30 a.m.

Cassie arrives with my much-needed breakfast and coffee, and Milly's put to one side whilst Cassie and I chat about the day ahead.

"When was the last time you cooked for me? This breakfast is amazing. Your culinary skills are definitely improving," I comment as I take my first mouthful after expecting something edible but not necessarily cooked to perfection.

"It's all thanks to Mum teaching me how to cook the perfect poached egg. You have to remember to add the vinegar."

"Why don't you see if Mum and Will are awake? We've got our kayaking at eleven-thirty, and we need to get there about fifteen minutes early for a safety briefing."

I'm pleasantly surprised when Cassie agrees without a huff, an eyeroll or any backchat. It gives me a few minutes to clear my browsing history. The last thing I want to do right now is upset Genie, and I'm beginning to think that it's too big a task for me to take on right now after seeing all those Google hits.

Cassie returns with Will and Genie, and she even offers to make breakfast for them. Perhaps we've turned a corner?

Kayaking was a great success, with Genie and me in one kayak and the children in another. Will almost tipped them into the inky water, but thankfully they both managed to right themselves without too much squabbling. Genie and I got into quite a rhythm with our paddles and managed to kayak around the lake quite easily without any mishaps. Afterwards, we picked up some burgers from Wendy's and then had a light meal of fajitas in the evening due to the big lunch. Cassie and Will have since retreated to their rooms, whilst Genie and I are enjoying a final glass of wine outside.

"What day is Maura flying out here?" I ask Genie.

"Saturday. She's getting the lunchtime flight, so she'll be here quite late. I said you'd pick her up from the airport. I hope that's ok?"

"Of course. Maura being here is going to save me from all that shopping," I say with my usual standard response. "Just let me know her flight number, and I'll track her flight." I swill the wine around my glass. "I've been thinking about when we met in that bar in Brighton that Maura used to manage."

"Oh yeah?"

"How did you end up in Brighton?"

"My friend at the church recommended it as quite a cool place to go to, that was easy enough to get to but far enough away from Bournemouth."

"Oh, yes, I remember you mentioning her to me. What was her name again?" I ask casually.

"Emma. Emma Hadfield. She was the only person in Bournemouth who ever showed me any kindness. She'd seen me at church and then we started talking because I took my O levels at her school. She knew what Mother and Auntie Maureen were like from seeing them at church. She even gave me some of her savings so I had a little bit of money behind me to get me away from Bournemouth."

"Did you keep in touch?" I probe.

"No. I felt it was better to reinvent myself, hence my name change to Genie. Milly was gone, and I had absolutely nothing to keep me in Bournemouth. Can you believe that Mother and Auntie Maureen had me volunteering at the church?"

I nod because I can believe it. Despite what an amazing grandparent Felicity's been, she's never cared as much about Genie, her beliefs and her wants.

"It was torture," she continues. "Even after giving the baby away, they still had control over me, as I had no money and they were always with me, even at the church.

"It was incredible how I ever managed to get away, to be honest. I waited until after my seventeenth birthday, as I wanted to see Dad one more time before I left. He came to visit me and slipped me some birthday money on the quiet.

"Once Dad returned to London, I feigned illness so I didn't have to do my shift at the church. Mother took my shift, and I slipped some laxatives into Auntie Maureen's cup of tea that I'd found in her bathroom cupboard. She was in the bathroom when I left. I was just so desperate to escape." Genie swigs the last of her wine and sits back, breathing in the night air.

"I called Emma the morning that I left from a phone box. I didn't call her again to let her know where I was staying, as I didn't want to get her in trouble. Her parents were also quite big in the church, and they would have been horrified to hear that she had helped me.

"I could never have done it without Emma's help. I do wonder how life has treated her. I've been lucky with my choice of friends, but I do feel guilty that I lost touch with both Emma and Ginny. Thank goodness I still have Maura and you," she finishes, leaning over and kissing me firmly on the lips.

I make a mental note of Genie's childhood friend's name for future reference and suggest another glass of wine, which Genie happily agrees to. With Genie and Cassie talking again, Genie now seems to be so much more relaxed. I will try my utmost to see if I can reunite Genie with Milly somehow, and as much as it irks me, Ed Nash deserves to know he has a daughter.

Chapter Fifty-four

Virginia

July 2018

The weather in London is still insufferably hot and stuffy. By the time the girls are up, I've already put on two loads of washing, showered, dressed and eaten my breakfast in the garden, and it's only 7:45 a.m. I leave the house just after 8:00 a.m., keen to get to work early in the hope that I'll be able to slip away early on the off chance Ed might be in touch. I know I shouldn't just keep myself available, but the way things have been going recently, I'm feeling optimistic.

I arrive and set about my day answering a series of emails that came in overnight from the States. I've worked at McKnight and Andrews, who are an international recruitment consultancy, for almost five years as a PA. Mr Bruce is my second boss, as my original boss ironically got headhunted for a rival firm. It isn't the most exciting job in the world, but the people are nice, the pay is good and it's local. Being a single mum, it's a peach of a job to have.

I'm just on my second coffee of the morning when a message from Ed flashes up on my phone: *Morning, gorgeous! Fancy dinner and a sleepover tonight? x*

I smile, knowing my senses were right. Not wanting to seem too keen, I wait ten minutes before replying: *On a school night? I'd love to! What time suits? x*

He replies almost immediately: *6:30/7? x*

Sounds great. I'll text you when I'm on my way x

The rest of the day typically drags, with Mr Bruce in and out of meetings. By lunchtime, he has quite a backlog of emails and correspondences to go through, so we both work through lunch to get everything under control. It's around 4 p.m., and I'm just sending off the final flurry of CVs Mr Bruce has selected for a very senior marketing role based in Hong Kong, when he pops by my desk to let me know I can finish early once the Hong Kong brief is sorted, as I worked through lunch.

I finish what I'm doing and leave, missing the rush hour traffic. As soon as I get home, I take a quick shower, style my hair and change into a pair of cropped jeans and a blue and white striped top. I pack a small overnight bag with some work clothes for tomorrow. I text Ed—*On my way x*—as I walk to my car.

I put my seatbelt on and check my phone to see he's replied with: *I'll get our caretaker to direct you to a visitor parking space x*

I chuck my phone on the passenger seat and start driving. It only takes me fifteen minutes to get to Ed's, and as arranged, I'm directed to a parking space.

"Thanks so much for that," I say to the caretaker.

"You are most welcome. I'm Sid, and any friend of Mr Nash's is a friend of mine," Sid says, holding out his hand for me to shake.

"So lovely to meet you. I'm Virginia," I say, returning his handshake.

"Lovely to meet you, Virginia. Let me get the lift for you."

The lift is airconditioned, which is a great relief from the heat. I check my reflection in the mirrored panels in the lift. As per usual with lift mirrors, I'm not exactly amazed by the reflection staring back. I never know if it's the lighting. I reach Ed's floor, and he's already waiting. He takes my overnight bag from me and kisses me passionately on the lips.

"God, I've missed you," he says as he almost knocks me off my feet.

"It's only been a day." I laugh.

"A day too long in my book. I gather you met Sid?" Ed asks.

"I did. What a lovely chap. He's obviously very fond of you."

"Yeah, we get on really well. He looks out for me." Ed takes my hand and stares at me intently. I sense he's eager to get back to the topic of 'us'.

"Where are we off to?" I reply, unexpectedly feeling a little shy under his admiring gaze.

"Fancy The Anglers again?"

"Definitely. Hopefully we can get a table outside," I say, remembering what a great time we had last time.

"I'll pop your bag in the bedroom, and we'll get going before it gets too busy."

We finally reach the pub after a bit more of a chat with the lovely Sid and manage to bag a table in the garden. The pub is already busy, full of yummy mummies making the most of a midweek glass or two of prosecco with their various bored and tired offspring. There's also a selection of office workers getting stuck into some post-work drinks. We decide to order a couple of Caesar salads.

"The question is, are we going to break our not drinking in the week pact?" Ed leans forward and smirks.

"I'm fine with a mineral water if you are?" I reply, shutting down his suggestive gaze.

"Sparkling or still?"

"Surprise me."

"Surely taking you out on a Wednesday is a special occasion?" Ed tries again, winking.

"You really are bending the rules, Ed Nash," I scold. "What about your health kick for the tour?"

"Mineral water it is," he finally concedes, defeated.

Ed only has to look slightly over at one of the servers and our order is taken care of. I'm getting used to how women react to Ed. A couple of the yummy mummies keep nudging each other and looking over in our direction. Ed ignores all the attention and keeps eye contact with me. Our salads and mineral water arrive, and we spend an enjoyable time just catching up on our day.

"Do you fancy a walk, or we could just go back to the flat and sit out on the balcony?" Ed asks as he pays the bill. He puts his wallet back in his pocket, nods a "thank you" to the waiter and takes my hand. As he starts to lead me out of the pub garden, one of the yummy mummies staggers over, dragging a rather grubby and tired-looking little boy behind her.

"I have to say, I really do lurve your music," she slurs, placing her hand on his arm. "I've got your photo on my fridge." Her lipstick is smudged and she's desperately trying to steady herself on her overly high heels.

"Oh, um, thank you," Ed replies.

"Any chance of a photo?" the drunk yummy mummy continues. "Otherwise, the girls at Pilates won't believe that I met you."

Ed glances at me, as if to get my approval. I nod.

"Sure, why not?" Ed replies with a fixed grin.

The woman sidles up to Ed, putting her arm around him. Her equally sozzled friend takes the photo whilst I stand to one side.

"Thanks sooo much. I really do appreciate it. It'll really piss off my husband too." She laughs, something that resembles a loud cackle, as she takes her phone back from her friend, eager to look at the photo.

"No worries. Have a great evening, ladies," Ed says, his hand making its way back to mine.

"Sorry about that. I wanted to say no, but as she was drunk, I didn't want to cause a scene," apologises Ed as we walk towards the pub gate.

"It's fine. It's part of your job. I mean, at least she asked, unlike the last time we went out."

"Yes, you get a much better class of drunk around Teddington, you know," Ed replies with a grin. "Now, let's get you back home so I can have you all to myself."

It's like an oasis of calm sitting out on Ed's balcony, enjoying the river views and continuing with our midweek no alcohol rule. Ed's fixed us a couple of iced coffees, and we watch the sun start to disappear behind the trees on the horizon. I can tell Ed has something on his mind—he seems a bit distracted, a bit fidgety.

"Everything ok?" I ask.

"Yes. Yes. All good. I, ummm... oh God, I don't know what to say really, Virginia, but you've had me thinking recently, and things are going so well between us, so I really don't want to rock the boat," he begins.

"It's fine. Is it because I said I thought Evie was pregnant?" I mean, I can't think what else it could be. If he said things are going so well between us, it can't be anything to do with that, can it? Unless Callum has put him off me and pursuing things with me. Oh God, it is that, isn't it? I take his hand in mine, as much for my benefit as his.

"Yeah, it is. How did you guess?" Ed looks down at the balcony floor, as if fixated by the pattern of the tiles.

I shouldn't feel relieved that I placed a thought in his head that's bothering him, yet I can't help myself, that issue seemingly being the better of the two. "I feel bad for going on about it. It was quite a major mind fuck to drop on you really. I'm sorry I ever said anything. If you want to talk about it, then I'm here for you," I say, trying to reassure him. "I may be completely wrong, of course," I add, hoping that I am.

"I'd like to have a look at those photos again, if you don't mind?" Ed says, a sadness in his eyes as he now looks into mine.

"We could drive to mine now if that's what you want?" I suggest. I'm not exactly in a position to say no when I'm the one who planted the seed. It's the least I can do.

"Are you sure you don't mind?" he asks.

"Of course not. Let me drive. It's the least I can do," I reply, hugging him close.

Ed nods. We make our way downstairs to my car. The traffic is thankfully fairly light, and we reach my house quickly. I open my front door and call out to the girls, but no one's home. We walk through to the sitting room.

Ed sits on my sofa whilst I get my secret book safe from the bookshelf. I've hidden it between my much-loved and battered copy of Armistead Maupin's *Tales of the City* and an equally much-loved and sun-bleached copy of *The Beach* by Alex Garland. After locating the key, I sit next to Ed and open the box, taking out all the photos. I leaf through, find the ones from Mark's pool party and lay them out on the coffee table in the shape of a fan. Ed picks up each photo and studies every single minute detail, searching for clues.

"What about this one?" Ed asks, handing me a Polaroid of Evie and me sharing a sun lounger, pointing at Evie's school shirt.

"Her school shirt does look a little tight across her stomach, doesn't it?" I agree. "Look, I'm probably wrong about everything. Maybe you were right—perhaps she had her period and was a bit bloated?"

"No, the more I think about it, the more I think you could be right. Why on earth would she just leave without saying goodbye to either of us? I need to find out if it's true, but there's no way she'll give me the time of day after all the unwanted publicity I've brought to her door," Ed says with a slight sniff, as if he's trying to stop himself from crying.

I feel so guilty having dropped this nugget of information in Ed's mind that is now obviously festering away. And to think I only used the photos as an excuse to get in contact with him again. I never thought we would become so close and definitely not so quickly.

"Ed... I can contact her. In fact, I already have," I blurt out before I can change my mind.

"What do you mean?" he asks incredulously.

"I looked her up on Instagram, like I did with you, and I sent her a message," I confess.

"Did she reply?" He immediately asks.

"Yes, but just with a very brief message saying she's sorry we lost touch and that it would be great to catch up one day. But I don't think for one minute she really meant it. It's just something you say to someone you've lost touch with, isn't it?" I remark, as I start to tidy away most of the photos.

"Contact her again. Try to meet up with her and per-suade her to talk to me. It doesn't have to be face to face. I just want to find out the real reason why she left and to see if she was pregnant. It must have been something pretty major for her to just leave. It's eaten me up over the years. I really thought we were happy," he says wistfully, still tightly clutching the Polaroid of me and Evie on the sun lounger at Mark's.

"And you were at the time, Ed. And I thought I was happy with Jamie, but it was just the thrill of first love," I explain, touching his arm, trying to get him back in the here and now with me.

"I'm sorry, Virginia, bringing all this stuff up about Evie again. It's not really what you want to hear. I want you to know that I still really like you, and to be honest I've never felt like this about anyone in my adult life, but I really do need your help."

It's as if he read my mind. His words reach me just as the insecurities start seeping through. It's refreshing to hear he is still interested in me but also needs to know the truth about why Evie left. I'd be more worried if he completely brushed off my comments and wasn't interested at all in finding out what really happened. Every step of dating someone and every situation you watch them experience shows what sort of person they are. With his drive to find out if he is a dad, I feel more and more willing to let him in and potentially take on the stepdad role.

And as was always inevitable, it's all down to me, who started everything off with my stupid Polaroids.

Chapter Fifty-five

Ed

July 2018

We drove back to my flat in almost complete silence and then sat together to pen another message to Genie: *Hi, Genie, so great to hear from you. I would really love to catch up. I live in Hampton Hill, so not too far away from you in Richmond. Fancy lunch one day soon? V x.* If my way of finding out what happened to Evie is through Virginia, then so be it.

Neither of us slept well that night, and the following morning, I'm awake at 6 a.m. I slip out of bed, leaving Virginia sleeping, and sit out on my balcony alone with my thoughts. Since being back in the public eye, I've set up a Google Alert for my name so I know when there's any mention of me in the tabloids. Since I've met up with Virginia again, I haven't even bothered to check any of the alerts. With plenty of time on my side, I check them. I'm shocked to see my name has been extremely popular.

I stop at one particularly very recent story, my mouth dropping. I frown and click on it to read it, not quite believing what I'm seeing. Callum, the shitty ex himself, has sold a story to a newspaper about how I'd always planned to hook up with Virginia and that's the whole reason they split up. There are photos of Callum and Virginia on their wedding day, together with a photo of him with Shannon and Sasha at the end of Virginia's World Cup final barbecue, and there, in the background, is me and Virginia. We're looking particularly cosy in the photo—I was reassuring her whilst she was telling me once again how sorry she is and getting worked up about Callum turning up how he did. Not that the readers would know that.

Heartbroken Callum Baker tells how Mountaineers' Ed "Nasher" Nash stole his wife!

"What the...?"

I read through Callum's outrageous lies, anger increasing with every word, hands shaking as I struggle to scroll down the page. The picture from after the World Cup and the falsehood not being enough, he's topped everything off by somehow getting hold of some of Virginia's old Polaroids. There's one in particular I *really* don't need people to see: me and Evie and Virginia and Jamie back at my house after Virginia's sixteenth birthday party. We all look extremely drunk and stoned, and Uncle Paul is in the background, taking a puff from a huge spliff. I really don't need this sort of publicity. God knows how Evie is going to take this latest bombshell, let alone Virginia. There are many, many lows people can reach. Selling a fake story on the mother of your child is surely right down there.

Things with Evie would probably never have worked out. We've been apart for a lifetime, and I have no idea what she's like now. She's made her life with her husband and her children, and I really should have respected that. It's only having spent time with Virginia that I've realised I've been going about my life all wrong, and a lot of that was down to the influence of my uncle Paul. At one time, we all thought he was so cool. In reality, my mother had been right all along. He's a complete waster and ingratiated himself into my group of friends, manipulating us all for his own gain. The paper has named him in the photo, so it won't be too long before they're knocking on his door for his side of the story.

I make a coffee for Virginia and take it through to the bedroom, stalling for time before I break the news of Callum's betrayal. I nudge her gently on her shoulder, trying to wake her, settling with a light kiss on the top of her head.

"Morning. I've made you a coffee," I say with a weak smile, sitting on the side of the bed.

"Thanks, Ed. I couldn't sleep for ages last night." Her eyelids can barely stay open, and her movement to sit up in bed is slow.

"I couldn't either, and I really appreciate what you have done for me, but we've got a bit of a problem." I pass Virginia's coffee to her, knowing she won't need caffeine to wake her up once she hears the news.

She groans. "What now?"

"There's no easy way of telling you really, but Callum has sold his story to the tabloids," I blurt out. While making her coffee, I spent the entire time working out how best to tell her what I've found out. I hit one big reality: there's no sugar-coating what he's done.

Virginia pauses as the mug is just about to touch her lips and instead puts it on the bedside table. "What do you mean, his story? He doesn't have a story." She rubs her eyes, trying to focus on what I've just said.

"I know that, you know that. I reckon they've paid big money for what he's told them." I pass my phone to Virginia whilst she reaches for her reading glasses, which are on the bedside table, right next to where she just put her mug. She starts to reluctantly read the article.

I watch her face as it turns from expressionless to shock to her jaw clenching. "I'll swing for that man, so help me, God," Virginia growls through gritted teeth. As predicted, she needs no help keeping her eyes open now. "He's even nicked some of my flippin' Polaroids. Who does that?"

"Calm down, Virginia," I say, placing my hands gently on her shoulders. "I'm fuming too, but it's out there now, and there's nothing we can do about it. I don't think it's going to help things with Evie either. I don't suppose she's replied?" I add as an afterthought.

Virginia checks her DMs and shakes her head.

"Ed, how can I go to work today with all this publicity? It's going to be a nightmare. But if I don't go in, I will only be adding fuel to the fire. Oh my God, I'd best warn the girls too," Virginia says, her mind working on overdrive, not at all sure what to do first. She throws back the duvet and gets out of bed to pace around the bedroom.

"It's ok, Virginia," I say, placing my hands firmly on her shoulders. I pull her shaking body close and just hold her. "Let's think about this carefully. Call the girls first and make sure they are both ok. Ask them not to talk to anyone about what Callum's done. My manager will deal with the press. To be honest, any publicity in his eyes is good publicity for the tour. If we remain silent, it may just all die down. Go to work as usual, but if it gets too difficult, see if your boss will let you leave early and come back here. I'm going to be here all day, so I could always drop you at work and then pick you up again." I feel her tense body start to relax slightly as she listens to my plan.

She looks up at me, on the verge of crying. "I'm so, so sorry, Ed, that Callum has done this. I should never have let him stay the other night after he'd had a barney with Amy. When her brothers' friends beat him up, I shouldn't have patched him up." She doesn't need to apologise; it's not her fault that Callum's a selfish and opportunist bastard.

"Look, he's Shannon's dad and has been good to Sasha as well, so hold on to that. He's made a few bob from the press now, so hopefully that will be the end of it," I say, knowing full well that Callum is the sort of guy that won't stop at just one story. I'm only now beginning to realise that I've been no different to Callum. I didn't consider Evie and her feelings at all when I was happily courting the attention of the press.

Virginia gets ready for work and then we have breakfast together on the balcony. For those minutes we eat, life feels normal. In the end, we decide that Virginia driving herself to work is probably the more sensible option. With this fake news already flowing around, we're hardly going to make things better for ourselves by turning up to her workplace together.

I escort her to her car and wave her off. I find Sid and warn him that I might have a bit of a problem with press attention. Being an avid gossip newspaper reader, Sid is already ahead of the game after Callum's bombshell and promises faithfully to get rid of any media hacks for me. I have a day to myself today, as we don't have any rehearsals for a couple of days, so I decide to chance going to the gym. There are a couple of photographers outside the flats, but I'm able to drive past them fairly easily through our underground car park, thanks to Sid giving them a piece of his mind.

There are a few sly glances and double takes as I enter the gym reception area, but I reach the changing rooms without anyone stopping me. I bust out a run on the tread-mill, not really wanting to stop, and then do some weights. The gym is always good for some headspace, and today it's really needed. I haven't heard anything from Virginia, so I guess everything is going ok for her. Workout complete, I skip the shower, grab my bag and leave. If there are any sneaky photographers here, I'd rather them not catch me at such a vulnerable time. As I sling my gym bag into the back of the car, I notice someone with a camera. Normally, I would stop and have a chat, but today I put my head down and drive off.

Back at the flats, the photographers have been forced to move further down the road by Sid, but their cameras click and flash at me as I drive back into the car park. I park up, and Sid's waiting for me, eager to talk.

"They're a ferocious lot out there today, aren't they? People shouldn't believe everything they read in the press, you know. Well, I don't anyway. Today's news is tomorrow's fish and chips' paper," Sid advises me.

"Thanks, Sid. I really do appreciate all your help. You're a lifesaver."

Back in the sanctuary of my flat, I take a shower, then grab a coffee and catch up on the headlines. Twitter is awash with comments about Callum's kiss-and-tell:

He deserves everything he gets that @EdNash. @Callum-Baker is just giving him a taste of his own medicine! #TeamEvie

@EdNash deserves to be happy. I heard that @CallumBaker has been divorced from @VirginiaBaker for 5 years after he had an affair! #UsedToBe

There's no point in reading any more. It's all out there now. Virginia and I know the truth, and that's the main thing. A couple of WhatsApp messages flash up on my phone, one from Mark and one from Jez, just letting me know they're here for me and Virginia. There's a message from Toby too: **Hey, Ed. Great publicity for the tour with the headlines this morning! I couldn't have organised anything better myself. See you at the weekend for rehearsals.**

It's all about the headlines with Toby. Always has been and always will be.

Chapter Fifty-six

Genie

July 2018

This first week in Jonesy's villa is rapidly running away with itself. In just a couple of days, Maura is joining us for the final week. It will then be time for me to let someone else in on my secret. I already feel Maura will be the easiest person to tell, as she's never critical or judgmental. When I escaped from Bournemouth, a kind lady on the bus told me about the job at The Hidden Snicket. A job that came with accommodation. Maura took me on based on a "good feeling" when I first arrived in Brighton and gave me a chance, originally as a cleaner. If that's not fate, I don't know what is. She's always joked that I was a far better barmaid than a cleaner, but she had to wait until I turned eighteen to let me work behind the bar.

Gray's jetlag has finally settled down, and it's me who's now awake early, alone and lost in my thoughts. I make a coffee and sit outside with my phone, checking for messages from back home. I have one Instagram DM. As expected—Maura and I use WhatsApp—it's from Ginny. She wants to meet up. I'm intrigued, excited even, at the thought of seeing Ginny again. I'll arrange to meet her when we return home. What harm could it do? It will also allow me to find out exactly what's going on between her and Ed. I compose a quick response.

Hi, Virginia. Good to hear from you again. I didn't realise we live so close! Let's meet up when I get back from holiday in about a week's time. Talk soon. Genie x

I send it before I can change my mind. I won't mention it to Gray—he'd probably be cross with me—but I want to feel in control of my own life again. I've always felt guilty for not getting in touch with Ginny after I finally settled in Brighton.

I pour myself another coffee, grab my iPad and check the gossip sites. I'm confronted with Ginny's ex-husband having sold a kiss-and-tell about how Ed supposedly stole her away from him. So, they're seeing each other. I'm not sure how I feel about it. Years ago, it would have felt like a betrayal, but Ginny always had a bit of a thing for Ed. Clearly, Virginia does too.

I spend the next half an hour poring over the photos that accompany the article. There's Ginny with her ex-husband Callum on their wedding day, then a more recent one of Callum with their daughters. In the background, you can just see Ed and Ginny looking deeply into each other's eyes. There's intimacy in that photo that shows the world they are more than just good friends. And then there it is, the sucker punch: a photo from Ginny's sixteenth birthday party of me, Ed, Ginny and Jamie all looking absolutely stoned. In the background of this one is Ed's uncle Paul, complete with a big joint between his nicotine-stained fingers. That man still gives me the creeps.

I continue to search online for photos of the old gang, but all the stories are a repeat, including the photos, of Callum's revelations. I send Maura a quick WhatsApp. I can't wait to see her. I don't have to wait too long for Maura to respond due to the time difference. She's busy finishing off some last-minute work things.

She's included her flight details for Gray so he can pick her up from the airport. I've just sent another message to Maura, saying how much we're all looking forward to seeing her, when Gray joins me outside.

"Morning. You're up early. Everything ok?" Gray asks, gently brushing my neck with a kiss as I try to stifle a yawn.

"Yeah, I just couldn't sleep. Maura's sent through her flight details. I'll forward them to you," I reply, pushing my hair out of my eyes.

"It'll be great to see Maura. You can get stuck into some proper retail therapy then. What do you fancy doing to-day?" Gray asks, scratching the ever growing stubble coming through on his face. I'm beginning to wonder if he packed a razor.

"Umm I don't mind, but I did want to show you the latest on the press front. It looks like Ginny's ex-husband has sold his story. There are also some dodgy photos of me and the gang looking very stoned," I warn Gray.

I bring up the story on the iPad, and he has a good look through the article, dismissing it almost immediately.

"Nothing to worry about there," he says, giving me the iPad back. "It's just a disgruntled ex getting his pound of flesh. Are you ok with it all?"

"I'm not particularly happy about the photo with me in it being used."

"I know, but we're lucky to be away, as we're in a bit of a bubble here. I was wondering if you fancy a trip to the beach today? Go for a swim and feel the sand between our toes?" Gray suggests.

"Yeah, why not? I know the kids will love it," I enthuse, needing a day away from the UK gossip sites.

It takes us just under two hours to get to the beach, as we've decided to skip the closest one for a more 'locals only' beach further away, and we park in the car park attached to a big surfing shop. It's selling an eclectic range of beach towels, surfboards, beachwear and typical must-have seaside souvenirs, which we almost have to drag Cassie away from.

We secure a couple of cabanas on the beach, complete with sun loungers for the day, and set up camp.

"Fancy a dip, Cassie?" Will asks.

"Sure," she replies, removing her sarong to reveal a stunning, but very small, silver bikini that doesn't leave much to the imagination. I almost gasp but button my lips instead. Now that Cassie and I are back talking, I really don't want to upset things between us by criticising her choice of swimwear, as much as I want to.

Our beautiful daughter certainly turns a fair few heads as she sashays towards the crystal-clear sea, closely followed by Will. Gray and I watch as Will attempts to playfight with Cassie, making it his mission to dunk her. And it's only a couple of minutes before he succeeds, Cassie completely disappearing underwater for a split second, jumping up quickly, her mouth wide, Will laughing.

Cassie stomps back towards us, water trailing from and behind her. "He's such a pain, Mum. He's ruined my hair," she moans, bottom lip jutting out in a sulk.

"You still look gorgeous, Cassie. I love your bikini. Is it new?" I ask, hoping my attempt at complimenting her choice of swimwear is working, when all I really want is for her to cover herself up.

"Yes, I bought it at Westfield with Mel," Cassie replies, lying on her sun lounger to dry off.

I put my sunglasses on, lie back and drift in and out of sleep as my early start begins to catch up with me. I dream of my carefree days with Ed, when nothing more than having a good time mattered before the sadness of living in Bournemouth with Mother and mean-spirited Auntie Maureen almost finished me off. And then I dream of my new life in Brighton, where I was finally accepted into a group of people, who, despite having no blood ties to me, only ever showed me love and kindness, all held together by Maura.

I wake to the children arguing again as Gray unsuccessfully plays peacemaker.

"Wha—" I begin.

"It all started because Will's hungry and his irritability is annoying his sister, as per usual."

Cassie shoots me a look, confirming Gray's words to be true.

"I noticed a McDonald's over the road. I thought it might fill the gap in Will's empty stomach," Gray suggests.

"I could do with another coffee and maybe one of those apple pies they do, please," I say, making it clear this is a case of lunch on the beach and I'm not moving.

"I'll have a cheeseburger, please, a fruit bag and a diet coke," Cassie adds, not budging either.

"I'll come with you, Dad, as I'm not sure what I want yet," says Will.

"Probably the whole menu," Gray mutters as they wander off.

"I think I'll have a quick swim once I've had my coffee and apple pie," I say to Cassie, Will and Gray now out of earshot.

"The water really is lovely. It's like being in a relaxing bath." The thought draws me in further to the idea.

"Do you fancy joining me after lunch?" I ask, trying to make an effort.

"You're not likely to try and drown me, are you?" she replies with a smile.

"Not unless you try and drown me first." I laugh.

There's silence for a while as we both close our eyes and soak up the sun, but then I hear a small, reluctant voice.

"Mum?"

I turn to Cassie. She's looking at me like she's got something to confess. I can tell it's on the tip of her tongue.

"Yes?"

"Did you see that Ginny's ex-husband has sold his story about Ed stealing her away from him?" Cassie blurts out. "And there's a right dodgy photo of you and your friends looking out of it," she adds, removing her sunglasses so she can look straight at me.

"Yes, I saw it this morning," I reply. My throat feels as if it's closing up, so I swallow before I answer. I sit up on my sun lounger.

"Obviously it doesn't show us in the best light, but in the grand scheme of things your dad and I don't think it's too much to worry about," I say, hoping Cassie will be reassured.

"I like that we're talking like we used to," Cassie says with a genuine smile. "I'm beginning to realise that you didn't really have any choice about keeping your baby, and that makes me feel really sad and also so shocked and angry with Grandma and Grandad," she adds, reaching over to touch my hand.

"It was more Grandma than Grandad as the driving force behind me getting my baby adopted. The way I acted was a disappointment to Grandad, but *I* was the disappointment to Grandma," I admit, gaining comfort from her touch.

"Sometimes I can't believe some of the things that you did when you were my age, you know?"

"I regret all the mistakes I've made, Cassie. I suppose I rebelled against my mother, as she was so strict. As you know, as a teenager, you always think you know best," I say as Cassie rolls her eyes at my comment. "And that's why I'm hard on you and Will sometimes—because I want the best for you both. I don't want you to make the same mistakes I did." I'm fed up of apologising for my youthful mistakes but I'm glad she's not mad anymore and I get to take the explaining route instead.

Cassie nods and is about to say something else just as Gray and Will return with our food, the moment now lost.

The rest of the afternoon is one of the most relaxing times we've all experienced together for ages, and once the beach starts to clear as people leave to go back to their hotels to get ready for dinner, we gather our things and walk along the pier in the late afternoon sun. We watch the fishermen fishing and marvel at the opportunist birds swooping down to see what the fishermen have caught. As we make our way back down the pier to go back to the car park, the evening stallholders are starting to set up, much to the delight of Cassie, who insists on buying a couple of handmade bracelets for herself and Mel.

The drive back to Orlando is easy enough, and after having had a full day of sun, Cassie and Will nod off in the car. Once back home and showered, I fix us some scrambled eggs on toast and then we all retire to our bedrooms to watch TV. Gray, bless him, crashes out almost immediately after the long drive. I check my phone and see a response from Ginny to my earlier reply. It's brief, saying she would definitely like to meet up when I return from holiday and apologising for her ex-husband going to the press and using one of the photos from her sixteenth. She's neglected to mention Ed. I immediately compose a reply.

Hi, Virginia. Please don't worry about the press article. I'm used to the press now, as I am sure you are aware! Hope you're coping ok. Genie x

I spend the next half an hour googling images of Ed Nash. Looking back at photos of us together when we were young still makes my stomach do a flip, but looking at the grown-up Ed, I feel absolutely nothing. I think it's more the nostalgia that has a grip on me. I can't deny he's still a good-looking man for his age, but he has nothing on my Gray. Gray will always be the one for me.

Chapter Fifty-seven

Virginia

July 2018

Callum always has a way of fucking up my life. I was fuming when Ed told me what Callum had done. I know exactly how Callum got hold of the photos—the night he had an argument with Amy and stayed on the sofa. When else would he have had time and been alone to find them? The photos are still here, so he must have taken copies on his phone.

I went to work as usual and had to put up with sneaky glances from at least half of the office. Thankfully, Caroline had a day off, otherwise she would definitely have given me the third degree. I had a quick chat with Mr Bruce to explain everything, and he was so understanding and told me to take some compassionate leave. He was concerned about the amount of press waiting outside the office though and said, "As much as I respect you as my assistant, the firm can't afford to have any adverse publicity". I cleared my desk as quickly as I could and slipped out of the back of the building to get to my car and dodge the press, then drove straight to Ed's, where the press were having a field day. Sid was on hand to guide me safely into the car park and even escorted me upstairs to Ed's floor. Ed had just got back from the gym, and we spent the day holed up in his flat.

It's now the day after the article, and copied articles, were published and I've been greeted with further lies in the press from Callum, with yet more of my polaroids being published. I've also received a message back from Evie. Neither of us have mentioned me being with Ed, but she obviously knows because of the press stories. Unfortunately, the next lot of photos that have been published are all from Mark's pool party. There's me in my lime green bikini—whatever was I thinking?—but worst of all, there for everyone to see, is Evie in her overly tight school shirt.

Ed's getting more and more riled up about Callum, and I'm finding it difficult to speak to him properly. I know I need to tell him about Evie, but with everything that's happened, no time has felt like the "right" time. But if there's no such thing as the "right" time, I might as well get it out the way.

"I've had a couple of replies from Evie," I confess.

"Why didn't you tell me?" he snaps. And there it is: the anger.

"I've had quite a lot to deal with, you know. Here, take my phone and read them for yourself," I snap back, practically throwing my phone at him. Here I am, feeling like crap, and once again Ed seems more interested in what his ex-girlfriend has to say than showing concern for me.

Ed scrolls through the messages, silently examining each one in great detail. With each of Evie's words, his anger seems to subside.

"Well, you didn't say anything about us. It's not really anyone's business though, is it? But at least she's up for meeting," Ed says, perching on the arm of the sofa I'm sat on. "Callum's really complicated things, hasn't he?"

"He's got nothing to lose and everything to gain."

"He has your girls to lose," Ed corrects me.

Ed's words about Callum potentially losing the girls comforts me in a way. I'm hoping this means he cares more about me and my daughters than his teenage romance with Evie. It seems he was thinking deeper than I thought. But it also hits home that my girls were not at the forefront of Callum's mind when he was taking those photos and grinning at the money he knew he could make. They weren't even at the forefront of his mind when he was taking photos with them after the World Cup—he was focused on the money signs and used them in his plan.

"What he's done has really made me think. I was in his position not that long ago, and as you said, I never really considered Evie's feelings, so maybe it's payback," Ed says, finally taking some responsibility for his past behaviour as he gets up from the arm of the sofa and paces up and down the living room. He stops in front of me. "Are you going to reply?"

"I will, but I want to think carefully about exactly what I want to say."

Ed spends the rest of the morning frantically googling his name to see what people are saying about us all. It ranges from people thinking Callum is a complete dickhead, just cashing in on Ed's fame, to people saying that Ed deserves everything he gets. One of the online sites has even compared photos of me and Evie aged sixteen to what we look like now. It's brutal.

Ed makes us some lunch, and we call a truce on talking about Callum's latest fake bombshell. I didn't sign up for this when I started seeing Ed.

"I want to go home and see the girls. I need to be with them, Ed," I mutter. I can't decide whether it's because I need to be there for the girls with how they must be feeling over Callum or because they somehow soothe my vulnerabilities.

"I thought you were going to stay here for a while until everything dies down," Ed says with surprise, trying to hug me.

"I thought that was what I wanted but... it's not. I'm sorry. My overwhelming feeling is to be with my girls right now." I pull away from him, trying not to cry.

After lunch, I gather my things and leave Ed's. He's quiet and subdued. Sid manages to get rid of most of the press, but as I drive out of the underground car park, several cameras flash in front of my eyes.

Thankfully, my road is quiet, and being able to park in my own space and return to the sanctuary of my own home is an incredible feeling. As soon as my key is in the door, it swings open before I have a chance to reach for the handle.

"Mum, I'm so sorry for what Dad has done," Shannon says, tears building in her eyes.

"Oh, Shannon, it's not your fault." I reach out for her and pull her towards me, holding her against me.

"But it is." She sobs into my shoulder. "I was the one who kept banging on to Dad, saying that you were dating Ed. I'm sure that's why he came over. I'm so sorry, Mum."

"Your dad's always been an opportunist. He's the one who chose to talk to the press." I remove my arms from around Shannon, take her by the hand as I shut the front door and lead her to the kitchen. "Let's get that kettle on and then you can choose what film to watch on Netflix."

Coming back home was definitely the right decision. My girls need me. Ed is old enough to look after himself.

Chapter Fifty-eight

Gray

July 2018

I naturally wake up at around 5:30 a.m. after falling asleep so early last night. I slip out of bed, trying not to disturb Genie, and check my phone whilst I make a pot of coffee. Yesterday, when Genie woke up early... I wasn't as asleep as she thought. Right now, I'm not sure whether I feel ashamed of myself or excited. I would never ever want to go behind Genie's back, and I usually wouldn't, but I can't sit back and do nothing knowing there's a guy out there who doesn't know he has a child and a woman who doesn't know her real parents. Genie didn't exactly want to give her child up, so what's stopping them from forming a bond now? Imagine the relief she could give to this woman knowing she was, and still is, wanted. Imagine the happiness she could give to Ed knowing he isn't childless after all. So, yesterday morning whilst I was in bed and Genie was sat outside, I hired a private detective to track down Milly. I gave him as much information as I could, including the name of Genie's friend Emma Hadfield in Bournemouth.

My finger shakily hovers over the unopened message from the private detective. He told me he'd get back to me with any information he could find. And here it is: a message. I don't know why but I'm really panicking that he was and is unable to find anything and the search is a dead end. I brace myself and open it, not sure what to expect.

The first half of the message states that the Catholic adoption agency was closed down not long after "Evie Del Rio's child was adopted" due to mishandling of some of the adoptions.

"Shit," I grumble, running my hand through my hair. If the agency closed down, does that mean all the files are gone too and finding Milly will be impossible? At least he's confirmed she was adopted though. That means she has a family and didn't remain in the system. The best we could have hoped for. But if there are no files, how would he know that? It's all so confusing. I'll have to make myself stop overthinking and let him do his job.

And then there it is, a nugget of gold: he's found Emma Hadfield, now known as Emma Hadfield-Jones. He's provided screenshots from her various social media accounts. She appears to be married with two grown-up sons and still lives in the Bournemouth area.

"Bingo, we have a lead," I rejoice.

It also says he's going to try to find out a bit more about Emma via the church where her and Genie first met. It's definitely a start. A big start. I quickly put my phone away, as I hear someone walking down the stairs.

"I can't believe you're up so early," Genie exclaims, rubbing her eyes. She definitely hasn't brushed her hair yet by the way it sticks up in places.

"Well, I had such a good sleep last night," I reply.

"You haven't been working, have you, Gray?" she says, her eyes focused on the rectangular shape in my pocket. "You did promise that you wouldn't."

"No, nothing like that."

"What have you been checking up on, then?" she asks.

Due to work, my phone is always glued to me. Since being on holiday, I've hardly even looked at it. Just left it on tables, the bed, the side of sinks—everywhere except in my pocket. The iPad has been my constant companion instead. Able to browse social media, staying away from phone calls and texts. And now here it is, in my pocket. My lifeline from accidentally not deleting the browser history on the iPad, since Genie seems to be using the iPad more and more, screwed over by the shape in my pocket. And I could lie. Easily. Because is it not normal to have your phone in your pocket? But look where lies have already got us.

"If I tell you, please promise not to get mad?" I say, knowing I need to start this conversation with honesty.

"I can't really promise anything until I know what you're talking about." Genie crosses her arms defensively, not sure what to expect.

"I've hired a private detective to try and trace Milly."

"Without telling me?" Genie shouts. "I wish you'd told me, Gray. You can't just do things that concern me and not consult me." Her face flushes bright red with complete outrage.

"Look, I did it with the best of intentions. They've managed to track Emma down," I explain patiently, as if I'm talking to one of the children.

She storms off, sliding the patio doors shut with extreme force behind her for effect, leaving me alone with my news. I'll let her cool off. Despite how cross she seems with me right now, I'm sure her curiosity will get the better of her. She tends to be quick to temper and then quick to calm down. True to form, it only takes ten minutes for her to return.

"I just wish you wouldn't take over, Gray," she criticises. After a rather large sigh, she relents slightly. "But how is she, Emma?"

"You're interested now, are you?" I say, trying to break the tense mood as she shoots me a steely glare.

I show her the screenshots the private detective sent me. She spends ages looking at the various photos of Emma and her family.

"She looks just the same. Well, obviously older, but I'd recognise her anywhere. I'd like to be the one to contact her," she says decisively. "I'm going to send her a direct message on Instagram."

"Ok. I'll get the private detective to hold off on his investigations into Emma," I agree. "Am I forgiven?" I ask with a cheeky smile, but Genie's not letting me get away with taking control.

"Not really. Please stop making decisions for me, Gray. You've always done it ever since I met you, and I've always allowed you to do it. But I want to be able to make my own decisions, especially on the possibility of finding my daughter," she replies, her cheeks flushing again with the little anger still left inside her.

I accept what Genie's just said, as I've spent the whole of our marriage trying to protect her. Maybe she's right; perhaps it's time for her to take back control.

Cassie's next up and brings our attention to the latest revelation from Ginny's husband. More photos of Genie, Ginny and Ed as teenagers at some sort of pool party. Genie looks up the article on the iPad and spends ages examining the latest set of photos. She says she remembers the pool party quite well, as it was the last time she saw Ed and the rest of her friends. The photos are quite faded and hazy, but Genie points out her pregnant stomach. She tells us it was the day her mother confronted her about her weight gain and potential pregnancy.

I leave Genie to her own devices, offering to do a coffee and doughnut run, anticipating Maura's arrival later. Genie's in a world of her own again, back with Ed and her friends—a world that doesn't involve me. I hope I've done the right thing in telling her about finding Emma. I still can't work out why Genie hasn't tried to find her friend before. Or her firstborn daughter.

Chapter Fifty-nine

Maura

July 2018

I'm thrilled to be joining Genie, Gray and the children for the second week of their holiday. The cats are staying at home, with a local veterinary nurse visiting them twice a day.

By the time I clear immigration and locate my suitcases, it's early evening. I spot Gray almost immediately at Orlando Airport, although it's extremely busy, as the last two planes from London have both just landed. He seems to have tanned pretty well, so I'm excited about what I'll be able to achieve in a week despite my pale skin.

"Well, hello, sir. Fancy giving me a lift?" I say with a cheeky wink as I approach him. We hug, and I can feel the tension throughout his whole body. I'm sure I'll find out sooner or later what that's all about.

"Hi, Maura. I am so glad to see you. Genie's been missing you. Here, let me take your cases. You do realise you're only here for a week, don't you?" Gray jokes, taking both suitcases from me, pretending to buckle under the weight of them.

"They're fairly empty, you cheeky sod. I'm nice and prepared for all that shopping," I say as we walk to find the car.

Gray's fairly quiet on the drive to the villa, and once we arrive at Jonesy's most-impressive home, I unpack and then enjoy a delicious Thai takeaway with the family, catching up on their holiday news. Once we're stuck into our second bottle of wine, the children make their excuses and go to their rooms. I'm fairly tired myself what with the time difference between London and Florida.

"Thanks, guys, so much for inviting me. I can't tell you how much I've been looking forward to this break," I say, settling back in one of Jonesy's comfortable leather recliner chairs, sipping my wine.

"We're thrilled you could join us," Genie begins. "But there is something I've been wanting to talk to you about for ages," she says, placing her wine glass on the table.

"Can I presume it has something to do with a certain Mr Ed Nash?" I reply, looking at both their faces for a sign that I'm right.

"Spot on," Genie replies before continuing. "As you know, Ed and I did date as teenagers, and yes of course it's all true that I was the inspiration behind a lot of his early songs. And it wasn't too long after that that I ended up in Brighton."

I nod, remembering the sweet, broken girl who found her way to me and the pub I was managing all those years ago.

"Well, I think it's time I told you the reason I ended up in Brighton."

Genie looks to the floor, the last word of her secret finally spilled. My mind is full of so many emotions: sadness that she went through what she did, anger at her mother and aunt... but mostly guilt that I wasn't able to be there for her and emotionally support her, knowing now that's why she ended up alone in Brighton.

"Oh, Genie. I had no idea, darling, no idea at all," I say, shaking my head in disbelief.

Genie looks up at me with her stunning blue eyes brimming with tears, whilst Gray just sits there with his arm wrapped around his wife.

"I'm a dreadful person, aren't I, Maura?" Genie says, trying to wipe her nose again with a tear-sodden tissue.

"Not at all. You were so young to have to deal with all of that: being taken away from your home, your boyfriend, your friends and being forced to give away your baby," I say, trying to console her. "I just wish you'd told me when you first came to Brighton." I feel completely inadequate. I'm a bit like Gray—I like to try and fix people.

We spend the rest of the evening talking about Gray hiring a private detective to try and find Genie's friend Emma from Bournemouth and Milly. I know from one of my friends who was adopted that it's so much easier for the adopted child to try and trace their biological parents than it is for the biological parents to trace their child—as long as the mother's known and doesn't tell any lies when she gives up her child, of course—but I keep that information to myself for the moment. I'm here to comfort and support Genie and the family. It's what I have always done and will continue to do. We stay up late, drink far too much, we laugh and we cry until my tiredness finally gets the better of me.

Chapter Sixty

Genie

July 2018

My relief in telling Maura my long-kept secret has finally brought me a kind of solace. Maura being Maura doesn't judge or criticise, she only offers comfort. She mourns with me for being denied a lifetime with my daughter. And just like Gray, I can see how devastated she is about not knowing and not being able to help me all those years ago. When I finally got away from Bournemouth and arrived in Brighton, it was my chance to start again and block out all that had happened. Maura was instrumental in helping me build a new and happy life, and I will always be so very grateful to her for that.

Despite the initial tears that my revelation caused, we do manage to have fun in our remaining week Stateside. Maura insists on treating us all to swimming with dolphins at one of the nearby theme parks one of the days—something the children have always wanted to do. We all take delight from our up-close encounter with such captivating creatures. We sunbathe, snorkel, swim and take it in turns trying to get into a hammock and not fall out. Will is the most skilled and successful in staying put, whilst the rest of us prefer the static comfort of a sun lounger.

Later, Gray catches up on some much-needed sleep under a shady palm tree, Will enjoys sampling a selection of the all-inclusive food that's on offer at the park and Maura, Cassie and I find ourselves mesmerised by the aviary, where colourful birds fly down to take food from your hands. We couldn't have asked for a more perfect day together.

With Maura here, the shopping trips have increased, and Gray finds himself being somewhat of a taxi service, but he never complains, often just dropping us off, giving him and Will some time together to play crazy golf, go to the movies or just chill at the villa. Everyone is happy doing things that please them. Surely that's the point of a good holiday: getting away from the usual routine, experiencing new things, having fun and relaxing. For us, for the first time in ages, we feel like a normal family again.

We fall into a new routine, and most evenings after dinner, Gray often nods off or goes to bed early, all those jet-lagged early mornings clearly catching up with him. Maura and I usually grab a bottle of wine, sit in the jacuzzi and just talk, reminiscing about times gone by, just as we are tonight.

"Who'd have thought old Jonesy would have made such a success of himself?" Maura observes, taking in the beauty of the illuminated pool and lush tropical garden, which both seem even more magical at night.

"I know what you mean. Even before I met Gray, Jonesy would always have a different woman with him at the bar." I agree, enjoying the jets of water from the jacuzzi soothing my body.

"He never settled down, did he?" Maura asks.

I shake my head, reaching for my wine glass. "He just can't seem to, but he's such a good friend to us as a family. And I owe him a lot. He was the one who persuaded me to invite Gray for an after-hours drink the night we met."

"I never knew that," Maura confesses. "But then, there were a lot of things I didn't know back then..."

"I'm sorry, Maura, that I didn't tell you sooner about what I'd been through. I guess I just cast everything bad that had happened to me away because I needed a new life." My eyes are unable to hold Maura's understanding gaze for too long, the guilt too much.

"I guess I would've liked to have had the opportunity to help you, look after you in some kind of way," she explains sadly, full of regret about what she might have been able to do if I'd perhaps given her the chance.

"But you did help me," I try to reassure her. "Together with Chef Rudi and his incredible food and lovely, patient Dom who taught me everything about being a good barmaid, who never tired in telling me the stories behind his numerous tattoos, you became my new family. We were all there because you took a leap of faith with us and gave us all a chance," I say with such conviction and love for a woman who I have no blood ties to but who loves me more than my own mother ever has.

Maura smiles at me through her tears. "We had such a good gang there at The Hidden Snicket back then, didn't we? I still get emails from Rudi and Dom to this day, and they always ask after you."

"I'm sure Rudi finding success with his restaurants back in Germany and Dom finally becoming a bar owner in Ibiza all has something to do with you. Dom always said you have a knack of finding the right people to take a chance on. I would never have met Gray if it weren't for you..."

"And I've always believed that you all had your own way of finding me because I needed you all as much as you needed me," Maura says as we both raise our glasses, celebrating our enduring friendship.

And just as we clink our glasses, we notice a group of fireflies lighting up and sparkling in the night sky. Their beauty is enchanting and mystical as they move together with their shining light. I remember once reading that the sight of fireflies is a symbol of light entering your life, and that's exactly how I feel right now, here with Maura. After a lifetime of holding back, keeping secrets from my loved ones, it's now my time to light up and shine and push forward to try and find my missing daughter, with the help of my ever-loving family and best friend.

Chapter Sixty-one

Maura

July 2018

The week with Genie, Gray and the children is a much-needed break, and I think me being there diffused things slightly between Genie and Gray. Gray has always been Genie's knight in shining armour ever since they met. He has to realise that he can't always fix things for her. Sometimes, she has to do it for herself.

My half empty suitcases have come in handy for the trip home, as I've had to accommodate some of Cassie's purchases, who really went to town at the outlets. During one of our nights sitting under the stars in the jacuzzi, Genie confided to me that Cassie initially reacted very badly to the news of Milly. Cassie's still being quite adamant and vocal about the fact Ed Nash has a right to know he has a daughter. I agree with her, as does Gray. Will, bless him, has been fine with it all. Gray and I managed to snatch a few private chats throughout the week about the best way forward. Gray knows it's a long shot to find his wife's firstborn but he's willing to give it a go.

It's now that awful time when you have to return home from a holiday, the week ending far too quickly. Once we packed up, Gray did a once-over of the villa. He only found a pair of Will's swim shorts left drying over one of the baths and a pair of Cassie's flipflops at the front door.

Gray booked us all into one of the airport lounges, where Will proceeded to eat his way through the entire buffet. We're on different flights, with my flight being an hour later. I insisted on buying us a bottle of champagne to thank them for an amazing week. We've now finished the champagne, and the first of our flights is fast approaching. Although it's been hard emotionally, we still managed to fit in a lot of fun.

"Thanks so much for inviting me to join you. That Jonesy's got an amazing home. It was so kind of him to let us use it," I say, embracing each one of the family in turn. "Cassie and Will, you both make sure you look after your mum when your dad goes back to work. And you're always welcome to come and stay if you fancy a change of scene."

"Thanks, Auntie Maura," says Will, giving me a big hug as he towers over me.

"How about a movie night soon?" says Cassie with a big smile.

"You're on. Now, get out of here before I start blubbing." I laugh, desperately trying not to cry. "Message me when you land, and I'll do the same," I call out as they leave the lounge.

I catch up on some work emails and then I flick through one of the gossipy magazines Cassie left for me for the flight. I stop at one of the articles, Ed "Nasher" Nash's face smiling up at me. It's an extensive article detailing Ed's love life over the years, starting with "Evie". I still can't get used to her being called anything other than Genie, but I can see why she wanted to distance herself from that name and all associated with it.

To be honest, Ed's love life over the years doesn't seem to have amounted to much after "Evie": a couple of models way back, a singer from a long-forgotten indie band and numerous unknown blondes. Virginia isn't included, as the magazine was printed before the press knew about their relationship.

I hope that, in time, Genie and Ed can be reunited with their daughter, if she indeed wants to be found.

Chapter Sixty-two

Virginia

August 2018

After Genie's last message, I left it a while to contact her again. I've spent the last couple of days trying to get it into my head that she's Genie now, not Evie. I've spent my whole life knowing her as Evie, so the change will take a while to fully settle into my mind, although I can understand why she did what she did, having done the same thing myself. Ed was chomping at the bit for me to meet her, driving me mad, but I understand that I'm the one who gave him the idea that he could possibly be a father. I'm also very intrigued to meet my former best friend again. I realise things can never go back to the way they were, but it's worth a try.

We've arranged to meet at a little pub in Walton that Genie recommended, overlooking the River Thames. She said it's quiet and discreet, so it sounds like the perfect venue for our reunion. Ed's insisted on driving to the pub, but he has promised he'll wait in the car unless I call or message him to the contrary.

Genie's already waiting for me, sitting at a table tucked away at the corner of the pub, nursing a cup of black coffee. She looks incredible; she's tanned from her recent holiday, her hair highlighted naturally by the sun. She looks nothing like the wild girl that I remember. I expected to feel more nerves than I do walking towards her, but she looks so different to how I remember that she somehow seems a different person.

"Genie?" I call out tentatively.

"Virginia, how are you?" she says. I wonder if she's had as much trouble as me trying to refer to me as Virginia instead of Ginny. There's that awkward moment where neither of us know quite what the etiquette is for this situation. She stands up, and we hug briefly.

"I'm fine, and you?" I say during the hug, taking a seat opposite her after.

"I'm fine too. Well, how weird is this, seeing each other after all these years? You look great. I love your hair colour."

"Thank you. You look good yourself," I say, returning the compliment. And she does look good. Despite everything she's been through, it looks as if life has been kind to her.

"Let me order you a drink. What would you like?" Genie asks.

"Just a coffee for me, thanks."

Genie orders my coffee, and as we wait for it to arrive, we talk about our children and how much time has passed. The waiter brings my coffee out and we make small talk as I stir it and wait for it to cool. I apologise once again for Callum's behaviour, which she seems to take quite well. It all feels quite civilised.

"So, you and Ed, then? You finally got your man," Genie says directly and unexpectedly. She crosses her arms on the table and leans forward expectantly. I can't work out if she's angry with me for being with Ed or just intrigued.

"Umm, well... we are seeing each other. It's early days though. I messaged him after watching *The Girl in the Song* and it just kind of developed from there really," I say quietly. Evie would have been livid, but I'm not sure about Genie.

"You always had a soft spot for him, didn't you?" Genie says with what seems to be a genuine smile, as if she's remembering back to what we were like when we were fifteen.

"I guess I did, yeah. I'm sorry if that hurts you, Genie. You always knew that I liked Ed, but once he met you that was it, I backed off and then I started going out with Jamie," I say defensively, the thought of Ed preferring Evie to me back then still a touchy issue.

"You're right, Virginia. I did know that you liked Ed, but the attraction at that time was too strong to ignore," Genie replies sharply, uncomfortable with being confronted with her past actions. She's definitely rattled by the way our conversation is going.

"When you left, Ed and I were both devastated. When you weren't at school, I went to your house and looked in our secret hiding place for notes, but there was nothing. Ed got so much stick from everyone for not knowing where his girlfriend was. It was brutal what he went through." I bite my lip, the conversation now going the direction I want it to. There's no need to bring up past jealousies. They're irrelevant. Today, I only need closure on two things: why she left and if she was pregnant. "We were left with so many unanswered questions, Genie. We were heartbroken," I add, pausing to take a sip of my coffee.

"I had no choice, Virginia. Don't you think I would have contacted both of you if I could have? And then when things changed and I was more in control of my life, I was scared to reach out because, in my mind, it was far too late. I was just concentrating on surviving. You have no idea what I've been through. No one does. Except for my family," she replies, trying to stifle her emotions.

"I think I do, Genie. I worked it out."

"You couldn't have," Genie says calmly, but I can see she's flustered, as her neck has started to flush red, and it has nothing to do with the August heat.

"Those photos from Mark's pool party that Callum somehow managed to get hold of... I only found those photos recently, as they were over at my parents' house. I spent one evening just going through them. You must remember that I got a Polaroid camera for my sixteenth birthday? It was great fun looking back on when we were young: the bad haircuts and our awful clothes. God knows what we were thinking." I laugh, trying to ease the tension in the air.

"I remember. You were obsessed with taking photos all the time." Genie nervously fiddles with her wedding band, trying to cover her emotions up with a forced grin.

"Well, I started to really examine the photos from Mark's pool party, as they were the last photos I had of us all together. I was looking for signs of things different with you, to work out why you might have left. You'd had another row with your mum, and you'd forgotten your swimsuit, so you just rolled up your skirt and dangled your feet in the pool. I looked at your tummy and at your waist. You'd put on quite a bit of weight. Your boobs were much bigger too." I'm shocked at the level of control and calmness in my voice. If I'm wrong, I've spent weeks pushing my idea into Ed's head for no reason. I could lose him. And I'll only have myself to blame. "You were pregnant with Ed's baby, weren't you? That's why you left, Genie."

Genie's face remains stoically impassive, but the constant flush on her neck betrays her. "You were always really clever at working people out, weren't you?" Genie whispers with tears in her eyes.

"I wish you'd told me, Genie. I could have helped you, supported you." I reach over the table to try and comfort her.

Genie shakes her head. "I didn't know. I didn't know I was pregnant until Mother confronted me after Mark's pool party. She was so angry with me, shouting at me, calling me names." Her tears are falling now. "A doctor confirmed it the next morning."

A slight gasp enters my throat. Having an inkling is one thing, but confirmation is another. I guess part of me prepared myself for Genie to tell me how wrong I am. "Why didn't you try to contact any of us?" I ask gently. I don't want to keep badgering her with my questions, but I want to know everything, to understand what she's been through. Maybe I selfishly need some sort of closure as to why she just upped and left, never confiding in me.

"I didn't get the chance. As soon as my parents knew, I was forced to leave London. I stayed with my auntie

Maureen in Bournemouth." Genie seems calmer now, as if unburdening herself to me is helping her relieve herself of the trauma to an extent.

"And then what?" I continue, getting up from my seat to sit next to Genie, taking her hand in mine to give moral support.

"I so wanted to keep my baby, but it was made clear from day one that that wouldn't be an option. My baby came early. A little girl. I was so poorly, I'd lost a lot of blood and she was so tiny." She desperately tries to wipe her tears away.

"I'm so sorry, Genie," I say sadly. To think that she went through all of that alone. Without me, without Ed and without any love or compassion.

"I only told my husband and my children recently. We've all been trying to come to terms with everything. That's why I've never commented whenever Ed's spoken about me in interviews," she explains. "I didn't want him to find out what I'd done." She can hardly look me in the eyes. I can sense her deep guilt, even though she doesn't need to feel guilty. She was just a child put into an adult situation that adults then took control of. Maybe *The Girl in the Song* documentary is really a blessing. Maybe they'll both be able to get the closure they desperately need, just as I'm getting my closure now.

"He deserves to know, Genie. You know that, don't you?" I say gently, pushing her to make things right. I think of Ed, waiting patiently in the car, aching to find out if he has a child.

Genie nods, facing down. A stray tear lands on the table.

"Would you like to tell him yourself?"

Genie's eyes shoot up, piercing into mine. "No, no, no, I can't." She shakes her head fiercely. "He'd hate me."

"Genie, don't freak out, but Ed is here. Well, he drove me here. He's waiting in the car, a couple of streets away."

Genie just laughs. From her desperate head shaking, I would have assumed a manic laugh. Instead, it's filled with coincidental humour.

"What's so funny?" I ask, slightly bemused.

"Gray, my husband, is also here. He's parked a couple of streets away too."

It's my turn to laugh, thinking of both men waiting for their respective partners, both anxious to hear how things have gone.

"I think I need to talk to Ed, don't I?" she finally relents. "But just me and him. I owe him that much," Genie adds, reaching over to grip my hand.

"Of course. I'll call him," I reassure her. "I'll tell him to meet you outside in the pub garden. You should probably call your husband too."

Chapter Sixty-three

Ed

August 2018

I walk into the pub garden, overlooking the Thames, and see Genie straight away, sitting at a table, looking out at the water. I've been so nervous about seeing Genie again. I still can't think of calling her anything other than Evie. It's almost like she's two different people. I know very little about grown-up Genie, and I wonder if there will be any signs of Evie, the girl who at one time meant absolutely everything to me.

"Hi," I say, not sure how to communicate with this person who's gone from the love of my life to practically a stranger.

"Hi, Ed," she replies, turning to face me, removing her sunglasses, as if she really wants to talk to me face to face, without any barriers between us.

"I can't believe it's you," I say, my voice sounding more like a hoarse whisper. I can hardly get the words out. I seat myself opposite her, taking everything in about her. I've dreamt about seeing this woman for a lifetime and now she's here in front of me, I'm in genuine shock. Gone is the wild, young, carefree girl I knew. She's been replaced by someone I hardly recognise: her once rebellious spiky blonde hair is now immaculately cut and coloured, she has fine lines near her eyes, but... those mesmerising blue eyes... they're still the same. There's some sort of familiarity there, but in some ways I feel as if I'm talking to someone I met briefly long ago.

"You look well, Ed." Genie looks nervous, bordering apprehensive.

"Thanks. You do too," I say, my voice returning to normal. And she does look good, just not in the quirky way she used to.

"It's been quite a morning so far..." she starts. "It was so good to see Virginia after all these years. She's still the same really, always wanting to help..." She trails off, fighting back the tears that are threatening to fall. Judging by her red eyes, she's already recently cried.

I nod in agreement, unsure where this is leading.

"I have to know why you left. It's been eating away at me for a lifetime, Genie," I implore, directing her to the track in my mind, willing her to finally tell me the truth.

"I'm sorry, Ed. I really am sorry for leaving you... for leaving everyone." She lets the tears fall, seemingly losing her strength from all of today's confrontations. Irrelevant of the time that has passed, it still hurts to see her so upset.

"Please, Genie, please tell me."

"I was pregnant, Ed," she whispers. "My parents found out the evening of Mark's pool party. I had no idea." She rests her elbows on the table and her head drops face first into her hands.

My heart is racing, as if I've just taken a line of speed, my head spinning. I feel lightheaded. Since meeting Virginia, I've mostly brushed off the possibility of a child, afraid to believe in it, afraid of how I would feel if she was wrong. But she was right.

"So, you left because you were pregnant? Why didn't you tell me?" I was a shithead in so many ways but I know for a fact I would have stood by her and our baby. All I can feel is this sort of internal panic. A need to somehow turn back time and confront her before her parents had the chance. Maybe if I'd just looked a bit harder and approached her first, things would have been different. "We could have brought the baby up together," I continue, knowing my suggestion of two sixteen-year-olds bringing a baby up in the 1980s is a ridiculous idea but it still being a possibility in my mind, nonetheless.

"You think I wouldn't have told you at the time if I had the chance?" This sentence squeezes my heart and just adds to the guilt that I should have taken more notice. Maybe my parents would have taken her in...? No, I doubt it. But Uncle Paul...? Yes, he would have. We would have all gone off together, and we would have raised our baby with the help of my drug-addicted uncle? No, no, no...

"I didn't get a say in anything," Genie says. "My parents drove me straight to Bournemouth to stay with my auntie Maureen. They didn't want anyone to know." She's almost robotic with her words, as if she's trying to hold herself together as she explains to me what happened all those years ago.

"Why didn't you call me? Why didn't you call Virginia?"

"They had me under lock and key. Between my mother and Auntie Maureen, I had no chance." Genie looks directly into my eyes, willing me to understand how it was for her.

"If only I'd known, maybe I could have helped you? Maybe I could have made your parents see sense?" I say, reaching out to take her hand. She pulls back, as if my hand is on fire. Her reaction stings. The last time we saw each other, we were in love. Now... she can't bear to touch me. But it's my fault, isn't it? Dragging her into the spotlight, all the unwanted attention.

"You couldn't have helped, Ed. My mother despised you. She put all the blame on you for the pregnancy, as if I had nothing to do with it." She laughs at the irony.

And here it is. The question I'm dreading the answer to. I'm not sure which would be the best option. Either way, I lose. Either there's a baby who didn't make it to birth or a child I've missed out on watching grow up. A family with Genie that never was. "Did you have the baby?"

"Yes," she confirms. "She came early. We were both very poorly." Her carefully applied makeup is running as she tries to wipe away her tears.

"She?" I have the overwhelming urge to reach out for her hand again, but I'm not sure I could handle a second rejection. "We've got a daughter?"

"She's almost thirty-three. I only saw her briefly when she was born, as I was so out of it. The midwife told me she had a lot of dark hair and the biggest, bluest eyes she had ever seen." Genie smiles, her mind miles away into the past. "I named her Milly. But I don't know what her actual name is. My mother had arranged for her to be adopted by a 'nice' Catholic family, who could give her a better life than I ever could."

Milly Nash...

"I'm so sorry that I've caused you so much pain since that documentary aired." I've felt guilty ever since Virginia pushed my actions to my attention, but hearing that Genie is the mother of my only child makes me feel so much worse about what I've done. "To be honest, my life meant nothing when you left. I was coasting for years, and when the song started getting popular, I just kind of seized the opportunity I'd been given. I had nothing else."

"Thank you, Ed, I can't deny that I've hated the attention. But I'm also so sorry that you didn't have the opportunity to see your daughter grow up. Being forced to give her away is my biggest regret."

"Thank you for agreeing to see me," I say tentatively, touching her arm, gaining comfort for us both. This time, she doesn't pull away. It feels natural and real. It's the most familiar she's felt today. She may look different but Evie is still within Genie somewhere. I can feel it.

"You've got Virginia to thank for that. She kind of railroaded me. But in a good way. You're lucky to have her," Genie says with a warm, genuine smile.

"You don't mind that we're together?" I ask nervously. I'm not sure if I need reassurance because I somehow feel like I'm betraying who Genie used to be or I'm worried she'll exit my life for the final time, just after I've found out all this information.

She shakes her head slowly. "Why would I mind? I'm happily married, and you deserve every happiness too." And I know she's telling the truth. There's a look of contentment at the mention of her happy marriage and I am genuinely pleased for her, despite everything.

"I dreamt about seeing you every day for years after you left," I admit. "I had so many questions that needed answers, but there was a big fat nothing."

"When I was in Bournemouth, I wondered what you were thinking and what you were doing all the time. It was heartbreaking."

Although it's hard to hear she was hurting too, it's a comfort to know it wasn't one-sided and that I really meant so much to her too. When your girlfriend disappears for over thirty years, it's amazing how much time you spend wondering what it is you did wrong. Even as a teen, completely in love, I always imagined what "more" I could have done to make her stay.

"Being pregnant with your baby gave me comfort at first, even though it was also the reason we were apart. Once I realised Mother was planning on having our baby adopted, I tried not to think about you too much. Mainly because I knew you would be devastated to think that I could allow our baby to be taken away. But I didn't have a choice," Genie says, this time not even bothering to try and wipe her tears away. "I thought you'd hate me. And that's why I never got back in contact with you. It was the easiest way to keep my secret."

"I would never have hated you," I whisper. I go to stand and embrace her, not sure if she'll want me to. But she stands too, and I pull her close to me. We console each other for some time, a quiet understanding of all that we've both lost. Despite the time that's passed, it feels the most natural thing in the world to hug her.

Genie pulls away first. "Gosh, I'm so sorry, Ed. I haven't been that close to another man in like... forever." She laughs nervously.

"It's fine. We're just a couple of old friends comforting each other," I say reassuringly.

We spend the next half hour just chatting, catching up on over thirty years of our very different lives and missed memories. It's so easy talking to Genie. Her appearance differs to back then but I feel the connection is still there. I'm absolutely devastated that she was forced to deal with the pregnancy all alone and bereft about the loss of our daughter.

Chapter Sixty-four

Genie

September 2018

I'm pleasantly surprised by my meeting with Ed. He was so understanding and supportive of what happened all those years ago. He was also extremely apologetic of how he'd exploited our teenage relationship to the press. We've both made choices we've later regretted.

Ed and I have kept in touch over the last few weeks, with our continued search for our lost daughter. Out of all the sadness, misunderstandings and wrong decisions, Gray, Ed, Virginia and I have somehow formed a kind of friendship. This is mainly thanks to Virginia, who's always making sure we have discreet dinner plans to catch up on everything in our search for Milly.

Together with Ed, Gray and I instructed another private detective to investigate the adoption. Every now and again, he has a lead, but as the adoption service has been closed down for quite some time, the search is seemingly futile. I've told my parents that I'm back in touch with Ed and that he's aware he has a daughter and we're trying to find her. My mother isn't too impressed with this latest development, but my dear dad is completely understanding. In fact, we've been spending a lot more time together, just me and him.

"It's so good to see you again, Dad," I say, placing two freshly made cups of coffee between us on the kitchen table before sitting opposite him. "To what do I owe the pleasure? It was only yesterday you last visited. Two visits in two days. I am spoilt." I laugh.

"Does your old dad ever need a reason to visit his daughter?" questions Dad playfully. "But actually, I do have an ulterior motive for being here today. You know that we've been visiting your auntie Maureen at her care home on a regular basis since we relocated her from Bournemou—"

"Dad, I don't want to hear anything about that evil old cow, ok?" The mere mention of her name still riles me. I can feel my neck spasming with tension, the memories of how her and my mother treated me throughout my pregnancy. The compulsory church visits. To this day, I have never entered a Catholic church again. "She made my life a misery together with Mum, and I honestly will never forgive her for her part in making me give my daughter away." I need Dad to understand that some things can't be forgotten and will never be forgiven.

"I know, darling. And you know how guilty I feel about my part in the whole thing."

I nod. And I do really believe him and his guilt because he always looks so desperately sad whenever Milly is mentioned.

"But things were so different in those days, and Auntie Maureen has been talking a lot recently about the past. She hasn't got a clue about what day it is or who we even are half the time due to her dementia, but she keeps talking about your baby," Dad continues, taking out his handkerchief from his trouser pocket to wipe his watering eyes.

"What do you mean?"

"Well, she keeps saying that she's sorry and that your baby was renamed Frances. She repeatedly says that she saw your baby at church. Then, she mutters about how the baby was saved by the Lord and starts asking for the priest," he says, shaking his head.

"My baby's name is Frances?" I ask breathlessly. "Do you think there's any truth in what she's saying, or is it just the ramblings of a demented old woman?" I finally take a sip of my coffee.

"I don't know, darling, but I think next time we visit her I'm going to try and record anything she might say on my phone. There could be some truth in what she's saying, and it's really the only thing she says that sounds lucid. I just thought you should know," Dad adds, deep in thought, full of remorse.

"God, that woman still makes my blood boil, but if after all these years she holds the key as to where my daughter is, then I'm willing to listen. Could you arrange for me to go and see her?" I ask. "Today."

"I'll see what I can do."

"Could it be just you and me, Dad?" I ask, not wanting Mother to be privy to any conversation I might have with her sister.

"I'll speak to your mother. She'll probably be fine with it—seeing Maureen nowadays tends to stress your mother out too much," Dad explains. Despite everything, he still considers my mother's feelings. It's so much more than she deserves.

"To be honest, I don't really care about my mother's feelings, I just want to find my daughter."

The residents' lounge area has an aroma of boiled cabbage about it, which the home has quite obviously been trying to disguise with copious amounts of lavender air freshener. I can't believe Mother agreed to this visit without her. Of course, she still had to seek control in some way—I am not allowed to upset Auntie Maureen in any way. I agreed, in principle.

One of the carers takes us to where Auntie Maureen is sitting. She's aged drastically since I last saw her. Her once bright blue eyes are now rheumy and vacant. As we approach her chair, she immediately looks up, as if she's been expecting us.

"Sit down, Evie," she instructs, patting the armchair next to hers. "Not you, Tony. Just Evie." She dismisses my dad with a flick of her bony, narrow wrist. I obediently take a seat, having been unprepared for such a direct, 'with it' greeting.

Dad's face is a detailed picture of shock. The shock definitely aimed at her alertness and not the way she spoke to him. She's never particularly liked him or given him the time of day. "I'll get us some tea," he says, walking away.

Auntie Maureen follows him with her eyes as he leaves the room and then suddenly turns back towards me, staring straight into my eyes, hardly blinking. I almost jump.

"I saw your baby, Evie."

"Where?" I enquire, keen to get this reunion over and done with.

"She was always in the church. Always," she mutters adamantly. "Such a nice family too. Couldn't have babies of their own, so they took yours," she says, almost with a childlike chant. I try not to flinch at the words "they took yours". I know they didn't steal my daughter, but it feels as if they did. A lot of things were stolen from me: first steps, first word, first day at school, maybe even grandkids.

"What is her name, Auntie Maureen?"

"Frances. Lovely name, just like the Saint, St Francis of Assisi." So, her story hasn't changed. Part of me was wondering if she was spurting imaginary creations, each time with my daughter having a different name, living a different childhood.

"Where did they go? What happened to them... to Frances?"

"I told Felicity and Tony already. Didn't they tell you? Took her to London, they did. The husband had a good job, and they all went," she continues.

"Do you know whereabouts in London?" I ask.

"North London. Near where you all lived when you were a baby."

"Do you mean Camden?"

"Yes, that's it. Felicity and Tony had a lovely flat in that mansion block. Very grand it was too." Her eyes turn even more vacant, and she smiles to herself, back in time with her memories of the lovely, grand flat in the mansion block.

"So, Frances' parents moved to Camden?" I continue, urging her on, trying to get her focus back.

"Yes, I told you that already," Auntie Maureen snaps at me, clearly irritated by the repetition, looking at me as if I'm the one with dementia. "My friend Sheila always got a Christmas card from them. Good Catholic family they are, the Whites, you know."

"Frances' surname is White?" I gasp at this absolutely massive revelation, if indeed Auntie Maureen is speaking the truth.

"Yes, that's right. Lovely family, Sheila said. They always sent such beautiful Christmas cards every year," Auntie Maureen repeats.

"Where does your friend Sheila live?" I ask, pushing, hoping from the repetition that I'm not losing her just as I'm getting somewhere.

"Oh, she's with the Lord now," Auntie Maureen says, lowering her voice and making the sign of the cross as she dabs a tear from her eye. "I'm tired now, Evie. Get the girl to take me back to my room. I need a lie down. You've made me feel very sleepy. You always were such a troublesome girl," she grumbles. Even in the midst of her dementia, she still has an acid tongue. But I don't care what Auntie Maureen says or thinks about me now. She no longer has a say in my life. Her dementia is punishment enough for all the hurt she's caused me. I decide not to push her further and potentially antagonise her, hoping the name "Frances White" and where she moved to is enough.

I signal to one of the carers, and she gently helps Auntie Maureen out of her chair.

I wince as a bony hand grabs my wrist. "You were such a naughty girl, Evie, but do remember God always forgives a sinner," Auntie Maureen hisses in my ear as she walks past.

Chapter Sixty-five

Ed

September 2018

Genie called me earlier to let me know she was going to be visiting her auntie Maureen to try and gain some news about Milly from her. I didn't expect much, if I'm being honest, but I'm now sat at her breakfast bar—Gray and Virginia are here too, as per usual—because apparently she has some news. I've spent the whole day desperate to know more, the anticipation gnawing at me.

"I'm so glad we're all here together," Genie starts.

"There's nowhere else I'd rather be," replies Virginia, smiling at Genie, knowing how important this moment is.

"As you all know, Dad told me that my Auntie Maureen has been talking about Milly. Her dementia has been getting worse but the one consistent thing that she talks about is our baby."

I nod, hoping she hurries up with the news. As much as I know she wants to tell us everything, impatience is overwhelming me.

"The adoptive family moved to London when she was about a year old. Apparently, they lived in Camden. Best of all, she told me Milly's adoptive name," Genie reveals with an excited grin.

"That's brilliant," I say, jumping off my stool with pure joy. We're getting so close now to finding our daughter. "What's her name, then?" I ask excitedly.

"Frances White," Genie announces. "Quite a popular name, but I've been doing a bit of digging on social media, and I think I've found her."

"Oh my God, I can't believe it," I say, shaking my head in disbelief. Could this be the moment we've all been waiting for, or has Genie just got too carried away with the idea that this woman is our daughter? I'm trying to hold all my internal happiness in just in case. I don't think I could handle Genie being wrong.

"I'm so pleased for you both," Gray says, hugging his wife close.

"That's wonderful news, Genie," Virginia adds. Although she's addressing Genie, it's my hand she's squeezing.

"I've been scrolling through the various social media sites, looking for a Frances White, but there were loads of different profiles. I tried Instagram and found this person. I understand I could be reaching, but don't you think she looks a little like me when I was younger?" Genie asks, proudly showing us her phone. "Although, she's known as Frankie."

We all look at the Instagram profile. The profile photo is a bit blurry, but it shows a young woman singing into a silver microphone. I can't deny that there are similarities between Frankie and Genie. And clearly her interests follow mine. There are some arty photos of sunsets and flowers and numerous photos of various bands.

"Do you think we should maybe message her to see if it is the Frances White we're looking for?" asks Genie, keen to push things forward.

"We might not have to," I say. "Look at this photo." I tap on one of the photos on Frankie's profile to enlarge it so everyone can have a better look. Everyone studies the photo in great detail, trying to work out what I mean.

"Sorry, Ed. You've lost me. What are we supposed to be looking at exactly?" asks Gray, eyebrows furrowed.

"Look here. She's tagged the band she's in. They're called Pulse." I click through to the Instagram account for Pulse. Bingo, there's Frankie White: a pretty blonde girl, who looks to be in her thirties, with electric blue eyes. She's obviously the lead singer.

"Ed, that's got to be her. She's a singer too, just like you," Genie says with tears in her eyes.

"Woah, woah, let's not jump the gun too much," says Gray, laughing awkwardly. "Ed's in a band, Frankie's in a band. Ed is the singer of his, Frankie is the singer of hers. But just because they have music in common, that *doesn't* mean she's the right person. I think you're both being very led by hope."

"But Genie's right: she does look like her when she was younger. I can also see Ed in her," says Virginia as she swipes the screen up, taking a look at the various other Instagram photos of Frankie White. "Surely, that's too much of a coincidence."

"What's our next move?" Genie muses. "Gray's right. As much as I want to have found Frances, it's true, we don't really know if she is the right one."

"I've got an idea, and it might just work," I say, my cheeks flushed with excitement. My mind is in overdrive, but I somehow find clarity in the chaos. A completely legitimate way of finding out if Frankie is indeed our daughter. "Why don't I contact Pulse and say that I'm interested in adding another support band for the reunion tour on our London dates and arrange a meeting? I can say that I'm impressed with their music from Instagram."

"That's genius," exclaims Virginia, with Genie and Gray nodding their approval.

"Well, there's no time like the present," I say. "I'd better check their music out. I bloody well hope they're good," I mutter.

"We could AirPlay the videos on the TV," Gray suggests.

After relocating to the living room and with a few clicks, we watch Pulse come to life, with Frankie White singing her heart out. The band are musically tight, and Frankie definitely has stage presence. Her voice is good too—slightly husky, and she can go from screaming some of the rockier numbers to singing with such vocal control, adding meaning to the slower numbers. Daughter or no daughter, she can sing.

Impressed, I DM a brief message to the band's Instagram account. Gray tops up our drinks, and we wait, all huddled together, eyes glued to the phone as Pulse continues rocking it out in the background.

Chapter Sixty-six

Genie

September 2018

Since my visit to see Auntie Maureen, things have progressed very quickly. We managed to track down Frankie White. The invitation of a possible support slot on the London dates on The Mountaineers' reunion tour did the trick with her band. A guy called Chaz from the band got in touch with Ed, and a date was made for Ed to see Pulse play. Ed arranged to meet Chaz and the rest of the band after their set in a North London pub. We, of course, all join him for the gig.

There's quite a buzz at the venue once a few people clock Ed but, being North London, most of the audience are used to seeing various actors, singers and musicians on a daily basis.

Frankie is the perfect frontwoman, and the resemblance to me in my younger days is even more uncanny in person. But it's the way she carries herself on stage that convinces me she's her father's daughter. From the way she holds her microphone to the way she works the crowd, it's all Ed.

After the final number, the band clear away their kit before joining Ed for a drink. Gray, Virginia and I are sitting at a table close by. Gray keeps nudging me, as I just can't stop staring at Frankie. I can just about hear their conversation with Ed enthusing about their music and the probability that they could support The Mountaineers for a couple of their London dates. Two of the band members make their excuses to mingle, leaving just Chaz and Frankie. Ed asks Chaz if he can get some more drinks on Ed's tab, leaving Frankie and Ed alone.

"Frankie, I'd like you to meet my very good friend Genie McNamara," Ed says, ushering me over. He doesn't need to catch my attention or call me loudly, very aware of my eyes fixed on Frankie the whole time.

I can see Frankie's puzzled but she's pleasant and shakes my hand when introduced. "Oh my God, you're *The Girl in the Song*, aren't you?" Frankie suddenly blurts out. "Sorry, that was really rude, but it is you, isn't it?" she adds.

"Yes, that's me," I admit.

"I adore that song. But I thought you two didn't even talk to each other anymore."

"Ahh, don't believe everything you read in the tabloids, Frankie," Ed says with a jovial smile. "There's actually a very important reason that I want you to meet Genie, Frankie."

Ed looks at me and gives me an encouraging nod, knowing I've waited a lifetime to finally meet our daughter.

"Frankie," I begin, taking a moment to breathe properly. I feel as if I've been holding my breath all evening. I have to almost force the words out. "Do you know if you were adopted as a baby?"

"Yes, I was. I only found out recently though when I had a row with my parents," she replies, her bright blue eyes darting quickly from my face to Ed's and then back again before adding, "how do you know that?" My heart begins to race when I hear Frankie's confirmation. Surely this all can't be a coincidence?

"Well, we think there's a possibility that you may be my daughter. I had a baby when I was sixteen, but I was forced to have her adopted. I gave birth in Bournemouth, and she was adopted by a local Catholic couple who were unable to conceive."

I can see the pure shock in Frankie's face as she tries to digest what I've just told her. "I was born in Bournemouth, but we left there to live in London when I was about a year old," she says. "Lynne and Tom have been really good parents, but I could never work out why I don't look like either of them. How on earth did you find me?"

I explain about Auntie Maureen and her dementia and how her friend Sheila from the church kept in touch with Frankie's adoptive parents until her recent death.

"I do remember Mum and Dad getting Christmas cards from a Sheila, and I'm sure they went to her funeral back in Bournemouth about six months ago. But hang on a minute..." Her brow furrows. "If you're potentially my birth mother, then, Ed, would that make *you* my father?" she asks, looking over at Ed, trying to piece everything together.

He smiles weakly and nods.

Frankie leans forward, arms around her stomach, as if the shock is travelling from her face and through her body, taking hold of her completely. She puts her hand on a table sticky with spilt beer to steady herself, seemingly unfazed by the feel. "Wow, I don't really know what to say. It's an awful lot to process. It all sounds feasible, but shouldn't we do some sort of DNA test or something just to confirm everything?"

"Yes, yes, of course." I reach out to touch Frankie's hand on the table, hoping to provide her some of my own strength. "We understand that this must be a shock for you, and Ed and I never want to come between you and your parents, but we would like to get to know you, if you'll let us."

She nods as she tries to make sense of what we've just told her. "I guess I now know where my love of singing comes from." Frankie laughs, trying to inject a bit of humour into this life-changing conversation. "Well, potentially, if the DNA confirms it. You have children, don't you?" Frankie asks me.

"Yes. Two teenagers. Cassie and Will."

"How much do they know?" she asks softly, the heat from her skin sending happy tingles through my own skin.

"They know that I had a daughter when I was sixteen, but they don't know about this meeting, as we weren't sure how things would go," I admit.

"I'd love to meet them one day." Frankie takes her hand off the sticky table, me removing mine from hers in the process. "And I have some news for you both too." Frankie pulls her phone out of her pocket and unlocks the screen. "If you really are my biological parents, then you and Ed have two granddaughters. Twins. Gracie and Billie," she says proudly, turning her phone around to show us her screensaver of two pretty little girls, one blonde and one dark, smiling back at us.

This time, it's our turn to be shocked. I feel giddy with excitement, whereas Ed is almost speechless for once in his life. A parent of two, and always knowing about a third child, I've always had it in my head that I'll be a grandmother one day anyway. I can't imagine how Ed's feeling. He's spent so long thinking he missed his opportunity to be a father, let alone a grandparent.

"Er, what did I miss? Did we get the gig or what?" Chaz asks as he arrives back from the bar with drinks to find the three of us hugging.

Chapter Sixty-seven

Ed

December 2018

Genie, Frankie and I all have DNA tests, and we're delighted when the tests confirm what we already thought: we're a family. Together with Gray and Virginia, Genie and I are really enjoying getting to know Frankie, who in turn feels that meeting us was like finding that final piece of a puzzle. Frankie's introduced us to Gracie and Billie as their "new grandparents" and, being kids, they're very happy to accept us into their lives. Whereas Genie flourishes as a doting grandma, I'm not quite ready to take on the role of grandad quite yet, but I do enjoy trying to teach the girls to play the drums and guitar, which leaves me constantly realising the limitations of four year olds. I often have to settle on teaching them how to play the tambourine instead on the occasions Frankie brings the girls to watch me and the band rehearse.

Frankie is like a sponge, wanting to absorb everything that I can teach her. We've even recorded a couple of numbers together. Frankie has fitted into our lives well. Genie and Gray's kids have really embraced her and the twins, and together with Virginia, Sasha and Shannon, we've all formed quite a tight little group.

My feelings for Virginia, despite all the recent events, seem to have only intensified, and I can't bear to be away from her for more than a night. She often tries to wait up for me after many of the gigs if they're close enough to London, and it's a comfort to find her curled up, fast asleep in my bed upon my return. She's the one who's kept me grounded; being with her makes me a much better version of myself.

Occasionally, I mourn for all the lost years of not having seen Frankie grow up, and I can't help but sometimes feel as if I've been cheated out of being a proper father. Mostly, I'm grateful that I've been given a second chance. Life is for the living, and I'm finally giving it my best shot.

The tour has been going well, and we're gearing up for the London dates. Pulse's rehearsals are sounding good too. Toby's very impressed with their addition to the line-up for the Camden Roundhouse. Genie's asked for some tickets for the last night of the tour for her and the family, as she's keen to see Frankie perform again. The more time Virginia and I spend with Genie and Gray, the more I realise just how well-suited Genie is to Gray and I am to Virginia. The woman Genie has grown up to be is poles apart from the girl I once knew. She will, of course, always be part of my life, but the thought of our past relationship is a distant memory, like a film you once watched but can't quite remember the plot of. I'm fully focused on my future, and at the forefront is Virginia and, of course, developing my relationship with Frankie.

The documentary makers of *The Girl in the Song* are filming some of our rehearsals and gigs, as they're making a documentary about our reunion tour. So far, somehow, we've managed to keep Frankie's parentage a secret. So, for now, our newly formed family is just for us. We're all determined to get to know each other out of the public eye. The Mountaineers' recent success has been due to all the publicity from the original documentary, and the irony isn't lost on me.

Chapter Sixty-eight

Frankie

December 2018

Pulse has been invited to join The Mountaineers for both London dates at the Camden Roundhouse. Thankfully, The Mountaineers' manager was happy to add us as an extra support act once he'd seen us perform. It's such a great coup for the band to be such a prestigious support act that Chaz has started calling me their lucky charm. For the moment, the band are unaware that I'm Ed's daughter. I don't know how they'd feel about it all if they knew.

My ongoing relationship with Ed is easy, as we have music in common, and he can't do enough to help me and the guys from the band feel welcome on the remaining dates of their tour. My relationship with Genie is taking a bit more time to develop though, as apart from our similar physical looks, we have little in common, but she's an absolute dream with Gracie and Billie. I don't resent Genie for giving me away. From what she's told me it doesn't sound like she had much of a choice, but being a single mother myself, I can't imagine ever being without my girls, whatever life threw at me. To be fair to Genie, things were different in the '80s and I was much older than sixteen when I had the twins. It's still early days, and I'm hopeful that our relationship will develop. She's everything a grandma should be though, and the girls absolutely adore her. They're also very taken with Auntie Cassie and Uncle Will.

Chapter Sixty-nine

Cassie

December 2018

I was so surprised when Mum and Dad sat me and Will down one evening towards the end of summer and explained that they'd found Frankie, our half-sister. It was amazing to finally meet her. She really isn't that much younger than Mum, they could have been sisters, and I suppose she looks a bit like an older version of me. It was mad to also find out that we have two little nieces. Gracie and Billie love coming over to stay at our house whenever Frankie has to rehearse. They like nothing more than raiding my wardrobe to play dress up.

Mum doesn't get to see Frankie that much now it's leading up to the gigs, but she's more than happy to look after Gracie and Billie. Frankie explained that her boyfriend split up with her as soon as he found out she was expecting twins. He was a drummer in one of her previous bands, but she was determined to go it alone. Her adoptive parents helped out at first, but the more she leaned on them for childcare as she tried to push her music career, the more they distanced themselves from her. It was during a row about childcare that she found out she'd been adopted. She said it wasn't much of a surprise, as she'd never really had a lot in common with them, but she'd had a happy and stable childhood.

Amazingly, after all the disruption we've had, I managed to pass a good selection of GCSEs, and I'm able to go to college to study drama.

So far, the press don't know that Frankie is Mum and Ed's daughter, but after the tour, who knows? Will and I have been sworn to secrecy about having a half-sister, so we can't even confide in Mel or Tommy. Auntie Maura obviously knows but that's as far as it goes. The rest of the guys in Pulse don't even know why they've suddenly got their big break, although I overheard Ed telling Mum that he's told the original guys from The Mountaineers who Frankie really is. Mum seemed ok with that, as they were all really good friends back when Mum and Ed were together.

I've grown up a lot since the summer and now appreciate just how difficult everything must have been for Mum when she found herself pregnant and was then forced to give her baby away. I feel ashamed about how rude I was to her when she first told us about our half-sister, but Mum has been only too happy to forgive and forget.

Chapter Seventy

Genie

December 2018

I feel so proud of Frankie whenever I see her up on stage singing her heart out, but more so for what she's achieved as a single mum of twins. How times have changed towards being a one-parent family. Our fledgling relationship is more of a friendship than a mother/daughter relationship, as we're so close in age. Ed and I always maintained that we never wanted to replace Frankie's adoptive parents, but as time went on, Frankie revealed that her relationship with her mum and dad had soured since she'd tried to resurrect her music career. We're both forever grateful that Frankie at least had a loving and stable upbringing. The fact we've had the chance to form some kind of relationship with Frankie at all is more than we could have ever dreamed of. There's been talk of a musical collaboration sometime in the future between The Mountaineers and Pulse, and I'll only be too happy to help out with Gracie and Billie as and when required.

Dad was thrilled to finally meet Frankie and overjoyed to meet the twins, although my mother stubbornly refuses to see them, much to my dad's dismay, but it's her loss. Auntie Maureen hasn't spoken of my baby since, as her mind's become increasingly confused. Frankie and the girls are yet to be introduced to Ed's side of the family.

I'm also proud of Cassie and Will in the way they've welcomed Frankie and the girls into our family. Finally, my family is complete. Although there's been many mistakes made along the way, I'm happy that we're all on track to becoming some sort of blended family.

I hope in time my relationship with Frankie will become closer, but for the time being, I'm just enjoying being part of her world.

Epilogue

December 2018

The excitement in the audience is now mounting at The Roundhouse as they wait for the main event. Sasha and Shannon are all dolled up, with Josh and Micky in tow, all proudly wearing their backstage passes in plastic lanyards around their necks. The girls share a bottle of prosecco as the boys neck their overpriced bottled beer in pole position at the side of the stage. Virginia's backstage with Ed, enjoying having a laugh with Mark, Jez, Andy and Simon before it's time for them to go on stage. Chyna and Cindy are busy getting ready in their dressing room, with Toby nipping in from time to time to make sure they have everything they need.

There's a buzz in the audience as the time approaches for The Mountaineers to finally take to the stage for the very last night of the tour. Virginia gives Ed a good luck kiss on the lips and wishes the boys well before joining Sasha, Shannon, Josh and Micky at the side of the stage.

Ed is incredible. Despite it being the final date of the tour, he has the energy of a much younger man, thanks to the personal trainer Toby hired for him. He owns the stage, and his voice is the best it's been in years. Chyna and Cindy really earn their money, and their added harmonies on some of the newer numbers only accentuate Ed's voice.

They've just finished performing their most recent single "No More Tears", enjoying the sound of the crowd singing along with all the words, when Ed says he'd like to sing a new number. The crowd quietens as the band explodes with the most intricate yet simple intro since Ed wrote "Used to Be".

As the band play and the audience sway, Ed addresses the crowd as they hang off his every word.

"We've never played this next song to an audience before, but I'd like to dedicate it to my incredible girlfriend." He looks to the side of the stage. Sasha and Shannon nudge their mum, who's almost rooted to the floor beneath her.

"This song's called 'Better with You'. This one's for you, Virginia," he shouts before he starts to sing the most heartfelt words. The audience erupts as the song progresses. It starts slow before ending with both a guitar solo from Jez and Mark having the final few seconds of the song with his distinctive style of drumming. It is, however, both the tenderness and the strength of Ed's voice that makes the song.

"And no Mountaineers gig is complete without this one. This is 'Used to Be'."

The audience cheer, finally getting what they've been waiting for all night.

Gray holds Genie's hand just that little bit tighter as the band plays the song that had until recently plagued his wife. But he does have to admit, even with everything that's happened, there's a reason this has always been one of his favourite songs. Genie turns towards Gray and pulls him close.

Frankie watches Ed from the side of the stage, the fascination of seeing her dad perform live in front of an audience still new to her. She's delighted that her new family are all here and got to hear her sing. Will's managed to get to the front of the crowd for the final number, while Genie, Gray, Maura and Cassie stand nearer to the bar.

As the song comes to an end, Cassie looks over at her parents, who are in a close embrace. She knows that for her mum, *The Girl in the Song* was not only coming to terms with her past but was embracing her future too.

The End

Lightning Source UK Ltd.
Milton Keynes UK
UKHW011159040722
405349UK00004B/1207